Some Months in 1968

A novel by
Baron Wormser

Some Months in 1968

A Novel
Baron Wormser

Woodhall Press
Norwalk, CT

woodhall press

Woodhall Press, 81 Old Saugatuck Road, Norwalk, CT 06855

WoodhallPress.com

Cover Design: Jessica Dionne Wright
Layout Artist: Zoey Moyal

Library of Congress Cataloging-in-Publication Data available

ISBN 978-1-954907-09-6 (paper: alk paper)
ISBN 978-1-954907-10-2 (electronic)

First Edition

Distributed by Independent Publishers Group

(800) 888-4741

Printed in the United States of America

In memoriam
Michael Steinberg

Writer, Teacher, Friend, Ballplayer

. . . *for there is no place / that does not see you.*

—*"Archaic Torso of Apollo," Ranier Maria Rilke*

"Try a Little Tenderness"

—*Song recorded by Otis Redding, 1966*

Time laughs at History

—*"Staggerlee wonders," James Baldwin*

1954

Dien Bien Phu
THEY NEVER DRANK THOSE BOTTLES

Before the year of this book—because there always is a "before," because that is how history is, though not the simple cause and effect of chronology but rather the ceaseless, frightening, inspiring drive of human invention, of philosophies and flying machines—a battle and then a siege occurred in a Vietnamese valley near the Laotian border called Dien Bien Phu. The village that had once been there had become an encampment filled with thousands of French troops who weren't all native French, who were Moroccan and Algerian in addition to the Foreign Legionnaires who included Germans, Spaniards, Poles, and Czechs. Professional soldiers, they were fighting the Vietnam People's Army—an army like the French army, with units and divisions, and yet not at all like the French army but rather a professional guerrilla force. This may have seemed a contradiction in terms but wasn't because they didn't have a nation yet to be part of, but that was why they were fighting, to expel the French from their homeland

and have their own nation. Ethnic native mountain people were fighting with the French too, along with Vietnamese who opposed the communist guerrillas.

The French, overwhelmed at the end, wound up surrendering. In the course of the months of fighting, hundreds of Viet Minh, as the guerrillas were known, got caught up on the barbed wire with which the French had surrounded their entrenched positions. Riddled by machine guns and rifles, the corpses dangled—mortal regrets begging their comrades to pull them down. Behind the barbed wire, the French were literally blown to pieces by the constant shells the Vietnamese artillery threw at them or were buried alive, their fortifications collapsing like sand castles. Not only were the French badly outnumbered, they were outgunned too. The Vietnamese had more firepower—the howitzers, mortars, flak guns, and rocket launchers they had trekked to the battle site through impossible terrain that wasn't impossible due to the determination of thousands of men and women who carried whatever needed to be carried—rice, weapons parts, gasoline—on their backs or on bicycles equipped with storage bins or with the help of draft animals. The French air force thought it would bomb the supply trails but never found them because they didn't, in the sense of being identifiable roads, exist. One more thing the French didn't understand.

To most of the French the Vietnamese weren't people, which was what the war was about. The French had owned Vietnam, and the people there were incidental and so less than people. The French thought they couldn't lose. They might lose a skirmish here and there, but in the grand sense of losing a war and what they called a "possession," based not the least on the opium trade that could be traced back to 1861, that was impossible. Even at Dien Bien Phu, where the writing was on the wall to any military person who analyzed the factors, the French commanders had bottles of champagne ready to drink and toast their victory. They never drank those bottles. Something in the world changed because of that battle. Some shift occurred, not just about the power of nations, since not many years later the United States was willing to pick up where the French left off, but something about how people thought about other people, how if you looked down at some people—even if you said that you respected them, even though you didn't because they weren't who you were—you did it at your own expense. Such shifts, of course, are slow.

January 1968

POETS DO WHAT THEY NEED TO DO

"So here we are," said Daniel.

Daniel and Helen Brownson sat on the couch in the den they shared—her desk by one window and his by another—and reserved as a no-television sanctum while raising their three children. They were facing their oldest son, Thomas, whom everyone called "Tom" and who stood before them, his left hand gripping the wrist of his right arm. He was tall but at the moment stooped, as if the weight of making a decision had pressed him down. Daniel had turned on two table lamps, but Helen, who followed him into the room, turned one off. Too bright too early.

"I couldn't stay there. I made sure you'll get almost all the tuition and room and board money, and I'll pay you back the rest. I'm going to wash dishes where I worked last summer. I called Joe before I left school. He said I can start right off." A prepared speech but spoken too fast. The announcing moment over, the grip relaxed a bit. He had come in late, let himself into the house with his key, gone to bed, woke after a fitful sleep, knocked on his parents' bedroom door, and now there was this.

"You realize," said Daniel, who wanted to finger-jab at the air but didn't, "there's a war going on and that you will have to inform the Selective Service that you no longer are a student and that you will be reclassified and in all likelihood be called up for a pre-induction physical." The consequences, all in a row and waiting.

"And why, may I ask, did you do this?" said Helen. "Don't you think you should have talked with us? We are your parents." Her voice, usually clear with maternal purpose, trembled: words she didn't want to say, a place she didn't want to be.

"If I'd talked with you, I wouldn't have done it."

"And that would have automatically been a bad thing?" Helen said.

"We've tried, Tom, to be there for you and to listen. I hope you know that." Daniel got up but then sat down—nowhere to go. The words in his mouth felt both real and stale.

Tom stuffed his hands in his jeans pockets. "I knew this would be hard. And it's not like I have a bunch to say."

"You just decided to blow your life up for no special reason." Helen looked away. Too many memories of her son at too many ages flooded her. He was two, five, eight, twelve, fifteen, seventeen, now twenty.

"It doesn't mean that. It means I need to live, and being in school was not living. Being in school was pretending, and I couldn't pretend anymore. I couldn't pretend to be interested when I wasn't. I know I'm going out on a limb. I know everyone is staying in school because they don't want to be on that limb." He stood a bit taller. Daylight began to seep through the room's farthest window. Another gray, depths-of-winter day.

"It's not a limb. It's a war. And lacrosse?"

"I told the coach. He said I was making a mistake but still said, 'Good luck.'"

Helen looked up—a cobweb in a ceiling corner. She cleaned her house herself. "Somehow I thought these things happened to other people.

I thought the path we had made in life was a reasonable one and that our children would see that and follow suit. What you are doing is not reasonable, but I suppose that goes without saying." She rubbed at her temples vigorously. "I really do not want you in that army."

"I don't know what to say. I haven't thought it through. But Dad was in the army. He lived."

"A different war in a different time," Daniel said. "And no one in war knows anything about living. War is about surviving."

"If you're thinking of going, then I have to say I will be disappointed. I will always love you, but I will be disappointed." Helen stopped. "I'm whimpering. How pathetic."

"Look, you both must think I've lost it, but I haven't. We'll see what happens." Tom edged toward the couch. "Don't cry, Mom. I didn't leave to make you cry."

"I know you didn't. I'm sure you made your mind up in a way that made sense to you and that if I begged you to go back, it would only make things worse."

"Yeah, my mind is made up. I packed up my stuff. It's still in the car."

Daniel reached a hand to Helen, which she took. "Minds of their own" was a phrase they traded back and forth over the course of their children's growing up. They hadn't understood the phrase, though, until now. They were just well-meaning words.

"We'll help you with your gear," Daniel said.

"Your room is as you left it. Except I put on some new sheets for when you came home later in the semester." Helen squeezed her husband's hand.

"Thanks," said Tom. "Thanks." He stood there rooted, an awkward, stubborn tree. Home again, home again. He had thought what it would be like, how there would be a feeling like seeing yourself in a broken mirror. He hadn't heard, however, his parents' voices.

A Sister's Voice, the Wheedling Needle of Kitchen Table Proximity /

"You always put too much milk in your cereal."

"Is it your business?"

"I have to sit here and watch it get mushy."

Sharon looked around for allies, but no one took her up. Daniel was shuffling legal papers while getting soft-boiled egg on them. Helen was riffling through a tome about slavery she was going to read for the course she was taking, the last before getting her master's. Tom was in his bedroom, the door closed. "Kix, to name the cereal in your bowl, is meant to be consumed right away. They'd make it soggy already if they thought it should be soggy. It's crisp and happy, and you make it soggy and sad."

"Don't be overly imaginative or anything." Her brother Herb raised a spoon. "Cereal doesn't have feelings."

Daniel looked up from his papers. "Anyone have a paper clip?"

"Did you look in your pocket?" Helen asked.

"You should wear a necklace of them, Dad." Sharon made a theatrical gesture, as if throwing around a long strand of pearls. Before various disenchantments set in, she had been in the school theater club and had a solo in a musical.

"Guys don't wear necklaces," said Herb.

"We know that," Sharon snipped back.

"All I wanted," Daniel said, "was a paper clip."

"Your cereal is getting mushier." Sharon made an aggrieved face.

"I figure you're going to be a lawyer and investigator like dad. You're so good at sticking your nose into other people's business. That's what you do, right, Dad?" Herb put a spoonful of the mushy Kix into his mouth. "Mmmm, good."

Daniel put on a weary frown meant to convey the hopelessness of parenting: "The Big Shrug," as his wife called it. Daniel thought of Tom, and the frown deepened.

"The law, as I've informed you on numerous occasions, is about lies and money. 'Fraud' is America's middle name. 'Justice' is the dog chasing the fire truck. People do indeed pay me to stick my nose in their business and other people's business, if you want to put it that way."

Herb beamed with vindication.

"What's with my other brother? I heard you guys talking. I heard Tom go back upstairs." Sharon took a bite of raisin toast. "I think they're cutting down on the number of raisins per loaf. Is that how capitalism works, Mom? Fewer raisins and more money for Wall Street?"

"As the daughter of socialists, which means I grew up on Jewish rye bread, I wouldn't know about the raisins. I do know your brother is home from college—for good it seems—and will be staying with us until further notice."

"You mean like a draft board notice?" Herb asked.

"I shouldn't have used that word, Herbert."

"Herb can't help making puns. You know that. But why did Tom leave? He didn't tell me he was thinking of leaving."

"You're his confidant?" said Herb. Another beam, this one ironic.

"He doesn't seem to have told anybody," Daniel said. "He got an idea in his head, although I don't know if I should call it an 'idea.'"

"In high school they call it a brain fart."

"Thanks, Herb. As I was saying, he's left school. What happens next none of us know, least of all Tom, though he did say he's going to wash dishes to earn some money."

"He left school so he could wash dishes and get drafted?" Sharon rubbed her fingertips together to rid herself of a few toast crumbs. "I thought Tom was the normal one in the family. You know—a jock. Did okay in school but didn't take it too seriously. More girlfriends than I could keep up with.

Plenty of drive-around-in-the-car buddies. Even a black buddy who played lacrosse too. A regular dude. Clear as a glass of water. And now . . ." Sharon paused, but no one spoke. "I'm waiting for some parental comment. Dad, you could say something like 'Well, Sharon, you're fishing in deep water.' Or, Mom, you could go for the low-key approach, as in 'Well, did you find a paper clip, dear?'"

"Maybe you could write scripts for us and we could stop living," said Herb.

"I don't know about scripts," said Helen, "but predictability looks pretty good to me. It beats going upstairs and crying, which is probably what I'll do when you all leave." She raised a china cup in a show of false cheer. "Well, did you find a paper clip, dear?"

"Thanks for asking," Daniel replied. "I found two."

Two Days, Two Weeks, Two Months /

In a dream an ancestor told him he was going to die soon. An old, ill man, he already knew that, but the dream was preparation for a death in bed, not a warrior's death. Many times Ho Chi Minh, the avatar of Vietnamese independence, might have died a warrior's death; many times he learned how others died that death. If he indulged his memory, he could see friends of his youth who perished in the struggle, whose bravery had helped to achieve nationhood, but not yet a full nationhood, a nationhood that was not North and South.

There was no shortage of proverbs about the futility of dividing anything. Division made no one happy. Everyone still wanted a full share. What was half a nation, particularly when one half was little more than a puppet? Yet people died every day for that puppet. To Ho's perpetual surprise, people pushed aside the truth of liberation. Or he wasn't surprised.

He understood how a person was born into a set of circumstances, however degrading, and lived with them and was willing to die for them. He, too, had been born into a set of circumstances and duties, but something in him rebelled. Something in him set him on his course, where many became his comrades and yet he was alone, a determined man on his own.

No one listened to him now the way people once had listened to him. He was a relic, a tie to the past, someone to be evoked, someone who had not just pointed the way but fought for it. What an idealist he had been at the outset! How life had hardened him! But that was to be expected. No one gave up power graciously. And no one in the West bothered to understand the simplest facts of regional history. Why should they when they could impose their notions by force? Why should they when their prestige and honor were at stake, to say nothing of their investments? Despite the glossy speeches, power only respected other power.

Someday in a not-too-distant future, his people would be united and would live together and help one another. No one would look down on them. No one would tell them who they were. They would define their own lives. Was that too much to ask of history? That's why guns spoke last and strongest. Guns had an answer. People understood death.

He sensed that his dream would overcome him so that waking would be a dream too. He didn't mind that. Once he would have, but not now. He had had his fill. Younger men with their own ideas had come along to pick up the struggle. They would succeed. He was sure of that.

He would die as Uncle Ho, someone who had steadily pushed forward, someone with a long-standing vision in his eyes and righteous blood on his hands. He could still receive visitors and talk courteously, while soldiers tramped the road named after him and fought to the death. Some nights those deaths came into his dreams, but he had the gift of faith. The deaths were necessary.

The Necessary Visitation, the Right Thing To Do, the Curious Inquiry /

Two nights after Tom's arrival and after finishing her homework—French and US history—Sharon knocked on Tom's bedroom door.

"Come in," he boomed, the bass of cheerful indifference, older-brotherness. "In" meant two baby steps.

"So?" Sharon said, trying to look bright-eyed, which was second nature in dealing with her brother, Tom being something of another planet, not serious the way she and Herb were. He tended to feign, roll off and slip away, airy despite being such a solid, muscled guy. Always "fine." For her, he took some work.

"So?" Tom answered back.

"Don't be your usual, amiable sphinx self. What happened?"

"What do you mean, 'What happened?'"

"I can be patient. I mean you left school. You're home."

"You notice everything, Sharon."

"You're not easy to love, but I do. So school sort of lost it for you? It sure loses it for me." She was still standing by the door. No invitation to come in further and sit down. A man's castle.

Tom, who was in jeans and a University of Maryland T-shirt, barefoot, walked toward Sharon and lifted his hands as if making a proclamation. "School was a drag. You sit in auditoriums and try to pay attention, but really all you want to do is party and get laid, which I did plenty of. Everybody sits there like the professors are saying the last words, but then everybody just wants a grade." He yawned and stretched. When he was a boy of seven or eight, Helen was struck by his gracefulness and sent him to dancing school, but athletics, running around in the fresh air and yelling, soon took over. "There's a war going on, but the radical types didn't do anything for me either. Making noise, but nothing more than that."

19

"That means you've thought about the war and about yourself?"

"That means I'm here in my bedroom in a suburb of Baltimore talking to my sister, who probably can't wait to go off and further her education. Hope you do better than I did." He stretched his arms downward, touching his toes.

"I can't wait, nothing against Mom and Dad, and I wouldn't mind going someplace where the professors had something important to say. I don't have to go fight in a war, though, which is the question in the back of everyone's mind in this house, even if it's not in yours."

"Yeah, well, it's like I said about a war going on." He stopped. "I haven't thought much through. I just did it. I need to start being an adult, and that's how I decided to do it. Might not have been the smartest move, but it's my move. That feels good."

"I get it."

"Do you?"

"Don't lay that trip on me. What does Mom say? 'I wasn't born yesterday.'"

"You're right, I'm being pissy. I'll tell it straight. I'm good, like I said— head on my shoulders, knee healed and legs ready to do laps, but I could use a map. I've got stuff going on inside me, but no idea where it's headed. I'm trying to take some time out, but I know there isn't any. Not now." Tom looked down. "Guess I need to cut my toenails."

"You're dodging me."

"I could be dodging you more. I could have just told you I like your hair that long, like Joan Baez the Second and left it at that."

"True." Sharon looked around the room where Tom's stuff from college—weights, a big transistor radio, lacrosse sticks—lay on the floor. What looked like his one real suitcase hadn't been opened. "Just keep me posted. We're living on the same dorm floor now. And, hey, if you're still smoking weed, think of your sister." Though her brother was just a few feet away, Sharon waved to him. She knew he had no questions for her.

Questions Annoyed Him. He Wanted Answers /

Lyndon Johnson had not asked for this war. He had inherited it when he inherited the presidency. He had taken power with the darkest of clouds over his head, but, as a master doer, there were no clouds he couldn't dispel. The war, though, was different; the war was like being caught in public with your trousers down. You could make excuses, but he wasn't a man to make excuses. Being the vice president was like making excuses, like being half a man. He was all man, and no man backed down from a war, much less one with the communists.

He'd known as much about Vietnam as most Americans, which was to say nothing: a place somewhere in Southeast Asia. Who lived there was irrelevant. There were the categories and the words—*democracy* and *freedom* being two of the biggest—and that was the end of any discussion. Kennedy had been an arrogant, Eastern son of a bitch, but he'd laid down the line about the nation taking on whatever had to be taken on. And Kennedy had been in World War II and knew what war was. He'd been a hero.

Lyndon had advisers, brains, to talk with, to say nothing of the generals, but none were much help. They had ideas, strategies, and assessments, and they had confidence, especially the generals. Yet the enemy didn't seem to care, as if to say, "Bring it on." He could bomb them and bomb them, but they didn't stop coming. Now he had to pay attention to Khe Sanh, where the United States had a base that might be overrun like what happened to the French. So the United States needed to reinforce and obliterate the hell out of everything around it, but how was he supposed to make sense of some place he could barely pronounce, that was a million miles from Austin and Dallas and everything he knew? The generals talked a good game, but when he lay in bed at night he had to wonder what good any general was. He thought of those brave Marines at Khe Sanh. The generals wanted more men and more weapons. America had both, but to what point?

America wasn't supposed to lose wars. The point of America was to win wars and show the world the value of the American way of life. That sharp point was stabbing a hole in him, but his power mocked him. Something in him, something almost physical, like an ache in his gut, suspected that he had been beaten. As a man, and as the nation's leader, that was a feeling he was not going to confide to anyone. As a wartime president, he had the duty of rallying and uniting the nation, but the nation was becoming more divided daily. Senators sniped at him, while the marchers—young people but not just young people—were letting him know how they felt about the war, which had become "Johnson's war." They did not believe in it. They did not believe in him.

One mirror he couldn't help looking into was the mirror of history. He had been the creator of the Great Society and landmark bills Congress had passed. In recent years he had seen some lights about civil rights and Negroes he could never have predicted he would see. The war, though, was something else. The enormous animus of the Reds was breathing down his neck. There was no going back, but there seemed no real going forward beyond throwing more bombs and men at people who weren't operating by the same rules as the so-called developed world. Frustrated, dismayed, and required to give a positive account of himself to the American people, Lyndon Johnson did not want to look into that mirror for too long.

❧

After Many Looks in the Mirror and Talks with That Image /

"From now on I want to be called 'Starflower.' It's my new name. I'm giving it to myself." In keeping with someone making a pronouncement, Sharon sat up straighter.

"Is it that one word or two?" Herb asked. "May I call you 'Star' for short?"

Helen, who had been washing breakfast plates, turned around from the sink. "What may I ask is wrong with the name Sharon? Your father and I thought it was a perfectly lovely name. You are named, as you know, for my grandmother Selma, who died shortly before you were born."

"I've kept the *S*, Mom, but the name isn't me. It's just some name."

"Isn't there some shrub called rose of Sharon? That must mean the name is in the Bible."

"No one wants your pointless information, Herbie." Sharon stuck her tongue out.

Tom, who had made it down for breakfast, looked up from his Cheerios. "You're a hippie, right? You're dressing like your idea of some south-of-the-border peasant woman and you're against the war and you'll probably stop eating meat one of these days, which means more fried chicken for me." He genially sneered.

"Sharon—" Helen began.

"Starflower." Sharon stuck her tongue out at her other brother. "You guys are both losers."

"I love your name the way I love you. I don't want you to become someone else or become some other name."

"I have to be who I am, Mom."

"But you are who you are anyway. A name isn't going to change you." This came from Daniel, who had put down the first section of *The Sun*, as the newspaper's morning edition was titled, as opposed to the afternoon edition, the *Evening Sun*, both of which came to the Brownson household, along with the Sunday edition.

"I didn't say it would, Dad. I said from now on I'm Starflower."

Helen made an unhappy face. Daniel returned to the paper. Tom refilled his cereal bowl. "Great to meet you, Starflower," Herb said.

"I realize that to my family this may seem like some stupid teenage girl notion, but it's not. I've been thinking about how I need to be freer inside me. Everyone's tying me down."

"I'm not interested in tying you down. I love you the way you are," said Helen.

"I know and appreciate that, but you're not me."

"Can't argue that one," said Herb.

"Will you butt out, Herb? I'm serious."

"So am I," said Helen. "And I'm more than a little upset."

Daniel could see a constriction in her face. Dismay, perhaps worse.

"Are you going to ask your teachers to call you that?" Tom asked. "Just curious."

"I am."

"And do you think they'll respect you?" Tom picked up the cereal bowl and tilted it to his mouth so he could drain the last drops of milk in it.

"Tom! You've been doing that since childhood. Won't you ever change?"

Daniel saw the constriction in Helen's face ease.

"Old habits die hard," Tom replied.

"I'm going to make them respect me," said Sharon, "the way you'll respect me."

"I'm good with that name. I may forget, but you can remind me," said Daniel. He started to refold the newspaper into something like the pristine shape it had arrived in that morning. "I'm sticking with my name, though. Anyone calling me 'Danny' gets fifty lashes." He started to crack a paternal smile but then took it back. "I'm afraid Johnson doesn't know what he's doing. He may even know that he doesn't know what he's doing."

"Who does?" said Herb.

"Point taken, Herbert." With both hands Daniel smoothed the front page flat on the kitchen table. The photo on that page showed the president answering questions at a news conference. For a big, confident man, he looked spent and haggard.

The Haggard Sought Signs of Divine Election /

In the United States, there was as a sort of perennial news item for a certain segment of society—the matter of the Second Coming.

Herb had read about what was called "Millenarianism" in the *Britannica* (a set of which resided in the Brownsons' den). If he had been asked to explain the matter to someone, which was unlikely—although he'd had some off-the-wall discussions with his friend Chuck on the school bus— he might have said, working along the "what would the immortal comic Lenny Bruce have said" line, that it had been on the back burner for a long time although sometimes, as various prophets and their disciples testified, on the front burner. Christ would return. There would be a thousand years of peace, maybe endless peace, because people would stop counting. People would return in their bodies, which would mean, if you thought about it the way Herb liked to think about such things, a lot of bodies. There would be the end of time in the way people knew time—eating Cheerios, joking and bickering with your sister—because there would be a different kind of time, a sort of suspended time, a feel-good time, a righteous time. No one could really exactly define that time because no one had experienced it, but people got the idea. More religious inexperience than religious experience.

For hundreds of years in the United States, many people had been walking around living their lives while waiting for the end of time. They looked for signs, which were plentiful, and they had a serious admonitory chip on their shoulders. The end-time could happen at any moment. Were you ready? Did you understand what was at stake? They had to put up with people who didn't believe in the end of time, who fornicated, blasphemed, and drank, and generally acted as though Jesus was irrelevant, which had to be, Herb thought, an insult. Such people didn't understand how life had a very big redemptive point to make.

They didn't understand that America had to make that redemptive point and keep the other nations on their toes. The other nations had been ruled by kings, queens, czars, and military dictators and didn't care about the end of time. They just wanted to squash other nations or groups within their own nation. America, however, was different. Many righteous Americans had their eyes on the prize and weren't wavering. They could laugh in that good-natured American way, but they were serious. Every day was fraught with possible news about the end of time, which could wear a person out. Still, it was rewarding, because anyone who was in on the deal had a special dispensation and was better than people who weren't in on it. It was like an uncanny ace in Christian America's back pocket. All of which the *Britannica* more or less explained.

Herb wondered about the effect of such thinking. If you carried that around in your head, were you a little pessimistic about human prospects? If a company stopped making a certain car the way Chrysler had stopped making DeSotos, was that a sign of the end of the world? If a black person became president, would that be a sign for many segregationists of the end of the world? Might a person become inflexible with that weight-of-the-end in his or her head? It seemed to Herb that a person might become skeptical too. If not now, when? Tomorrow and tomorrow and tomorrow. Did hope run that strong? Or was it a matter of being ready, like the two umbrellas in the downstairs hall closet? When he was a boy and told Helen he was bored, she told him to go read the encyclopedia, which he did. The reading caused him more questions than answers, which pleased him.

He thought of asking his father, because Daniel had dragged his kids to church at various points in their upbringing, which was joyful at Christmas, exciting at Easter, and dull the rest of the time, but he wasn't sure how to broach the topic. When would the situation present itself? When frogs started raining from the sky? When the president said he was taking time off to sit around and listen to Aretha Franklin records because all this relentless importance got him down? Surely, those would be signs. The encyclopedia soothed in its blah-blah way, but Herb could imagine Lenny riffing on the theme: "Now, how long have you been waiting for this bus? The number what? Are you going to need a transfer? You say that God is the conductor?"

∞

A Hard Object Can Be the Conductor of Terrible Force /

"Why would someone hit someone with a club—isn't that what you call them, 'billy clubs'?—who isn't making any trouble, who is being peaceful and nonviolent in protesting the war. I saw the pictures in the evening paper." Starflower hadn't touched her brisket or her lima beans. Some nights she avoided the lima beans, but she usually went after the brisket with fervor.

"Well," and Daniel drew the word out as if looking for what might be on the other side of it. "The police are sworn to keep order—"

"Which means they're sworn to whale on people?" Herb asked.

"Of course it's not right. I don't mean that. I mean that their patience gets tried and they lose their patience—"

"They aren't losing their patience. They're like massacring people. How many photos have I seen of white cops beating whomever they could get their hands on? I can tell you what America is: blood running down faces in black and white."

"So," Herb said, "then they go home after a day of beating people and kiss the wife and chuck the infant under her adorable chin and ask what's for dinner. Maybe brisket and lima beans? And then they talk about how they have to hit these lousy protesters who don't mind their own business and shouldn't even live in America if they don't like it."

Helen began to hum softly, a sound the others recognized as Helen-in-conflict. "I'd like us to enjoy this meal that I made and took some time in preparing. That doesn't mean I'm immune to what you two are saying. It troubles me and keeps troubling me, because it feels that the assumption is that it's okay to break a few heads, which is what Herbert's saying: 'All in a day's work.'" She looked from one child to another. "Hard to eat a quiet meal these days."

"You could pass on becoming a history teacher, Mom, and sign up for home ec," Herb said.

"Thank you, Herbert. Your sarcasm is always appreciated."

"I know," Starflower said in a low, almost-talking-to-herself voice, "that no one really can answer me. What I wonder is how I'm going to grow up and live. How can I keep turning the page?"

"Pass the anger," Herb said, but no one laughed.

This was a point where Tom might have pitched in. He was good at turning the conversation onto harmless pathways.

Starflower looked around as if expecting her older brother to materialize. "What's with Tom?"

"What do you mean?" asked Helen.

"Come on. You know what I mean. He's mostly not here, and when he is here, he doesn't necessarily come down and eat with us. It's like he came home to be a hermit."

"I think," said Daniel, "he's thinking."

"That means you've talked with him?" asked Herb.

"That means he's told me he has to get some ground under his feet. He'll come along."

"Oh, Daniel," Helen said. "What are you saying? As if clichés could make things right. He's going to be drafted whether he has ground under him or not. I hate it when you talk like that."

Herb and Starflower exchanged looks. It felt as if Tom had parachuted into some enemy country and was carefully reconnoitering, as if some weird fate had come into the house.

"Tom's always kept it simple: Catch the ball and throw it," said Herb.

"Get a girlfriend, then leave a girlfriend," said Starflower.

"I appreciate the commentary, but it's fair to say that he's confused. Maybe embarrassed some too," said Daniel. "In any case, he's made a decision and has to live with it."

Live. The word felt harsh and starkly electric. No one said anything.

Anything That Does the Job, You Use /

Words couldn't say, but they followed along, indicating, gesturing. Bodies lost their skin. Bodies became charred. Bodies became torches and flew through the air. Bodies suffocated. Bodies disappeared. Bodies became statues.

Before that happened, the bodies screamed in terror. Seasoned soldiers screamed in terror before the flames and heat. Mouths opened but were black caves; no words came out. Only the screams that came from a nightmare that was real.

As a weapon, napalm was unanswerable. Its flames mocked any extinguisher. When the United States bombed Tokyo in World War II, people jumped into ponds, but the atmosphere was so hot that the water started boiling. The people were scalded to death.

People had been setting fire to people for a long time, so napalm was not new in that sense. What was new was its all-around potency: intensity of the heat, extent of the fire, and efficiency in delivering the weapon.

Governments justified their use of napalm by saying that war was war and any means were permissible. The United States was killing communists in Korea and then in Vietnam, and how the communists died was irrelevant. If anything, napalm may have made it harder to actually count corpses, since bodies might no longer be identifiable as bodies.

Looking at scenes of firebombing, it was hard to fathom what happened. Atomic bombs were not the only twentieth-century invention that could cause utter devastation. Tokyo after the bombings did not so much look like a ghost city as a city that hell's breath had blown away. No city remained, not even ruins. Virtually all the dead were civilians.

Fire cleanses, but the people who were burnt up by napalm were not cleansed. They died in the utmost agony, their lives reduced to the sharp, unbelievable pain of those final, tortured moments. Pilots who flew close to the sites they bombed often vomited afterward. They could smell flesh burning. "A sickening, sweet smell," one of them said.

Meanwhile, words floated in the air above the corpses—*democracy, aggression, empire, constitution, nation, liberation*—seemingly endless words floating serenely, abstractions that had no smell or color but that men were more than willing to die for, banners they held up when they inflicted death on others. The shrieks of agony disappeared, though in more than one psyche—a child watching her mother burn or a soldier feeling, even at a distance, the terrible heat—the shrieks lodged and never left.

❧

Left to Their Own Conversational Gambits, the Family Wanders, Though Not Aimlessly /

"Flog the frog this morning, Herbster?" Tom leered. He looked chipper in a button-down shirt and khakis.

"No, I thought I'd beat my meat instead." Herb leered back.

"Hey, I wanted to pound my mound, but there wasn't time." Starflower raised both hands in a what-can-you-do gesture.

"Children," said Helen.

"Which is one thing we definitely are not." Starflower lowered her hands and gripped the edge of the kitchen table as if about to deliver a speech.

"You're up early this morning, Thomas."

"Thanks for noticing."

"No need for that tone this early in the day. I'm cutting you a fair amount of slack, but I don't want you to think I'm not paying attention." Daniel fingered the Windsor knot of his tie, one way he put a physical period on his words.

"You and the draft board, Dad."

"How's work going?" Helen asked. As parents, Helen and Daniel worked in tandem. Two draft horses. Two card sharps. Two debaters. Two short- and long-distance haulers.

"Washing dishes in a pizza joint doesn't change much from day to day. It's what any self-respecting guidance counselor calls a dead-end job, but it's a dead end that puts gas in the VW and lets me do some thinking."

Four people paused in their breakfast routines to listen.

"I haven't made up my mind. About anything."

"Well, keep us posted. Time, as you know, stops for no one." Daniel reached for the sugar bowl.

"Since you're not afflicted with school, like some of us, got any plans for the day?" Herb asked.

"Think I'll drive around B-more and see what's happening. Enjoy my freedom. Maybe stop and see a couple people."

Four people wanted to ask, "What people?" but knew they would not get an answer. Tom tended to vagueness about his doings, not exactly secretive, but not forthcoming. As a boy he'd gone off on walks by himself and when asked by Daniel or Helen what he'd been up to would reply, "thinking about nothing."

"If you're downtown around noon, why don't you stop by the office and we'll have lunch? I'm in today," Daniel said.

"Thanks. Could happen." Tom shook out some more Cheerios into his bowl. "I could live on Cheerios."

"You could have been a horse," said Starflower. "Maybe in another life you were."

"Or just something round with a hole in it," said Herb.

"I sure missed sitting down for breakfast when I was at college. No wonder I came home." Tom set the box down before him and ducked his head as if walling himself off.

Helen and Daniel deployed "we'll have to bear with this" glances. On these mornings their older son felt to them not so much a son as a palpable apparition.

"Drive safely," said Helen. "It may snow today."

∞

Today Sifts into Gray, Hard-Pressed Songs /

After Starflower listened to *John Wesley Harding* on the stereo in her bedroom, she came into Herb's bedroom, bearing the record with her. "I know you're a big fan, but Dylan's gone wrong. Here, you can have it back."

"I didn't think you'd like it. It's not *Blonde on Blonde*, which I know wasn't your favorite anyway, since you tend to be stuck on 'Blowin' in the Wind.'"

"Don't patronize me, Herbie." Starflower put her hands on her hips, elbows out, ready to confront.

"I wouldn't think of it—"

"Yes, you would."

"But maybe he's a poet. Maybe poets do whatever they need to do." Herb had been sitting on his bed, noodling with his acoustic guitar. Each day he spent an hour or so picking and strumming. "Listening to myself" was what he told the other members of his family.

32

"It's like he's got a secret but can't tell it." Starflower gave her long black hair a casual, dismissive flip. "So he has these little songs that just sort of come from nowhere and end up nowhere. Like all he can do is whisper."

As co-editor of the school paper, Starflower occasionally wrote about music. Those columns were relatively tame. Simon and Garfunkel going to Scarborough Fair were not the revolution. Her editorials about the war in Vietnam, civil rights, and the numerous hypocrisies of her high school ("How about emphasizing the 'adult' in 'young adult?'" was a typical jab.) earned her sit-downs with the assistant principal who, as the tough cop, informed her there were "limits." Starflower stood up for her journalistic rights; Mr. Klausmeyer told her she had to abide by "the rules," which meant she had no journalistic rights. Finally Starflower would nod contritely ("Why argue with a moron?" as she said to her co-editor, Ruthie.) and go back to the little office that was not much more than a closet that housed the student paper, the ridiculously titled *Lamp*. She had been playing this game since September of this, her junior year.

"*John Wesley Harding* is sort of keeping me going," said Herb. "I don't mean that life here at 28 Lincoln Road is unbearable. I mean that it's telling me stuff that no one else is telling me. It's bone music—you know, so spare, so haunting, so intense. I read on a liner note somewhere that some music was like 'the near side of darkness.' That's what this is."

"Maybe you should start writing for the paper. I forget how many words you have inside you. I still don't agree, though. He's just sitting back and acting like he's above it all, or maybe beside it all, but," and she gave her brother the benefit of a significant pause, "there's room for other points of view."

"That's big of you, but you're missing something, even though I know you never miss anything. You want him to keeping doing what you liked the most. But what I think, although Bob Dylan would never say it because he never says anything, is that this is his Vietnam album. It's the album of the dead soldiers, the guys who are already gone and aren't even voices in the wind. It's grief. And that's why I'm learning to play 'All Along the Watchtower.'"

"What do you know about grief?"

"Not much, but I can imagine. You die young, that's grief."

"You thinking about our brother?"

They looked at the album cover that Starflower had deposited on Herb's bed, how gray it was. How quiet. How Bob Dylan looked barely there.

"I try not to think that," said Herb. "I try to think everything will be okay. Maybe that's why I keep listening, because it's telling me things aren't okay; but he's singing it, which means something is okay. Like Dad says about trying, how you have to do that for anything to happen."

"You need to write for the paper."

"One crusading journalist is probably enough for this family." Herb picked up his guitar and brushed his fingers across the strings.

⁂

Strings, Chains, Bonds /

In a dream he had after Kennedy's death, Lyndon Johnson saw himself on the floor of the Senate walking toward JFK. When he reached him— and it took a strangely long time—he extended a hand to shake Kennedy's hand. Kennedy seemed to be a body, but the hand Johnson shook was a ghost's. Nothing was there, only a clumsy, wrenching feeling, like missing a step on a staircase. Then Kennedy looked down at his phantom hand and flashed his winning smile, a smile Lyndon could both mimic and envy. Then there was something like a scream but coming from far away, as if a tunnel were between the two men.

When you inherit a presidency after an assassination, no one gives you a time-out to assess your feelings. Being a vice president was an errand boy's job, but no one wanted the presidency on the terms that it came to Lyndon. Yet there it was. In college he had more or less read Shakespeare's *Macbeth* and *Julius Caesar* and learned something about the thirst for power that he recognized in himself. Power could be wanted for the sake of power, or to do great things or to impress and manipulate people or all those things at the same time. What was bound to occur first was the wanting. Macbeth wanted; his wife wanted.

What surprised Lyndon after he took on the presidency was the emptiness he felt. Men of action were never supposed to feel like that. They filled life up with energy. The camera was on them, and they showed they were equal to whatever events occurred. Yet what followed him around was a feeling of unsureness, of something not of his making. He was used to affairs being of his making, but Kennedy's death had created another dynamic, something beyond him, yet something he had to inhabit. In the rare moments when he was alone, he even found himself looking around, as if Kennedy were going to appear, as if he hadn't died and the whole awful train of events had been a mirage.

He never told anyone about such visions. Presidents had other things to do. The nation's trust resided in him. He had assumed the mantle, but the mantle was more insubstantial than people thought. He was thrust into a spotlight that he had craved and prepared for. He was on a stage. The lines were his but weren't his. He, as substantial a man as there was, found himself dealing with a ghost in a world that no longer believed in ghosts.

⌘

Ghosting the Streets /

Each day Tom let his car lead the way. Although he had grown up in Baltimore, he had never spent any serious time wandering its streets.

35

Now he would drive the mile or so to the city proper and say aloud, "Turn right," then go a while longer and say, "Now left." Drive for the sake of driving until he pulled over at whatever block beckoned to him, locked up, and started walking. The weather tended to be unpleasant—cold rain and sometimes snow, lowering skies and stiff breezes. He kept his hands in the pockets of his high school varsity jacket and trudged onward, more or less lost in the city whose uniformity was strangely appealing, brick face after brick face, as homely a city as men ever made.

He felt calmer than his parents told him he had any right to feel. In their different ways—Daniel wary, observant, concerned with a small *c*; Helen caring yet overbearing, as if he were a child again—they were perturbed and wanted him to be perturbed. What had he done? For starters, he had liberated himself from a sense of life that had become a straitjacket. He had studied enough to get by, but nothing more. He had the requisite good times, but hangovers got tiresome; while pot, which he'd become fond of, made him introspective: inhaling on his own, listening to a record, or watching how random his thoughts were. He had recovered enough from a knee injury to play lacrosse, but he didn't care anymore about being on a team. Something in him had snapped, which surprised him. Maybe the big commotion beyond the campus—the war—had touched him. Maybe he needed to meet that commotion and not pretend. Too much of college had come to feel like pretending, more of "when I grow up."

Meanwhile, he found his way among the eateries and coffee shops of the city. He walked beside the endless row houses and the block-by-block checkerboard they constituted—blacks here and whites there. He'd talked about that with Reggie, the lone black kid and his roommate at a lacrosse camp he went to between his sophomore and junior years of high school, about how segregated Baltimore was, how a black person had to watch his or her step. Tom had known next to nothing about that, but sitting there that week in the cinder-block dorm room, he had listened.

The dishwashing job started in the late afternoon, leaving him with hours to walk and think. He'd broken up with a girl over Christmas vacation. They were let's-get-it-on physical, which was good until they got out of bed and tried to talk. He'd started rereading *Huckleberry Finn*, which was as involving as he remembered it, Huck so unencumbered. He read the newspaper each day, but it made no special sense to him—wartime, but you wouldn't know it from people in the street. Communists were not running up and down Fayette Street.

The freedom of his aimlessness pleased him. He sat in whatever luncheonette he walked into and listened to the buzz and patter around him: gossip about people he didn't know and never would know. He ate his pastrami or grilled cheese or submarine and drank his coffee or Pepsi and felt that consoling feeling that went with the city—everything reduced to the workaday, the frankly unmemorable. More than one waitress looked twice at him—not a regular, his hair on the long side though neatly combed back. Nights, after work, found him driving around more or back in his parents' house, reading Mark Twain and fantasizing about heading off one morning to see the Mississippi. A marked man, he was marking time. That seemed how it had to be: exhaling more than inhaling.

☙

Inhaling the Sexual Impulse /

Last year at the art cinema in town, Helen saw the movie *Belle de Jour*, about a woman who has sexual fantasies and goes to work in a brothel. For Helen the film felt like a species of anthropology, an hour and a half about an idle woman in Paris who was not connected with her husband and who seemed to have no thoughts about the world she lived in. Yet as she sat there before the omniscient screen, she felt the movie had everything to do

37

with her—a mother, a wife, a woman on the verge of menopause, a woman who had gone back to school to prepare for a teaching career, a woman who had many unholy thoughts about herself and the world she lived in, a woman like and unlike.

She thought as she sat there that she, so different a person in faraway Baltimore, was the reason such a movie got made: someone who was buried by responsibilities, yet moving along more or less serenely each day. Each person must have buried parts. Time did that; convention and decorum did that. A person could forget she was a body, but not forget. That night she lay in bed, and her head, which was terribly connected to her body, ran riot. She wanted to be taken in violent ways, to be ravished by a stranger while being coolly complicit. She wanted to know she was still alive as a woman. She wanted such a night to go on forever because she was weary of the daytime.

The woman in the movie worked in the brothel in the afternoon when her husband was at work. In the brothel she, too, worked and developed something like pride. Complications ensued and matters, inevitably, turned out badly. And since it was a movie, there had to be a degree of exaggeration: someone getting shot. There was that edge of violence that sex couldn't contain.

That was part of what haunted Helen as she lay in bed beside her husband. She knew that exaggeration. She could feel how it could consume her in the way it consumed the woman in the movie. The movie wasn't prurient. If anything, it was grim. Watching, Helen felt that, as a species, humans were ill-fated, compounded of catastrophe. The director was not American. Optimism need not apply.

The man beside her liked Westerns and adventure movies and didn't have much to say beyond Catherine Deneuve being "pretty nice as blondes go" but "cold." He had accompanied her because she liked to see "arty" movies, a proclivity he was determined to honor.

The woman Catherine Deneuve portrayed wasn't cold; she was a woman. In bed, after the movie, Daniel fell asleep quickly, no touching or fondling. He'd done his duty by sitting there and reading the subtitles. Helen, however, lay there, almost rigid with tension, her life playing as a movie in her head. She saw herself as a girl listening to her mother, who, as a fount of Jewish knowledge, told her how to be an appropriate woman ("If Emily Post were a Jewish leftist" was how she once explained it to Daniel), and she saw herself as an adolescent trying out womanhood, starting to understand how socially confused and confusing a woman could be (the sexual fuse Emily Post overlooked). Now she was moving into another stage, yet sensing it had all gone by too fast and that she wasn't the woman she wanted to be—who would not be Catherine Deneuve but someone who, in her own Helen-Brownson-née-Shapiro way, acted out her desires. She wondered whether that was a fairy tale, an out-of-reach yet consoling latitude, the ever-hidden ecstasy. *I wouldn't be the first*, a phrase her mother favored when explaining how the world worked. For more than two decades, Helen had been busy taking on the accoutrements of marriage and motherhood, a fate she had actively embraced, a good fate. And the movie's moral wasn't lost on her: Disaster was only an impulse away. Impulses ruined lives, didn't they? That, as she struggled in the small hours, was their wretched beauty.

⚬⚬

On the Beauty of Daily Sustenance /

On the large, round ("No one sits at the head of the table" was a Brownson truism) wooden kitchen table that served the family for all of its meals, there sat through the earth's seasons, the nation's historical trials, and a family's emotional vicissitudes a small glass salt shaker, slightly oblong at its base—a wedding present from one of Daniel's law school classmates who had gone on to become a lobbyist in Washington and each year sent a Christmas card enumerating his behind-the-scenes political achievements.

The salt in the shaker came in a round, cardboard container from the Morton Salt company and featured on its blue exterior a girl holding an umbrella. The company's slogan, "When it rains, it pours," spoke to the presence of the umbrella, as did the unadvertised calcium silicate that went into the salt to keep it from clumping (which Herb's chemistry teacher explained to the class one languorous afternoon), as did iodine (which he did not explain) to keep everyone healthy and free from goiter, which Helen claimed a great-aunt of hers had suffered from.

Salt caused twinges and puckers. Salt caused reaching across the table and being told not to reach but to ask. (There could have been two salt shakers on the table, but there was only one.) Salt spoke to the chthonic depths of the earth, to the savor of food, to the ache for its bite, to hands performing a little back-and-forth motion or quick downturn and then upturn, to measurement in quarters of teaspoons, to taxes levied on peasants, to physical necessity, to spillage and wiping up. Salt spoke to the powers of American consumer assumption, for there always must have been salt, and salt must have always been available to everyone.

"And where," on one evening among the seemingly uncountable evenings, asked Sharon who was years from becoming Starflower but rivaled Herb as a questioner, "did salt come from?" "The sea," said Daniel. "The planet," said Helen. "Salt is evaporated from the ocean's brine," said Daniel. "Salt is mined," said Helen. "But that doesn't answer my question," said Sharon. Blank parental stares, as in *Didn't we just answer your question? Haven't we always answered your questions?*

"What I meant to say is 'Why is there salt?'" Before one of the boys could ridicule her, Helen praised her daughter for her "philosophical mind." She went on to say, "There is salt because salt is the depth of our being here.

It's one of our elements, and we can't live without elements. There is salt because of time, because salt is the reality of eons and, as an unmistakable taste, almost a cry out loud."

"What are you saying, Mom?" said Sharon.

"I'm saying that we look at the salt shaker each day, and we take salt for granted the way we take being here with one another for granted, but we shouldn't. Salt is a mystery."

Daniel felt a fond twinge—his wife's instinctive poetry, part inspiration and part exasperation. "For my part," he said, "I'm glad we have salt. In the war we went times without salt and you could feel how flat everything you put in your mouth was, not that we were eating great food anyway."

Helen shivered. *The war* was ever foreign to her, but long ago it had become an up-to-a-certain-point-but-no-further familiar, a frame of carefully mundane reference. "And did you know—because I learned it in a class once that touched on the history of American advertising—that the Morton girl has had her hair style changed a number of times?" Helen asked this in her bright, let's-switch-the-topic manner.

"Why did they choose a girl?" asked Sharon. "Would a boy with an umbrella give it a homosexual overtone?"

The boys snickered. Daniel said nothing. Helen sighed. She could only do so much rearranging of table talk. Indifferent to mystery, a sea of questions always lay before her, beckoning and daunting.

∞

The Daunting Agendas of Revolutionaries /

The communists were great explainers. Every chapter of history could be analyzed at frightening length and then challenged by another communist as deviationist, revisionist, and other terms of esoteric yet potentially bloody opprobrium. No one, however, bothered to explain to

Ho how cold it was in Moscow in the winter. He knew something of cold from his time in France, from his room where he brought a warmed brick wrapped in newspaper to bed with him, but he had never experienced cold that went far below zero. He was being tested.

He was tough, a reed that bent in the wind but did not break, but he mused more than once about what such cold did to people. To him there was something stolid in the Russians that could only be thawed out by their vodka. Full of rhetorical shrillness, they remained essentially wary people forced by the winters to move slowly and carefully, lest they fall and freeze. How many did fall and freeze on the way home from a vodka-drinking session? The Russians promised a world revolution but were used to life happening to them. Oppression was like that.

Yet they had fought a bitter, successful war and invited him to Moscow to help him further his revolutionary goals, which were part of world revolutionary goals, although they barely knew where he came from—his nation only one more square on the overthrow-of-capitalism chessboard. Meanwhile, they spent much time plotting against one another and giving long speeches. He, too, gave an occasional speech. Diligent, he wrote articles, including one on the Ku Klux Klan and lynching. White Americans treated the Negroes as disposable, the way the French treated the Vietnamese who worked in the rubber plantations and mines. Meanwhile, he attended enough meetings to decide everyone's fate for the next five thousand years.

Surrounded by comrades, he was solitary. That was how his exile from Vietnam had been—of necessity, no doubt, because no one had taken the path he had taken; no one had put himself through the school of revolution in France and in Russia that he had. No one had stood up the way he had. To convince others to stand up with him was a life's work. Leninism stressed that conditions had to be ripe for there to be a successful revolution. Oppression alone was not sufficient. There must be revolutionary consciousness. It had happened in what was now the Soviet Union. Yet all the sureness of the communists was improvised, and Ho knew it. They had a nation. He had one ruled by the French, a nation where if he set foot, he was sure to be arrested and likely executed. That was as it should be—he was their enemy—but as a situation it often left him, for all his tactical energy, doing little more than waiting. At first glance, a revolutionary might seem impetuous, but that was wrong. A revolutionary was patient. A revolutionary put up with much worse than cold and bad food. Every day was strategic. Or so he told himself.

February

THE QUESTION HUNG IN THE AIR

Himself, Himself, Herself /

"On the rag?" asked Tom.

"Got the curse?" Herb chimed in. They both indulged in brotherly leers.

Starflower looked from one to the other. They were two; she was one. They were older; she was younger. They were impenitent males; she was supposed to be the penitent female. They took their status for granted; she somehow had to earn hers. "What's it to you?" she replied.

"Nothing beyond how much you tied up the bathroom this morning." Tom touched his hair. "I needed to primp."

"You look like something the cat dragged in."

"I spent some time with an old girlfriend." Tom paused to indicate no more details would be forthcoming. "How's your name doing?"

"Some teachers are good with it, some aren't. Some kids are cool with it, some assholes aren't. Thanks for asking."

Herb poured milk into his cereal bowl. "Do you think Mom and Dad still do it?"

Starflower suspended a spoonful of Rice Krispies in midair. "Can't you tell by how Mom looks some mornings? Dad's drilled her."

"What would you know about it?" asked Tom, his voice mock polite.

"As much as I need to." Starflower resumed eating her Rice Krispies.

The thought, and more than the thought, of sex remained. Their parents were elsewhere: Daniel at his desk in the den and Helen upstairs.

"Don't let yourself get pregnant, kiddo." Tom hunched in toward his sister. Some wry speculation on his face and some concern, which surprised her.

"You're full of wisdom this morning, aren't you?"

"Enough to see me this far."

"But maybe not farther." Her brothers, who had been mildly animated with banter, sat there, suddenly still as the boxes on the table, still as the sugar bowl, still as the ceramic milk pitcher. "I'm sorry I said that." Starflower looked away from them—the lives of men right there before her—and out one of the kitchen windows. They joked and teased, and then there was this ancient, ineradicable presence, the invisible weight they bore. "I wasn't thinking. I mean about the war."

"What war?" Tom didn't smile, didn't wince, didn't draw back. Starflower recognized him at that moment in that deep family way of knowing—her brother who refused to take anything too seriously. Or seemed to. He had a depth, maybe as the oldest, that eluded her.

"That's a question we could leave hanging in the air," said Herb. "Like they do in books. You know, like 'The question hung in the air between the two of them.'"

"You read too much, Herbster," said Tom.

Starflower pictured her brother sitting across from her in his habitual jeans and T-shirt in an army uniform, hefting a rifle and shooting someone. "I feel sick," she said. "Excuse me."

The brothers watched her head to the downstairs bathroom.

"You have a clue?" asked Herb.

"Some," replied Tom. "She sees stuff we don't. It doesn't help her, and doesn't help us."

No Help for the Dreamer /

What Daniel saw in the dream that had been recurring for more than two decades was Harper falling. Their unit was more or less marching down a road in France, no enemy around. Harper fell slowly in that way that happens in dreams, where time is at once exaggerated and irrelevant, things occurring at their own deliberate, frightening speed. There was no noise, no gunfire, no planes strafing or bombing. And Harper had been walking right beside Daniel, a foot or two away, talking about horses and the farm he'd grown up on. Daniel felt him falling, and then he was lying there in a heap, crumpled as if some giant had squeezed him, shaken him, and then tossed him aside. What happened to him wasn't human. But that notion—the human—was a joke, wasn't it? No one hollered, "Man down." Daniel didn't holler either. He stood there—rooted, unbelieving, stunned, pinned by the weight of his own body. The soldiers around him had disappeared. Daniel stood there—he could feel himself saying to himself, *Do something*, but when he went to move, to bend down toward Harper, he couldn't. Immobile.

He wished—again he could feel himself thinking—he were in a movie, because then Hollywood and the cavalry would come, but this wasn't a movie. There was only Daniel and what had been Harper, the words all gone out of him.

Then Harper started to move, sort of wormlike, sort of writhing. *Why*, Daniel thought, *did I think he was dead?* Maybe he just fainted. Guys fainted from exhaustion all the time. Boom! Down they went. But Daniel knew that was not what had happened. Something stranger had happened, something from behind war's closed door that had gotten out and had come looking for Harper and could come looking for Daniel. At any moment.

Daniel was still trying to lean down and trying to speak, but there were no words. Nor sounds. Part of Daniel knew this—that he was in a dream—and didn't seem surprised or upset. But part of him was very upset. Part of him was ready to scream and cry. He needed to help. Harper had been walking beside Daniel for miles through France, and they'd shared cigarettes, chewing gum, and memories of life before the war—Harper grew up in Tennessee—and the usual bitching about the Germans, how they wouldn't give up. Daniel needed to help.

That was when Daniel called out and Helen started to shake him. That was when he did something called "wake up" and felt her hand on his shoulder and heard her soft voice.

"Daniel," she said. "Daniel. You're here in our bed in our house. Our children are here too. Do you hear me?"

Daniel nodded to the darkness around him. "I hear you. Thanks." Something inside him heaved, a terrible wave of feeling, something that was never going to leave him, something that had endless variations but only one scenario, something waiting for the daylight so he could go on leading what he called "my life." But there was this other life that lived inside him that his wife could never understand and that words could never reach and that he carried around like a stone on his heart. Only Harper could understand.

"You had a bad dream," she said. "The war dream you've told me about." She kissed his head. "You're okay, though." He lay there on his back, and suddenly she got on top of him. "You're okay," she said, and pressed her body against his.

⁂

His Humor(s) /

Lyndon Johnson grew up with a good share of instructive humor: Always drink upstream from the herd, make sure you look back to see the herd is still there. Cattle and Texas; they went together. Some of what he was taught he liked to insist, humorously of course, that he still hadn't mastered, as in there were two ways to argue with a woman and both were wrong.

There was in him and countless others the intimation that a person couldn't understand America if a person couldn't understand its jokes. That didn't mean the nation was a joke. Far from it. It did mean that everything had a humorous side—or almost everything. It meant that there was a species of self-deprecation that was good-natured and helpful—for people not to take themselves too seriously. And in the legion of jokes, it was natural for a Texan to feel that Texas jokes came first, because Texas came first in so many ways, because Texas was the heart of the nation. Without Texas, America was just a confederation, a bunch of miscellaneous states. Texas supplied the mythology. When Lyndon started out in politics, he knew that instinctively: where he came from. If he played his cards right—and he grew up playing cards—he knew that Texas was an advantage.

The jokes were often about how big everything was in Texas and how Texans bragged about their bigness. The jokes about the ranches that went on forever and how long it took to drive from here to there, jokes about trying to explain the geography to someone who wasn't from Texas and didn't understand the vastness, those jokes were right in the center of a sense of life and destiny. You had to laugh, because the Texan was so sure of how great everything was about Texas. The joke Lyndon often told was about the rancher who told the visitor from New England about how he could drive his car all day and not reach the edge of his property. The visitor replied, "I had a car like that once too, but I got rid of it."

Lyndon was incorrigibly proud of Texas, so when he left Texas and started hearing jokes about people from Texas and how stupid they were, how bad-mannered, how violent, how prone to boasting, he was taken aback. How could they make fun of Texans? Lyndon with his big ears and too-long face heard plenty of people making fun of him when he was growing up. Part of his armor revolved around that, but as the decades in public life went by, he started to understand how the joke dial turned on everyone. That was as it should be.

You grew up hearing the adults tell jokes, and you learned about the world in those jokes. There were not many Negroes around where Lyndon grew up, but he heard jokes about niggers and how worthless they were. He could see men's faces (because it was almost always men, not women) when they told those jokes, how pleased they were with themselves.

He could see something else in their faces, a self-satisfaction that went with their sitting in judgment of other people. He was trying to get along, and he must have snickered when he heard some joke about watermelons and coons, but clearly those jokes weren't jokes. They had an evil edge to them; they came from a small, hard place. If Texas was about having a heart as big as the land, then those men weren't Texans in the way Lyndon felt a Texan should be. Yet those men slapping their knees and acting as though they had said something hilarious were citizens he would someday be representing. What was a man—a white man—to do?

⁓

Do-or-Die Double Talk /

"So where do we go with this? That 'It became necessary to destroy the town to save it.' Any thoughts, Dad?" Another brittle winter morning. Herb already in what was coming to seem a never-ending, indignant political gear; Daniel trying to not feel the weariness brought on by more wretched news, trying to carry on—whatever that meant.

Daniel laid down the front section of *The Sun* while making an unpleasant throat sound. His sinuses had been bothering him. He took a sip of cold coffee, a hazard of getting lost in the paper. "I grant you that it sounds stupid. What you like to call 'absurd.' Our government is, as I understand it, trying to get people into safe places so they won't be preyed upon by the enemy." He raised his cup but remembered the coffee was cold and put the cup down. "That makes fair sense, I trust." As a lawyer he sought resolution; as a private investigator he believed there was very little.

Starflower (Daniel was conscientious about trying to keep that name in his head, however ridiculous it felt) was upstairs. Helen had left the house to have coffee cake and "a catch-up chat" with a girlfriend. Tom was asleep. Daniel wondered how he had come to have three children.

"It's not just absurd. It's loony bin. What's the point of a war that destroys what people need?" Herb didn't sneer; he wasn't like that. But despite the comforting abundance of another breakfast on another day, he plainly was in a sort of empathetic pain.

"That's what wars do. I walked across a certain amount of Europe in '44 and into '45. You wouldn't believe the devastation I saw. I still look at a building and see it in ruins."

"But that was one side fighting the other side. This is our idea of helping people. It's not about them. It's about us. Can't you just say it's wrong?" Herb rapped a spoon on the table for pissed-off emphasis.

Daniel looked down at the front page—more fighting and more death. "No, I can't, because I've been to war. I understand how things get confused, how up becomes down. You can get killed by your own forces." His voice had an edge that he didn't want it to have.

"'Friendly fire' they call it. I've read about it."

"We mean well but . . ."

"Do we 'mean well'? Do you really think that?" He was not yelling, but he was not just talking either. "I think Johnson doesn't know where to turn, so he listens to the generals, who want more troops."

"Generals live in their own world, like presidents." Daniel paused, almost absentmindedly. "You have to understand—"

"But I don't have to understand!" Herb was yelling. "Why do I have to understand what's stupid and wrong?"

"I was going to say that the military is a world unto itself. Whatever they say is always an order. You give an order, it becomes a reality. Or is supposed to." Daniel reached across the table to touch his son's arm. "You're right about what that guy said. It's nuts. Lost. Hopeless. But that's only the half of it. The other half is even worse."

"You mean our sitting here and talking about it?"

"Something like that." Daniel drew his hand back. The ruins loomed, not so much before him as within him.

⌘

Within the Murderous Annals /

"Killing defenseless black folks, nothing new there." Reggie glared, but not directly at Tom, more at a spot in the air to the left of him. He was standing in front of a bookcase that was the main feature of his bedroom in the off-campus apartment he shared with two other students at Morgan State.

Tom said nothing.

51

Reggie continued. "A wonder this made it into the papers at all. What do you think? If some highway patrolmen shot three white kids at Johns Hopkins, do you think the news might be a bit bigger? Just a bit. But then again, there's no way in God's sweet world that Johns Hopkins is going to call in cops with guns to deal with some peaceful students. I don't see the governor of Maryland calling in the Highway Patrol. Maybe those Highway Patrol guys in South Carolina didn't understand what guns do. Maybe they weren't content just to beat up on some black skin."

"The paper said the authorities mentioned 'outside agitators.'"

"You don't need a PhD to know that in the annals of white bullshit, 'outside agitators,' is right up there, like there's some boundary separating Orangeburg and the rest of the known world. Of course, in plenty of those white minds there is a boundary. It's our South, our town, and our niggers—who used to be good niggers until 'outside agitators' got to them." When Reggie finally looked at him, Tom understood a word, *baleful*, he had never understood before. "I understand Malcolm," said Reggie, "'the white devil.' They are the curse of this planet."

Tom felt the air in the room contract. "Guess I need to look into some skin darkener, like the guy who wrote *Black Like Me.*"

"That is one lame joke."

"Agreed." Tom shifted in the chair Reggie had offered him, recrossing his long legs. "I wanted to hear your take on the shootings because the papers are mostly about the war and how it's getting worse, about some place called Khe Sanh. It's like the shootings, the students, that was just small change."

"If I were you, Tom, I'd hold onto that whiteness. Handy when a cop pulls you over. Handy when some white woman looks twice at you. At the least, a good short-term investment. Those three young men who were killed, their lives are over. We're fighting for democracy in Vietnam.

Imagine what that sounds like to me. And you're telling me you're thinking of taking your sad ass over there. You must be a natural fool."

"Or a man who thinks men have to step up and be men."

"Same difference." Reggie made a low sound, almost a groan. "Those men who were gunned down had families, loved ones. But they were black, so that doesn't matter. Black people don't have love that matters. They don't have bodies that matter. They don't have grief that matters. What's the phrase? 'Beneath contempt.'"

"I knew when I walked through the door that both my choices were bad—avoiding you was bad, acting as though these killings were nothing, like I could know you and never say a word about it to you and things would be just fine between us. But so was my showing up with really nothing special to say." Tom wanted to look directly at Reggie but couldn't. "I'm kinda sick of myself, to tell the truth. How I've got nothing special to say."

"I get it. White people have dilemmas too. You could have predicted what I would say, and I know you know that. But you came by because you had something on your mind, something more than 'Let's get high and listen to jazz.' I sure as hell don't have to thank you, but I get it. The hard thing to explain isn't my outrage. No. It's how numb I feel."

"I'll split." Tom rose slowly. "Not exactly a social call today. Like I said, I needed to touch base. Maybe that's selfish."

"It's all hard," said Reggie. "Like black people are specimens or something. But, yeah, let's keep it short and not sweet."

"I'll stay in touch. I'm around and you're around." Tom stood there, almost relieved to have heard the reality beyond the newspaper but not moving toward the door, waiting for a further cue.

"If you're looking for a last word," said Reggie. "I don't have one."

⌒⌒⌒

One Female, One Male /

"Ruthie has the hots for you. She told me yesterday."

Herb and Starflower were seated together on the school bus. Most days they sat separately; Starflower usually with Francie Hancock, with whom she went over French homework, and Herb with Chuck Carranza, with whom he talked baseball, Bob Dylan, and the war, among other topics. Starflower had made a point of sitting next to her brother because she had something to "confide." Herb wondered where she got that word. Maybe it just wafted around in the teenage-female-drama air.

"Just because you were born with a clubfoot and had surgeries and braces and stuff and you walk a little funny and can't do the more challenging stuff in gym doesn't mean girls don't think you're cute. I mean you won't be going into the army, so no one's gonna have to worry about you the way I'm worried about our brother. And that sort of lift step you have, which is barely noticeable anyway, is sort of sexy."

"Are you done?" Herb asked. He had the window seat and noticed very tiny snowflakes starting to fall. Maybe school would be dismissed early.

"Don't get snotty. I'm doing you a favor. You can't do it yourself forever. *Playboy* only goes so far." Seated as she was, Starflower gave Herb a sideways, as opposed to full-on, smirk.

"I'm glad to hear Ruthie is interested in me."

"Don't you listen, thickhead? She's more than interested. Do you want her to lie down on the cafeteria floor and say, 'Bring it on?'" Starflower lifted her wrists that were encircled with several silver bracelets and shook them, as if to ring some sense into her brother. They jangled enough for the bus driver to look in his rearview mirror.

"Okay. I get you. I'll move on it." Though he had noticed her, Ruthie, who was Starflower's co-editor on the school paper, best friend, and fellow frustrated revolutionary, hadn't previously shown any particular awareness of his existence. He was just part of Starflower's sibling decor—Herb the guitar-playing gimp and Tom the handsome jock. Herb didn't blame her. He'd learned to make jokes about himself and how he walked—the Herbie Shuffle. He'd mastered the art of self-deprecation as much as a seventeen-year-old could master anything. He'd gotten used to himself because he didn't have a choice. He'd been through an ordeal when he was small, but he had been small and didn't really know it was an ordeal. It was just his life. And he'd had time then to do not much more than learn to read. "Bookworm" was a happy phrase for Herb. But, as his sister knew, he lacked confidence with the opposite sex. With girls there was that physical bar of who he was and who they were. They were all there—way there—and he had been damaged. Not that his organ didn't work. He was okay in the boner department, but felt he was always going to be a step behind—literally. Herb coming up in the rear. The braces he once wore stayed in his head. Sometimes he dreamed of them—metal manacles.

"I'll tell her you're interested." Starflower put a hand on Herb's arm. "I love you. I want you to be happy. You get too gloomy."

He never knew what his sister's next feeling was going to be. Maybe that was how it went with women. Maybe he needed to start learning.

Starflower got up at the next stop and went farther back in the bus. Herb looked out at the snow and thought about Ruthie's body. How to talk to that body? Fencing with her about teachers and whether you liked the Rolling Stones more than the Beatles didn't cut it when what you wanted to say was "You turn me on." But that's what the Stones were singing about. He had that trace of a limp, but he wasn't deaf.

The Deafness of Habit Poked and Prodded /

"Swiss steak again?" Herb asked.

"We did have it last week," Starflower added. As a mother, Helen carried a catalog in her head of each child's gesture and tone of voice. Herb was in his biblical affliction mode; Sharon (Helen was having a hard time thinking of her as someone named "Starflower") registered world-weariness.

"I need hands in this kitchen, not comments. If you want to hire a chef, be my guest." Helen wagged a mildly admonitory finger at the two of them. "Meanwhile, I need someone to dice celery and someone to pound the meat with the tenderizer hammer."

"Good you didn't say 'beat the meat.' Herbie's already—"

"No one asked you, Starpower." Herb reached out. "I'll use the hammer."

"Starflower is my name, and I'll use that hammer." Slowly, displaying her graciousness, she moved to the counter where the meat was sitting. Helen always wondered about theater. Was it all based on life in a family? Endless cues, half-heard lines, and significant glances.

"Where is Thomas?" Helen asked.

"Don't know," they bleated in near-chorus.

Helen felt an echo of their childhoods: *Who did it? Not me.* "He's hard to keep track of. He lives here but he doesn't live here. I get it. He's old enough to go off to war, then he's old enough to go where he pleases and not tell his mother about it."

Starflower hefted the metal hammer and started whacking. "What do you think is going to happen?" she asked.

"The draft board is going to come get him or, as he's told us, he's going to beat them to it. I don't like either option. I didn't raise him to go to war."

"But wars happen," Herb said.

"They do, but they don't have to. That's one reason I want to teach. It's not all dictated to people. They can do different things at different times. The book I'm reading now for my class—it's about Jim Crow—makes that clear. There didn't have to be Jim Crow. There were other paths."

Starflower looked at her mother hard—a summoning of history. "I only know a little about that, about how blacks couldn't use restaurants and trains and stuff that white people used. They had to sit out back all the time or go through the back door."

For a moment, Helen saw, as if it were right in front of her, a picture of some well-dressed black people boarding a train and going to their assigned car; they were talking to one another and settling down as best they could on their allotted seats. She saw the women in their hats and dresses and the men in their jackets, and something lethal grabbed her, something vanished but tragically true.

"If those celery pieces were any finer, Herbert, they'd disappear." She turned to her daughter. "You're right. They had to endure indignities and much worse than indignities, and the South and the virtuous North just went about their business because there was no reason to care if it didn't pertain to you, because as long as money was being made, that was—and is—the main thing in America. White people went to their church on Sunday and black people went to their church, and supposedly they were praying to the same God. Maybe even in the same heaven."

Both her children looked startled. The fierceness in her voice wasn't Mom defrosting dinner rolls.

Too bad. Too bad. Too bad. She was trying to raise them to think twice. And the lessons kept coming, which was the nature of the living, breathing text.

Once More, Herb Considers a Text /

"Look, I need to tell you what I told Dad that I read, because it's not going away in my head: An army guy said, 'It became necessary to destroy the town to save it.'" Herb gave his brother as hairy an eyeball as he could: *Take that.*

"The army goes about its business the way it goes about its business, Herbster," said Tom, who was reclining on his unmade bed. Shortly after he took up residence, Helen had informed him that she was not doing his housekeeping. He reeked of pot.

"It's about killing the so-called enemy. I get that. But we don't know who the enemy is. All we do is make more enemies."

"Nice you've got it pegged out. Call Washington and ask to speak to the president."

"May I ask you why you are so fucked up about this? Is it because you're older and have to be right about everything? So when I tell you something that's plainly crazy, you can act as if it's not crazy because you know something I don't, when all you're really doing is tying yourself up in a knot. Let's face it: Anyone who says something like that has lost it. Do you want to lose it too?"

"I want to live in truth, brother. I know it's a grand statement from a humble jock, but that's what I want. When I was sitting there at U of M, I knew enough to know I was very far from that. Sometimes when I was playing lacrosse, I felt it. Sometimes when I've had sex, I've felt it. But lacrosse is a game, and sex is a wheel we're all on." Tom raised his hands as if testifying. "I'm at very loose ends."

"I'm listening."

"That's good. I appreciate it. Everyone here is always butting into everyone else's business. I guess that's what families do." Tom's hands went down. "So I don't know where I'm bound, as the song once put it. I mean you're good at school and books, and that's okay for you; it'll work out for you one way or another. But I don't care about that stuff the way you do. I want life to tell me some things I didn't know. And I don't want to wait."

"So joining up . . ."

"It's dumb, isn't it? I know that. But it's not dumb. Those guys over there aren't dumb. I know you can say they don't know what they're doing. They're just kids with rifles."

"Can you shoot someone? Someone you don't know? Someone who never did anything to you?"

"Once they kill someone on your side, someone you've lived with, they've done something you can't forgive. You don't have to read books to figure that out."

Herb looked at the travel posters on the walls: Italy, Peru, Japan. Helen had gotten them from a girlfriend who worked at a travel agency. Tom had put them up four or five years ago and never changed them. Their edges were brown and curled.

Tom nodded at the posters. "Maybe I just need to get out of here. No, not 'maybe.' I need to definitely."

"I guess you do," Herb said, trying to put some force into his voice, as if he knew something when all he knew felt wrong. That was something, but too much like those maps they gave you to fill in back in grade school—too much blankness. Tom was making his own bed, even as he sat on an unkempt one. He'd forsaken the shelter of routine and expectation. That, Herb had to admit, was in character. Even when his answers seemed screwy, he admired his brother. When Herb had been taunted as a boy for his foot and how he walked, his brother had stood up for him. Tom would take on anyone. Was that what he was looking for? Someone to take on? The army? Death? The unknown?

"You might want to disperse the aroma before you come downstairs," said Herb as he moved toward the door.

"Good advice. Anytime you're interested in inhaling, just let me know," said Tom.

"My one weed experience didn't go well. My head got too big for my body."

"Occupational hazard."

They laughed an easy laugh, the years they had been through together.

Together with the American People, He Deliberated /

Day and night, Lyndon Johnson did a lot of figuring. Some of it was practical—how many votes needed to pass a bill or win an election—but some was down-to-earth philosophical, as in how to best swim in the social sea, the one each person was born into. No one amounted to anything by him or herself; people were social animals. Lyndon believed you might as well own it. There was no sense in pretending and standing off to the side like Hamlet, a character in a play by Shakespeare that he never got around to reading but who a woman he was close to once told him about—how this Hamlet character complained about everybody, which meant he was complaining about himself. Did anything bother Lyndon more than futility?

What mattered was not so much the nature of the sea—the world wasn't going to become perfect tomorrow—but what each person was doing in that sea, also known as "America." You acted friendly—even if it was put on—and people would act friendly back to you. Or you didn't act friendly, the way a Yankee president like Cal Coolidge was: frosty as a winter morning, reticent, as if words cost money, and you let people feel some Puritan rectitude was at work they could endorse. As the son of a politician, Lyndon gravitated to the openness of words, the spoken glad hand. Democrats like Al Smith, who lost a presidential election to Herbert Hoover, had the language. Lyndon could quote him: "The American people never carry an umbrella. They prepare to walk in eternal sunshine."

Lyndon's forte was persuasion. Any idiot could be a bully. Persuading people, getting them to listen to you, was something else. What he learned early on was that you needed to make them feel you would hear them out. He made a point of patiently listening and saying things people wanted him to say, but he rarely committed to their point of view. Instead, he kept turning their words so that something else would emerge, something like "Don't you think?" or "Well, that's true, but . . ." There was always another turn of the wheel; if he played his cards right, he could control that turn.

The biggest persuader, however, was not words but power. Power made men listen who otherwise wouldn't have given Lyndon Johnson—a hick from Texas—the time of day. Power resided in money and knowing what to do with money, how to make money talk, how to get contracts for people, how to get laws made and unmade, all the coarse wrinkles that went into politics. Lyndon didn't come from a line of horse traders, but he understood that you needed to be a horse trader and that if you had money behind you—not in your own pocket necessarily, but behind you—then the world was yours to mold.

For two decades, affairs had worked that way; but by 1968, time and history were showing Lyndon Johnson that he was wrong, that a man could overestimate his powers and that people reading their daily newspaper could see that. Those powers were considerable—he could lean hard on people and cut them as if he had ice for a heart. He didn't brag about that, but he was not ashamed of doing what needed to be done. But when the whole society started to shake and quake, he didn't have an answer and, at more and more moments, felt almost quaint, another good old boy pretending he could buttonhole history and make it listen to him. His way of doing business depended on everything staying in place so that when he made his moves, he knew exactly what the playing board looked like. But the board had gotten thrown up into the air and the pieces scattered. Instinctively, he knew that when Kennedy was murdered, but he went ahead because he had to go ahead. And for that he suffered.

❧

Of Peripatetic Suffering /

When he was not driving around in search of "information," which, contrary to the popular private investigator image, was as much about people committing embezzlement as adultery, Daniel liked to walk to lunch, especially in good weather. On the edge of downtown, conveniently near a few linen-napkin restaurants, but more to luncheonettes and delicatessens with first names like Lil's and Jack's, the granite-faced building that housed his one-room office evoked, with its Renaissance details, the more or less ancient. When he walked down the three flights of worn marble stairs to the street, after a morning of taking notes that would help prove or disprove some legality or run-of-the-mill sordidness (though the two often converged), he tried to empty his teeming head and prepare himself for the urban clamor, the purposefully striding crowd. He would take part in the parade but a little more slowly. He liked to amble, to take time out to take stock.

Though Helen sometimes asked, he couldn't exactly say what he was taking stock of. "The law" joined with his private investigation work was a middling fate. He didn't begrudge his position. He'd signed up for it and not been disappointed. The two roles allowed him to use different parts of his head, though both had to do with a talent for patiently following a lead.

He'd signed up for marriage and fatherhood too, and hadn't been disappointed there, either. Yet his life nagged at him. After the war, he imagined that God (he very much believed in God) would recognize his devotion and leave his mortal life in humdrum, churchgoing peace. That was wrong. God had not so much failed him as he had reduced God to a personal equation: God equals my safety and my family's. Unfortunately, the God-fearing nation was not God-fearing, as the current war and increasingly apocalyptic peace illustrated. Human purpose always seemed to get in the way of both praise and humility. The creation was never enough, but then his investigatory work testified to that abundantly.

When taking that lunchtime walk, more times than he wanted to count, he thought of Doc Hafner, whom he'd gotten to know in the army and who committed suicide in 1954—a long time ago but still feeling like yesterday, getting the call from Doc's wife, Jill, and holding the phone and mumbling that he was sorry and then not able to say anything, stunned and nauseated. He and Doc had exchanged Christmas cards and sometimes called each other to chat. No war memories, just moving forward with marriages, kids, and jobs; what returning veterans were supposed to do; getting with the American program. And then his wife had called. And then, as if forever, there was the memory of Doc saying after a man died, not of a wound but of pneumonia, "Lots of ways to go, aren't there?" Out of all the words Daniel heard his friend say, those were the ones that stayed with him.

There were moments on his lunchtime walks when Daniel saw someone who was apart, someone standing on a street corner looking around, bewildered. *Where am I? Where was I? I was in pursuit of something. I had an errand. I had an office to return to and work to do.* "Shell shock" they used to call it. Probably they called it something else now. Progress did that to everything, came up with new terms. But the situation didn't change. Your country needed you and you went. His oldest was right in the line of that fire.

Like cowboys with six-shooters, except their weapons were infinitely more lethal, nations brandished their power and didn't relinquish it unless they had to. But what was the point? People lived their particular lives amid whatever political realm they inhabited—eating a corned beef sandwich, falling in and out of love, walking along the street, wondering what time it was and whether it was going to rain. Couldn't the basic situations be enough? What did power have to do with anything that was real and human? Daniel kept thinking of Nixon and Kennedy debating about two islands off China, Quemoy and Matsu, and how Nixon was ready to raise the issue of war about them as "a matter of principle" because they were "an area of freedom."

Often when Daniel reached his lunchtime destination, he was surprised. There already.

Already Known /

"Ever think about all the people who have lived on the Earth?"

"No." Starflower was diligently spreading grape jelly on rye toast. "Sounds profound but kinda pointless. Sounds like a song you might write. Or maybe Bob Dylan already has written it."

"Tom got in late again last night. I was up around three and saw headlights in the driveway." Daniel spoke from behind the newspaper, a habit Helen deplored.

"Catting around," Starflower said before taking a bite.

Herb was tempted to say, "What do you know about it," but knew he said that too much. He continued: "I mean so many people have lived, and they had names and lives and worries and beds where they had dreams every night. I mean, think of all those dreams. Where do they go?"

"Perchance to dream," Helen said. She was frying bacon, her back to her family. Daniel deplored her habit of talking with her back to people.

"A little early in the morning to quote Shakespeare, dear," Daniel said.

"Somehow I don't think anyone is taking my question seriously." Herb looked around, but no one was looking back at him. "If we don't have a sense of how many lives have gone before us, how can we live our lives? Think about someone in a village in Italy in the year 1683 getting up to feed the chickens."

"You think about it. I'm thinking about what shade of lipstick I should put on. What do you think, Mom?" Starflower puckered her lips.

"Are you feeling pink or red?" Helen asked. She never went out of the house without her lipstick on. Being without lipstick was "like going out naked."

Daniel put down the newspaper. "How about Eugene McCarthy? He's starting to wake some people up. And who would think it? He reminds me of someone in math class who gets the answer before everyone else and has to sit there waiting. People that smart get bored."

"I hope he wins," Herb said. "I hope every person in New Hampshire votes for him. And I hope he becomes president and ends the war."

"Not everyone in New Hampshire is interested in voting for a Democrat," Daniel said. "They're mostly conservatives up there. Probably wish Coolidge was still president."

"Probably. Meanwhile, I'm still thinking about everyone who ever lived. That's a lot of names. Just think about how many Herberts there have been."

"Thrilling." Starflower puckered again. "I'm going to go with something purplish. I feel purplish."

"You look purplish." Herb puckered for parody's sake.

"I'm thinking I should go to New Hampshire and work for McCarthy," Helen said. The others started from their semi-soliloquies and came to attention. "I'm in school, I know, but what am I doing to help? Really help?"

"I think it's a great idea," Starflower said. "I'd miss you, though." She took a final sip of orange juice that gave off that draining-the-glass sound. "Time to do my face."

Herb tried to think of his mother knocking on doors or talking up McCarthy on the phone. He thought of her as his mother, as if she weren't anything else. It wasn't as though he called her "Helen," even though she had a name like all the people he had just been speculating about, everyone having a life and feeding the chickens. He felt childish. "I think it's a great idea too," he said, but didn't mean it. He wanted her to stay there and keep frying bacon and be the person she was meant to be, even though beyond being his mother, he didn't know who that was. She was just there. He felt selfish but didn't have to tell anyone how he felt. He loved her. Probably that made up for everything.

"I don't know, dear, about your going." Daniel said. He considered McCarthy's thoughtful face in the newspaper. "I'd miss you. I know that. But I understand. Here we are in the winter of our discontent."

Herb recognized those words. They were from a play by Shakespeare (*Richard II* or *Richard III*, some Richard) he had seen in a downtown theater last year, where even the simplest phrases trembled and shook the theater's dusty air. He didn't understand every word, but that didn't matter. Importance hovered and more than hovered. Time, in and of itself, became a speech.

The Refusal to Be Speechless /

Born in the nineteenth century, Ho Chi Minh was tutored by his father in an ancient philosophy, the Confucianism that remained with Ho through the many ideological vicissitudes of the twentieth century. How did a man of virtue act? What did the Master say? What is the path of the Good? How were the rituals observed in the ancient days? What is the wisdom with which we can live? The permanent questions of human behavior. The long way home.

At times, when Ho stood among the Soviet communists, he was the only Asian there. What was he to them? A revolutionary, a comrade, an indication of a world beyond Moscow, an exotic? Yet the Soviets were always clear about who was teaching whom. What did Confucius have to say to Marx and Lenin? To the communists, Confucius was some long-ago ethical claptrap, some inscrutable Asian worthlessness, shuffling, bowing, and averting an inevitably filial, ancestor-worshiping face.

As a revolutionary, Ho made common cause with those who would have him. The colonialists, who by definition were imperialists, had no use for an independent Viet Nam. There was too much for them to appropriate, too much money at stake, too much civilized vanity and cachet on their side. No one was going to throw up official hands and say, "You know these people aren't children. We should respect them. We must learn who they are and treat them as equals." Perhaps such an attitude would come with time. As far as the colonialists were concerned, centuries were fruit that could slowly ripen. Meanwhile, they—the people, the natives, the others— must be patient. The colonialists' gain, even as they literally enslaved the Vietnamese, even as they kept them illiterate, even as they turned a blind eye to opium addiction (while profiting), all that wrong-doing was mere policy. The conceit was clear: The Vietnamese were fortunate to have the French, pinnacles of culture that they were, as their rulers.

How did the French—or any colonialist—dare to think like that? Evil, as far as Ho was concerned, was bred in their bones by their one true religion, by their belief in what they had the nerve to call "reason," by their political slogans that did not apply to "lesser peoples," by their sheer greed. Confucius stressed moral action as a governing principle, which meant sharing with others, not hoarding or accumulating more than you needed. Moral action was socialism in the true sense: better for people to be fair with one another. Nothing was limitless. Yet the French took and took.

When you experience contempt, you do not forget it. You may live with it—accommodating yourself or hating yourself—but you do not forget it. At a young age, Ho decided that he could not live with it. Did he compromise himself? Many times. But he was true to his conviction: a free nation among other nations and a just society for his nation, no more of the few rich and the many poor.

If you have to go to war to show you are serious, then you go to war. What was the phrase? *Dead serious.* The teachers Ho knew from the Confucian texts were warriors—unafraid to die. If you have a just cause, why fear death? With your comrades you have legs much longer than your own and a heart much larger. You have a strength that can't be measured in tons of bombs. Ho stood there among the Soviets, who had their own aims and demons, and kept his eyes on the seemingly intangible prize before him. If it seemed ever out of reach, one of the Confucian virtues was steadfastness.

∞

Steadfastness Being of No Use on a Sluggish February Morning /

"I jerked off twice this morning." That was Chuck ("Rhymes with You-Know-What") Carranza. He made a point of being matter of fact. Reporting the autoerotic weather.

"Your hands will turn green and fall off. The strength of your seed will weaken." Herb invented new punishments each time Chuck made this announcement, but he was running low.

"The stuff'll come out my nose if I don't. I'll be sitting in Spanish and blooey! All over Laurie Hanscomb."

"Spare me," said Herb while making a shooing gesture. "Plus, she'll love it."

"Why, asshole, should you be spared? You aren't part of the male condition. You aren't hanging so heavy that your balls are scraping the ground?" Chuck paused to brush dandruff off his shoulder, another of Chuck's plagues. "Anyway, I got bigger shit than my dick. My parents are gonna get divorced. Or I hope they do, because all they do is argue. I hide in my room and I don't have a car, so I can't really go anywhere, and my little sister cries her head off." Chuck bared all his teeth in a full grimace. "What do you think of my storybook family? I'm a regular misery-a-thon. Maybe you were upset this morning because your toast got burnt."

"I like it on the burnt side. Comes from my Jewish mom. But weren't you looking for a job?"

"I have to have a car to get to the job, and living as we do in the burbs, a car is as vital as having two good legs." Chuck looked down at Herb's legs. "Or two any legs."

"Can you help your parents? Be like a mediator?"

"You're too thoughtful for your own good. My parents must have loved each other. That's why I'm here, right? Assuming sex has something to do with love. Which, given the free will of my dick, is a big assumption."

"Maybe sex can lead to love."

"Maybe we don't know what we're talking about. But it seems like they hate each other. They yell about how worthless the other one is. Doesn't make me feel too great about either one. If they get divorced, I may have to choose. In which case I'd choose neither. Maybe I'm lucky there's a war on. I'll get drafted and have an excuse to be grown up."

Herb wondered how bad was "bad" for Chuck. He knew Chuck had his inner flights that kept him something like sane. Herb sang Dylan songs to the mirror in his bedroom, while Chuck perfected Lenny Bruce routines. Since Herb was half-Jewish, Chuck asked him about the fine points of intonation: "Should I make my voice go up or down when I deliver the punch line?"

Lenny had died not that long ago. "Are electric stoves snobs?" "Don't get the idea that I'm trying to *sell* you anything." "I was wed to a stripper!" Those were some of the texts. The variations, as Herb and Chuck saw them, were as endless as their school bus rides. Lenny's routines came out of a desperation they intuited and somewhat understood: People were crazy, but people asserted they were anything but crazy. Lenny's jokes were keen but futile. Chuck's parents kept arguing. The school bus led to another day in so-called high school. Male biology kept asserting itself. And Lenny was dead at forty.

Hard to Be Dead to Commercial Blandishments That Constituted the Imaginative Life, Such as It Was, of a Substantial Part of a Great Nation /

In the days of black-and-white TV, because for a time those were the only days, a man dressed to play tennis (viewers first saw him helping a girl they presumed to be his daughter hit a forehand) spoke to the world at large in a forthright, deep voice. He was your teeth. Behind him was something called "the Gardol Shield." Someone served a tennis ball that bounced harmlessly off the shield. Hard to know what the shield was made of. Seemed as though glass would shatter, but a tennis ball was not a hard ball. Maybe Plexiglas, whatever that was made of. Still, the ball bounced off and the man never winced, the way you might if a tennis ball were coming your way and you were talking to some people and not going to do something awkward like duck or move aside. The announcer was holding his position. His daughter seemed to have disappeared, but he informed the world at large that you "can't learn too early" about the benefits of Colgate dental cream.

For those like the members of the Brownson family, who in their various ways were interested in the deliberations of reason, asking what ingredients went into Gardol was a fair question. As a word, *Gardol* was one of those invented nouns that advertising and technology tossed up like so much clever confetti. Men made Gardol the way they made Plexiglas. It sounded sternly indicative of the power of protection: "Things are A-okay here. My teeth are guarded." Viewers could imagine those walking around with unguarded teeth—innocents, dupes, and unfortunates who invited tooth decay and bad breath, the prey of dentists who wanted more patients so they could earn more and buy a new Cadillac.

The Gardol man tapped on the shield to show you it was there. That was believable. You heard the sound his knuckles made. The power of metaphor was never to be underestimated. That was how human beings learned, by associating one thing with another, though you could associate tennis with tooth decay and never learn how to hit a decent forehand. And you could associate the palm trees waving in the background with bad breath. That was unlikely, since people rarely thought about the lives of trees and their exhalations. But children were imaginative and alert, and you could imagine a child in Florida becoming nervous about going outside.

You could also imagine how comforting it was to have an invisible shield around your teeth. The world was full of communists, but your teeth were safe behind a hygienic version of the Iron Curtain. The nameless man on the TV, who might as well have been called Mr. Expert, informed America that this product offered the "surest protection." How were Americans to know that? They had to believe him the way they had to believe Gardol was something special and not just some ingredient in tooth powder or some similar, old-fashioned, unscientific nostrum. And there was a jingle at the end of the commercial, because nothing was quite real in its unreal way unless there was a jingle to reinforce the message: "Fight tooth decay the Colgate way." Not the world's most inspired jingle, but it did the rhyming job.

Some Madison Avenue adman dreamed that line up and, maybe as a perk, got all the Colgate he and his family could use. Maybe when he did his "one brushing" that protected him all day, he felt a certain contentment. Other things may have been going to hell—Negroes going to white schools, the Soviets threatening America, the Chinese getting redder and redder, the war over there in Southeast Asia—but there on his toothbrush was that strip of Colgate doing its anointed job. Maybe, as he brushed, he heard that telltale tap on the Plexiglas ministering to his beleaguered psyche.

The Brownsons used Crest, known as a "cavity fighter."

⌒⌇⌒

The Fight Continues on Several Fronts /

"The Beatles are gonna break up. I read it." Ruthie scrunched up her face to show her dismay. Her textbook covers displayed a forest of Beatles photos cut from magazines, particularly of Paul McCartney. Starflower had moved on to the psychedelic bands and Art Nouveau lettering.

Around them in the school lobby, before classes began, dozens of predicaments were being acted out, some subtly, some not so subtly, amid dramatic yawns—"Stayed up too late"—or sidelong glances to see who was talking with whom. Everybody was supposedly there to learn, but that was the adult reason, the world's reason, the dull blanket of necessity. As so-called students, they were really there to probe one another's emotional temperature or slight one another or pretend they didn't know one another or show off or commiserate, along with a few hundred other calculated

72

yet seemingly offhand behaviors that not infrequently spiraled into brief operettas of implacable egotism. As self-styled counterculture politicos, Starflower and Ruthie were spectators at the circus.

"Maybe they're sick of being Beatles," Starflower said.

"How could you be sick of being a Beatle? Everyone loves them. How could you get sick of being loved?"

"Maybe you just want one person's love and not the world's?" Starflower didn't quite know what that meant, but it sounded deep. "I like your bandanna, by the way."

"My mom doesn't. She thinks I look like a farmer."

"Moms are sort of in the dark ages."

"If the Beatles break up, I'll cry. They made me who I am." Ruthie sighed her stage sigh. She was in the school Thespian Society, which the jocks called the Lesbian Society.

"I guess that since I'm your friend, I'm supposed to console you. I'm supposed to say, 'They're just a band' and 'You'll get over it.' You know the stuff parents say to you." Starflower looked around. A sophomore girl was raising her voice to another girl. A girl fight might be looming. "But I'm not going to say that to you."

"How come you don't like the Beatles?" Ruthie looked at her friend gravely, as though she had a disease.

"I do like the Beatles. I especially like John Lennon. He's smart and cute. I wish he were here this very moment. I'd start talking to him and, even better, I'd listen to him."

"I like Paul the best." Ruthie's eyes became far away. "Your brother reminds me of Paul. He's polite the way Paul is polite."

"My brother is shy and awkward, not polite. Paul's okay, but I think he'd get on my nerves."

"Paul would get on your nerves? Someone that cute would get on your nerves? My problem would be doing something other than fainting."

The homeroom bell rang. The girl who had raised her voice stalked off from the other girl. Part of Starflower's head recognized that time was moving—the presidential primary in New Hampshire, the claims and counterclaims about the war—but another part of her head felt that time had stalled and that high school went on forever, a second skin you could never shed, a doom.

"Oh, shit," Ruthie said. "I forgot to brush my teeth this morning. I can feel the germs in my mouth."

Starflower gave her a stick of Juicy Fruit. She carried gum around, though she didn't like gum that much. She just liked to carry things around in her big woven bag that came from Central America and that she bought at a little import store downtown. As Ruthie started to chew, Starflower wondered if she could figure out how to smoke pot before she went to school so that no one in the house would know. A few tokes and then maybe gargling with that stuff her Dad used, Listerine. It had to be good for something. For a few hours she'd be both pleasantly high and germ-free.

"Wake up, Star. Time to roll," said Ruthie.

"I did wake up. That's the problem." Starflower hefted her textbooks in preparation for the trudge toward Room 119. When would life be more than a number?

 ❧

Unnumbered Soldiers /

"You're a good dishwasher, but probably this is not gonna be your life's work. You thinking about your next move? Not that I don't want you to stay here. Help's hard to find this time of year." Joe Dinunzio leaned against the doorjamb of the back room where the sink with its flex hose stood. Tom was listening to the radio—one of the R & B stations. Time passed agreeably. He wasn't in his dorm room studying something he didn't care about. He wasn't in the gym getting ready for lacrosse season and wondering if his knee could take it. He was scraping food particles off plates and admiring soap bubbles. *Peace* and *freedom*, two limitless words he rarely used spoke to him as he submerged himself in the music-abetted moments. "I don't know," Tom said while trying to dry his hands on a wet towel.

"I was in Korea. You hear of that one?"

"General MacArthur."

"A turd in a monkey suit. Anyway, Uncle Sam came and got me. He'll come and get you. The thing is—you think you know something when you're your age. I thought I knew quite a bit." Joe looked at Tom's hands. "I need to give you two towels back here, don't I? You must think I'm cheap."

"No, I just think I need to be more careful how I use this towel." Even when it was small change, talking with Joe made him feel like a man among men. How-the-world-worked talk.

"The army does what it wants. You turn into a soldier, which, believe me, isn't like anything you've been through. You've seen movies, but you can't really get ready for it. And then when it happens, you're blindsided because whatever you thought it was gonna be, especially combat—I mean fighting, real fighting—it's different." Joe had put his hands together, palms pressed against each other, as if they were thinking too.

"Like I said, I don't know. I don't really believe I'm going to make a difference—"

"You don't make a difference to what happens in any big picture, but you make a big difference to the guys you're with. Your buddies." Joe separated his hands and thrust his right toward Tom. "Italian hand talk," he had explained to Tom early on in Tom's employment.

"I can't say I've been walking around thinking about shooting anyone. There's not a gun in our house." Tom put the towel back on the little rack beside the sink. "But maybe I could. But why should I care about what's going on over there? That's what bugs me. I try to care; I listen to the news and think about guys like me who are dying there, and I get nowhere. It's like some kind of hole I keep digging."

"You can think too much. They tell you to go, you go. You live here, it's what you have to do. Go." Joe reached in his shirt pocket for his pack of Kents. "Sweet Jesus. This war shit never ends, does it?" He took one out but didn't light it.

Looking at Joe's face, Tom could feel something flooding into Joe, something large and something he knew nothing about, even though Tom's own father had that face sometimes. Tom tried to imagine himself in Joe's place, standing there talking to a young guy, trying to explain and not getting very far. Two guys in Tom's high school graduating class were already dead. No later wisdom for them.

"Take another towel out of that locker over there," Joe said and pointed. "Least thing you can have at the end of the night is a pair of dry hands." He made a flipping motion with his right hand—palm up.

The flood hadn't stopped, maybe never stopped. Tom wasn't going to ask. He had, after all, the opportunity to find out firsthand. On the radio, Aretha was singing "Chain of Fools." What a voice she had.

***

Different Voices Arising from Different Depths /

"Ulrich came by yesterday. You know, the guy from across the hall."

"The coffin-chaser, as you like to put it? Wills and estates? Has gotten his hands caught in the cookie jar a couple times? Superpatriot who's never seen active duty? That guy?"

"I guess you listen to me."

"Sometimes."

"Well, this time he starts in about Gene McCarthy. How McCarthy is un-American and doesn't stand a ghost of a chance, and even though he, Ulrich, is a Republican who knows America would have been much better off with Barry Goldwater, Johnson deserves better than having some—and I quote—'worthless senator' running against him. And—"

"Hold on," said Helen. "I want you to bring the vacuum cleaner upstairs. And I also want you to understand—or at least ask yourself—why I should care about what Ulrich said to you. Just because you're my husband and I love you doesn't mean, as a woman, I want to hear every male blow-by-blow. Do you have any idea how pointless it is for me to hear about some blowhard when, as a woman, I have a spent a good deal of my life listening to blowhards tell me what they know and I don't know while I'm supposed to be at their service?" Helen, who was wearing an old housedress, dipped down while holding onto the skirt of her dress to make a sort of peeved curtsy. "My hip keeps bothering me. I must be too young to have a bad hip, but apparently my hip doesn't feel that way."

Daniel made a wry face, but not from picking up the vacuum cleaner. "I thought what I was saying was important because this time—"

"I'm sure this is important to you, and I'm sure you've listened to me talk about chats with my girlfriends where you've wondered why does any of this matter? But somehow, I seem to be developing a low exasperation threshold, particularly when it drops onto my doorstep, which, I suspect has something to do with spending my life as a woman listening to politicians, who are virtually all men, tell the world what they think when they don't think much of anything. They're just men and assume that whatever comes out of their virile mouths has value."

"Wow, you're wound up. Believe me—"

"That's the trouble. I'm not wound up. That's just something a man would say when a woman troubles the waters. I go around in a constant state of frustration that I smooth over because that's what women do—smooth over. And I don't mean to dump all this in your lap when you were willing to help me with some cleaning. But when I hear about some guy in your building—and I don't care if he's Jesus—it gets to me, which I hope you can understand."

"I do." Daniel paused. "I thought I'd try a short sentence you couldn't interrupt."

"Glad you can retain your sense of humor, because you obviously are part of what I'm indicting, which I realize you didn't bargain for, but then again you were born into it, weren't you?"

"I suppose but—"

"There are no *buts*, sweetie. That's the point. It's all terrible and funny and sad, and I think I have to sit down on the stairs and have a little cry, because now I *have* gotten all wrought up about nothing, even though it's not nothing." Helen sat and put her head in her raised hands.

Daniel looked at her: *Portrait of Distraught Woman with Vacuum Cleaner Accompanied by Hopeless Mate Ever Ready to Plead Well-Meaning While Quietly Asserting Whatever Prerogatives He Can Get His Hands On.* He was going to tell Helen that he'd basically told Ulrich to go fuck himself, but reporting that would probably only have confirmed more male ridiculousness. He needed to stop while he was ahead, but, as the sight of his wife illustrated, he wasn't ahead.

Ahead and Behind in the Color Line /

"What's with the white boy?"

Tom stood in a room he had never been in on a street he'd never been on looking at a tall black man wearing a beret whom, it went without saying, he'd never met.

"He's cool." Reggie made a dismissive, don't-bother-with-it motion with his right hand.

"Ain't no white boy cool. That's the last thing any white boy is. All these white boys do is make wars and then tell black boys to go fight them. You buy that, white boy?"

"His name is Tom," said Reggie.

"Like I said, 'You buy that, white boy?'"

"Yeah. I do buy it."

"You looking to score some extra weed, no doubt. Black folks grow this stuff. Been mother's milk to black folks. Then along comes white folks. 'We want some too.' Take, take, take."

"Nothing wrong with anyone wanting some. That's the way I see it." Reggie lowered his head a bit, an affirmative to the gods of marijuana. "Recreation for everyone."

"How you know this boy?"

"Lacrosse. We played some together. Stayed in touch."

"La-what? What kinda crazy shit? You can't play basketball like a normal black man? You are one strange cousin."

"Look, Tough, I know you want to start in, because you like to start in, but we got cash money and not all the time in the world."

"I bet your friend's got time. White people got everything. Except smoke." The man smiled. "Girls come around here and pull their skirts off. Maybe your sister."

"Okay, man, we can leave." Like Tom, Reggie had not sat down. He moved toward the door.

"I'm hospitable. Just telling the truth. Black man tells the truth there's gonna be trouble." Tough turned to Tom, who was trying to somehow be there and not be there, standing still but twitching around inside himself. "You probably think all black guys like me have names like what Reggie called me. Well, that's just shit. My name, you want to know what my name is?" He moved up to Tom, chest to chest. "My name is Clarence. How you like that?"

"Seems like a good name to me. Hard to find a nickname for it, though." Tom drew back a step.

"You right there, Mister Tom. That's how Tough came easy to me." He chuckled then moved to a small table in the center of the room.

"How much weed you boys interested in? This white boy got to be studying like you, Reggie?"

"I dropped out of college."

"You dropped out of college? Might not be the smartest move. Me, I got in and out of the Armed Forces before this Vietnam shit. Was in Germany, me and Elvis. Fucked my share of fräuleins. Of course if you want to find yourself beside a bunch of black asses with rifles—"

"Maybe I do," said Tom.

"Let's hope for your sake they share the smoke." He reached into a large brown-paper grocery bag.

"You feeling political these days?" Reggie asked.

"I ain't feeling nothing but good 'cause I got this. I paint houses for a white man and I play my saxophone and I got some money, and I feel good 'cause I decided when I came back from Germany that I was done with believing in anything except what was in front of me."

"There's no world of shit in front of you? You stopped being a black man?" Reggie's tone was almost speculative, classroom-like.

Tough stopped putting the weed into little plastic bags. "Don't talk fool. You know what I'm saying. I'm keeping myself in my line. The other lines can go to hell. Mostly they already have." He looked over at Tom, who hadn't moved an inch.

"Loosen up there, Mister Tom. No one gonna bite you. You know, Reggie, you must know something. Probably you two boys get together and talk like talk is money and you millionaires." Tough resumed his measuring.

Ever Measuring the Rules of the Game /

In an election there has to be a loser, someone who typically gives what is called a "concession speech," some polite, earnest words about his opponent along with some spirited words about his wife, family, supporters, and all the good people who voted for him. There's a script and you follow it, because—unless you are a demagogue—you never know when the tables might turn. The show of civility is to control those tables so that you don't find yourself fumbling for kind words when, in your heart, you don't feel kind at all. You feel disappointed, and if you have any balls, you feel frustrated because you lost and no one likes to lose.

Lyndon Johnson judged himself on the unforgiving basis of winning and losing. People would say, in what passed for wisdom, that a loss now and then was part of the mix, but Lyndon disagreed. Lyndon had no use for either resignation or grace. Whatever it took to win, you did. Although that might sound crass and unethical, American democracy was not a clean endeavor. It had always been dirty, rife with vote buying and election fraud. Lyndon did not see how it could be otherwise. You take a lot of different people, all of whom are trying to get ahead, all of whom want their tribe to get whatever their tribe can get, whether they're Irish or Italian or Jewish, while still being 100 percent American, and you're going to have the opportunity—as long as you are white—to make your power actual, because America was too big to be controlled by just one gang. You could say the organized parties were that gang, to say nothing of the money behind the parties, and Lyndon would not have argued with you. Every expedient day showed how right he was. The task was to keep maneuvering; even if you lost sight of your aim, keep maneuvering.

A few politicians pretended to be above the fray, but that pose bit you in the end. FDR, whom Lyndon made a point of playing up to, was one shrewd operator; his patrician ways allowed him to play ball with some down-and-dirty bosses. *Altruism*, a word Lyndon learned in college but never had any use for, did not go very far down the political road. The genius of the nation was self-interest, and people discovering that their self-interest had something to do with their neighbors. Or some of their neighbors. That was the glue that made the USA stick. It could be amiable, and it could be nasty.

As Lyndon saw matters, if you stuffed a ballot box, bought votes, kept people from voting, curried favor with people who were little more than hoodlums, vilified your opponent and just plain lied, you had to understand that if you didn't do it, someone else would—and that someone would beat you. Your principles were not going to get anything important done. They were not going to build dams or schools or highways. They were not going to promote the wealth that lifted the standard of living. Your honesty was just a badge that you could wear so others could admire you, even if they then talked about how you were not as honest as you made yourself out to be, because who could be?

The many people who were not amused by Lyndon Johnson said he was only rationalizing his bag of dirty tricks, but, as Lyndon would have been quick to assert, there was more to it. America had gone through a civil war and numerous fierce local conflicts. Politics could break down and people break down with it. If you played the game, though, and if people understood that there was no perfection out there, only degrees of imperfection, then the society had a chance to keep being one society and not a miscellany of people who wanted to kill one another. A certain number of them wanted to kill one another anyway, but unless you were Negro, which always was the low card in the deck, dirty business as usual took the edge off the hatred. Lyndon didn't grow up with hatred, but as the son of a man who had lost his way and been disgraced financially and politically, he knew what contempt was.

Stealing an election, as Lyndon did when he was elected US senator in 1948, seemed small potatoes compared to that contempt. Bad acting did not make Lyndon a better man, but it made him a shrewder one. Losers called for fairness; winners took the prize and moved on. Winners knew how the game worked and how to work the game.

❦

Not a Game Show /

"Hey."

"Hey."

One brother standing in the bedroom doorway, one brother lying on his disheveled bed. Herb and Starflower made their beds each day. Tom, according to his mother, was "above it all," while his father thought he was "beneath it all." Tucking in sheets each day was not part of the bargain. *Casual* was the word Tom liked to use.

"What do you say if we hang out some? Maybe I drive around with you? I don't know where you go, but anywhere is okay." Herb looked from his brother to the bookcase above Tom's desk. Paperbacks from high school: *1984, Of Mice and Men, A Farewell to Arms,* and Tom's favorite book from childhood—*Winnie the Pooh.* He loved it when his brother would tell him how much he liked a book, as in "This is a really good book. You should read it." Almost always Herb had.

"I may not be the best company these days. I'm kinda chewed up inside. Or I'm like that story by Poe where the walls are moving in on the guy. What a creepy story. I think Mrs. Kaufman made me read that back in eighth grade." Tom glanced at the bookcase. "One story was enough."

"Makes sense to me how you feel. You turn on the TV and there it is. Weird. I mean seeing what your life could be, there, on the evening news. One of those guys."

"Definitely not a situation comedy. Definitely not a game show." Tom propped himself up and leaned back against the wall, a habit that an amorphous smudge testified to. A few years before, Helen had bought him a bolster, which Tom had put in his closet and forgotten about. "It is weird. It's like that word you use—*absurd*. That's not a happy word. That's not a word that carries you from day to day."

"May be the truth, though."

"May be. My ticket may be getting punched this very minute." Tom yawned and stretched his arms out in front of him. "What's shaking in your life here in Happy Suburban Acres?"

"I'm wearing out my *Moby Grape* album. That and *John Wesley Harding.*"

"I lost track of Dylan. Shows how scrambled I've been. You'll have to play it for me."

"It's good. Different, almost eerie but good."

"Eerie? I don't know if that's the kinda music I need these days. Weird and absurd seem like enough."

"Sharon, also known as Starflower, says a girlfriend of hers is interested in me."

"And you've done what?"

"Nothing."

"You think she's gonna just jump on you?"

"I wouldn't mind."

"Got to step up, man. I been preaching that to you for a while. Got to lay down whatever it is that bugs you. No government's breathing down your neck. You're free. Or free enough." Tom picked up a pillow and gave it a punch.

"Where did that come from?" Herb took a half step back.

"It came from where I told you. Problem is, there's a whole lot more in there. I made a decision and I gotta live with it, which means I gotta make another decision, but I don't know what it is." Tom sighed. "Check out this chick. Women are why God made this world. You can quote me." He took the pillow and began to smooth it. "We'll go somewhere together. I promise. I'm trying, but what did Bob say? 'No direction home.'"

∞

Home Is Where the War Is /

Helen had gone to bed to do some course reading and "take some time out," but the other Brownsons watched the "Walter Cronkite Special Report" because it was Walter Cronkite, the newscasting eminence—living exemplar of the comforting, measured tone and as reliable and steady a televised presence as America had in 1968. After the show was over and Cronkite had delivered his opinion that "it seems more certain than ever that the bloody experience of Vietnam is to end in a stalemate," everyone sat there, silent, as if waiting for the next show. Finally, Daniel turned off the TV and said how he grew up before TV and that it was hard to imagine there was a time before TV, that TV had become like water and air. He was standing with his back to the set—a Motorola—and felt suddenly woozy, as if the weight of what he had just seen and heard was on top of him and he needed to slough it off but couldn't. A few seconds passed, but then he rallied because that was what he did—kept rallying. Perhaps a flicker of buried feeling had crossed his face; perhaps his children had seen it.

Cronkite, who had been a supporter of the war, based his remarks on the time during the prior month when he visited Vietnam. The Brownsons knew the images he was talking about. They had seen the GIs, the enemy, the captives, the villages, the napalm, the helicopters, Saigon. They knew that people, including children, were not only being killed but maimed, terrorized, and poisoned, all in the service of a "stalemate." Up until that night, however, Cronkite merely reported what had happened. Now he had stepped out of that role. Daniel couldn't remember when he had started to listen to Walter Cronkite, but Cronkite seemed—as he told the nation what he thought on a Tuesday evening in late February—to have become someone else, a moral presence intent on pulling away the pose of objectivity.

"I don't think he should have done that," Tom said. "Guys are dying there this minute. You don't make a judgment like he just made. That's not for some news guy to make. That's for the president to make." His voice throbbed. Upset.

"You think he should just keep his mouth shut and live with it." Starflower's voice throbbed too.

"Yeah, I do. People are gonna take him for the gospel, but how much can he know based on being there for not very long? And what's the alternative? We just leave and let the North kill as many people in the South as they feel like?" Tom paused. "Those people have trusted us."

"They may have made a mistake," Herb said. "We may not have had a clue. It wouldn't be the first time."

Daniel imagined this conversation going on for a while: three talking points. He could see himself refereeing and offering, if it seemed relevant, his I-lived-through-a-war opinion. But it might not be relevant, because this war was different. As in: Who were we helping? Where did the agony end? Where did justice abide in such a movable landscape? After Pearl Harbor, no one thought about the war he had been in. This war was all about thinking.

The other morning Tom had informed the family that he was thinking of joining the Marines, that whether America was right or wrong, we were there and that was what mattered. As a man, he needed to pick that up and not turn his back. "That's what men do," he announced to the others at the kitchen table. "Some guys I played ball with are there right now. Buzzy Coryell. Ronnie Braxton. Maybe you didn't know that. Things are pretty cozy here." No one replied. He waited for someone to speak, scowled and opened his mouth as if to say more, but then put his head down and went back to his cereal bowl. After more uneasy seconds, Helen said sleet was in the weather forecast.

Daniel had wanted to explain to Tom how he didn't have to do that, how his life could proceed without hefting this particular pack and rifle. But maybe his life wouldn't proceed.

There was the draft. And the Marines offered what they offered: the proud manhood ethos. Daniel listened as his children kept talking about what Cronkite had said, but what he thought about was how when Tom was a boy he had spent so much time by himself outside; how Herb was inside with his bad foot and his operations; and then Sharon, a girl, had taken to dolls right off and created her own world. Daniel remembered Tom being both the cowboys and the Indians, both the Americans and the Germans. When sometimes he asked Tom what he had been up to, he used to say with an expression both serious and abashed, "Oh, you know. Taking care of business." Where had he gotten that phrase? It wasn't all that long ago.

"Do you know that you make no sense at all?" Starflower asked Tom.

"She may be right," Daniel said. He wanted the words to be somehow gentle, but they couldn't be. And he had to say more. "Damn it, Tom. Being a man doesn't mean you have to sign up for the full plan."

"I guess I don't," said Tom, "but maybe I should." Turning his back, he took long, decisive steps to the staircase in the front hall. They watched him ascend to the second floor as if he were not so much a brother and son as some foregone phenomenon, a boat disappearing on a horizon. When the siblings looked at their father, their frustration leaped at him, a dark twist in their eyes.

"Do you think Tom knows who he is?" asked Starflower.

"No. Probably not. I doubt it," said Daniel. The enormity of what his son faced gaped before him, an incommunicable abyss. "Bedtime for me too." As he walked away, he could feel his children's eyes on his back. They wanted better answers. He couldn't fault them.

∞

Fault Lines /

"And what did Tom say to you?"

Daniel was sitting on the bed, taking off his socks. He wore argyle socks with patterns that had something to do with Scottish clans. Or maybe someone in New York designed them to look like patterns of Scottish clans. Daniel's maternal grandmother had emigrated from Scotland. She was gone before Helen came on the scene—"the Jewess," as Daniel's mother put it more than once, as in, "Now, as a Jewess . . ." Helen didn't know the word *presbyter* until she met Daniel, who was full of such words. A restless Christian, he "churched around," in his suitably offbeat phrase, sporadically intent on tasting another sectarian flavor, adjusting the God-lens. Lawyer, private investigator, combat veteran, seeker.

"He said he thought we had an obligation to the Republic of South Vietnam. He said we couldn't just leave. And he seems to feel he's part of this nation that owes that nation. And he's willing to pay with his life. Although he doesn't understand that, because he's young and doesn't understand death, hasn't seen death."

"And what did you say?"

"I said nothing. No, that's not true. I affirmed what our daughter said, which was that he wasn't making sense. And I spoke about being a man, the price he didn't have to pay. And I swore."

"You swore?"

"Mildly. But I felt—or I think I felt—that anything I said would be held against me: all-knowing Dad. That sounds lawyer-like but that's how I felt. Tom was going back and forth with Herb and Starflower, and he wasn't giving any ground. He's the oldest, after all. There's that pride of place. The problem is—he's not afraid. Far from it. Yet he doesn't really believe in the war. He knows it's all made up. He knows it's not like Hitler. Ho Chi Minh is not trying to take over Southeast Asia." He stared at his feet, one sock on and one sock off. "Christ, I wish there were no history."

"How could we be here if there were no history?" Helen, who had just put on a nightgown, moved toward him, not wanting to console him but also not wanting him to feel more isolated.

"We'd be bugs who lived from moment to moment. There are worse fates. We wouldn't try to make things out to be more meaningful than they are. We wouldn't carry grand packages on our backs and pretend the future of life on Earth depended on them." Daniel turned to his wife. "That's probably not sufficient for a woman who's going to become a history teacher."

"Don't you think you can counsel him?" As she moved a bit closer, she had the odd thought how this was like that game from childhood—Mother, May I—where you gradually inched up on someone. Approaching My Mate. And there she was, broaching the topic of one male advising another male. A puzzle that came with missing pieces.

"Of course I want to say something that will keep him safe, but what can I say? He's full of his own feelings. Why should he care about mine?"

"That awfully fatalistic, isn't it?"

"Fatalistic or just truthful? I've spent a certain amount of my life parsing out what people say and what they mean. Almost every initial interview has some serious snag to it, the famous 'doesn't add up.' And I've learned there are some walls, for all my good intentions and yours, that can't be scaled." He tugged the other sock off. "That doesn't mean it's a good thing." He threw the sock on the floor and put his head down. "It's not a good thing at all." He started to sob, a dire animal sound, his chest heaving. He never cried.

Helen sat down and put a tentative arm around him, but what had taken hold of Daniel took hold of her as well. She began to moan, the image of her son as a ghost rising up, his young life already spent and dooming her to a world with no consoling words, an irrevocable fate.

America-Fate /

Ho Chi Minh lived for a time in the United States of America, working, for instance, in a famous hotel in Boston and developing a sense of who these people—Americans—were. He liked them. They were happy-minded, sometimes like children, petulant and grasping, but energetic and imaginative too, the way children were. They put great vigor into their work, building their skyscrapers, their trains and cars. Their bustle and energy impressed him. Here were people who were not being told what to do. Here were people who truly were creating a new world, who were something more than the ruled.

The full picture was subtler. Innocence in a child is ignorance in an adult. Although there were many newspapers proclaiming the news each day, they said nothing of importance. Or they said what they were told to say. If Ho had started to explain to any of his employers or fellow workers anything about where he came from and what it was like to be subdued by another society, they would have looked at him with indifference. What was that to them? What was the conceit of the West to them? What was the face of exploitation to them? Americans had their tasks; many had their rights. That was sufficient.

He didn't hate them for their ignorance, but he grew tired of their automatic assumption of virtue. To stay among them and make America his home would have been pointless. They were materialists in the strict sense of the word: dominated by things. If you took away their machines, they had no culture. His nation had a culture that went back thousands of years, but the United States of America, like a machine, was an invention. Americans could afford to be efficient like machines. They could say that business and manufacturing were the sum of life. For them that may have been, but not for him.

His bosses would ask what he thought of America, and he would say something ingratiating, something polite that savored of the etiquette of the fabled Orient. Ho believed a young person needed to see the world of which America was part. He could see that Americans' goodness depended on their freedom. He wanted that for his country, yet Americans' goodness was simple-minded. They not only wanted others to be like them, but assumed others wanted that too.

When he wasn't working, he sat alone in his rented room and considered how his country could become free. America had been created by a revolution, but an old-time revolution, a revolution about independence, not about how men might live together. What good was a revolution that didn't deal with how men lived together? In America everyone was busy taking because there was so much to take—the best part of a continent. But they had created the old troubles in a new land—landlords, owners, appropriators, all the misery of possessiveness. Ho wanted his country to be different; he wanted a true revolution, one where equality was thorough.

He looked out his window at the crowds on the streets. For them life seemed easy. They hustled and bustled and sang the popular songs. For him nothing was easy. He had neither a nation nor an anthem.

March

ALL OF US BEING LEFT OUTSIDE

Without a Relevant Anthem but Full of Questions /

"I asked Mr. Fuchs, you know he's my history teacher, how come we never talked about the war. He said it wasn't part of the curriculum. I said what's the point of the curriculum if it doesn't deal with what is happening right in front of our eyes. He said first we have to learn about the past. Then I said I didn't care about the Alamo, and what about how we never read about how many Vietnamese are dying. 'Are they like ants we've stepped on? Are they just insects?' That's what I said. Mr. Fuchs tried to keep his cool, though you could tell he was kind of bananas, because he grabbed this yardstick he uses to point stuff out on the blackboard and told me I was 'out of order' and that we needed to 'move on.' I said, 'Move on to what? More dead ants?' That's when Joe Zimmer told me to shut up, that I wasn't a good American; that if I didn't love it here, I should leave. Mr. Fuchs told Joe he was out of order and then things got wild, because Cathy Powers, who usually sits there admiring her fingernails, told Mr. Fuchs that 'out of order' sounded like we were all like the Coke machine in the lobby of the gymnasium that they turn on before basketball games because we can't drink Cokes in school during regular hours. 'How can people be "out of order"?' she asked. 'How can you say that, Mr. Fuchs, like we're machines? We're people. We may just be students, but we're people.' She sounded like she had just had a real thought, which I guess she had, and Mr. Fuchs told us all to calm down, that he knew we were people. He tried to smile, but it wasn't real convincing, and then David Prentiss said he wanted to get back to doing the work we should be doing, that we weren't going to get into college talking about what he called this 'dumb stuff Herb brought up.' I told him he might think differently if he were living in Vietnam and he was getting shot. 'But I'm not,' he said, and snickered like he said something smart. I wanted to hit him."

Everyone at the table waited to see if Herb had more to his story. Then Helen said, "I'm glad to learn that the person here in this house is also that person at school."

Starflower asked why her brother hadn't told her on the bus ride home what had happened. Herb reminded her that she got a ride home with Ruthie. Daniel said Herb had every right to speak out. Tom, who was home that night, looked slowly at everyone at the table, one by one, as if he were considering prizes at a fair booth. "Herb's right, but he's wrong too, because school isn't about thinking. School's about doing what you're told to do. That's why I left. I don't mind being told to do some things, like how to throw a lacrosse ball, but I do mind being told when there's no reason to do it."

"The army may not be for you, son," Daniel said.

"I get it, Dad, but the army's different. If you don't do what you're told to do, you endanger others. In school there's no danger beyond falling asleep."

"To repeat—the army's not strong on reasons."

Herb waited to see if more was going to happen between his father and brother. They weren't glaring at each other, but they looked far from pleased, the way people looked when they wanted to be heard but weren't: aggrieved. He went on. "More stuff happened. You know, this person weighed in and that person weighed in because talking like that was something different, but I wound up feeling what Tom just said, that what I did was dumb because I acted as though Mr. Fuchs cared about what was happening to some people on the other side of the world. So, I was wrong."

"You weren't wrong, Herbert," Helen said. She smiled bravely but didn't say anything more, nor did anyone else until Daniel announced that he would clear the table but would welcome helpers. The soft clatter of plates, glasses, and silverware made a reassuring sound as hands got busy, except for Tom, who sat there the way he did in church when he went with Daniel or to synagogue, where he'd been a few times with Helen's brother Bernie—his hands folded in his lap as if he were praying, as if God were listening.

"One of us might see those people fairly soon," he said.

∽

Said What? /

He'd been talking with the waitress in a diner on the other side of the city, a random point in his random drive after his dishwashing hours, about how for her this was "the tail end of a slow night." When he left, as he was paying his bill—coffee and a burger—she slipped him a scrap of paper with a phone number on it. Tom took it, walked out, didn't look back, but called her the next day—why not? And now, the day after that, he was sitting in Sharlene Ricks's kitchen in a row house in a white neighborhood he didn't know, but then Baltimore—white and black—was a big city.

"I should remember how you like your coffee," she said to him. "But that's just something a waitress would say to make conversation. What I want to know is how old are you?"

"Twenty-one in December."

"God, I'm robbing the cradle. I'm twenty-five." She grinned and moved her head side to side in a show of disbelief. Her teeth were on the crooked side, not unlike his. Too many girls in his high school had flashed perfect smiles.

"You probably think I give out my phone number to all kinds of men, especially ones I trade five sentences with at the end of the evening."

"I haven't thought about it. I just wanted to come by and see who you are. My life's kind of a slow-playing record right now."

"Curious, huh? You're okay. I could feel that about you, how you're okay." She took a seat at the kitchen table where Tom was sitting—not right next to him, but not far either. "I lost my husband a year and a half ago. He died in Vietnam. He was a car mechanic. He didn't have to go, but he wanted to go. I loved him. I didn't screw around when he was gone, and I still miss him. I had a kid with him who's at my parents' house tonight." She took a sip of her coffee. "I need to make a fresh pot. You'd think, given what I do for a living, I'd be on the ball about that. Oh well." Another sip. "This is a little crazy—you being here. I've dated a couple guys, but it was no good. They were respectful like I was a disease. Like they couldn't just talk to me as a woman. But why am I bothering you with this? You're brave to show up here. I could be an outlaw."

"I've been driving around Baltimore, waiting for the city to tell me something, which is pretty nuts if you know anything about Baltimore, so slips of paper with phone numbers fit in fine." Tom looked around. "I like your kitchen clock. I like clocks that have big hands. Makes time seem more important."

"But time is always important. That's one thing I've learned."

"How old is your child?"

"You're sweet to ask. He's three. Three and without a daddy." Sharlene got up and walked the two steps over to Tom. "I'm not going to lie. I don't care what you think, because I'm desperate. I need some love. That's an unconditional fact. Do you have any love to give?" She started to sway. Tom thought she was going to start crying. Had he walked into a movie? What movie was it? The movie called *Life*? Big cast, but no extras. He got up quickly.

"You're a pretty woman."

"You're right. And a sad one too, who's putting her stuff onto a total stranger who I'm sure has his own problems. Right out of the blue. Crazy. Like in some cheesy romance book. I'm so embarrassed." She put her hands on Tom's shoulders. "But I'm not embarrassed, because I got a feeling that I'm right about you. Sometimes if you're gonna live, you have to be crazy." She pulled him toward her and pressed herself against him.

Her words didn't surprise him. Not that he thought he was irresistible, but when he had looked at the phone number and the name, he felt that a fraction of mystery had fallen into his lap. Mystery could go in any direction.

"You don't know what it's like to lose what I lost. I wouldn't want you to." She pressed against him harder but then pulled her face back. "You think you can kiss me like you mean it?"

He felt the deep instinct arising and hugged her as hard as she hugged him. "I'll try."

Trying to Make Further Sense /

"Did you ever want to be a politician?"

Daniel and Herb were in the cellar shucking oysters Daniel had bought at a fish market near the harbor. Oysters on a late Saturday afternoon were what Daniel liked to call "a Brownson tradition," which meant—as his family pointed out—a few times a year.

"Like Richard Nixon or Lyndon Johnson? Heavens no."

"Eugene McCarthy is a politician too."

"As your mother keeps reminding me." He looked over at his son. "Keep a wary eye out for what you're doing with that implement."

"I am. I may be better at this than you." Herb flourished his knife. "What I wonder is whether you think the world can be a better place and whether politicians can make that happen. You know like 'The Great Society.' Though I can't say I know what LBJ means by that. Doesn't seem so great if you're a black person who can't go into a bowling alley."

"I learned to shuck oysters from my father. These gloves are his. A few cuts in them, as you can see, but still serviceable. We lived out in the country, but he liked his seafood." Daniel looked down at the pail that contained the oysters. "Oysters depend on the Bay, you know. They need just the right conditions."

"I do know. They taught us that in school when we studied Maryland."

"Glad to hear it. But I'm evading your concerns, aren't I?"

"As usual."

"Let's say that I'm skeptical. I'm skeptical about promises, which is a lot of what politicians spend their time doing. I'm skeptical about how much government we need. Most people—though, believe me, not everyone— would agree that the New Deal was necessary and more than necessary. Working people needed help, and the economy does not revolve around working people. It revolves around capital making more money. You don't have to be a fan of Karl Marx to know that. What I'm saying—or trying to say—is that there doesn't have to be a New Deal approach all the time. I'm a lawyer and believe in laws, but laws aren't the answer to everything."

"But they're the answer to people being able to go into a bowling alley, right?" Herb frowned. He had an oyster that didn't want to open.

"Right. But laws can step all over people on the one hand and, on the other, make people feel they're going to be taken care of. But only people can really take care of one another."

"But what about money? If the government doesn't support workers, won't money step all over them? Isn't it about power?"

Daniel put down his oyster knife, took off his gloves, and put a hand on his son's shoulder. "Probably I should be asking you, not you asking me. It's like this war. The politicians have got us into this war. We don't need this war. We don't even know what it would mean to win this war because we aren't Vietnamese. We're Americans. Two wrongs don't make a right. But that's what too much politics is to me: two wrongs trying to make a right."

"That's kinda hopeless, isn't it?" Herb looked into his father's face—a frown there, too.

"I guess. I guess I believe in people caring and"—he looked down again at the metal bucket—"in oysters." Gently, Daniel squeezed his son's shoulder. "But you can't make people care."

Herb nodded. He'd been at this point with his father before. He recognized the feel of it—his father's voice, the hand on his shoulder. A comforting path, but one that only went so far. And maybe that was how it should be. Knowledge wasn't some magic penny you carried around in your pocket that kept you safe. "I hear you."

Daniel took his hand off. "Good," he said, but the word was soft and low, as if lost before it was spoken.

In Search of a Few Spoken Words /

Weary of the Presbyterian Church he had been raised in—the feeling that God became lost in the repetitious avowals, the dumb show of faith, and wary of the evangelism that placed so much heavenly and human weight upon Jesus's slim shoulders—and needing to consider himself as a soul not just a self, a soul who was still experiencing nightmares twenty years after the shock of war; in short, seeking something spiritually fresh, especially in the face of yet another war, Daniel took himself one Sunday morning to an unprepossessing wooden building where a congregation of Friends met. As he came in, he nodded to a few people, none of whom he knew, but who in turn nodded to him. He sat down on a folding wooden chair and waited. As Helen pointed out to him when he was leaving the house, Daniel Brownson sounded like a Quaker name. He thanked her for her Jewish insight. "Hope God is there," she added, her agnostic idea of a joke.

He had known a Friend in college and attended two meetings with him. The silences perplexed him—what was everyone waiting for?—and so did the often halting words that interrupted the silences. Back then he had been little more than a curiosity seeker and remembered making an excuse when asked if he wanted to attend a third time. He had been ashamed and still felt ashamed. He should have been able to say that he was uncomfortable, that it was all too bare, too inward. Now he was sitting and listening to his thoughts, which were the usual jumble of tasks, random memories—a girl in his third-grade class who excelled at the game of jacks—and worries, beginning but not ending with his son Tom. He suspected that Sharon was experimenting with drugs because that would be something Sharon would do. The drugs were a mystery to him—he'd grown up in the days of booze and more booze—while the notion of experimentation seemed scientific, yet clearly wasn't. He needed to talk with her, assuming she wanted to talk about something likely to fall under the category of "my business." She seemed more inclined to talk when he addressed her forthrightly, as in, "So, Starflower, I've been thinking." He hadn't told Helen, but he'd actually come to like the name. Part of a great awakening.

A middle-aged man in khakis and a striped, button-down shirt (though one of the collar buttons was not secured) had gotten up. "More and more I have looked for conscience to guide me in these troubled times in my listening and talking to others. I think, though, I have been wrong. I think I have not trusted the light that led me to this room to begin with. Conscience can become too easy: He's wrong and I'm right. Conscience can feel like nothing more than the glamour of my self-interest." The man picked at a shirt cuff as if removing an iota of lint. "I look glamorous, I know." A few people laughed softly. "I despise the war, but there have always been wars. Do I despise people? Does my conscience allow me to set myself apart? Am I nothing more in God's eyes than indignation?" The man looked around but vacantly, as if he did not see the others in the room. Then he sat down.

A modest, lulling, between-winter-and-spring light filtered in through the few windows. Daniel listened to his heartbeat—faint but discernible. Somehow, and no doubt having something to do with the suspended state of being he found himself in, that taken-for-granted rhythm morphed in his head to a song that Herb played over and over, the song about the sound of silence. After the tax returns, TV shows, meetings with clients, and vacations to the shore, what had become of what the speaker just evoked—his conscience? He had come to the meetinghouse in the spirit of openness and with a longing to listen; not to pray, but to listen. How tired he was of bearing what felt unbearable. Yet the words that a stranger spoke so clearly claimed no special authority unless it was the sense of struggle. They offered no saving certainty. More doubt. More quiet agony.

Who knew how much time passed? *Hope God is there.* Someone shook his hand. He shook some hands. Yes, he said, he was a visitor. Yes, he was glad he came.

⚮

She Came to Dinner with a Pin /

"I have something," Starflower held out a fist for the rest of the family. "Gonorrhea," said Herb.

"Herbie! I don't need that." Schoolmarm prim, Starflower touched the top button of her blouse with her other hand—securing her dignity. "As I was saying before I was interrupted, take a look at this." She flipped her hand over and opened it. A campaign pin lay on her palm, the name *McCarthy* printed in the pin's center. Above the name was *Peace*, below the name was *Equality.* "Ruthie's brother Kenny, who goes to Yale, has been working in New Hampshire on the campaign; he brought these back, bumper stickers too. I'm going to wear this to school and go up to idiots like Joey Tolland, who wants to drop nuclear bombs on North Vietnam."

"Wow!" said Herb. "Don't tell Lyndon," said Daniel. "My hero," said Helen. "Pretty cool," said Tom, who had the night off from dishwashing. "Peace, what a concept. I like it, though. Kinda like what Dad told us about his being with the Quakers."

"He's going to win," said Starflower. "Kenny is sure of it. People he talks to are sick of Johnson and sick of the war."

"I don't know. McCarthy isn't exactly a ball of fire. He sounds half asleep."

"He's calm, Dad," Herb said. "He doesn't have to pump up every word. If you're for peace, then you should be peaceful."

Food—lamb chops, creamed corn, mashed potatoes, and dinner rolls—was being circulated while the family talked. Helen cooked from what she called "old-fashioned cookbooks"—*The Joy of Cooking, The Settlement Cookbook, Fannie Farmer.* Herb was the most interested in learning how to cook. Daniel couldn't boil water.

"He was a monk once, "Tom said. "I've read about him, how he's what you would call 'a spiritual person.' That's sort of mind-blowing—that someone who's running for president, someone who's political, could be like that. I don't mean to give a speech, but since JFK died, I've sort of given up. His death was so awful. You kept thinking it didn't happen, but it did. It was like some big door being shut and all of us being left outside. But the more I read about McCarthy, the more he gives me hope. He's different. He's thrown away the script. He's standing up and being counted."

For Tom, it was a speech. A brief silence ensued, respectful and surprised.

"Actually," said Daniel. "He's linking himself to JFK, trying to bring back that feeling."

"Johnson is crude, and he thinks crudely," said Helen.

"He's from Texas. What can you expect?" said Starflower.

"He's better off with cattle than people," said Herb.

"I'm not going to stick up for Texas or LBJ, but you may be going overboard," said Daniel.

"Whoops!" said Starflower. "Here comes the lawyer to sort us out."

"I don't intend in the least to do that. I do intend to—and will—praise your mother for this delicious meal. Have you ever thought about how many meals she's made for us?"

"A lot," said Herb.

"Thousands," said Starflower.

"A plethora," said Tom. "Vocabulary test, February of my junior year."

"Thanks for the testimonials," said Helen, "even if your father put you up to it."

"Hear, hear," added Daniel. "Nothing wrong with a little prodding."

The visage of Eugene McCarthy, senator from Minnesota and presidential aspirant, looked on benignly from a spot beside Starflower's dinner plate. He looked thoughtful but somewhat far away, almost dreamy. More than one pundit, in the news magazines that came each week to the Brownson household, opined that to challenge a master politician like Lyndon Johnson, you had to be in a dream.

⌘

Dreams and Near-Dreams /

Some nights Tom lay in bed but couldn't fall asleep. He didn't want to read or listen to music or go down to the kitchen and eat some leftover. He lay there, eyes closed, and let whatever might appear in his head appear. Open-minded—random school days' memories turned up; the feel of the woman he'd just met pressing herself into him; arguments with himself about what he should be doing. And some nights he was visited not by thoughts and feelings but images, images from the war. This didn't surprise him. He had seen hundreds, maybe thousands, of photos but not known any of the people in them. Strangers. Yet they weren't, because they came from the same place—"The War"—and in that sense were known to him. Vietnam might as well have been the house next door, and in the drowsy space between consciousness and sleep a few Vietnamese spoke to him. They weren't images he was somehow summoning, though. They were present to him, like a Vietnamese woman who had lived in Hue and who told Tom that her husband had been killed by the communists and her two children had been killed in the shelling of the city. One week she had a husband and children, and then she had none. She said the word *none* a couple times. She asked Tom how people could be so cruel. Then she asked *why* people are so cruel. She wore a long dress; her hair was long too, longer than his sister's, down to her waist, but messy and tangled. Was she a dead person or was she alive?

Tom had listened to her and seen her more than once. At first as he lay there, he thought, even as she was speaking, that this wasn't happening or he was already in the dream world. And as he lay there, he told himself that maybe he was in the dream world. It wasn't as though this woman was physically there in his bedroom. But she seemed more than an illusion. She told him she had been sent to him—"I know you," she said—but there was no asking on his part who had sent her. What was happening was a one-way street.

The woman vanished, and then there was the silence of his room. He lay there and felt a sort of panic. How could he protect himself? Should he *want* to protect himself? What was he being told? Some intuition was making itself known, but there was more there than that. This was a person who was there in the world or had been there. She was testifying to Tom. And she wasn't the only one. There was a GI from Oklahoma, a black guy, who told Tom that he would never know what the war was like unless he went there, and then "It would be too late." He assured Tom, though, that "it wasn't all bad. It's pretty exciting sometimes. When you know you could die any second, you get with life more." He had a wicked scar across his right cheek but wasn't sinister. He was calm, as if talking about what was for dinner or about a ball game. He didn't tell Tom what his name was.

Tom didn't tell anyone about these visitations. They seemed intended for him alone, as if something was being entrusted. What was he supposed to learn? That the war was real? That he shouldn't go there? That he should go there? How had the war come so deeply into him? He was more or less living his life in Baltimore and waiting to see what he would do; watching himself, as if he were outside his life looking in. Maybe that was why these visions had found him.

In the daylight hours the people receded, but their words lingered. He didn't forget the woman saying "cruel." How could he? It wasn't a word he heard much. His family tried hard to be good people. He tried in his way, too. But what if he couldn't help himself as a human being? What if he put himself in a situation where he had to be cruel, where it was part of what he was supposed to do? That started to feel intolerable, because he could see this woman—her face twisted in sorrow—and had heard her. How was she going to go on? She had been wrecked. No one could bring back her husband and children. And what had they died for? In the name of what? What monuments would there be to them? They were just *casualties*, to use a word in the news each day, as if people existed to be discounted.

He wasn't afraid of these visions. It was more as though he was curious. They came from some elsewhere about which he knew nothing. And they might stop. There was no telling. He wasn't in charge, but the people seemed to be telling him that it was his life, and he was in charge of that, at least the daylight side. Sometimes he waited and nothing happened, and eventually he drifted off to sleep. The visions only came at a certain moment when he was in-between. Where was he in that moment? Part of him wished he knew, but part of him was glad he didn't. As a boy, he liked secrets and still retained that feeling. Though he had played on teams throughout school, he liked being on his own and being responsible for his aloneness. He was the only one who could be Tom Brownson, which sounded simple but wasn't, because he was somehow connected to a vague yet insistent network of feelings. The invisible could be visible. That daunted him but also pleased him. He would make up his own mind about the war. He had advisors, not people like Lyndon Johnson had but, still, advisors.

◯

Advisor to Stricken Humanity /

When Lyndon Johnson was a boy, he often heard someone say, "Well, it's a sin how he treats that horse," because Lyndon lived in a place where many people had horses. That was how he came to know that religious word, casual-like, not a big deal. He was one of the Protestant masses, and though he knew about the hellfire preachers and their talk of sin and damnation, that kind of fear never got into his bones. Whatever retribution he came to know happened in this world and wasn't accompanied by anything as definitively menacing as sin.

And yet if something was sinful by definition, it must have been politics, an endeavor inherently venal: malleable opinions posing as forthright beliefs, unprincipled accusations matched by principled justifications, pious statements matched by underhanded ones. You went around so long posing in public that you forgot there ever was a private person. And you started to believe everything that came out of your mouth. They weren't even lies anymore, just how you saw whatever and said whatever. The terrible truth was how Lyndon loved every inch of that dubious terrain.

Politics was always talk about going forward (or pretending to), but Lyndon came to understand that politics was the opposite. It was always stuck: stuck in money, in prejudice, in worshiping power, in talking about a better world when it offered no real way to that world. He could throw around words like *great*, which something in him could believe but something else in him knew was false, that he was just one more huckster selling whatever uplifting potion came to hand.

Lyndon denounced the communists as godless barbarians when he was coming up in the political ranks and had never so much as met one. Whatever manias your era offered became your certitudes. He couldn't say to what end. By 1968 he should have been able to, but he couldn't, as if he were an onlooker to his own life. He had enjoyed the melee, getting people to do what he wanted them to do while making them think they were acting in their own interest. He relished matching his conceit against another man's. The most conceited didn't always win, but stood a good chance. Confidence, along with blame, impressed people, who in their daily lives were full of stifled resentment. A politician gave people the vicarious chance to snigger, to scapegoat, to impugn. If that wasn't sinful, what was?

Protestants didn't go in for confession. They let the good and bad times rip and then worried (or didn't) about the next world. Or they felt their salvation ticket had already been punched. When you were out in the American world, you had to deal with a scrim of religiosity. You put your hand over your heart and bowed your head. Lyndon wasn't smirking on the inside, but he wasn't believing either. Men made their destinies. All the appeals to the Lord were just that—appeals. Considering how many people that life ground to dust, the Lord could have used a hearing aid, but Lyndon went along and said the righteous-seeming words.

Lyndon had been called a hypocrite, but he never had any principles to betray. Politics, at least in America, didn't work that way. For all the talking, politics in a democracy was about listening to what people said they wanted and then trying to do something about that, which meant that most of the time you didn't do anything. Lyndon voted against making lynching a federal crime. Why, he asked, was one sort of murder worse than another? Privately, he could admit that the reasons he summoned were sophistries and nothing more, ways to indulge people in their confirmed opinions, because that was where they lived. As someone who wanted to be known as a mover of men, he preferred to acknowledge opinions while manipulating them. Yet, as he came to see, time was the great mover. The pleasures and pains of political contention were just so much froth, while the permanent dramas—greed, exploitation, class, national mythology—churned on, obdurate and often savage. It was almost humbling.

Humbling Moments on the Parental Path /

"What do I know about anything?" A glass of Donald Duck–brand orange juice made from frozen concentrate stood before Helen, untouched. She had told the rest of her family—everyone but Tom, who was upstairs in his room sleeping—to "go ahead and eat."

"What do you mean?" Herb asked back. "Do you mean you don't trust your sensory impressions? Or is it something epistemological about the nature of the mind?"

"Cool it," Starflower said. "Mom doesn't need that kind of talk. Right, Mom?" She offered an encouraging, child-to-parent smile.

"What I mean—and I thank you both and am always glad to hear your vocabulary at work, Herbert—is that I sit in this class on African American history and almost everyone—I mean almost everyone—in the class is white, including the professor. We read about these horrible things like slavery and race laws and lynching, and I sit there and try to imagine what these people—African Americans—have gone through and realize that I can read books to the end of time but I don't know, which is probably not a huge realization; but it is troubling me this morning when I glance at the paper and see that Martin Luther King Jr. is once more being reviled for wanting to make our government live up to its promises."

"You can't be in another person's skin, is that what you're saying?" said Daniel. He had put down the newspaper he had folded into quadrants.

"Of course I'm saying that, but it runs deeper. It makes me despair when we're all studying for tests and writing papers because we want to get academic credits. It seems so insipid."

"Maybe we should move into the city," said Starflower.

"Maybe we shouldn't be white flight," said Herb.

Everyone paused to let the emotional dust settle.

"I like this house," said Helen. "This is the house I always wanted. I like having a flower garden and trees. I like walking down to the kitchen each morning."

"You get to have your own bedrooms in this house, don't forget that," said Daniel.

Starflower and Herb refrained from commenting. They had had their own bedrooms in their prior house.

"I don't think anything is going to happen in America until people actually live together," said Herb. "We could practice what I think Mom is preaching."

"And for people to live together, they may have to make sacrifices so that living together comes first, not second or third or not even on the menu," said Starflower.

"That sounds good," said Daniel "but there's something called reality. I doubt if you would much care for living in the ghettos of Baltimore."

Again, silence all around the table.

"Maybe we would, Dad," said Herb. "I more or less hate it here. Everyone has his little castle with a lawnmower and a garage. Who cares?"

"And I'm not 'more or less' like my diplomatic brother. I just plain hate it," said Starflower. "It's like this big nowhere. Like it was made for cars, not people. The suburbs suck."

Helen put her hands out in front of her, a gesture that meant *Stop*. "That's not the world's best word, Sharon—yes, I mean Starflower—but I didn't intend to start a confessional. And I feel you aren't listening to *me*.

Reverend King has talked many times about the importance of hope, but there has to be more than hope. There has to be agreement. We all have to reach that place. Or at least try to. But that probably means Starflower—there, I did it—is right. To agree we may have to give things up." Helen lowered her hands and looked at her daughter, then her son, appraising them. "Maybe you already know more than I do." She picked up her glass of orange juice. "Not that I plan to give you credit. We're the parents, right?"

Daniel peered down at his coffee as if might hold an answer. "If you say so."

The Mind Says So, the Un-mind Says So Too /

"Chris Patterson," said Starflower.

"What about Chris Patterson? He's cute but knows he's cute, so he's bound to be trouble. Unlike your brother, who doesn't know he's cute."

"I did acid with him over the weekend."

Ruthie gasped. "You mean LSD?"

"Don't shout it out to the whole school or anything." Like insects with their insect purposes, students milled around her in the school lobby. "Not that anyone's listening."

"And?"

"And what?"

"You didn't tell me to just drop the subject. Come on, Star. What was it like? Were you afraid?"

Star sniffed. "Have you ever noticed that wherever you are in this school, it smells like farts?" She sniffed again. "Ugh! But no, I wasn't afraid. I was too excited to be afraid. You know me. I don't want to be left behind."

"You're up there with the Beatles now. You could talk with John Lennon."

"Don't get swoony, Ruthie."

"Did you do anything with him, with Chris?"

"I sort of forgot I had a body. It's hard to talk about. It's like what you've heard and read, but what you've heard and read are just words. It's like you feel everything swaying around you and you're swaying too. You disappear but you're still there, but you aren't you."

A voice came over the loudspeaker: "Debby Jackson, please report to the office."

"Probably that doesn't make sense. I got afraid once, actually, because some part of my head told me I wasn't coming back from wherever I was. I was going to stay there forever. But that went away."

"Did you talk with Chris? What's he like?"

"I think I talked with him. That sounds stupid. I must have talked with him. I know we listened to music—Hendrix, The Who, the bands Chris calls 'love-thunder'—and we walked outside his house. This was in the middle of the night, so no one was around. It must have been cold, but I didn't feel it. His parents were off somewhere. I think they were in New York City. They go to the opera." A bell rang. "Shit, the bell. He's an only child. Empty house. He drove me home in the morning. I was still kind of high, but I mumbled my way past my parents. They thought I was sleeping over at your house. Chris left me off a block away. He's cool, very cool."

Ruthie leaned in to whisper. "Would you do it again? Do you think I should do it?"

"I would. It was beautiful. I wasn't there anymore. I wasn't in my own way anymore. But it wasn't like what I imagine being dead is like. Not creepy. I was part of everything. It was like this word an art teacher I had in junior high used—*vibrant*. Everything was vibrant. And humming. I heard the hum. The colors are all humming."

"Wow! I want to hear that. All I hear is dumb chatter from dumb girls."

"I was on another plane." Starflower took some strands of her hair and began to finger them. "I wonder if a person can live there."

⟨∞⟩

To Live the Ideological Life /

What the revolutionary world offered Ho Chi Minh to slake his ambitions was the porridge of ideology. He picked at it. He downed it. He excused himself from the table. He asked for another helping. He could not get enough of it. He wondered why it was tasteless. He hoped it would explain everything the way it was supposed to. He offered his portion to the person seated next to him. He learned every ingredient.

Ideology—to change the metaphor—was etched into stone. Monumental, impervious, ultimate, unchanging. Yet ideology was written on the air and was variable, flighty, uncertain, words that had nothing to do with actions. Ideology was carried from one person to another—a virus, a baton, an open secret—and lodged in texts that were crammed into human minds and regurgitated with alacrity. Ideology was science, or so it proclaimed. Ardent as hope. The necessitous fuel of betterment.

If the capitalists had shown any sympathy to his goals, he was not averse to working with them. The point, above all, was to establish a free, self-determined nation, but the capitalists had no use for what interfered with the proprietary rights, which to them were almost divine. Democracy was a fig leaf, something to cover the economic rapacity and racism. In the West, he had lived among them and walked through the days that a working person walked through. He was offered a bit of money and the entertainments that could while away a lifetime. He chose not to linger.

Ideologues tended to be humorless. They were, after all, involved in what they considered a life-and-death struggle. The French had put a price on his head; a number of times they almost had gotten him. Willing to believe, he had signed on to the millennium of the communists. For a revolutionary, what other faith was there? And yet he realized again and again how laughably imperfect the faith was, how the winds of doctrine blew in contradictory directions, how one year internationalism was correct and the next year incorrect, how popular fronts came and went. The party line never used *good* and *bad*, which were obsolete words. Instead, there were terms that explained the changes strategically, but they seemed like very poor inventions, caprices.

Ideology was like a game of chess where the squares on the board kept changing but the pawns remained pawns. He wrote and wrote, and what he wrote made sense to him, but sometimes the game seemed senseless. He, too, could have been liquidated at various moments of ideological frenzy. And when he came to power, he liquidated his enemies without any qualms. They had been reactionaries, counterrevolutionaries, imperialists, lackeys. The words tumbled off his tongue and the tongues of others like so many agile acrobats.

Perhaps the lure of ideology was that it dwarfed death. That was why so many were pleased to die in its name. He would have died without a second thought. He was right, and no one could take that rightness from him. Revolution was struggle. Ideology was a handhold to maintain that struggle. He listened and wrote and spoke to a dream that almost seemed real.

⁓

A Dream You Can Chew as If It Were Real /

"Yipes, stripes, Beechnut's got 'em. Am I on target?" Chuck was holding forth on row eight, right side of the school bus. "It's not just gum. It's the classic pickup ploy. 'Wanna stick of gum, sugar?'"

"You're too slick. Do you think *yipes* is a word?"

"Of course it's a word. If it's in advertising, it's a word. But chicks like questions like that. Makes you seem sort of smart. Not that you aren't smart already."

"My dad said chewing gum helped get him through the war. Took out some of his worry. He chewed his way through western Europe."

Chuck turned to Herb and relaxed a bit from his broadcasting mode. "Your dad was in World War II?"

"Weren't all our dads? Isn't that what dads did?"

"I guess. My dad never talks about the war. It's like a hole. When I asked him once, he said, 'I'd rather not talk about it.' For my dad, that's a long sentence."

Mutual silence. Holes and precipices all around them, and they were doing nothing more than riding a school bus on a dreary March morning. Herb reached into a jacket pocket. "How about some Spearmint? It's not the same as stripes. And the stripes are cool, I admit it. But Spearmint does it for me. Though there's a lot to be said for Doublemint."

"You sound like an ad." Chuck deepened his voice: "Here's Herbert Brownson on the school bus talking to his friend Chuck Carranza about the wonders of Wrigley's chewing gum. Take it away, Herbert."

"For a long time, I led a languishing life. I lingered in corners and backs of dingy classrooms. Droning teachers never knew my name, nor did those bubbly cheerleaders for whom I not-so-secretly pined. Then one otherwise uneventful day I discovered Wrigley's chewing gum. Yes, I had heard about doubling my pleasure. But what if you don't know what pleasure is? What if you are among the lost, the misshapen, the readers of too many books? Nonetheless, I took a deep breath and gave some of the pennies I had saved in a quart jar to the man behind the counter at my local drugstore. Bravely, I opened the pack and then carefully opened a stick of gum enveloped in paper and foil. I inserted that stick of gum, an anonymous thing—but I too lived in a mass society of status seekers and manipulators—into my mouth and began, slowly and then more insistently, to chew. Instantly, a dazzling new world opened up to me. I felt fresher, more alive, more vital, more confident . . ."

"Okay. Man, you really can get into it. When you grow up—"

Herb squinted. "I'm something like a grown-up already. And when I really and truly grow up, I wanna be a chimpanzee."

"I was gonna say you could be one of those advertising guys *MAD* magazine makes fun of. You know—buy a new Veeblefetzer. Even if you don't know what it is, it's good for you. In the meantime, got any gum, chum?"

They gave each other a gleeful, vaudevillian shove on the shoulder—confirming, in the face of the long odds against nonconformity, their solidarity.

∞

The Solidarity of the Forsaken /

"You smoke pot?" Sharlene hunched over the table toward him, but didn't particularly lower her voice. Her son, Travis, sat beside her, playing with some sugar cubes. The luncheonette she had chosen was near her house. "Everyone will see me sitting here with some good-looking young guy who's not from around here, because everyone here knows everyone else. That's great, because I'm sick of being who they think I am." She turned to her son. "That's wonderful, Trav, but drink your milk too." Travis said, "Yesh"—he lisped a bit—but didn't reach for his milk.

"Yeah, I do," replied Tom. What was he doing? Talking to this woman with a little kid and a shaky hold on life had that stoned, hyper-real feel to it, but then the words *why not* flashed across the screen of his mind. These days that phrase seemed to sum up everything. As far as he could tell, the draft notice wasn't going to catch up with him in the near future, because he wouldn't be reported as having officially dropped out until the end of the semester. But he could be wrong. There were many stories out there about draft boards. One size did not fit all.

"I didn't used to. I heard about it in high school, but I was a jock and drank beers with the guys. Pot was for the longhairs. Then last year I got turned on by a girl I met. I liked her and she smoked; if I wanted to hang out with her, I needed to start smoking too."

"Led astray by a woman. An old story." Sharlene drew back and tapped two impatient fingers on the table. Travis pushed his sugar cubes onto the floor. He stared down as if asking: "How did that happen?"

"So I did, and I liked it."

"Because?"

"Because it slows your head down. Because you start looking around in a way you never looked around. Because it made the world seem pleasant even when the world wasn't so pleasant."

"Shangri-la?"

"Not exactly. People have been smoking marijuana for a long time. I just joined up. Not a big deal. It takes the edge off. There's a lot of edge to be taken off."

"You can get busted."

"I can, but I'm careful. And it's not like where I live is crawling with cops."

"Will you smoke with me sometime?"

"You're a pretty fast mover." Tom took her drumming hand and held it.

"Time has not been on my side. I didn't think the word *widow* was going to enter my vocabulary at this age." Travis had gotten down and was retrieving his sugar cubes. "Get up on your chair and drink your milk, Trav. We're going to Nana's house."

"Sure, we can do that. I don't have a place of my own but—"

"We'll go to some neck of the woods around here. Only the deer will smell it." Travis was crawling under the table. "That lady over there is noticing your hand on mine. That's good."

"Should I know how your husband died?"

"Everyone always wants to. Why shouldn't you?" She picked her hand up and made a flicking motion. "Get up, Travis." Her face looked quizzical, searching for an answer to an impossible question. "He died in the war. In the line of duty. When the military comes to your door, that's all you learn. Like they're telling you something you didn't know already, but you get to hear it from them, all serious and official. Not that words could make a difference." Sharlene swiveled and bent toward her son, who was building a sugar cube structure on the floor. "You've got a mind of your own, don't you, little boy? Wonder where that comes from."

"It's okay if you don't tell me."

Sharlene kept her head down. "I have told you. But you get that. It's like something that comes out as nothing. I wasn't there. What the hell do I know?"

Tom got it, didn't get it, half got it, wanted to get it. "Hey, Travis," he said, "what are you making there?"

❧

There on the Speculative Curve Plus Cat /

"Do you think adults, grown-ups, have feelings?" Herb asked.

He and Starflower were eating Tastykakes, Butterscotch Krimpets, to be exact—a late-night, after-homework snack. In Helen's words, the family in a week "demolished an untold number" of Tastykakes. Helen and Daniel had already "retired," a word Daniel favored. Tom, as usual, was out.

"You've got a milk mustache," she replied.

"Answer my question." He took a swipe at his lips with his shirt cuff.

"Of course they have feelings. What kind of question is that?"

"A good one. It seems to me that you have to become brisk when you grow up. You have to be all-business. Your feelings disappear."

"Our parents have feelings."

"Do they?"

"Oh, come on, sure they do." Starflower pressed down on some crumbs on her plate and inserted her finger into her mouth. "God, I could live on these."

"You do live on them, but I wonder about Mom and Dad. You know the expression Mom uses: 'I've got a lot on my mind.' Does that mean your mind overcomes everything? Does that mean you're nothing but a mind?"

"Look who's talking."

"How come they never tell us what's bothering them beyond things we shouldn't be doing? How come they don't stare out windows and do nothing and just sigh the way someone does when he looks out a window?"

"They're not in school every day, for one. School is made for staring out windows and sighing."

Herb pushed his plate away. "I think Mom and Dad are unhappy."

"And what makes you think that?" Absentmindedly, Starflower dragged an index finger around the plate in search of further crumbs.

"Just how they go from one day to another and are always so busy, like they don't have time to feel anything."

"What do you expect them to do? Sit on the sofa and start crying? I mean it. I don't see your point."

"They're worried about Tom, but they don't really say anything."

Starflower pushed her plate away. The refrigerator hummed. Cleo, the Brownsons' tabby cat, padded into the kitchen to investigate the late-night confabulation.

"What can they say?" asked Starflower. "It's bigger than they are. They didn't make the war."

"But they're here. We're people, not flotsam and jetsam."

Cleo jumped onto Starflower's lap. "What do you think, kitty?" she said while starting to stroke Cleo's back.

"You touch her and she purrs. She's got her feelings right there," said Herb.

"She's wise," said Starflower. "But I'm worried too. Sometimes it's like my feelings don't matter. Like school is telling me the way it is, which is do the work. Stick to the straight and narrow, if you know what's good for you. But that's crap. Like Mr. Klausmeyer knows what's good for me? What a joke."

They sat and listened to the refrigerator and the cat.

"Maybe you're right," said Starflower. "Maybe they are unhappy. But maybe it's just average unhappiness, like feeling groggy in the morning, only it's your heart that's groggy."

"That's what we have to look forward to?"

Starflower stroked Cleo's head. Cleo purred even louder. "I guess we'll find out."

⌘

Out, Out /

Each year (assuming there would be another calendar year in the so-called civilized, orderly, ongoing world), the *Bulletin of the Atomic Scientists* issued a clock that showed how many minutes the human race had before a nuclear holocaust led to unparalleled loss of life and destruction of the Earth's sustaining environment. A press event and an article in the newspapers heralded the full report. In 1968 the clock read "7 minutes to midnight."

Beginning at the age of thirteen, Herb Brownson drew a clock each year and pinned it to the bulletin board in his bedroom. One of his heroes, Bertrand Russell, who had been president of the Campaign for Nuclear Disarmament, had spoken often about the "peril" facing humankind. And Herb had read *Hiroshima*, an account of what happened to people on the ground when the atomic bomb was dropped. That bomb had much less force than the bombs available in 1968.

Why anyone would want more force or why anyone would want such bombs in the first place seemed to Herb a fair question. What, however, could any little, talking-and-walking life say to such an enormity? And what was "humankind" beyond existing as a word? People and nations were defined by their differences not their similarities.

The bomb shadowed Herb. How was anyone to live under such a shadow? He knew that for most people, there was no shadow. They pushed the clock away, because the notion of such a catastrophe happening was inconceivable. Yet the planet was studded with missiles. The missiles had been in Cuba; the United States and Soviet Union had been locked into what seemed the ultimate confrontation. There was no forgetting those days in October 1962.

Once upon a time, the legend said, there had been a tree of knowledge that humankind was supposed to avoid. That was a legend, but it seemed more than a legend because it showed how helpless humankind was before the prospect of knowledge. People wanted to know. People were curious and inventive. People believed in science as a value in its own right. People wanted to go forward wherever that led and whatever that meant. Meanwhile, nations threatened one another and resorted to death and destruction that was—unlike those bombs—paralleled.

Sometimes Herb's mother or father or sister or brother would notice the clock on his bulletin board. Sometimes one of them would say something like "You don't forget the clock, do you?" Herb would nod and say, "Yeah, I don't." The conversation tended to end there with unvoiced questions. How could there be such a world? Why didn't the nations devote themselves to removing such weapons? Was every life tattooed with futility, no matter how a person spoke and strutted about?

The scientists were in earnest, each fraught year, when they updated the clock. The nations made a show of being earnest. Everyone wanted life to go on—or so it seemed, since midnight had not yet struck. But one day, who was to say? Herb did not have an answer and did not talk about the clock with anyone. It sat there on his wall and inside him. But the minute hand moved.

∾

Dance of the Minutes /

"Got a minute?" Starflower stood on the landing where the staircase turned, three steps up from the floor of the front hall. Tom was putting on the varsity jacket he wore in all weather.

"Sure. What's up?"

"I don't get to see you much. You're either out or holed up in your room."

"Keeping the low profile."

"Should I worry?"

"Everyone else does, why not? I can't say I'm worried, but that doesn't mean much. I'm getting used to limbo."

Starflower came down the three steps. "I need to ask you something special."

"Yeah?" Tom jingled his car keys.

"Can you get me some pot?"

He started to laugh. "Do I smell that strong?"

"You dropped out of college. What else could be going on?"

"What does Dad say? 'A first-rate mind.' You and Herb, a couple of brainiacs." Tom put the keys in a jacket pocket. "Sure, I can help you out. There's something called money that's involved, though."

"I'm gonna start waitressing in the summer. Meanwhile, there's my allowance and some babysitting."

"Forget it. Just for you, though—personal stash. No dealing in the girls' room."

They stood there observing each other. They had lived in the same house for what felt like forever. They knew each other from thousands of meals and looking at the same television programs and talking and listening to music and knocking on the bathroom door. It had all seemed so substantial, but there in the downstairs hallway with its photos on the wall of the three Brownson children as toddlers and then in grade school, they could feel, and sensed the other felt, how insubstantial their life together was—how they were moving away from each other and how that was inevitable but made everything they had shared seem hopeless and lost so that, involuntarily, they both shook their heads as if ruing something that had somehow happened to someone else, sharing a sympathy that felt both close and already gone.

"I gotta be going." Tom pulled the keys out. "What are you listening to these days?"

"Janis Joplin. The band is called Big Brother and the Holding Company, but it's Janis Joplin that lights it up. But you know who she is."

"Mostly I'm listening to soul music these days. Some jazz too that Reggie put me onto. Lee Morgan. But, yeah, I know. She's a white girl from Texas."

"Tom?"

"Yeah?"

"Do you think it's stupid that I want to be called Starflower?" She moved a step sideways.

"No stupider than anything else."

"That's not much of an answer."

Then it came to him, that beseeching look that he remembered from childhood, his little sister being serious. "You know, I like that you did that. I'm trying to make myself up too." He secured the top fastener on his jacket then moved toward the door.

The Doors of Shaky Perception /

"Where is the draft board?"

A Saturday night. "The three," as Helen sometimes referred to their children, were out. Helen and Daniel sat in the den drinking Scotch and nibbling Planters salted peanuts.

"Towson."

"And who's on it that decides about these young men's lives?" Helen held her drink in both hands, cradling it. The glasses came from Daniel's family. "Gentiles imbibe," he had told Helen. "It's part of their religion."

"Patriots. Men who served in World War II."

"Like you?"

"No, not like me. People who have been vetted through the American Legion or the VFW or continuing military connections or political connections. People who know people. You know how that works. And most of them have been at it. They take pride in it."

"And our son—"

"Is in the crosshairs. When he gets his notice, however, is uncertain. Draft boards are a crazy quilt. Each one is going to be different, because each one is in a different place with a different population. And he's got options. That knee he had fixed in high school could keep him out."

"You mean he can run up and down a lacrosse field but can't be in the army?" Helen gave a quizzical head shake.

"Ever hear of Joe Namath? He's a professional football player who was classified 4-F because of bad knees. And I'm sure he does have bad knees, and I'm sure, given what an army pack weighs, he's not the guy they're looking for."

"If Tom goes to a doctor?"

"That, dear, is up to Tom."

They took contemplative sips of their Johnny Walker. How could they have imagined such a discussion when they brought Tom home from the hospital on an early winter afternoon in 1947? How could they have conceived of more wars? And why, looking at their firstborn that day, would they have ever wanted to think such a foreboding thought?

"Is this close-at-hand experience we are having with our son radicalizing you? Or is that too radical a word?"

"Scotch wit." Daniel raised his glass in acknowledgment. "I seem to be a small step from debilitating sadness about the human race. Of which I am very much a part. Also, a small step from blind anger at human stupidity, myself included. Will I march in the next march? I guess I will. I have this feeling, though, of the inconsequence of protest. Small fists banging on a large gate."

"Your political commentary has always been bracing. Good thing I checked my idealism at the door." Helen raised her glass. "Many small fists can make a difference."

"You know me—I'm from the lesser-evil school. But this isn't what I went to war for. This is something else. Our son—to begin in this house— is ripped up inside."

"Has he talked much to you? He doesn't say a real word to me."

"I wouldn't say he's said anything substantial. He's sincere—that's why he left school, but I doubt if he knows what he's sincere about. And it really is his life now. That's a big one for him to get his head around."

Helen tried to speak, but her voice caught. She waited. "I have the feeling that we're sitting on a stage set when we have these conversations, that it's not our days of the checking account, the oil change, and the grocery list. But it is our days and plenty of others. And it's become real to me whether I like it or not." She got a startled look on her face, the onset of tears, but then heaved out some words: "I keep looking for an exit, but it's not there. And I keep feeling that at any moment, I could start screaming."

They regarded the bottle that stood on a little folding table tray midway between them. They knew the bottle held no answer or, if it did, that the answer was a wrong one. Daniel put a hand out to his wife and she took it.

Later that night, their lovemaking was fierce. Their desperation surprised and relieved them.

∞

Unrelieved Hamburgers /

While Tom waited in his car for Reggie, he had the car-feeling—how much time he had spent in cars and how that time seemed like sand that went through his fingers; how even if he tried to hold the sand he couldn't; how some would slip through, the unconscious waste within the purposeful moments. Maybe that was why he was reading *On the Road*. The book made car time seem real and important, something more than shuttling back and forth between here and there. As if there were a romance to something mindless. Or a willed intensity. He could use some of that.

"Man, you are like a bad penny. That's an expression my momma uses, but I can't say I understand it. Probably you're in need of some more minority counseling." Reggie closed the passenger door of Tom's VW Bug. "I never understand why a tall guy like you has such a small car."

"I bought it off a guy at school who needed some immediate cash." Tom started the engine, which puttered to life. "And it's kinda cozy. I like that."

"These seats are like teacup saucers. Germans don't have any asses? But just press down on that pedal. I need a hamburger in the worst way." He sighed. "I've been studying too hard." Another, more-pronounced sigh. "But what's with you, my dropout friend? Need more smoke? Did I explain how Tough is a relative of mine? Cousin on my daddy's side. Black people fall into all sorts of holes. Though to black people they aren't holes. They're life." He gave Tom a confirming poke on the arm.

"If you had to go to Vietnam, would you?"

"Oh, that's what's on your mind. What else could be?" He turned on the radio, heard five seconds of a song, and turned it off. "The Temptations have lost it. Hate to say it. I used to worship them. But about this war, like I've said, I'd have some serious mixed feelings. Very mixed. When I walk into White Castle and one of those white waitresses looks at me, I know she wishes she didn't have to look at me, much less serve me. It's hard for me to think about dying for a place that's still having trouble giving me a hamburger."

"I get it. That's sort of my problem."

"Considering the color of your skin, it would have to be 'sort of.'" Reggie made a low sound, somewhere between a chuckle and a groan.

"My dad was in the Second World War. In combat. He never really talks about it. I've tried to bring the subject up, trying to just hear something, but he clams up or makes a joke or just says something that says nothing."

"Maybe he saw some bad shit. Maybe some bad shit happened to him."

"I know. But I don't know. And I don't know how it made him who he is, how it made him a man in a way he wouldn't have been a man if he hadn't gone to war."

"That's what you're thinking? About being a man?" Reggie whistled. "How it works is this: If a woman tells you you're a man, then you're a man. That's how that works."

"I've gotta hand it to you—you have the answers. You should be on one of those TV quiz shows. But I'm feeling there's something I need to know out there. Maybe the war is my answer."

"That's crazy. You hearing me? That's crazy. You want to get yourself a letter from some head doctor and kiss this war goodbye."

"Maybe." Tom reached for something more to say but couldn't find it, feeling at sea and then further at sea, mumbling "Not many cars this time of night" as he pulled up in front of the White Castle. Entering, he made a point of opening the door for Reggie. A waitress behind the counter grimaced.

"That's a look that might not kill but sure could disable," said Reggie. "Maybe she thinks we're civil rights workers."

"Like something she saw a few years ago in *Life* magazine?"

"Or maybe she's nostalgic. Wants to relive the glory days of cops bashing Negro heads. Fire hoses. Police dogs."

"Maybe she doesn't know what to think."

"Maybe she's afraid. That's what makes me want to sit down and cry a river." Reggie slid into a booth and took a menu. "You multiply her times a big number, and you get a sense of what's watching me. And who's watching me."

∞

Watching the Big Words /

In the constellation of American politics, some words shone more brightly than others. Guiding stars, they led people forward. Above the citizens' heads in the vast night of importuning abstractions loomed *prestige, honor, integrity, commitment, faith,* and *values.* Someone might come along, a Lenny Bruce–like comic, and do a stand-up routine:

"So, if the nation lost a war, its 'prestige' was at stake. What was this prestige? Some other nation might say, 'You know you've lost some of your prestige. We're not going to bother with you anymore. You're sort of slummy. You're just another down-at-the-heels nation.' If the nation lost a war, its 'honor' was at stake. Some other nation might say, 'You've been dishonored. That's crummy. We're not going to soil our hands with you and your dishonor. Phooey!' If the nation lost a war, its 'integrity' was at stake. Some other nation might say, 'Look, your integrity doesn't amount to much. What is a nation without it? Do you expect us to take you seriously? Are you running some kind of cut-rate nation? Are you running a racket? Our nation is dripping with integrity.' If the nation lost a war, some other nation might say, 'Your commitments don't mean much, do they? You say you're going to help and then just because you have to spend millions and your soldiers start dying, you back down on your commitment. Who is going to believe you when you say you are going to come to some other nation's defense?' If the nation lost a war, some other nation might say, 'You've lost your faith. You've lost your way. We thought you had it in for the communists until the end of time, no matter where they showed up, but look at this—faithless. Cardinal Spellman said the Vietnam War was a war for 'civilization.' He had faith. If the nation lost a war, some other nation might say, 'What happened to your values? Are you going to stand by and let some communists and not just communists but Asians, little gooks, take over a nation?'"

What were these shining words? Could you find them in a store? Did they grow on trees? How did the nation steer its course through the historical waters by such words? What did they portend? And could the nation live without them? What if the words were merely rhetoric, words that made people feel better when they shouldn't feel better, words that did nothing but create an aura of something important, words that were not appropriate in the first place to a nation-state, which was an inherently compromised entity. In what sky did this constellation exist? Did these words go out into the void of the universe, far from Earth, and send signals back?

Some other nation, a cynical nation, one of those nations that was an outright oligarchy or a simple despotism, might say, "Our integrity is shaky because we've been known to take bribes. Our honor is available to the highest bidder. Our values are strictly mercenary. Our prestige is not an issue because we aren't powerful enough to care about such a thing. Our integrity depends on what you are asking for. Our faith is cash in a Swiss bank account. Our commitment is to what is best for us. Nations are realists not philanthropists."

There were such nations, but the United States, although not above railroading smaller nations for corporate interests—as when Franklin D. Roosevelt called the Nicaraguan dictator Anastasio Somoza a "bastard" but "our bastard"—liked to think of itself as steering according to the constellation of good words, the words that indicated the nation amounted to something, if not moral, then at least full of moralizing righteousness.

Some of these words showed up at the funerals of soldiers; some didn't. There were other words available of a similar tenor. For a time, they lingered in the grief-stricken air, then they disappeared.

◦◦◦

Chocolate Ice Cream Disappeared /

"You see any chocolate ice cream in there lately?" Daniel peered into the recesses of the freezer compartment.

"I lost my taste for both ice cream and beer in college." Tom was eating a Swiss cheese and lettuce sandwich he'd made for himself. A late snack—1:30 in the morning.

"I would too, if I had them together." Daniel stuck a hand in tentatively. "I woke up with a yen for chocolate ice cream."

"The ice cream came from the cafeteria; I don't know how you can screw up ice cream, but they did. The beer was like water at every party, but after a while water tasted better." Tom took a hefty bite.

"I guess I'll have to pass. Someone must have beat me to it." Daniel closed the door. "So . . . ," he said, pausing significantly.

"I've been meaning to ask a question. What's with you and the Quakers? I didn't know you had them on your religious radar."

"I haven't taken up Buddhism yet, but don't sell me short." He looked at his son's plate. "Maybe I need one of those pickles you've got there on the side. I need something."

"The Quakers just sort of sit there, don't they?"

"They're waiting for a guiding light to speak. Some arrow of spirit." Daniel opened the refrigerator. "I guess pickles are a poor substitute for chocolate ice cream."

"'Arrow of spirit'? Where did you get that from? That's like something Mom might say when she's in one of her highfalutin moods."

"I must have read it somewhere, but not in a law book. You been reading up there?"

"I read *Huck Finn* again. Huck and Jim on the raft, that must be the dream that keeps us dreaming. Free."

"I seem to recall they had their troubles."

"They did, but they still were free."

"Must sound good to you at this moment." Daniel pulled out a jar of olives. "A couple of these should do the trick."

"It does. But I wonder about you sitting there with those Quakers and not saying anything, just sitting there and waiting. I can sort of relate to that—the sitting and waiting. People must have gotten up and said something?"

"They did. Someone talked about being angry about the war, the waste of it. Someone had a dream about being on a desert island with Lyndon Johnson. Not exactly what you think of as church." Daniel took out an olive. "Your mother saves these for cocktail parties, but she won't miss a couple."

"You haven't had one of those since I came home, have you?"

"You mean cocktail parties? We haven't been in the mood." He took out another olive and screwed the lid back on. "What can I say?"

"You said it, Dad." Tom picked up his plate and went over to the sink. "I just can't wash another dish today." He turned to his father and smiled. "You know—I like being here with my family. See you down the road."

Many Times the Revolutionary Road Seemed to Go on Forever with No End in Sight /

One of the words that followed Ho Chi Minh as he made his fugitive way from one country to another, a wanted man who used aliases and disguises, was *subversive*. What did that word threaten? Foremost, it threatened Order: how things were done and arranged, the sanctimony of power, those men seated at desks in Paris who ran companies that used rubber and rice and cloth from Vietnam; those other men who sat at government departments in Paris and pursued national prerogatives, ruling, as they did, peoples who had not achieved the level of civilization that France, a light unto the world, had achieved. Those men had wives and children and went on vacations and bought automobiles and ate dinners where they talked about the parlous state of the world but also about whatever entertainments were coming along in the cinema or on the stage. They were at the center of a regulated endeavor that, as far as they were concerned, would go on forever. Why not?

Such men slept in comfortable beds each night. Ho slept many times on the earth, be it bare ground or a pigsty. He might have a mat; he might not. He trekked long before trekking became fashionable. He knew the ground beneath him because he had to know the ground beneath him. His life might be described as spartan or minimal or modest or simply that he was uninterested in materialism, because materialism led men to lose track of their consciences. No photographer was going to take pictures of his office or country house for a glossy magazine.

He came from another approach to being on Earth, one that belonged to the discarded, the looked-down-upon, the forgotten, the ridiculed. And the hated, he being someone who wished to overthrow the established order and was willing to stop at nothing to accomplish that end. A number of Ho's comrades had been caught and killed, each execution a cause for congratulation on the part of the colonial powers—one less troublemaker. Murder called for murder; revolution called for suppression by any means.

Ho was resolutely cheerful about his task. To be a subversive in the twentieth century for someone who came from where he came from was something like a higher calling. That may have seemed ludicrous when one looked at the brutal machinations of the Soviet Union and the millions of lives that were thrown away like grains of sand. Perhaps Ho looked hard at those machinations, perhaps not. His mind was set on his nation's freedom and his desire to build a communist society in which his people would not oppress one another, in which no one would sit at a faraway desk and make decisions that wrecked lives that were, to the person making the decisions, fundamentally unreal.

Ho slept in jails that were more like dungeons. His body was never that strong, and he suffered from various maladies, including tuberculosis. Sleeping on the ground and making arduous journeys on foot did not help. Yet they did help. Unafraid, he did whatever the situation demanded. The Westerners had a long list of fears they papered over with their power, but they were vulnerable. They were too accustomed to having the world go their way. They had no steel inside them. All the Frenchmen and then Americans at their desks and sleeping at night in their orderly beds lived in a fool's paradise. An ugly paradise at that. A ruined paradise.

Paradise (as in Where Eve Lived) Was a Long Time Ago /

"Women is losers." Starflower intoned the words across the cafeteria table. "Janis tells it straight." She and Ruthie were talking before the next class after eating the bag lunches they brought to school.

"That doesn't seem fair," said Ruthie. "I mean really."

"Who said anything about fair? What about your period last month, when you thought you were gonna die from the pain? What about these guys who expect you to open your legs when they look at you? What about your older sister who tells you about her love life and then cries to your mom? And what about your mom, who keeps warning you about getting a bad reputation? Does any of that seem fair?"

Ruthie tilted herself back twenty or so degrees on the cafeteria table bench. "It's too bad we don't have a debate team. You know how to sock it to 'em."

A voice—self-consciously mellifluous—loomed above them: "Hello, girls. How is the hippie clique today?" Tracey Sanders, a school icon, loomed above them in all her orthodontic glory. Possessed of a relentless, metallic smile, she won every election she entered. Students got to "participate in her self-love," as Starflower put it.

"We're high on our peanut butter sandwiches right now," Star said.

"I bet. As you know, I'm running for senior class president, and I'd appreciate your vote. Any concerns you have about this school, you can just let me know. Of course you two represent the power of the press, and though you can't make an out-and-out endorsement, you can insinuate."

"I want to insinuate that most of the people in this school are dopes and that some days I think I'll die from boredom; outside of that, I have no concerns whatsoever." Ruthie smiled at Tracey's smile.

"You two are so funny!" Tracey clapped her hands.

"I wish we were." Star raised her hands as if to clap but didn't.

"Well, ta-ta you groovy girls." Tracey sashayed off in search of more votes, her careful blonde bob moving ever so slightly—no long peasant tresses for her.

"Ever feel that life is one big indignity?" Star asked.

"All the time. And I get what you're saying about Janis. She's hip to that. I wish I could sing like her."

"Maybe you can. Have you tried?"

"Only in the shower. Next time you're over to my house, you can hear my version of 'Down on Me.' I can get right down in the basement with that song."

The girls eyed the clock on the cafeteria wall. Last year someone had thrown a carton of milk at it. Now the clock was protected by several thin metal bars.

"Is prison like this?" asked Star.

"The paint colors in prison are probably better. But we get to leave at the end of the day. Don't forget that." Ruthie started to gather her books.

"You're right. More like prison on the installment plan. Or a factory. Here I am—an unhappy robot off to her next class before the bell rings and

I get a detention for being late." Star began walking to the cafeteria exit. "If only someone in charge would just occasionally tell the truth."

⧔

Truth Rebounds, Skitters, but Doesn't Stop /

"You came back." Sharlene gestured with one plastic-bracelet-spangled wrist. Her hair was piled up bouffant style. She wore pink lipstick that matched her nails.

Tom thought how his sister would make fun of her. Starflower was bohemian and hippie; Sharlene was 1958 record hop. But as Reggie put it, "A nice-looking woman is a nice-looking woman."

"Like I said, I'm kind of aimless at the moment. I might as well aim here."

"That's what they call a left-handed compliment. Though left-handed people may be okay with it. I'm one of them."

They were seated on the couch in Sharlene's living room. On the floor, Travis was playing with some wooden railroad trains. Occasionally, he made a delighted sound: "Twoot, twoot."

"Women don't slip me their phone numbers every day."

"You're an easy catch. But what do I know? You're sitting here looking at that table across from you with the photo of my husband who didn't have to go to war, who could have stayed here and been a mechanic because he had a deferment; but he had to be a man and a patriot because his dad was in the war, the one against the Nazis and the Japs, and he felt he couldn't just sit on the sidelines. Those were his words, about the sidelines." Sharlene sniffled and pulled a tissue from her blouse sleeve. Her blouse was white and had a frilly front. Starflower would have made fun of that too.

"You're gonna get sick of me, aren't you? What do you care about me and the man in that photo? It's not like I'm the only widow or he's the only

136

guy who's died there. Everyone has a story. I've met a couple other widows. They talk about how it happened and who their husband was and what they were gonna do in life. It's sad, but what I wanna say is: 'This cookie has crumbled. Time to get over it.'"

"That a little harsh?" Tom watched her carefully.

Sharlene ran a hand over the lap of her skirt.

"Everyone told me I should be proud. I was here with this little boy, and his father was dead and I should be proud. And then time goes by, and where does my pride go, which I never had in the first place? That's their stuff, not mine. I'm left holding the emptiness."

"Twoot, twoot," exclaimed Travis. "Twoot, twoot."

For Tom, since wonder seemed to have become a permanent state, there was no surprise in listening to Sharlene. He could imagine his mother sitting with one of their neighbors in a year or so and talking about her late son Tom. He could see Helen crying. It didn't take a lot of wonder.

"Are you there, Tom?" Sharlene took his hand. "I'm just overwhelming you, an idiot pouring out her troubles who hasn't even offered you a cup of coffee." She gave his hand a squeeze. "But, hey, we've got to cheer up. And I know how to do that." She looked down at Travis. "Travis, you stay here and keep playing. I like it when you make those train sounds. I'm going to show Tom what the upstairs looks like." Still holding Tom's hand, she rose and led him toward a staircase.

One wonder led to another.

❧

Another Point of View /

Helen ordered a grilled cheese sandwich with an extra slice of dill pickle on the side and looked around the luncheonette, crowded at noontime with elderly women who lived in apartments near the university and were having a sociable lunch, a few businessmen between appointments, and a smattering of students, one of whom was seated beside her at the marble-topped counter. Basquette's had been around forever, but she had lunch there rarely. Today, however, no errands were pressing her. She would have the luxury of a few hours in the library.

"You're in the African American History class, aren't you?" The young man beside her was speaking. "I'm John Tobin, and I'm pleased to meet you."

"I am in that class, and I suppose I stand out. Not many women my age there. My name is Helen Brownson. I'm pleased to meet you."

"Not many women period. If it weren't for the master of ed students, there wouldn't be any. Going to an all-male school can get a guy down." John sighed a heavy sigh. "But I want to ask you, what has been your favorite book thus far? You know, as one student to another."

Helen took a second to regard John Tobin. He was dressed very neatly—well-shined penny loafers, slacks, a V-neck sweater over a dress shirt. His hair was short. She thought of how her sons looked. Tom hadn't had a haircut since who knows when, and Herb wasn't far behind. They both favored jeans or rumpled khakis. "Hands down, *The Souls of Black Folk*. I can't believe every American isn't made to read that book. It made me feel some of the depth of—what should I call it? The African American experience." Excited to be suddenly talking, Helen reached to feel her pocketbook in her lap, a familiar, calming gesture. "When I think of my not having read that book, I feel embarrassed. Where was I?"

"I agree," said John Tobin. "It's so real. But kind of elegant, eloquent, how he writes. Like a gentleman."

"And you are studying what?" asked Helen.

"Classics and history. I plan to go to divinity school. I want to become a Presbyterian minister. I'm studying Greek now so I can read the New Testament in the original."

"Goodness, I'm seated next to a potential man of God. And someone connected to my husband's church of origin. We were married in a Presbyterian church."

"Is that right? We share something then. And not to get too serious with you, ma'am, the fact is I've wanted to preach since I was a boy. Something in my blood, I guess."

"Yes, but that makes me wonder, John, given your goal in life, what you make of this war. I mean, how Christ is the bringer of peace." Her words surprised her, the jump into that fraught place, but her words were unhappily natural. "You don't have to answer. I'm afraid I'm being intrusive."

He pulled a bit at the base of the V in his sweater then waited some seconds. "I've thought about it. To me, we're fighting people who are opposed to our way of life and who, if they had the chance, would take away our liberties. Communism is evil. It's godless. Probably you know that, though. You've seen more history than I have." With those words he loosened the tone in his voice, as if trying to go easy with something he didn't feel at all easy about.

"They're very far away from us, though," said Helen, "and I'm not sure we understand anyone over there very well. They aren't Americans."

"You're right, ma'am." John pushed away a large, empty milkshake glass. "I have to get going, but it's been a pleasure to have met you. I look forward to seeing you in our class. I grew up down South with a lot of black people around me, but I didn't know anything about their history. To tell the truth, I took the class as much out of shame as anything." He got up while bestowing a courteous nod in Helen's direction and headed to the cashier by the door.

"*Ma'am.*" No one had called her that in a long time, maybe ever. She hoped that God would look out for someone as mannerly as John Tobin.

Mannerly Approaches /

"Hi."

"Hi."

"Mind if I sit down next to you?" Herb motioned at the cement bench with the hand that wasn't holding his school books.

"It's a free country," said Ruthie. "Or used to be."

"I guess the newspaper kept you after school."

"Deadline looming. Not much to put in it—student council elections and wrapping up winter sports. I wrote an editorial with Star about Gene McCarthy. He's a hope."

Herb had sat down—not too close, but not too far. Ruthie had on a scent with something like vanilla in it. The smell made him giddy, but he had to be cool.

"Yeah, he's a hope, and we need hope."

Students who also were waiting for the late bus jabbered variously around them. Someone called out, "Hey, asshole!" Someone guffawed.

"Speaking of hope," and Herb sat on the word for a few seconds, "I was wondering if you're doing anything Saturday night. I thought you might like to go to the movies and see *The Graduate*. Probably you've already seen it, but I know I wouldn't mind seeing it again and thought maybe you would feel that way too." Herb had rehearsed this little oration at least a dozen times. It still came out too fast.

"Sure, I'd be happy to do that. You're right. I've seen it, but I could see it again. I don't know about you, but I had a feeling when I saw it that I was watching something important about my own life, even though Benjamin is a guy. I mean that feeling of being caught."

Herb sighed internally, an easing of the anxiety that wasn't exactly eating him alive but was doing some serious gnawing. "Yeah, you mean how Ben gets entangled with Mrs. Robinson and how he wants to do that—have sex with an older woman—but he knows it's not going to amount to anything, how she's using him."

"Do you think Ben and the girl Katherine Ross played—I can't remember her name, which probably says how little she really registered with me—will stay together? Screwing your girlfriend's mom doesn't seem like a great way to start a relationship."

They exchanged amused glances.

"If that movie were now, Ben would be thinking about the war and being drafted. Like my brother Tom. Already, the movie seems like a long time ago, like something open that's been closed."

"But the movie seems like forever too." Ruthie threw her head back some, trying to concentrate amid the talkative noise around her. "How the music and the feel of being at that age are forever. They go by, but they are forever." She started to sing "Scarborough Fair" then stopped. Her voice had the lovely lilt the song had. "Does that make sense? What I said."

Herb felt so good to be sitting and talking that a discussion about Martians would have made sense. Ruthie's being so tight with his sister was forbidding. He knew girls talked with each other, and they probably talked about him. But he wasn't a girl, so it was hard to imagine what they said; probably there were some true things that he didn't know about himself and might not want to know. But he wanted to spend time with Ruthie. She had long wavy brown hair that drove him crazy just looking at it. As if the perfume weren't enough.

"Makes sense," said Herb. "Makes real good sense."

⧡

The Sense of Time Moves Forward Suddenly /

Starflower and Herb stood before Tom's bedroom door for a few seconds before they started knocking. "Hey, Tom, wake up!" they shouted. The door stayed shut. They began pounding with the sides of their fists. "We've got news!" shouted Star. "Let us in!" shouted Herb. Tom, in his boxers and a T-shirt that had "Varsity" written on the chest, opened the door. He made a show of being barely awake, extending his arms and yawning. "What the hell? Shouldn't you kiddies be getting ready for school?" He ran a hand through his sleep-confused hair.

"McCarthy almost won in New Hampshire!" another shout from Star, though she was only a foot away. "He did what nobody thought he could do," said Herb. "He almost defeated a sitting president in a primary. That means Lyndon Johnson is in trouble." "That means," said Star, "the war is in trouble. People don't want this war, and they don't want Johnson." "That means," said Herb "that the war could start to be over and the draft could ease up. No need for more bodies."

Tom stepped back. "I guess you guys do have some news."

"You guess?" said Star. "What do you mean 'I guess'? There's nothing to guess about. What happened has happened. People voted and other people counted those votes and a whole lot of those votes were for Eugene McCarthy."

Tom shrugged. "What I'm saying, sister, is that I'm glad McCarthy has shown that peace is something we don't have to be ashamed of. But what I'm also saying is that just because some politician is interested in peace doesn't mean the North Vietnamese have any interest in any peace that is going to deny the blood they've already spilled. Just because we may want something doesn't mean they want it. It's not like ordering hamburgers."

Herb and Star both looked startled. The reality of McCarthy's almost winning seemed, at the moment, to be everything.

"You're entitled to your point of view," said Star, "but given the situation you're in, I expected you to be a little happier. There's some real hope."

"It's not—even though I'm still half asleep—that I'm not glad. I would love the war to go away today. Abracadabra! But like I said, it's not that easy. Each nation has to save face. And a lot of people can die before they have saved their faces. Even though they're countries and have no face."

"It's weird," said Herb, "how expressions sort of take on a life of their own."

Star, who was in her socks, jumped up and down in place. "I'm glad no matter what. I feel energized."

"You're always energized, kiddo," said Tom. "You were born energized."

"We can make a difference," said Herb.

Tom put his arms out to bestow a hug. "I like the sound of that. I do." He felt irretrievably older than his sister and brother, but not a whit wiser.

∞

A Wiser Man in a Realm Not Noted for Wisdom /

The presidency, a democratic throne, beckoned in the neon haze of promises and pleas, evocations of the nation's destined striving, the pure indeterminacy denominated by the presumptive word *America*. There was no sword to pull from some legendary stone, only the regard of the people— the "canaille," as the likes of slave-owning Thomas Jefferson had called them—and the power to not merely act upon the stage of history but to make and break others, the courtiers and critics, along with the sycophants a candidate wanted to believe but shouldn't. At the raw, emotional level, far below the blandishments of speeches and slogans, seemingly distant from the public realm, lay the appeal for something so visceral it might as well be called "love," something that spoke to a need in both the wooer and those being wooed.

Most candidates were marked by their ardor, the backslapping, ever-smiling, folk wisdom–spouting genius of American bonhomie. Eugene McCarthy was the otherwise candidate, almost reluctant to enter the proverbial tussle, though full of the self-regard necessary for anyone who chose to isolate himself so forcefully from others. "Almost" formed a halo of sorts around him. Almost a philosopher-king, almost a spectator to his own actions, almost inclined to believe his own rhetoric, almost interested in what others had to say, but in the end a man utterly unto himself who, nonetheless, took the challenge the war in Vietnam presented and met it. His way.

That way was glancing, offhand, unprofessional, yet shrewd, yet sincere. He did oppose the war. He had no great ideas to get the nation out of the war that would placate those on both sides: the metaphorical hawks who wanted to escalate by any means necessary and the metaphorical doves who thought the war a bad idea to begin with, a war based on nothing more than a metaphor about some dominoes falling in Southeast Asia. Dominoes! Nations falling over in order, one nation shoving another nation in the back, toppling to the force of communist physics, thousands dying for a far-fetched metaphor. And he, McCarthy, someone given to the spell of poetry, knew what a metaphor was—air with a thin tongue of fire—and was not impressed. To simply withdraw would be to deny the sacrifice of those who had already given their lives in the nation's service. To stay was to make more corpses for no compelling reason.

He held his honor about him as if it were a scepter, yet (there was always a "yet") he was quick to make fun of himself and his effort, one that so many had labeled "quixotic": a Democrat challenging a Democrat president who was still very much in office and who was prepared to run for another term. Everything indicated that McCarthy had no chance to become president, but that didn't matter, did it? The effort wasn't about the main chance. The effort was about the wisdom of his days as he entered the unhallowed spotlight. Those days stood for commitment of a special sort—emphatically not the everyday commitment of senators keen on their share of the public limelight but something higher, something he could barely articulate but had goaded him from his modest origins as a school teacher in rural Minnesota (though Lyndon Johnson's origins were even more modest and he, too, had been a school teacher). McCarthy believed in elevation and was pleased to offer that elevation to others, even if it seemed, at first glance, the most preposterous of political gifts, the exact opposite of the famous leveling impulse of democracy.

If people chose to be interested, then they chose to be interested. If they weren't, he wasn't going to lose sleep over it. There was none of the savior in him. He was, for better and for worse, on the far side of persuasion. He was who he was and, as an evolving soul (a distinctly nonpolitical category), eschewed the definitive. It was easy to feel with him that at any moment he was going to quote from *Hamlet*, that he was someone who was most at home with the fraught gravity of moral probing. One of the ironies was that he came across well on TV: composed, articulate, using the distance TV promoted to his advantage. To some, his reluctance played well. And he had walked onto the stage when no one else was willing to do so. If, as he suspected, he was bound to be a historical footnote, he would be his own footnote. In the meantime, he was putting forward a message that was surprisingly unequivocal: Give peace a chance.

The Chance of a Lifetime Is Examined, However Randomly /

"Eugene McCarthy—"

"I know," said Chuck. "He almost won." Chuck lifted his hands in a show of exasperation. "Big deal. Do you think Coach Brown would get excited if the basketball team almost won? What a joke. I bet Lyndon Johnson is quaking in his cowboy boots."

"You're being—"

"I'm being a pain in the ass, I know. Who wants this war? And it's not a fair war. They're not bombing New York. How can we pretend it's a fair war when we have all these weapons and money and an air force? Do they even have an air force?" Chuck tried to get comfortable on the bus seat by burrowing the back of his WWII bomber jacket that he'd bought at Sunny's Surplus. Herb was wearing a GI jacket too, but olive, standard-issue stuff he'd also bought at Sunny's and that the guy at the store said had come from guys who were stationed in the Aleutian Islands. Herb and Chuck both thought the salesman liked to make up stories because he was bored selling war surplus to suburban kids who couldn't tell a firecracker from a hand grenade.

"I don't know," said Herb. "You don't hear about their planes. They must have some. Every country has an air force, right?"

"Beats me." More burrowing. "Anything else on your mind?"

"Sure, you know me. I've been thinking about how weird it is that companies advertise their products as being part of a 'family' of products. You know, like the 'Heinz family of products.' I like their ketchup, but what kind of family is that? Is that something about America, like we can't tell people from bottles of ketchup?"

"This been eating you up?" asked Chuck.

"Not just that, but what's with the other stuff, what they call 'catsup'? It's always too thin and doesn't feel like real anything. It's not spelled real."

"I guess this stuff takes your mind off other matters, but yeah, I have thought about how companies throw the word *family* around. Gives everyone a warm feeling. Happy America. One big hand in the refrigerator."

"I wonder," said Herb, "what sort of warm feeling we would have if the bombs were coming down on us. Try Heinz Ketchup Blood."

In the seats ahead, Cathy Sherbow and Susan Prescott were discussing their weekend plans. Cathy was a cheerleader and Susan might as well have been one, always peppy. "Do you think he's gonna want you to do it?" asked Susan.

"You're not in the best mood today," said Chuck.

"I felt great because of McCarthy, but my brother got me thinking about what has to happen for the war to end. A lot." Herb made his right hand into a gun shape and pointed at Cathy Sherbow's head. "Meanwhile, the sex lives of teenagers grind on." He pointed at Susan Prescott's head. "And how are you doing?"

"I wish the North Vietnamese Air Force would bomb my house. With me in it. That's how I feel. You know I'm supposed to show up every day and act like I care. I do like talking with you because you're my friend, but really I could not show up and I'd be okay. I could just stand by the side of the road and stick my thumb out and see what happens, because anything is better than listening to people argue who are convinced the other person has nothing to say."

"Like nations," said Herb.

"Like nations," said Chuck.

∽∾

The Ways of Nations I

Looking back—and that was what history was, a looking back at circumstances and grappling with the consequential reality of those circumstances, which was too wordy a definition but felt true to her—Helen felt that the trouble began with John F. Kennedy, a man for whom she had voted, when he said, and she could quote the words: "Let every nation know, whether it wishes us well or ill, that we shall pay any price,

147

bear any burden, meet any hardship, support any friend, oppose any foe, in order to assure the survival and the success of liberty." Any price? Any hardship? Did he understand his words? Was he so full of the wind of rhetoric that it wasn't rhetoric to him? And what did "friend" mean in the world of nations? The Russians were friends in World War II, as Kennedy well knew. Then they weren't friends. And what was "liberty" during the reign of Joseph McCarthy, when lives were destroyed in the name of fear?

Helen could hear her father, a tailor who then started a dry-cleaning business but who was also, as he liked to say, "an armchair historian," talking about how in America every politician had "to play to the crowd and tell the people what they want to hear whether it's right or not." Sorting out right from wrong was a task for wary minds, not impulsive ones, and sometimes Kennedy had shown that. He'd managed to be calm during the missile crisis in Cuba. He hadn't gone in with planes and bombs. He'd waited and been firm but not rash. But maybe something that began slowly like Vietnam never felt rash until it grew and grew like a snowball rolling down a hill and there was this mass of commitment at the bottom of the hill that no one seemed to know what to do with, except to accept it as inevitable, as the "price" and the "burden."

She thought these things during her busy days, but especially in preparing herself for the interviews she would be having for a job teaching history or civics or social studies—whatever they called it at the particular school. Would they want to test her patriotism? She was glad to live in America, but she had floated on a sort of current she had taken for granted: the rising tide of prosperity and the feeling that the world around her made sense. Yet now, as she studied the history of African Americans, an ongoing history as the civil rights movement made plain, and as she witnessed the televised war each night, she was not sure about that current, which felt more like mindlessness than anything, as if buying a new Plymouth were the American sum of life. Her parents had been fierce FDR believers who lived and died with "our truly great president," according to her mother. Would Roosevelt have allowed Vietnam to happen? Would he have become the prisoner of his words? Roosevelt seemed to understand that everything with politics and nations was provisional. Some fights were worth joining and some weren't.

And there was her older son bobbing on the sea of events and speeches. He seemed more cheerful than when he had come home in January, but he didn't talk about his plans, assuming he had any. When she thought of him, Helen had a hard time concentrating. All those days of raising him could go up in sudden smoke. Already it had happened to many mothers who remembered their son's first steps or first words or first birthday and a thousand more occasions. What did "burden" have to say to that? What could it ever say? There were the lives of women and then the lives of men.

Three Young Men in a Restaurant /

"This is my brother Herb. Herb, meet Reggie."

The hand Reggie put across the booth's tabletop was open and vertical, not horizontal and flat, a call for a clasp not a shake. Herb got it and did it.

"Nice to meet you," said Reggie. "You got the same cheekbones. And you both haven't visited a barber in a while."

"And nice to meet you. I've heard so many things about you." An unsettling perception came to Herb: He'd never touched a black man's hand before.

"Good things, I hope." Reggie turned to Tom. "How's it hanging?"

"Still dangling, if that's what you mean."

"Dangling a couple ways, huh?" said Reggie. "A wind's gonna come and blow you away."

"You're cheerful," said Tom. "You hitting the books too much?"

"If I never see the inside of a chemistry lab again, it won't be a loss. But as to hanging, I've got three women chasing after me. Who could resist?" Reggie smiled a resplendent, born-to-please-women smile. "How about you in that department?"

"I met an older woman. She's different. For one, she has a kid."

Herb felt an inner gasp. He hadn't heard a word about this woman.

"Watch out," said Reggie. "She'll reel you in. You're still a rookie."

"Thanks for the warning."

Reggie craned his neck as if to take in the whole restaurant. "You think anyone would show up if they called this place Black Castle? Somehow, I doubt it. White is good and black is bad. Keeps things simple." He caught the eye of a waitress. "I think Miss Segregation is coming over here. That's good. I didn't want a sit-in today. I just want a hamburger."

Herb spoke to Reggie: "You following the news about McCarthy?"

"He just about beat Lyndon Johnson. I bet Mr. Texas is none too happy. But I have to tell you that black folks aren't jumping up and down about Mister McCarthy. He just seems like one more well-meaning white man. And black folks have met a few of those."

"Who do you follow?" asked Herb. He put his elbows on the tabletop and leaned toward Reggie. He wanted to hear what Reggie had to say. About anything. There had been one African American student in Herb's high school, but she left. Not hard to figure out why.

"I pay the most attention to Ali. Nothing against Martin, but Ali is in the white people's faces. Martin is eloquent. I love that. The whole church is in him. But Ali is eloquent too. And he can hit a man so the guy never knew what happened. Bam!" Reggie struck his open left hand with his right fist.

"The government's trying to bust Ali's ass," said Herb.

"The boxing business stripped him of his crown. He can't fight. He can't leave the country. A man of principle, and he's treated like a criminal. But," and Reggie waved at the rest of the people in the restaurant, "what would white people know about it? Like Ali said about how he had nothing against the Viet Cong. How he said it wasn't his war and how it was against his religion." Reggie stared down at the paper place mat in front of him that displayed ads for local businesses. "Damn."

They all were silent as if listening to the restaurant—glasses placed on counters, cash register clanging, doors to the kitchen whooshing open and shut—then Tom let out a soft, slow whistle. "One man of principle who won't bend no matter how hard they lean on him."

"A lot of black athletes are behind him: Jim Brown, Bill Russell, Lew Alcindor," said Herb.

"You're right," said Reggie, "but no matter what a black man becomes, he's still a black man."

The waitress stood before them with her pad out and pencil ready. "Can I help you gentlemen?" Her face showed how hard it was for her to say those words, as if on an otherwise unremarkable late weekday afternoon, the weight of American history was right there—alive, trembling, and something like explosive.

"You can take our order," said Reggie.

∞

The Pecking Order /

Lyndon Johnson believed in himself in that almost magical way that many politicians believe in themselves, an agency that was his alone and that could do virtually anything. When he looked back at his career and the modest circumstances from which he emerged, his attitude was understandable. Who would have predicted that he would have the career he'd had and achieve what he had achieved? A few of his longtime colleagues might not have been surprised, but they had the sagacity of hindsight. Lyndon was not the only ambitious man in Texas, but he was the one who wound up as president of the United States. Given the disinclination of the rest of the nation in the first half of the twentieth century to elect a Southerner as their president, that alone was an achievement.

If you cajoled and punished people, you could get what you wanted, and Lyndon pushed that to the limit. People knew they were being cajoled; they certainly knew when they were being punished for crossing him, but that didn't stop him. He had the belief that he was ever right, that he was an essence of America, and America was ever right. The two went together. Politics wasn't about self-doubt. Politics was assertion and more assertion, something Eugene McCarthy, to name one politician with whom Johnson was familiar, did not grasp. McCarthy questioned certainty, and that made him seem weak. Yet many voters in that first presidential primary preferred McCarthy.

In the Vietnam conflict, as it was properly called because it was not officially a war, Lyndon ran into a very unforeseen curve. Ho Chi Minh was not interested in being cajoled, and he was willing, along with his people, to endure savage punishment. The bombs that rained on North Vietnam were Lyndon's version of arm-twisting. Depriving people of offices they wanted and bills they wanted to pass or not pass was different, however, from the terror of massive bombing. Did he understand that?

Senator Fulbright of Arkansas, whom Johnson came to despise, used the word *arrogance* to characterize Lyndon's performance and beliefs. That wasn't a permissible word to Lyndon. America, as it upheld the ideals of freedom and liberty, was right. The communists were wrong. Nothing more needed to be said, especially by some grandstanding senator. The circumstances where this drama might play out—another nation in Southeast Asia with its own complex history—did not matter. To some who had seen something of the world, that must have seemed an incredible notion, one that was somehow supposed to be papered over by raw power, machines, money, and the loss of many young lives. Someone who had written a book like *The Quiet American*, which inserted a disabused knife into American virtue, was not president.

The insights of literature could be dismissed. Who, of any consequence, cared about such things, particularly something by a Brit who had his own scores to settle? Yet there Lyndon sat, the proud occupant of the White House, listening to "Hey, hey, LBJ, how many boys did you kill today?" He, who believed he could talk people into anything, wanted to go out there and talk to those mistaken, confused people and explain how wrong they were, how they were subverting the great American enterprise and offering consolation to the enemy. Yet he couldn't brand millions of people "traitors." Some of them were veterans who had returned from the war and were now opposed to it. You didn't have to be a syndicated columnist to understand that was a bad sign. One among many.

Many Female Tatters /

"I need some Mom time," said Star.

"I can do that, and we can do that. Just let me find where I put my car keys."

"Have you tried your pocketbook and coat pockets?" Star asked.

"You are my practical girl. I have, but I haven't tried this place." Helen opened the top drawer of the desk in the front hall. "Bingo!" She scooped up the keys. "Sometimes they seem to have a life of their own. Want to go grocery shopping with me?"

"Sure, but first I want to talk." Star did a modest plié to focus herself, a gesture left over from a year of childhood ballet lessons. "I need to know some big stuff, like how you've managed to do what you've done. How you've managed to be a woman, because it's getting me down, how in school I'm supposed to follow the girls and be interested in every girl thing. If it weren't for Ruthie and a few others, you'd never know there's a war going on. All the talk is about the next date and who's going out with which guy, and have you heard what so-and-so and so-and-so did? Maybe I just can't stand the gossip. And meanwhile I read the news, and what am I supposed to do—blow up the White House? I understand why Tom left school. It may not have been smart, but I understand. Frustration—pure and simple."

Helen scrutinized her daughter, who stood there in her fancifully patched jeans and peasant blouse and saw, as she was accustomed to seeing, the child she brought into the world and helped to raise. Once more, the years jumped out at her, brimming with feelings. "You're high-minded. It runs in the family."

"Am I?"

"I went through the Depression and World War II, but it didn't stop girls from gossiping. Or guys from talking baseball to the exclusion of what seemed like everything else. Maybe we can only take so much reality. And yet I have to say, when I sit in my class and listen to what black people have been up against, I feel like an idiot." Helen clutched her keys. "I should have looked harder. And that's one more thing I love about you. You look hard."

"Thanks, but it feels more like life is grabbing me and won't let go. So much is happening, and that makes school feel even dumber. Was school that way for you? I mean high school?"

"It's a while ago, but I remember sitting and passing notes and looking at the clock. I wasn't cut out to take chemistry, I can tell you that. And I have to admit—I was boy crazy."

"I think about that too, boys, but that's the problem. They're boys. And when they try to act like men, that only makes it worse." Star made a face that Helen recognized well—trying not to cry. "There's so much more to being alive than what we do in school. It drives me crazy. I don't want to be in a box."

"You don't have to be." Helen moved to hug her. "You won't be."

"Everything feels like weight," Star said. "And impossible, because so few people care and I'm supposed to act as if that's okay. But it's not."

Helen opened her arms to her daughter's embrace. They hugged in a medley of immediacy—a bit desperate, a bit consoled, and a bit perplexed, ease and tension registering simultaneously. And they felt how close you could be to someone but distant, another body and life, the tingling moments leading inevitably to separation. They felt—all this unvoiced— more than a little sad. And so they hugged harder.

Hard Not Soft /

In the background, although ready at any moment to rankle the political air, like a taunt hurled on the playground, was the almost-magical phrase: "soft on Communism." Sometimes the phrase seemed like a product, like a box of Saltines or Ritz crackers that a person would pull off the grocery shelf and put into a cart. And the phrase was meant to elicit that feeling, since there was that sensory word in it, something tactile and palpable, something that evoked squeamishness, moral rot and cowardice, something no real man—since it was men hurling the taunt—would countenance.

The men using the phrase were eager to raise the specter of whatever insidious fantasies might come to mind. One dreadful size fit all. Very few people in the United States had actually experienced Communism, but the intentions of Communism—world revolution, overthrow of the ruling class, destruction of private property, abolition of individual freedom in the name of the state and the party, godlessness—were enough to elicit a primal revulsion. That millions were sacrificed to such goals was, in the eyes of those who used the phrase, small, human change. The United States had not gone to war over the rebellion in Hungary in 1956, but no one accused Dwight Eisenhower of being soft. He was merely prudent.

Richard Nixon, a Republican candidate for the American presidency in March of 1968 was fond of the phrase. He enjoyed acting tough and enjoyed ridiculing anyone who did not meet his standards of rhetorical toughness. Whether using such a phrase took anything like courage was irrelevant: A constant alarm must be rung. Senator Joseph McCarthy had rung it too stridently but had been on the right path. A cold war was nonetheless a war; vigilance was vigilance.

Why did the nations think they were civilized? Because they had sophisticated airplanes or automobiles or radios? Or was the notion of civilization extraneous, so much cotton wadding that graduation speakers dispensed with diplomas? The playground remained, as did the need to belittle anyone who might be weak, who might be led by something "soft," something confused or insidious or seditious or whatever un-American feeling had crept into the person. Anyone "soft" had betrayed a more or less sacred trust. Every American politician had to deal with softness, and so the easiest path was to protest his hardness, as in "hard-liner."

If there were an adult on the playground, someone who had read a few works of world literature, he or she (because in this situation the person could be a woman rather than a hectoring male) might point out that human societies lurched from one mania to another and that it might be prudent to abandon ideological goals and downplay patriotic ones. Human greed, for instance, was not going away, no matter what anyone did. Notions such as ownership of the earth, whether by the state or individuals or corporations, also showed a powerful lasting force among the civilized. The economic spear was going to be hurled by someone and justifications were going to accrue, whether for Wall Street or the politburo. Life outside the walls of Eden had always attracted explainers.

Meanwhile, people like the Brownsons had been picking up the morning and evening papers for what seemed like an eternity and reading about some Republican politician raising the specter of softness and some Democrat attempting to refute it. Were Americans going to be impotent? Was that the ultimate question? Was American manliness going to fail, its men averting their heads in shame, their women thrashing in unsatisfied anguish? Any comic who joked about this could be jailed for what amounted to political obscenity, as happened to Lenny Bruce—nothing remotely funny there. A look at Richard Nixon's painful face, ravaged by discord, loathing, and ambition, confirmed that there was nothing funny, while in the background, the intercontinental ballistic missiles were patiently waiting.

⌒∞⌒

Waiting for No One /

"Now I know what a backdoor man is." Tom grinned.

"A what?"

"It's from the blues. It means a guy who comes in through the back door so no one sees him. Like how you make me park two blocks away and knock on your back door."

"I guess you think I'm crazy."

"No, just cautious."

Eleven p.m. and they were sitting in Sharlene's kitchen, where Sharlene was holding forth: "For months and months after my husband died, I was miserable, like I was curdled and dried up at the same time, but I was angry because, like I told you, he didn't have to go there." Sharlene stared off, far beyond the kitchen clock on the wall above Tom's head. "I think he wanted to die. Probably you think that's crazy too, but I think there was something in him that wanted to tempt fate. I pleaded with him. That's what women do—plead. I asked him if he loved me. He said he did, but he loved his country too. 'Did your country give you a child?' I asked him that. He hated when I said something like that." Sharlene took a paper napkin from a holder on the table and began to twist it. "You know what? It's men who are crazy. I'm not crazy. It's men who are crazy, and then women have to live with them and their craziness. Probably you're crazy too. Probably you think you should tempt fate and see what death is like." She gave the napkin one more twist and threw it at Tom. It didn't fly far.

Tom got up, walked the few steps to her, crouched, and put a hand on her shoulder. "Hey, you're right. One thing I like about you is that you're not crazy."

"That's not what I'd call a big plus. I'll have to laugh to keep from crying." She picked up the napkin and dabbed at her eyes. "I could give Travis to his grandparents—my husband's parents—tomorrow and they'd raise him and be happy to do that. It's like he's their child more than mine, because he's their tie to their son."

"How come you never say your husband's name?"

"Because if I say his name, everything comes back too strong; all my feelings come back too strong." She shook her head as if to chase away the tears. "You know who I've started listening to? This hippie woman, Janis Joplin. When she sings, it's like the whole universe inside me is coming out of her. Only a woman could sing like that."

"Look, I'm thinking I'm not going into the army."

"You just dropped Janis, but that's okay. What does it mean, what you just said?"

"Means I've been thinking. Means I've met you. Means I'm sitting here in this kitchen. Means we're different from each other and never in the probable world would have met each other. Means you're having an effect on me. Means I need to be a man in a way that makes sense to me. Means I don't know exactly what I'm going to do." Tom took a breath—another speech delivered.

"Wow! You let something out. I like that; I mean you're kinda buttoned-up, but I have to say, when I hear you, I don't understand the world we are living in." Her voice, Tom realized, had gone through at least four registers of feeling in a matter of what felt like moments. Her last few words were clear, almost hard. "I thought I was going to be married for a lifetime and have a bunch of kids and bake pies and buy gifts for baby showers and go to the shore in the summer and kinda watch life go by. Be a woman, I guess." She leaned toward Tom and started to nuzzle her head in the crook of his neck but drew back. "I have no idea what you mean to me, but you keep showing up and I want you to keep showing up. Probably that's enough." She stared off as if to summon the right words. "But at some point, I have to deal with the front door. I have to say I'm not a war widow forever. I have to say what I think and feel." She started to nuzzle with determination, softly boring into him, her words becoming muffled: "And I've started tonight, right now."

❦

The Tragedy Now /

After Mrs. Billings told the class that they should go over Act IV of *Macbeth* and be ready for a quiz about who said what in that act, Herb raised his hand.

"I have a question."

"Yes, Herbert." Mrs. Billings was the most formidable of the school's English teachers. She had gray hair that she parted on one side and secured with barrettes from the five-and-dime, often spoke while holding a demonstrative pencil in her right hand ("Pencil" was her school nickname), wore moccasins year-round, and, when exasperated, was not above resorting to sarcasm. Her students gave her a wide berth and tried to find her amusing or eccentric or something that would alleviate the uneasiness she cultivated. If she ended the class a few minutes early, that meant she wanted to get ready for the next class or just breathe out. She did not want to answer a question. As the teacher, *she* asked the questions.

"How come there are no more tragedies? We're reading this play by Shakespeare, but as far as I can tell from reading the *Encyclopedia Britannica*, tragedies haven't been written for centuries."

Mrs. Billings made a face, showing amused perplexity. "That's quite a question to answer a few minutes before the bell. The short answer is that there are no more kings, and tragedies are about the downfall of kings. We've talked about that. As you know."

"I do, but we have presidents who have enormous power—like they can blow up the world this afternoon—and if something happens to them, like recently Lyndon Johnson sort of lost an election to some senator from the Midwest, that doesn't qualify as a tragedy. But could there be a tragedy with someone like President Johnson in it?"

"Cool your jets, Herbie," Tracey Sanders said from three seats over.

"Shut up," said Herb. "I'm talking to Mrs. Billings."

"You're in a classroom with other people," said Tracey. "Not in your head, where you seem to spend all your time anyway."

"That will be enough, Tracey," said Mrs. Billings. "And no need to be rude, Herbert. I'm taking your question seriously, and I would advise the rest of you to take Herbert's question seriously. In fact, I may have you write an essay for your final grade on *Macbeth* that is devoted to Herbert's question."

Everyone stopped rustling paper and gathering books. Someone in the back of the room said "What the—" but then thought better about saying the last word.

"Is it that no one has the stature that a king once had? Is it that even someone like President Johnson is just a politician and not much of a big-deal person?"

"You seem to be answering your own question, Herbert."

"Sure, I have my thoughts, but I want to know what you think." Herb pursed his lips to indicate a degree of befuddlement. Tracey Sanders made a show of dropping her biology textbook to the floor. Mrs. Billings glanced over at the clock.

"Are we different from the Elizabethans?" Mrs. Billings asked. "They didn't even have indoor plumbing or electricity. But that's not the measurement of what you call 'stature,' is it? That's the measure of invention and comfort and practicality."

"And tens of thousands of people die," said Herb, "for what seems like no reason, and we just go on and keep saying it's okay and send more troops. Is that a tragedy?"

With that the bell went off. Like genies released from a magic lamp, everyone sprang up at once. The words in Mrs. Billings's mouth became a throttled whisper.

"Saved by the bell," chortled Tracey.

"Thanks," said Herb above the hubbub of everyone's leaving, "for taking my question. I think about stuff like that. I thought you might think about it too."

The teacher, who had started to busy herself with some mimeographed papers on her desk, stopped. "I do. That's why I come here every day." An abstracted expression came over her face for a few moments then disappeared. "And now we each have another class to deal with."

Herb took the cue and headed for the door but stopped at her voice.

"And Herbert," she said, "thank you. I know what school is like. There's nothing wrong with thinking."

⨳

Thinking about Another Candidate /

The announcement came via the television: Robert F. Kennedy was running for president. In the Brownson household Starflower made the announcement, going from room to room to alert the other family members who were home, Tom being "out." They abandoned their miscellaneous, apolitical tasks on a late Saturday afternoon to gather in the living room.

As the direct recipient of the news, Starflower held forth: "He said a lot of good things. Like we are on 'a perilous course' and we need 'new policies,' and that these 'are not ordinary times' and that he could not 'stand aside.' He's right, but I still don't understand why he's doing this. McCarthy just almost won and showed that there are people out there, many people, who are unhappy with Lyndon Johnson. Why do we need Bobby Kennedy? It's like McCarthy baked the loaf of bread and now Kennedy comes along and wants to eat it."

"Because," Daniel said, "he's a Kennedy and that's what they do. Even though he was waiting for 1972 to run, when he saw what McCarthy did, he must have decided that it was time to do it now. Time stops for no man and, as a Kennedy, he would know that too well."

Everyone understood his words, an emotional pall that went with the name "Kennedy" or the mention of "Dallas."

"What is that gonna mean, Dad?" Starflower looked over at her mother. "And Mom?" She sat down on the living room couch while the others remained standing, but all of them feeling, in whatever pose or attitude, self-aware, more history leaping out at them.

"Your father," said Helen "seems correct to me. Politics is principles—and the principles can be terribly wrong, more like prejudices than principles—and ambition. You don't get into politics, particularly at the national level, unless you are ambitious. You don't have to look any further than Lyndon Johnson or, for that matter, Richard Nixon. They are men who try to act polite, though it's obviously an ordeal for them, because they will step on anyone to get their way."

"But what's gonna happen to McCarthy now?" Herb sat down beside his sister. "People go crazy when they hear the name Kennedy. But isn't he like what Star was talking about, like what you call a 'Johnny-come-lately'? Or, I should say, 'Bobby-come-lately.'"

"I imagine," Helen went on, "that McCarthy has no love for Robert Kennedy but is not going to give up. Still, there's no telling. Do we need two candidates who are opposed to the war? Is Kennedy opposed to the war? I haven't kept up with what he's been saying."

"I remember more," said Star, "how he ended. How he said something like it's not just an election, it's our right to the moral leadership of this planet."

"Holy moly! How can he talk like that?" Herb threw his hands up in the air. "Who does he think we are? Like Americans have the answers to everything?"

"He's a politician—"

"You say that word, Dad, like he's a leper. But Senator McCarthy was brave to run against Johnson. There's nothing brave in what Kennedy is doing. He's just an—" Herb paused. "Opportunist." Herb winced at his own word.

No one spoke, the moment transfiguring them but feeling unwieldy, another bend in the road that would create another map of possibilities, until Helen, who felt an abrupt surfeit of historical feelings that was becoming second nature—a war inside her mirroring the war out there— told Herb and Star she could use their help in preparing dinner.

"Does every country want to run the planet?" Herb asked.

"Only countries that believe they can," his father answered.

⁓

The Dark Answer /

Death for Ho Chi Minh was a familiar. He never sought it out, but the terms of his life—a revolutionary—dictated that his death by violent means was a likelihood. And he caused many deaths, though the cause he espoused was larger than any individual death. When the Americans counted corpses, they didn't understand. They thought each death was a grievous, irreplaceable loss. Each death was grievous, but one death could be replaced with another. One death ended a life but did not end the dedication to liberation. Or the fact of death.

Was it death that made people cruel? The French routinely tortured the Vietnamese. That was part of how the colonial world worked: A Vietnamese life already was less than a French life, fractional in the way that slaves in the United States had been defined in their constitution as fractional, less-than-human creatures. The French would never say that, but that was the understanding. The cruelty was justified. He would not have argued with that. One hell created another. Anyone who romanticized the chain of wrongdoing was a simpleton.

He was on his own but inextricably social: one of the cadre, the cell, the party, the underground, the movement, the shadow nation, the people. Strictly speaking, he was not responsible for anyone's fate but his own, yet he was tied to a web of allegiances that created a virtual mountain of death. Revolutions did that, beginning with the French. Ideals went hand in hand with death. The imperialists and capitalists who made the First World War created a mountain too, but they had no ideals. Their kings and queens, parliaments and munition makers, flags and newspapers were quite sufficient. Pinning death wholly on the revolutionaries was unjust.

Everyone in modern times shared in the making of death. The Americans called their war department the defense department, as if there were some difference, as if that prevented them from going anywhere to pursue their enemy—a long-reaching "defense."

He had heard about the play by the great English writer Shakespeare where the queen could not get the blood off her hands and went crazy trying to do so. That was only a play, but he understood. What justifications could there be for pursuing death? He had many, and he followed them to wherever they led him. But lying on a mat or thin mattress or bare ground at night, he found himself staring into the peopled void of human history, a history he was creating. A very long trail of deaths went with that history. That weighed on him, but the weight was not even or sensible. The weight was like a thin sound of a woman wailing, a sound he imagined but that spoke for something all too real. The weight was nothing you told another revolutionary about. The weight went with being human and understanding that any life was bound for death and that each day was only a pretext, a forgetting.

For all his native kindness, the iron of his commitment was bound to diminish him. He accepted that as he accepted his own death. Increasingly, the gist of modern times in the West seemed to be devoted to avoiding death, as if each death were an unexpected calamity. How foolish! The Americans lacked any perspective about the depths of death. They refused to recognize the shadows that mocked each living moment. Would they learn anything? Did they want to learn anything? That was no business of his. He had his own death to live with.

Living with Spiritual Dissatisfaction /

Once in a very long while, when his obligations let go of him, Daniel liked to imagine not a trip to Europe, which as a continent remained a charnel house in his memory, nor a long laze around the house, but rather a month of churchgoing Sundays. No daily work, no daily news, no daily conversation, only time devoted to perennial matters, to mysterious ends and sanctified means, time accompanied by a devotional aura that would suffuse the very air. Such constant Sundays would abolish the distractions and offer a large chance to pay serious attention. He listened carefully to clients, to his children and wife and to the television news reporters. It was true that the unadorned meetinghouse didn't feel much like a church, but then he had had a hard time settling on a church and residing there. Even at those moments when he felt something like a healing presence, he could feel it retreating, Sundays disappearing into Mondays, the God of his forebears not his God.

Helen, in her historical mode, had given him a brief lecture about the Quakers' past. They were much "milder" than they once had been but still were "determined" people. The Puritans had hanged Quakers on Boston Common for what, in the eyes of the Massachusetts Bay Colony, amounted to religious sedition. That had been long ago, but it didn't feel so long ago to Daniel as he sat in the silence of the meeting room and waited for something inside himself to stir. What dispensation was the man identified as "Daniel Brownson" waiting for? He wished he knew. He had witnessed much suffering and had created a family in part to oppose that suffering, to affirm life, but now there was more suffering, more war and the reasons that surrounded war, the words that reeked of certainty.

What the Quakers talked about weren't exactly feelings. They were spiritual thoughts, but ones that seemed honed by the fabled inner light. His jack-of-all-trades father and the modest farm on which Daniel grew up instilled in him a reverence for practicality—how things got done. On that count, he took to the law naturally, while the investigative side kept him, as he liked to put it, "on his toes." But seeing how one thing affected another only went so far. Some things you couldn't see. Or some things you saw but only the externals, the husk and not the core.

His family, accustomed to his bouts of churchgoing, treated his recent interest with tolerance—"Dad likes his Sundays"—another one of "Dad's things," like putting up birdhouses and building bookcases, though Tom had raised the matter a couple times. Therefore, he wasn't completely surprised when Tom asked to go with him to a meeting, that he wanted to see "what it was like." That was Tom—curious.

On the way over, they made small talk about the pizza joint and how Tom kept in touch with a fellow he had met in his "lacrosse days." Tom's talking about those days felt strange to Daniel, as if they were irrevocable. Everything had been so regular. He had stood in the stands and cheered. No sigh on Daniel's part could have been deep enough.

Though Daniel would have been the first to admit that he didn't have much experience to go by, the meeting seemed a particularly quiet one. Only one person got up, and she talked about how her mother was dying and how she felt a sort of peace with that dying. A few times, Daniel looked over at his son, who seemed to naturally draw into himself. He didn't fidget or yawn but seemed focused on the task at hand, though it would have been hard to define what the task was. Afterward, Daniel introduced Tom to a few people that Daniel recognized from other Sundays. Everyone was polite. Tom nodded and smiled. Seeing his son among these people gave Daniel a new heartache. The depth and decency of the silence and the attendant speech were so far removed from each imperative day. There was so much human work to be done and so little true time to do it.

Doing the Death Stick Routine /

"If I smoked Tareytons, then—" Herb paused to give Chuck an opening.

"You'd rather fight than switch. And you'd have a black eye to show you meant it."

"But I'd be wearing a coat and tie and have a neat haircut too."

"And if I smoked Winstons, then—"

"I would know that Winston tastes good, like a cigarette should."

"Even though Mrs. Billings would correct you for using like as a conjunction."

"She's a stickler."

"And if you smoked Marlboros, then—"

"I'd wear a cowboy hat and ride a horse and be a total Western guy, and I'd have a license plate from a state that doesn't exist."

"And you'd look into the distance in a meaningful way that had something to do with smoking a cigarette."

"Is that why the settlers killed the Indians, so some fake cowboy could ride around and smoke a cigarette?"

"That's a Herbie question if I ever heard one."

"And if I smoked Pall Malls, then—"

"You'd be having an experience that was outstanding and mild."

"And if I smoked Lucky Strikes, then—"

"You'd be the truest American you could be, because Lucky Strikes went to war with you. C-rations and Luckies. I bet your dad smoked them."

"I never asked him, though it seems like a harmless question. He doesn't smoke now. But I wonder if we send cigarettes to our guys in Vietnam."

"They already see a lot of bad smoke there."

"Yeah. Cigarettes are death, puff by puff."

"Smell crappy too, but if you want to be cool—"

"Then you need to smoke Kools, but you'd have be in the country where the air is clean even though you'd be polluting it with your stupid cigarette."

"Menthol! What do they put in those cigarettes?"

"They put advertising in them, that's what they put in them."

"Right. What do you think? Who can name the most brands in a minute?"

"Are we counting just American cigarettes or British, too?"

"How do you know about British cigarettes?"

"I read books. They have their own cigarettes."

"How come? I mean they don't grow their own tobacco, do they?"

"Maybe the cigarettes get made here and we send them over there with a different package."

"What a life we have that we talk about this stuff."

Both of them peered around the bus, explorers who wondered where they were and how they got there.

"And if you smoked Old Golds, then—"

"Not a cough in a carload."

"What?"

"That's an old one. I'm studying the history of human wrongheadedness."

"Come over to my house then." Chuck gripped the bar on the seat in front of him as if to steady himself.

⌘

The Steady Drumbeat of Historical Determination /

Helen scanned the room for the young man she had met at the luncheonette but didn't see him. She took a seat next to a woman who also was a master's degree student and who also intended to become a history teacher. Her name was Margaret Martin; they had joked about her having the same initials as Marilyn Monroe.

The professor, who was young, no more than thirty-five, tapped the microphone on the podium. "I am going to be lecturing today, as you know from your syllabus, on the migration north and will be showing you some slides of the migration series by the painter Jacob Lawrence. As slides, they are just notions of the paintings, which I would urge you to see for yourself in Washington and New York; but then again, much of life is notions."

He touched the knot of his tie, a ritual gesture. Helen thought of her husband. Men and knots.

"But before I start, I want to say some words about what is going on right now. As you may know, if you have been following the news, Martin Luther King Jr. is in Memphis, Tennessee, to lend his support to a strike on the part of sanitation workers there. Again, as you may know, on February 1, two black sanitation workers were crushed to death when the compactor mechanism of the truck they were working on was triggered accidentally. This happened on a rainy day, and the men were sitting in the back of the truck to keep out of the rain. Some people refer to these workers as garbage men, and there is no doubt that what went into that truck could be foul and disgusting. They were doing work, however, that needs to be done and is as important as what any person does in this world—more important in ways, because there were no notions in their work. They were doing something actual that this society depends upon."

Every face was turned forward. There were two black students out of seventy or so.

"Since then, the workers have rallied to seek better conditions, wages, and pensions. The mayor has been adamantly opposed to their demands. As far as he is concerned, they have no right to strike. They should be satisfied with their lot. His philosophy, a word much too high-toned for what is occurring there, is *paternalism*—a word with which you are familiar in our studies in this class, if you weren't familiar with it already. He thinks he is doing those workers a favor, and he thinks he is doing white people a big favor by keeping these men in their place. A reverend in Memphis who is a veteran of the civil rights movement invited Martin Luther King Jr. to come to Memphis and focus the nation's attention on what is happening. He spoke to the workers and their supporters and has promised to do more, to lead a larger march. Meanwhile, garbage is piling up, and many men who didn't have much to begin with are doing without that. And I, a white man and a professor to boot, am standing here talking to you."

Not a sound in the large room.

"I don't know what you think about Martin Luther King Jr. I think it is extraordinary that we have such a person among us. I was raised in the Episcopal Church, and some days I am proud of that and some days I'm not sure at all about the God I worship. Dr. King is sure about that God, and he is sure of the nonviolence he has espoused and lived by. There is hate all around us and hate within us, waiting patiently to be activated. It takes a great deal to get beyond that hate and to see that peace is a place where we could live. Dr. King's vision is about that place. Right now, Memphis is not that place, but we must hope—which I assume is the reason we are all here today in this room studying the history we are studying—that there can be such a place."

He looked out at his students then wagged his head a bit, as if waking from a dream.

"He needs to compose himself," said Margaret Martin to Helen, "to go on."

"In speaking of the migration north, we need to first interrogate the word *migration*, what is in that word, what were the circumstances of so many people leaving the South?"

Once more, Helen felt there was nothing as strangely visceral as history.

✒

History Speaking /

Sometimes Tom picked up the newspaper on his way upstairs after work and after a few cursory words with whomever was up, although sometimes more than cursory, sometimes about the news. He more or less kept up in that department. Too much could swamp a person: wars, refusals, denials, disagreements, filibusters, denunciations, all acting as if they were achievements. And there loomed his personal news, that envelope from the government, the Thomas Brownson Special Edition.

The excerpts from a speech that Martin Luther King Jr. had given in Memphis, Tennessee, made him pause—something worth his time. Settled on his bed, he placed the page in his lap and read:

> We are tired of our children having to attend overcrowded, inferior, qualityless schools. We are tired of having to live in dilapidated, substandard housing conditions where we don't have wall-to-wall carpet, but so often end up with wall-to-wall rats and roaches. We are tired . . . smothering in an air-tight cage of poverty in the midst of an affluent society. We are tired of walking the streets in search of jobs that do not exist. We are tired of working our hands off and laboring every day and not even making a wage adequate to the basic necessities of life.... We are tired.

Reverend King wasn't addressing Tom's life, but a human bridge was there, along with the unspoken question about what he would be fighting for on behalf of the United States. Oppression? Indifference? Racism? Those were words, but they weren't. People's lives stood behind those words, people such as those Reverend King was speaking to. Tom read the passage again. There was that cadence to the words. What was it called? A litany? "We are tired." And where had he, Thomas Brownson, been?

He had eyes, but he didn't have eyes. He'd been busy passing the buck, minding his own business, looking after number one. He hadn't seen into the heart of anything.

He put the paper on the floor and lay back on his bed. Reverend King was someone who not only told the truth but lived it. You could hear his voice come off the newspaper page, that solemn thunder. Tom lay on his comfortable bed in his comfortable house, but that could change. No—it *would* change.

∞

Change Moves through a Person Like a Dark Cloud /

"We've known the Shiptons for what seems like forever. I know they will ask about our children, and that means I need to say something about Tom. They have a daughter in college and things are going more or less swimmingly; and I have a son who has dropped out and put us in a state of dread so that when I go to the mailbox every day, I feel that I'm walking on hot coals or to the guillotine like in *A Tale of Two Cities*, but meanwhile I'm supposed to say, 'I'm fine and pass the broccoli.'" Helen gulped and rolled down the passenger side window. "I think I'm getting sick. Pull over."

Daniel maneuvered the car into a driveway.

"The whole thing is that a lot of this nation is getting sick. It's not just you and me. It's millions of people getting sick but having no place to really go and get over it, because we're all in it and we can't get over it. We're stuck, even though many of us can't really believe we could be stuck because we went to college, the way I went to Goucher, and studied civilization and its outpourings and thought that life would proceed along a reasonable and sensitive path." Helen opened the door, staggered out, and started retching but nothing came out. Dry heaves.

Daniel came around to her. "Take your time."

"What else could I do?" she said between gasps.

"Nice that your sense of humor hasn't abandoned you."

She picked her head up and then raised her torso. "I feel a little wobbly."

"Lean on me and inhale." Daniel extended an arm.

"I'm afraid I'm not the best candidate for a dinner party."

"As I said, no hurry. The hors d'oeuvres will wait. Probably squiggles of Velveeta on bologna slices."

"Daniel! You'll make me throw up more. I need to sit down. Help me back in the car." Helen moved very slowly to the still open car door. "Cold out tonight. Or maybe it's just me." She dropped down onto the passenger seat, more falling over than sitting.

"No, it's cold. That March-cold that we get sometimes. Not real spring yet." Daniel stood by the open door.

Helen hoisted herself up some. "I can't stand this waiting. It's like waiting to see if he's going to be executed."

"That's a bit strong. I've told him about counselors who can help him figure this out. He's said he'll go to one."

"He says lots of things and he says nothing. He's so up in the air, I'm surprised he hasn't floated away. Probably he's smoking his share of pot, too. He's got a funny smell to him sometimes."

"Could be, though that seems a lesser matter at the moment. I gather our soldiers over there smoke a fair amount of it."

"Oh, Daniel." Helen started to cry, hesitated, and then gave into it. "Why these wars? What is it about people?"

Daniel listened to her weeping. How to explain to their hosts how they had been detained? How to explain to anyone, how circumstances could be so much larger than a mere, driving-down-the-road life? He pushed in next to his wife and put an arm around her. He resisted the urge to speak.

Visionary Speaking and Singing /

"I did it again."

"Did what?"

"Dropped acid with Chris."

"You are too fast. Did the sky explode again or whatever you were telling me?" Ruthie, who was on a weeknight sleepover and sitting with Star on Star's bed, drew herself up a bit to receive the illicit psychedelic news. Helen and Daniel had turned in with some words about not staying up all night. Herb, after making awkward small talk, pleaded "an avalanche of chemistry homework" and retreated to his bedroom, leading to giggles on the girls' part. Tom was working and then going "oh, somewhere." Spinning around on the turntable at a modest volume was *Surrealistic Pillow* by Jefferson Airplane—love songs and drug songs.

"I wrote some poems about it, but I don't want to read them. They're dopey. It's hard to get into words. Maybe it's not supposed to get into words. Maybe that's what it's about. But it turned into a bummer at the end because Chris got real upset and curled into a ball like a fetus and wouldn't say anything, so I had to kinda keep an eye on him, even though the world around me was a lot less than solid. After a while, or it felt like a while, because time just sort of gets up and hides when you take acid, he started talking in a real small voice as if he was a little boy. It was sad stuff."

"Bad-parents sad? Stupid-school sad? No-friends sad?"

"Maybe worse, but you have to promise not to tell."

"Who could I tell? Some idiot in school who wouldn't talk to me anyway?"

"He likes boys, but he can't tell anyone because he's afraid; because you know what happens when guys think someone's a homosexual. They

175

almost kill him. All Chris wants is for high school to be over so he can go to college and be a person. So he takes acid on weekends and he draws a lot—he's a good drawer—and at school he tries to be inconspicuous."

"When I think of him," said Ruthie, "you know—walking the corridors and trying to fit in—my problems don't seem like big-deal problems. What did you say to him?"

"I thanked him for telling me and told him things would be okay, that he'll get there. What could I say?" Star picked up one of the stuffed animals on her bed, a monkey, and clutched it to her chest. "I'm not gonna take acid again. It's too crazy to go to school and then know how everything is so made up, how there are dimensions we barely know about and we're sitting around memorizing verbs. It's a help but it's not a help, because everything's still the same when you come back from it. And it can turn you inside out, like with Chris."

"You know what the song says: 'Feed your head.'" Ruthie got up and put the turntable arm down on "White Rabbit."

"The San Francisco bands are the best, aren't they?" said Star. "They get it, about the flow. The thing is, like with acid, no one knows what to do with the flow. But that's not the bands' fault."

"Speaking of which, do you have any Mary Jane?" Ruthie started singing along: "One pill makes you larger."

"I've got a joint from Tom I've been rationing. Let's take a walk and put it to use." Gently, Star put down the monkey. "Got to go out for a while, Roscoe, but I'll be back."

"Roscoe?" said Ruthie.

"Who knows if I'll ever be naming kids. In the meantime, there's Roscoe, Mona, Shrimpy, Dozy, Patricia, Teddy, and Wally the Walrus." Star gestured with an open hand to the other creatures on her bed.

"Go ask Alice," sang Ruthie.

Star began to bob her head with the music. "Wild isn't it, how this song is on the radio with the ads for deodorants and Tums: 'Here's your favorite antacid and a song about mind expansion and, wait, here's a news flash about how many died today in a place called Vietnam.' You wonder what's going through the disc jockey's head. Like truth is rolling sideways, downhill, and backward all at once."

"Yeah," said Ruthie. "It's wild. Let's get stoned."

⌘

The Blind Stones of Memory /

"Before we do what we both seem to need to do, I'd like to play a little game with you." Tom reached across the table but Sharlene drew back.

"I don't like games. Probably I shouldn't be a mother on that account alone."

"The game is 'Truth or Lie.' Harmless."

Sharlene cocked her head to examine Tom closely. "What's got into you?"

"I just need to know a few things before we go further."

"Further? We haven't gone anywhere. I'm just some wacko waitress who writes down her phone number, and you're some waiting-to-be-drafted guy. We're not a 'we.' Sorry." She pointed upstairs to where Travis was sleeping. "I've got enough on my hands right now. Plus a ghost."

"Is Travis your husband's kid?"

"You don't beat around the bush, do you? I should slug you. What kinda shit is this?"

"You can just say, 'Travis is my husband's kid,' and that will be that."

"You're not stupid, are you? That's why I picked up on you right away. But you're wrong. He is my husband's kid."

"But you were ready to leave the marriage."

"I'm what you might call impulsive. I knew after a half year that I wasn't cut out for marriage. But that's what you do after high school if you come from where I come from, and that's what I did. And I married a good guy, a decent guy."

"And he went to war to get away from you?"

"He wouldn't be the first guy, would he? Things weren't going well, and even with a child to fix things up and make us parents, things didn't look good. Maybe they looked even worse, because I was pissed off and let him know it. Not that I hid it before. I can be irritable. Probably you can't imagine that."

"Actually, I can, but I'll skip over that. Do you feel guilty?"

"Of course I feel guilty. I didn't make him go, but I did. He had all these reasons, but they weren't reasons. We could have just gotten divorced like regular people, but he was stubborn. He always said he saw something in me, that I'd make a good mother and a good wife. Oh, Christ, I'm gonna start crying. Look what you've done. Some damn game."

"You're for real. There's no crime in being for real."

"You wanna make a bet? It's a big crime, one of the biggest. And it's such a bad joke, because I barely ever paid attention to the war. What was it to me? They don't need girls except what they have over there to spread their legs."

"And now you're a war widow."

"And now I'm sitting here with some guy I barely know because I'm just a lost soul, when I should be coming to attention and bearing down and generally acting as if I know what I'm doing because, front and center, I have a little boy to raise."

"You tell other people this?"

"Just guys I give phone numbers to."

Tom reached over and held her left hand up. "You still wear a ring."

Like a child, she repeated in a singsong, "I still wear a ring."

❧

A Ring in a Drawer, Stamps, a Baseball Card, the Shadow of Futility /

Helen stared down into the second drawer of the front hall desk, the one she designated the "catchall" drawer because the family put this and that into it and then, more or less promptly, forgot. She had asked Herb to help her with a "second opinion" about what to keep and toss.

Underneath an envelope from the Humane Society, she found a condom in its foil package, which she displayed to Herb.

"Not mine," he said. "Must be Tom's."

"Good he's taking precautions," said Helen. "As to you—"

"No teenage guy talks to his mom about sex. It says that in the Bible."

"Thanks for the theological update. Does that mean I shouldn't ask you about your date with Ruthie?"

"That means we enjoyed the movie and talked about it. I like her, and she seems to like me. Stay tuned for further developments."

Helen made a sound like hmmmm, which indicated awareness and dismissal at the same time. "Look at this ring. It must be Sharon's. She should own a silver mine. But how did we get all these miscellaneous stamps? Look at them." There were six-cent stamps, five-cent stamps, one-cent stamps, even a four-cent stamp.

"They're all from the United States," said Herb. "Seems fair to me."

"School going OK?" Helen was rooting around for more stamps.

"You want an agreeable response, so when I say 'OK' it means abysmal. I'm hanging in there because what else can you do? Throw a tantrum? And

I'll say I've had a few talks with Mrs. Billings, my English teacher, that have been something more than what happened in act four, scene three."

"That's good to hear. But basically, more of growing up absurd?"

"That's the book's title. Maybe I'll give our principal a copy." Herb stood a little taller and cleared his throat as the prelude to assuming a voice of dignity: "Sir, here is a book that tells about how we systematically shortchange young people in this society because we have nothing of real worth to pass on, and what we might pass on gets devalued because it's not going to make anybody any money."

"Well, we can't start over. When societies try to do that, even worse things happen."

"I'm lucky to have a historian mom." Herb stuck a hand out. "Hey, here's the combination for my locker in freshman year. Why did I keep that?"

"For historical purposes, I assume."

Herb tore up the scrap of paper.

"How's school going for you, Mom? I'm gonna read some of your books this summer."

"One of the best classes ever. I wish all white people could learn what I'm learning. I'd begin with the senators from Mississippi, Alabama, and Georgia."

"You could throw in some other states too." Herb looked harder into the drawer. "Wow, that's an old baseball card. That's Gus Triandos. How—"

"Does anything get anywhere? I wish I knew." Helen picked up the card and handed it to Herb. "Seems absurd, doesn't it? Or what I really mean to say is that I wish I could straighten life up like this drawer. I wish I could apply what I'm learning. Maybe teaching will do it. Once I get a job."

Herb carefully moved two fingers across the photo on the card's front, as if removing dust. "We could move back into the city. There have to be some blocks of Baltimore where the races live in something like harmony."

"You're right, there have to be."

"But you don't believe it?"

"I want to."

There were moments, Herb had learned, when you seemed the parent and the parent seemed the child. Those moments had enough passing truth to them to make both parties uncomfortable.

Mother and son looked at the partially tidied drawer. Herb was going to comment about how it was going to get messy again but didn't.

He Didn't Expect Him to Get Up and Talk /

All at once, like quick little knives, Daniel felt elation, surprise, and trepidation as his son rose to speak. He pitched forward as if to listen better.

"This is only the second time I've been here, so I apologize if I'm speaking out of turn. I realize many of you have been attending this meeting for years, but I needed to speak. And that seems the point of this meeting, as I understand it, that when a person needs to speak, he should speak. You can probably just look at me and tell what's on my mind, how there is a war going on and I am what's been called 'cannon fodder.' That's true, but what I'm feeling and thinking, what's been growing inside of me since I left school in January, is wondering about what I'm doing here in the United States as someone responsible for some big things—his soul and his conscience. This has been coming over me gradually with the news each day, sort of like a slow landslide within me, but the simplest way to put what I've come to feel is that the nation is not God, and that it's a big mistake to think the nation is God. I know it's on our money, and we believe we are fighting godlessness in fighting Communism. I doubt, though, whether God would applaud us. I don't think militarism—and that to me is what we're guilty of, nothing more complicated than trusting to guns and war to make something right—has anything to do with God. Or at least the God who has spoken to people's inner voices in this meeting room. I've been wondering whether there is a voice inside me that can speak for something more than doing what gets called 'my duty.' I'm not a big talker, so I've been chewing on this and keeping it to myself, but today I needed to get up and say that however this turns out for me, I won't go. I have nothing against those men who do go; in fact, I respect them all the more. Their insides are their insides, and it's not for me to judge. But I have to live my life, and my life looks too dark if I give in to the demands of my nation, because those demands, for all the words accompanying them, seem to me to be confused. And I have enough confusion inside me already without adding more. I need to simplify and find what God's spirit has to do with me. It might not have much to do. I can understand that. But what's the expression that people use? 'Something is better than nothing.' I guess that's where I'm at. I don't know if I'm supposed to say, 'Thanks for listening,' but thanks for listening." Tom ducked his head and sat down quickly.

Silence. Daniel thought to reach out and shake his son's hand, but this wasn't the moment. He did look sideways and made that puckered face of concern people make to quietly acknowledge each other—a passing concentration of feeling, usually to a stranger on the street, the tug of shared humanity, but here to the son he had spent two decades watching, loving, and caring for. Daniel suddenly felt uneasy, the breadth of this other person opening up before him, the feeling of how much his son's life was different and would take its own path. That was to be expected, but expectation and feeling the reality were two different things.

A young woman got up and began speaking in a very soft voice about despair and how "oppressed" she felt, but how when she walked out of her apartment building that morning and stood on the street and didn't do anything, just stood on the street, she felt "strangely better." She talked about how full she was of purposes and how those purposes seemed to make her "farther from life not closer."

After she sat down, no one else spoke, and after a certain amount of time, Daniel feeling the spaciousness of the silence, the meeting ended. He hugged his son before they left the room and said he was proud of him. Outside, a man came up to Tom and began talking about how Tom's words "resonated." Daniel stood slightly to the side, glad to wait. He noticed the breeze, a warmth he hadn't felt for months, and looked around cautiously as if to see the wind, sensing that, somehow, God was near.

<hr />

Near the Hard Matters /

"You ever think about how at this moment, while we're sitting here spreading jelly on our rye toast, that someone over there is dying a violent death? And that supposedly that death is making it possible for us to sit here and eat breakfast in peace? Or do I have it all wrong?" As if it were an exhibit at a trial, Herb held up his plate for everyone to see.

"Yeah, I have thought about it," said Star. "I think about how when I want to run a photo in the paper from the war with the caption 'Is this part of your world?' Mr. Klausmeyer cans it as 'not school relevant.' I think about it when I'm sitting there in trig and feeling barely alive, and yet someone over there is dying. Right then. And I'm just fucking yawning." Star looked at her parents but didn't apologize.

Daniel took a long sip of his coffee and made a face. "Too dark this morning. The coffee, I mean." No one laughed. "Poor joke, you're right. But what I was going to say was that you get into a frame of mind. The basic one is indifference, lack of imagination about anything outside your corn

183

flakes and toast. But there's another frame of mind, and I know it because I was there. That's thinking of other people as the enemy and wanting them to be dead, because if they're dead, that helps you somehow. You aren't any richer or, God forbid, happier, but they're your enemy, and so the less of them the better."

Everyone paused to listen.

"But you can get consumed by hate, which happened to the Nazis, a whole nation, but happened to some of our guys. I once saw a guy, one of ours, shoot a German prisoner in cold blood, and we all looked away and waited for life to go on. That wasn't right. That was hate, revenge, weariness—call it what you want. We didn't lift a finger. Because we understood."

Helen, who had been thinking that she was unhappy with the earrings she had put on, regarded her husband with awe, fear, and love. How many years had it taken for him to calmly say what he had just said? How often had she imagined herself as a supplicant before a closed gate marked "Daniel's war?" "I appreciate," began Helen, "what you just said, each of you. It feels to me that it's too much, what you are telling me this morning, yet I'm glad to hear it. Not because of other people's suffering but to understand my own. No, it isn't too much. I've never wanted to push life away. But . . ." Her voice trailed off.

Everyone waited, then Herb jumped in. "To return to where I began, even when I'm doing something like studying or learning a song or joking with Chuck, the war is in the back of my head, with that equation between them and us, that they have to die so we can live."

Tom, who had been eating his second bowl of Wheat Chex, raised his hand, which seemed an uncalled-for gesture but somehow wasn't. His face was grave, almost official.

"I need to tell you all something, though Dad's already heard it. And we agreed that he wouldn't say anything, that it was my call. Maybe I've been selfish trying to figure things out and not including you, even though I've been living here. But what I need to tell you is that I can't go. I don't feel great about it, because I feel like I'm passing the obligation onto other guys. Even if they throw me in jail, someone will be taking my place. But I can't do it. I don't want to kill anyone."

"I guess this isn't something," said Star, "where I say 'Congratulations.' I mean who knows what sky is gonna fall down on you. But I'm glad you're my brother." She went over and put her head on his shoulder.

Daniel exhaled, a whistling soul-whoosh. Helen looked away—too much feeling. Herb, as if dutiful, nodded, though he couldn't have said what he was nodding to.

Nodding to the Ubiquitous, Impersonal "They" /

"I want to read this to you." Star was holding a piece of typewriter paper.

Ruthie took a Tootsie Pop out of her mouth. "Grape really does it for me. Sure, I'll listen." With a smacking sound she stuck the lollipop back in.

"This is an editorial, except it's not exactly like an editorial." Star held the paper up in front of her, as if she were delivering a speech. "It's called 'They.' Here goes." She opened her mouth but didn't say anything.

Ruthie continued to suck on her Tootsie Pop. They were the only two people after school in the newspaper office.

"My emotions are clobbering me. Hang on."

With a flourish, Ruthie removed the lollipop. "I can wait. My oral gratification is getting gratified."

"Okay. This is called 'They.' I know I already told you that, but I needed to back up. Here goes:

"When my brother's draft notification comes there will be a name on it from the person who is in charge of the Selective Service, but the people involved in the decision are never going to be personally known to my brother unless he decides to go before them and somehow appeal. 'They' are just doing their job. A lot of the world now is unknown as to who does what to whom. A lot of the world is 'they,' as in 'They said so' or 'They like it like that' or 'They make up the rules.' A lot of the world now is faceless. Maybe that's why my bedroom walls are plastered with faces. The faces console me. They are real people, not a vague pronoun. But I've grown up in the world of 'they,' and that's not going away. It's like driving a car but the steering wheel is in the backseat and receding out through the trunk. Soon the steering wheel won't even be in the car. Everything will be remote. When the Vietnamese people look at the airplanes, they must say, 'They. The Americans.' That is all there is to say. Death comes to them from a distance, and the people who fly the planes will never be known to them. Nor will the pilots know whom they killed. I know it wasn't better when one soldier stabbed another soldier with a bayonet in the Civil War. But I also know that there's something eerie that's been going on, and that I have inherited that eeriness as part of who I am and how I'm supposed to live my life. I'm supposed to be good with that sense of 'they.' But what if life becomes so remote that people can't even live anymore? What if our faces become faceless? You may not think that could happen but I think it's happening right now."

Star put the page down on the small cluttered table that was the newspaper's one official piece of furniture. "What do you think?"

"I think," said Ruthie as she pulled the lollipop out of her mouth, "this school doesn't deserve you. I mean it. Maybe you should get your parents to send you to some private school where the teachers listen to the kids and, even more, the kids listen to the teachers." She lifted her lollipop and waved it as if it were a flag. "Maybe you'll become a writer."

"I don't want to become anything. Right now, I just want to be something other than a high school child. But thanks for listening. I'll show it to the boss and see what he says. I can see him wrinkling his forehead but being relieved because there's nothing seditious here. Just a high school child being sensitive." Star looked around the tiny space as if remembering where she was. "Oh shit, oh shit, oh shit. I wish I could sing the way Janis can sing. I wish I could pour my heart out like that."

"I don't know how happy Janis is," said Ruthie. "She sounds kinda desperate sometimes."

"I wouldn't care if I was happy. I just want to let everything go."

"Maybe you need to get laid."

"Fair, but I need a good layer."

"Maybe you can place an ad in the *Lamp*: 'Wanted: Guy who can do me right but has more on his mind than balling another chick.'"

"Which reminds me . . ."

"Herb? I'm working on it. He's working too."

The Endless Work of Making the Truth Known /

Very carefully, aware of his body approaching another body, John Tobin sat down next to Helen. His trousers were creased and his shoes polished. Once more, Helen marveled to herself—a neat young man.

"Hi, Mrs. Brownson." He gave an amiable nod.

"Hi, John. And you can call me Helen. I'm just another student here."

He halted for a second—Helen could see him realizing he should obey her despite his polite instincts—and then recovered. "What do you think?"

"About what?"

"About Memphis and the march there—how it became violent and people got beat up; how one person was killed and Reverend King had to leave; how the mayor is all agitated and doesn't want to give in; and how troops are being called in."

Helen took what she had come to recognize as a political deep breath. "That was a lot to tell me, but you've got most of what's been reported. It seems vague as to who started breaking windows and how the police started to beat people up."

"It must have been Black Power types. They have no use for Reverend King and his peaceable ways. They think they need to show white people that you don't get anything by turning the other cheek."

"That's from the Bible, isn't it? About turning the other cheek."

"From Matthew. Everyone quotes it, but it's a hard thing to do."

"And what do you think?"

"About what?"

They both paused, amused at the circle their words had made.

"I think that what Reverend King has been trying to do, with marches and everything, can only go so far," John Tobin said. "I mean black people have seen that, and some things have definitely been accomplished, but people get angry. And when people get angry, then violence happens." He opened his notebook and pulled out a pen from a trouser pocket. He clicked the pen—ready to write. "That makes me sad. That makes me feel sometimes that Christ is too much for everyone. You know, like he's impossible. And that makes Reverend King sort of impossible too."

"There must be a middle ground," said Helen.

"But how do you make people respect people they're not used to respecting?"

"Maybe only time can do that. Time and a chance for people to be with other people and see they're human, not demons."

"I guess that sounds good, Mrs.—" He stopped. "That sounds good, Helen, but we only have so much time in this world."

Helen tried to focus harder on this person who was talking to her. He had parents somewhere and a goal in life. He had doubts, even as he intended to do work that required sureness. You could live a lifetime in the United States and not consider what she and John were talking about in this minute or two before the professor began speaking. There seemed to be many minutes like that in recent months, minutes where the pressure of events felt heart-stopping, where it was natural to ask: Can this go on like this?

"You sound like someone much older than your years, but maybe the war makes us all older. Who knows how old those soldiers over there have become? You see some of the photographs of their faces, and they look as though they have seen beyond the end of the world. I have a son your age. There's no telling what's going to happen to him." Helen watched the professor head up to the lectern. "Reverend King has known what he's doing, but many other people don't know. Maybe they don't want to know. And you're right—people get angry."

"I need to say a few words more about what's happening in Memphis," the professor began. Helen could hear the slight tremor in his voice. She sat back. This was like some movie, where moments kept hurtling forward, but this wasn't a movie.

∞

The Movie in the Middle of the Night /

He was following a line of children, boys and girls in ragged clothes and wearing no shoes, along a dirt path. Around him were ruins, no buildings standing, only a masonry wall here and there, a column jutting up into nowhere, a telephone pole leaning at a dangerous angle, its wires dangling. The children were singing and he was singing with them, some sort of nonsense syllables, very lively and happy. They skipped along, and he could feel a freedom in himself as if his bones and flesh were lighter. Then the children stopped before a church. A girl at the head of the line beckoned to him to enter, pointing at a massive door with an ornate handle. The building was immaculate, not a broken window or a pock from a howitzer shell. He doubted he could open the door, but the little girl said very gravely, "You can, signor." The door opened easily. Inside it felt like twilight, a few shards of light coming from somewhere above, a few candles guttering by the doorway. As he moved slowly forward, he could hear his footsteps echoing with a stony clarity. At the end of the hall stood Mills, a guy in his outfit. Mills waved to him, a hand moving back and forth in front of his chest. He, the person in the dream, knew that Mills was dead. That person had seen Mills shot by a German sniper. But there seemed to be another person in the dream who was walking in Daniel's body but who wasn't Daniel. That person didn't know that Mills had died and greeted Mills as if Mills were alive. Mills started to reach out to that person, and then everything jumped as if there were an earthquake. Daniel's waking mind could feel the jump, something that happened in unreal time but a real space. He heaved a bit, his body thudding upward, emerging.

Then he was in his bedroom with his wife sleeping beside him and the little glow-in-the-dark clock showing it was 3:20 in the morning. Helen was snoring lightly.

He lay there and tried to collect himself. The phrase was literal, because he had the feeling that there were more parts to him than he knew what to do with—not just conscious and unconscious, but the war parts of him. He had been supposed to hand in those parts like a rifle at the war's end but had never done that, and they were still racketing around inside of him like loose gears in a machine, and he was supposed to ignore them because he had to in order to go on with his daytime life. He could see himself lying there in the pajamas that Helen dutifully bought for him at Hecht's, his forehead a bit damp, his hair a bit mussed, his heart a bit excited. He was alive, and that seemed the crucial feeling that came over him after one of these dreams where he was visited by the dead. He was alive but had no idea what to do about that. Life was a condition and he was just one more example, inventing aims and discarding them for other aims. Meanwhile, he had dreams of churches and soldiers and children. He knew very well the passage from Matthew: "Except ye be converted, and become as little children . . ."

He was more awake than he wanted to be, but that seemed ungrateful. Wasn't that what Mills was telling him, Mills who could yodel and used to win most of the poker games and had a girl back home with the "sweetest gash in east Texas." Everyone was alive inside him. Even as he felt he would never get back to sleep, he knew he would. And dream.

∞

No One Would Dream That He Would Do Such a Thing /

Anyone could give up. Anyone could get tired. He, however, was not anyone. The imperative thrust of his life, his rising from almost unimaginable obscurity, the fullness that went into becoming and being Lyndon Baines Johnson, was opposed to being "anyone." With age he felt himself coming into some degree of self-understanding, a strange feeling for someone who was so wholly an actor on the public stage. He acknowledged the fact of his acting—backslapping bonhomie being the better part of false humility—and despised the likes of Gene McCarthy and Bobby Kennedy, men who pretended that vanity was beneath them. Why were they there in front of those cameras, imploring and inveighing? To do good? To better the world? Of course, of course, but that impulse came from the person. All the talk of "forces" and "currents" was just talk, the bunk of history. People did it. And people had feet of clay.

He knew, accordingly, what made people tick, but he hadn't grown disgusted with people. That would mean he would have grown disgusted with himself, which would have been unfair on all counts. Not because of his failings, which he had a wife to remind him of, but because he was painfully aware how tenuous his stature was. He wanted to see himself as one of those statues you saw in Washington, DC, of presidents and statesmen—the truly great, those who strode through time and put their imprint on everyone's days. That wasn't an idle fancy. Over decades, he had worked at his stature. But as the war in Vietnam went on, he came to realize that he only could stride so far. He might even come to a standstill—one more confused man looking around vainly for help.

That bothered him more than he could say. As an American, he believed he was infallible. The nation's blessings were geographical, economic, political, and he partook of all of them. How could he be wrong when he had such wind in his sails? If, as was the case, the United States opposed Communism, then Communism would have to fail. American convictions were unassailable; American reality was the only reality.

When he told the nation he was done with being president, he felt relief. It wasn't that the job was too much, although the strains were, at times, colossal. It was that the world was changing, and he saw that he already was in the past. America did that to people, superannuated them, the American pace being relentless, almost inhuman, as if harassed by the fabled freedom. Something like that had happened to his father and wrecked him. His son, whom his father did not live to see as president, had gone to the heights and dwelt there but still heard the motley voices below, protesting and complaining. They didn't understand how much the nation's grief and ire rested on him. And he, more the fool, had asked for it.

∞

The President Gives the Nation a Gift of Sorts That Many Asked for but Never Expected to Receive /

"Whoa!"

"Jesus Christ!"

"Yippee!"

"Well, I'll be damned."

Helen walked into the living room with a glass of Welch's grape juice she had fetched from the refrigerator. "What did I miss?"

"LBJ isn't running."

"He's done. He just told America on national television he's had it."

"Can you believe it? It's like he's tossing in the towel."

"Does that mean the war will be over soon? Did McCarthy get to him? And Kennedy, how he has gotten on Johnson's case?"

Helen walked to the couch and sat down. The others were standing up, as if ready to go somewhere. "You're all talking at once. May I hear you one by one? I seem to have missed a historic moment because my throat was dry."

The Brownson children all looked to their father to begin.

"I admit," said Daniel, "that I'm stunned. Unlike others in the room, I almost don't have an emotional response. I will say that strangely, LBJ puts me in the mind of Shakespeare. 'Uneasy lies the head that wears a crown.' That's from *Henry IV*, part 2."

"We just did *Macbeth*," said Herb. "Maybe Lady Bird is named for Lady Macbeth."

Daniel gave Herb a two-finger salute—one smart-ass kid recognized. He went on: "As I was saying, the burden of the war seems to have become more than the president can bear. Now a great uncertainty opens before us."

"You sort of sound like Shakespeare," said Star.

"I have to say that my mind is somehow relieved." Tom looked at his mother. "It's not like anything is going to get better tomorrow, but you know about the light at the end of tunnel you hear about. To me, Johnson has been the tunnel. He definitely has not been the light."

"I'm afraid you're right," said Daniel. "It's as if he's run out of gas. He's had it. Should I say 'defeated'?"

"As a member of the press," said Star, "I need to speak. I don't know about you, but I saw this coming. How much could he take? And he is someone who, as a politician, as LBJ, has spent his life knowing what to do, and here he was—in the middle of nowhere."

From her perch on the sofa, Helen waved. "Okay, how about my turn now?"

"Just so you use an official-sounding voice," said Herb.

"I'll try. What I think is that we should have some compassion for Lyndon Johnson, who has done many good things as a president and deeply loves his country. He ran into something bigger than he was."

"But didn't have the sense to understand that," said Star.

"Or he did," said Helen. "And that's why he just said what he said."

"I keep thinking," said Tom, "of all the people who are sitting here tonight and talking about this and wondering what happens next. Like it really is some kind of play. But it's not. Or if it is, then I'm in it, too. But the script keeps changing."

"And I feel the way I used to feel on the roller coaster at Gwynn Oak," said Star, "when it came to the top of a rise and then you were going down so fast it took your breath away."

They talked for another twenty minutes or so, full of an unsettling excitement, each one of them examining what had just happened—the most powerful man in the nation relinquishing his hold on that power—and trying to believe it.

To Believe in Others /

As someone who had lived in the United States and fought on the American side in World War II against the Japanese, Ho Chi Minh had liked Americans, their openness and optimism. Who would have thought that Protestants, with their lacerating, hellfire preachers, could have created such an optimistic nation? And a lawful democracy—not a mere willful oligarchy, but a nation in which laws could be enforced evenhandedly. As Ho had witnessed, not everyone was accorded the benefit of those laws, to say nothing of laws that were enacted in the American South, where Negroes were denied elementary rights. Prejudice, about which Ho knew something from the French, spanned all societies. Utopias were never nearby.

America was a nation but not a people; Vietnam was a people but not a nation. Apparently, a nation had the right to suppress a people. America was brimming with rights, but there was that atomized feeling in America, that feeling of so many individuals but nothing coming together in a meaningful way, that feeling of everything being at the mercy of commerce, as if commerce were a god in its own right. Each individual had the right to imbue his or her life with self-created purpose, but how much value was there in that striving? People barely recognized other people on the street. "In a hurry" was a phrase he had picked up quickly.

The backwardness the French had inflicted on the Vietnamese, the refusal to educate them and make them part of the society the French controlled, the eagerness with which they dismissed the very humanity of the Vietnamese people, had made the United States seem preferable. The Protestant tenor honored each person because each person had a soul and a Bible and the dignity that a soul and a Bible conferred. In practice, the nation was glad to look the other way, as with the Negroes, but the premise was a powerful one. What value did one Vietnamese life have in the eyes of the French? In the United States, news stories would focus on the tribulations of one individual, someone who fell down a well or became lost in a cave. Such a story seemed preposterous but wasn't. Each life had its value.

He never would have said the Americans were especially sensitive. They paraded their rawness and made that a virtue. Like children at a fair, they esteemed every kind of novelty. There was something charming and innocent about that pose, but something desperate too, like the too-ready American handshake. What did the friendliness of Americans mean when they were going to turn around and use some degrading epithet, every Asian regardless of provenance being a "Chink"?

Walking the throbbing urban streets, he had felt the welter of individuality, how each person was pursuing his or her destiny, even though a cursory look at economics and politics would have informed each person that destiny was not an open book. The weight of that individuality was massive, each person trying to adjust dreams with realities, each person believing or trying to believe in him or herself, as if the society at large were a conjurer's trick. Little wonder the Americans could prate of liberty and then oppress others. Their nation was an abstraction that no amount of individualism could complete.

After the Second World War, the Americans had to choose between the Vietnamese and the French. They chose the French. That was not surprising. Ho was a communist. The French were traditional allies. The situation ran deeper, however. Ho stood for those who had been despised. To speak on behalf of the despised, much less support them in a war against a Western power, would demand a belief more spiritual than political. And so, Ho had bade farewell to the Americans, to their cities, their souls, and their Bible. Their omniscience was partial.

April

AND NOW, ONCE MORE, THE CONVULSION MADE ITSELF KNOWN

Impartial Wisdom Variously Dispensed /

"You're gonna trust yourself to the government on account of some words by a writer? Not even the Bible?" Reggie picked up his glass and drained the last of his Coca-Cola. "No offense, but they are gonna send your ass express delivery to Vietnam."

"I'm sending a letter to the draft board explaining my beliefs. I'm quoting Henry David Thoreau's essay on civil disobedience. And I'm writing about Quaker meetings."

"Tom, this is the government. From what you tell me, you've just started going to these meetings, which I have to say don't seem like any holiness church to me. What kinda Christians are these people?" Reggie waved to a waitress and held up his glass. "Another Coke, please."

She looked at him blankly but headed off to the counter.

"Not that I have anything against these people. But the draft board is full of regular Christians, Methodists and Baptists, that kinda shit, and I bet you that's what they're looking for when someone comes in and says he can't do it, can't kill anyone. He better have their God on his side. And even then, I doubt they'll buy it."

"'Must the citizen ever for a moment, or in the least degree, resign his conscience to the legislator? Why has everyone a conscience, then?' Those are Thoreau's words." Tom picked up a french fry but didn't bring it to his mouth. "What can I say? That's where I'm at. The words aren't empty. This is what's made sense to me. They'll do what they do, but to me conscience is real." He waggled the fry. "Real as a french fry." He shoved it into his mouth.

"I hope there are no black folks on this panel—though of course there won't be—because black folks know that conscience is just a word for white folks. Nothing to take seriously. White folks might as well be spitting out watermelon seeds."

"What about the abolitionists? They had consciences."

"They did, but that was a long time ago. Look at Martin pointing over and over to what's going on in America. Do you think those crackers down South or those bigots in Chicago have a conscience? A conscience is for the high-minded. I love Reverend King because he's high-minded. But I have to tell you, some of these Black Power guys at school think he's a fool, almost an Uncle Tom, believing that white people will listen to what black people have to say."

The waitress arrived with a Coca-Cola. "Well thank you very much," said Reggie. He looked directly at her, a white woman in her forties with piled-up hair and a pencil stuck in it. She turned around and stalked off.

"Case in point," said Reggie. "Do you think she has a conscience? She doesn't have a 'You're welcome' in her apparently."

"Everyone has a conscience. It gets lost, but it's there."

"Sort of like buried treasure? All we need to do is find the map. You know, Tom, I like to keep it up with you because, as a member of a nation within the nation and attending a black institution of higher learning, I can lose track of what's going on with the white folks. Not that today isn't like yesterday with them. But you keep me on my toes. And, to tell the truth, I admire you for what you're about to do. Because, like I said, I think you are gonna get whupped."

"It's not like I don't get you. I do." He closed the edition of Thoreau, placed it on the tabletop and then ran a hand over it. "When I read what he wrote, it was like he wasn't dead. That's kinda incredible: me—now—and him speaking to me from the past and showing me there's more going on than the evening news. That these situations don't change."

Reggie held up his glass as if to examine it. "You think some white man stole Coca-Cola from some black man? Wouldn't surprise me. Wouldn't surprise me in the least." He winked. "Not your man Thoreau of course. What do they say? 'A credit to his race.'"

The Political Race, the Going-Nowhere Race /

"Dad?"

Daniel looked up from the legal pad on which he was taking notes. Getting home late, he had eaten the baked chicken, oven potatoes, and iceberg lettuce salad Helen had left for him and gone to work at his desk.

"What's up, kiddo?"

"I know I've asked you before, but do you think the name I gave myself is stupid? Tell the truth."

"Frankly, I've gotten to like it. It wasn't in the realm of names your mother and I considered, but times change. And you're still Sharon to me.

The fact is that you get to have two names; actually, when I count Star, you have three. But not an alias, unlike some of the characters I deal with. You'd be surprised how many bigamists there are out there."

"That's like two marriages at the same time, right?"

"You pass the vocabulary quiz."

"Should I go with you and Tom to the Quaker meeting?"

"Your call."

"Do you like bell bottoms? I think they're ridiculous."

"They've gone by now, haven't they? Or maybe I just don't pay enough attention to fashion."

Star sat down in the Windsor chair beside her father's desk. "You ask me something. It's only fair."

"What did kids in school say about LBJ's decision?" Daniel placed the mechanical pencil he used to write with on the pad, parallel to the lines.

"They don't think anything. You'd think they didn't live in America or know there was a war. High school is about put-downs." Star struck a crooked-arm-at-the-waist, elbow-out pose and waggled an index finger. "'Have you heard?' and 'Can you believe it?' and 'I always thought she was whatever.' You fill in the blank. Really dumb."

"How do you manage?"

"I have Ruthie for my best friend and I have the newspaper, and I try to practice being good-natured but mostly I fail."

"How's Ruthie doing?"

"She's keen on your son Herbert. What can I say? Herbie's smart but immature. I don't see it as a match made in heaven. Not to put them down." Star yawned. "I need to get to bed earlier. What did they say around your building about LBJ?"

"Not much. One person, who is something like my nemesis, made a point of telling me that it was too bad how—and I'm quoting here—'hippies and Negroes have driven a good man out of office.' I told him that

LBJ was a big boy who could take care of himself. The conversation went no further."

"What's going to happen?"

"I guess we'll stumble along. I imagine Humphrey will get the nomination because he's the best positioned. No matter who the Republicans run, there's a fair chance that George Wallace will throw the election into Congress to decide because the South wants segregation forever. It will be like something they teach you in social studies class in junior high school—an election with no clear winner." Daniel looked off past his daughter. "That's not much of an answer. A category I seem to specialize in. We're all in the dark."

"And Tom?"

"Tom's sending a letter to the draft board. Something's changed inside him. Or maybe something that was there has clarified."

"How can millions of people be going through this stuff and still be walking around pretending everything is okay?"

"TV? Sports? What's for dinner tonight? Cars? Movies? Inertia? And there are plenty who aren't pretending." Daniel picked up his pencil. "And then there are our old friends: work and money." He gave his daughter a brief, resigned smile they both knew—time's up.

⤫

Time Out of Mind /

"I'm so wet, but I feel like a pile of rubble. Like I'm liquid and solid at the same time. Like I'm run over and feel good. Like you empty me out and I empty you out. And then we're lying here and we have to find our way back to our lives, but we don't know where our lives are and we don't care."

Sharlene propped herself up on her elbows. "It's like our bodies know more than our heads. Way more."

"Bodies are like that. I played lacrosse. On my best days, my body was way in front of my head."

"Lacrosse? I'm the daughter of what people call 'hillbillies.' When spring comes, you play baseball. Not that I don't like guys running around in those little shorts." Sharlene collapsed back on the bed and spoke to the ceiling. "What I'm feeling is that someone is going to come through the bedroom door and shoot me. And shoot you too. This isn't allowable."

"How do you mean? Were you planning to be a widow forever?"

"That's a shitty thing to say."

"Is it? We eat each other up, and then you go into this song and dance." Tom reached over and traced a finger across her brow.

"You don't get it. I'm caught. People know I'm up to something with someone. That's how it is around here. I'd have to just split with Travis. But I can't just split. I need a man to stand by me. And there isn't a long line of guys excited to take on someone else's kid." She took his hand and moved it to a breast. "Touch me there while you're at it."

"You think about leaving?"

"Every day. My little boy is my in-laws' connection to their son. Do you know how much I want to tell them that he didn't have to do what he did? How they filled him up with the flag and being a man." Sharlene rolled over on her side. "Keep your hand there. It feels good. I need good."

"I have to tell you that the man in bed with you is going to tell the government that war is against his conscience. I'm not going."

Sharlene said nothing then pressed herself up against Tom, body against body. She drew her head back to speak. "You aren't a coward, are you? It's that you really don't want to go there and kill people?" She pushed herself away, shook her head hard as if clearing it, then pushed up against him again, but wriggling as if trying to get into him.

For some seconds they stayed like that—Sharlene rubbing, Tom unmoving—until she pushed off again but not far, still close.

"I need to feel your body so much. It's not even about your dick. It's you being alive, here. How you're not what I knew about. And how there's so much I never thought about." Sharlene went on, her voice wavering but dense with feeling. "It's not that you're some kinda light to me. How could you be? It's like I was trapped or caged up and didn't know it. Didn't care. To give myself some credit, though, which I need to do, something was circling around me, and now it's started to get into me. And from what I read and see, I'm not the only one. It's almost as simple as being able to say no. Because I wasn't brought up to have a mind of my own. If you met my folks—and you're not going to—you'd see what I mean. Plastic slipcovers on the furniture, the cleanest people and tight-mouthed. Like a pair of human closets. No wonder I run on like I do."

"My parents both talk. I grew up with talk. Every breakfast and dinner—there's talk. Good talk. But it's been hard to get to my own talk. That meant something. To me."

"Jesus," and Sharlene almost shouted the word, "we're serious aren't we? The thing is, I like being serious. Almost as much as fucking. Maybe more."

"As my dad likes to say, 'No joke.'" Tom pulled her to him. She smelled of sex and what she called "good department store perfume." "No use being too serious, though."

Sharlene flattened herself against him. "This is best. When there's no space between us. There shouldn't be any space."

∞

The Narrowest Space /

Upon hearing the news on his favorite soul station—the disc jockey's voice throttled, frantic with grief—Herb knocked hard on his sister's door and shouted, "Martin Luther King has been murdered!" before running downstairs to where his mother, father, and brother were sitting at the kitchen table and shouting those words again, screaming, but not at them so much as at something inside himself, something already lost, something he thought was strong but was weak. Star lurched downstairs, clutching the banister, asking, "What did you say? What did you say?" as if her question could undo what her brother had just told her. Then she and the others were keening in their different voices, there in that moment but ancient, the bottomless vowels of sorrow—except for Daniel, who felt a numbness, the wartime feeling, the shutting down in the face of what could not be borne. Then Star fell in a heap at the base of the stairs; Helen bent over her as if somehow to minister to her. Herb and Tom looked at each other and shuddered, a dagger plunged into them. Weighted by a despair that had, at once, descended upon him and rose up within him, Daniel put his head down on the table.

For a further time that no one could have reckoned, time having abandoned them, they were silent, each of them struggling with the leavings of desolation. The memorable events hovered: the family going to the March on Washington in August of 1963; Kennedy's murder that November; and then the uncertainty and uneasiness that accompanied every day, exaggerated by the confounding mire of Vietnam, so that there were no more regular days, despite the going-to-work-and-to-school of their lives. Inside the days, a convulsion lurked, a dark, injured thrum, and now, once more, the convulsion had made itself known—the worst surprise, and no surprise at all.

"Why is there so much hate?" Star asked, her voice hoarse, her face contorted. "Why don't people have anything better to do? What is it with people? And why do we all go along with it?" She was still on the floor, seated with her legs crossed and staring but not focused on anything, dull with pain.

"I read some of Reverend King's speech he just gave." Helen stopped to try to gather her feelings. "He knew he might not get to where he wanted to get to, but he believed that he had to keep trying." She stopped again. "He didn't have an answer to those questions. No one has that answer. We're all thrown into life, and we start paddling or we sink or we do both—sink and rise, sink and rise. But that's just my words, not an answer."

"Someone almost killed Reverend King before, and now someone has. If you step up the way he stepped up," said Daniel, "you have to expect someone will take it upon him or herself to avenge the goodness that he represented. That goodness offends many people because it refuses their prejudices. Their dignity—that's really not the right word—depends on those prejudices. It's like money—they hoard it. For some, his life was not permissible."

Cautiously, the Brownsons looked around, as if nothing could remain the same, as if the very furniture must have changed, as if their skin were now thinner.

"I'm thinking about Reverend King and what he kept telling the world and what's been in the back of my head," said Tom. "How the answer to violence is nonviolence. I'm thinking how hard that is, how you just want to pick up a rock and throw it. But he was right, even though you can say he was wrong, that his death shows he was wrong, that a gun is always louder. A gun offers the simplest answer. A gun says, 'No.'"

"And maybe," said Herb, the last to speak, because they were being careful about taking a turn, alert to one another's agony, "we shouldn't say 'nonviolence'; we should say 'peace' and use that word every day and try to be in that place where peace is, the way Reverend King did."

"I wonder where that place is now," said Star.

Everything wanted to be said—the chasm of experience they had entered—yet the sudden force of his death kept insisting itself, pressing in on them. They remained in their places, as if held there, not pushing the horror away yet already self-conscious, knowing that eventually, even on this shattered evening, they would reconvene their lives but wishing there were no "eventually," that something so ultimate should remain ultimate.

Ultimate Songs /

"Knock, knock."

"Come in. I'm dressed."

"How you doing?" Herb walked a few feet into his sister's bedroom. Surrounded by the array of her plush animals, she was lying back on her half-made bed. "Gathering your people?"

"I need all the help I can get." She picked up a teddy bear. "And they're not people. Teddy doesn't shoot anyone, and he doesn't hate anyone."

"Good Mom told us to take the day off."

"We would have done it anyway but, yeah, good of her."

"Been listening?"

"Been lying on my bed staring at the ceiling. Been thinking more than I want to think. You?"

"Same. I put on 'Dock of the Bay.' Then I started thinking about how Otis is gone. Then I thought about how the song is still here, the whistling, his voice, how he's singing but talking too." Herb saw himself in the mirror above Star's bureau. "I look as wrecked as I feel."

"We both need some help."

"What would you listen to?"

"Something sad, something quiet. Look in the bin." Star gestured to a milk crate where she stored records. Years ago, she and Herb had decided "what's yours is mine"; which record was in whose bedroom was fluid. They both lived in part—sometimes a large part—through the songs.

"Leonard Cohen?"

"He passes the sadness test, doesn't he?" Star hugged the little bear. "I feel almost woozy, like someone punched me, like I'm gonna have a hard time walking out of this house and going anywhere and looking at people because I don't know how they feel; and that frightens me, because I know enough to know there are people who are glad he's dead or they don't care. He was just some bad actor."

Herb examined the record jacket, a suitably dark photo of the great, gentle melancholic. "I was thinking that too; how it's gonna be hard going back to school, how the stupidity is gonna feel even worse." He hadn't taken the record out. "Hard to believe isn't it? Elvis and Leonard Cohen on the same planet."

"Let's hear 'Stories of the Street.' Please. But what I was thinking about was how much I take for granted, like I took Reverend King's being here for granted, like he was going to go on making speeches and leading people and bringing up stuff that needed to be brought up: like why do we have all this wealth and all these poor people have nothing. What's the point?" Gently, she put the bear down beside her.

"'One hand on my suicide and one hand on the rose.' I guess Leonard got it. 'One eye filled with blueprints, one eye filled with night.'"

"I thought I was the only one who remembered the words."

"I'm your brother, remember? Your older brother."

"I know; I'm just the baby of the family. Little Sharon."

"Funny to hear you say your name."

"Feels funny to me. But maybe I was wrong, too, about naming myself. Maybe I should just listen more. But maybe what I hear will be worse."

"That wouldn't be Leonard. He's dialed in, how his voice is so wrung out, so patient. Like he's been to the end of the world, and not as a tourist. And he's come back to sing to us."

Star gave Teddy a loving pat on his head. "Put that song on. We need him."

～

The Nation's Need, Quoted and Interpreted /

"Before we start to consume the pot roast and potatoes I cooked this afternoon, I'm going to give a short talk. You'll have to curb your appetites a bit longer. I read Robert Kennedy's brief speech that he gave yesterday in Indianapolis upon learning of Reverend King's death. It made me think. And I wrote something out on the typewriter." Helen plucked the paper that was lying on her dinner plate and stood. Her hands trembled slightly. "Senator Kennedy was going to give a campaign speech to a group of voters, mostly African American. He threw that speech away and gave an impromptu speech, a very moving speech in which many things struck me, such as his stress on kindness and love, topics that don't come up much in political discourse. He also is a straight talker, because he acknowledges this shooting is not the end of anything. There will be more violence, lawlessness, and disorder—to use three of his words. But what struck me the most, maybe because of the African American history I've been studying, is that he doesn't talk about freedom. He doesn't say Martin Luther King Jr. died in the cause of freedom. He doesn't go to that put-your-hand-over-your-heart place and act as though our freedom is the most important thing in the whole world. No, he doesn't." Helen looked up from the paper at her family.

"Teach it, Mom, teach it," said Star. She gave her mother a fisted power salute.

Her brothers and her father nodded in captivated agreement. This was a first.

"The words he focuses on are fair and fairness. He said about white people and black people that—and I quote—'They want fairness for all human beings that live in our land.' I think that may be the hardest goal. We can talk about freedom because it's built into the rights we have and part of our mythology of individualism. But do we want fairness? Do we really care about others? Isn't it their problem that their skin is a different color or they were born into poverty and thus lack the opportunities to make something of themselves? Don't we say automatically that life isn't fair? Life isn't fair, and that's why I had to type this up, so I could say that fairness matters and that no one can really look anyone in the eye without feeling the importance of fairness. That's why it's so hard for anyone to look anyone in the eye who is different from them, because everyone who thinks twice knows how unfair this society is and how it often makes a virtue of that unfairness, often applauds its own meanness. Yet fairness seems the most important animating principle I can think of, and it's one that Reverend King strove to put forward every day. We act as though we have a great deal here in America—and in some material ways we do—but without fairness, we have nothing. We have selfishness that does no one any good. And I want you to know, dear family, that I don't think I'm better than anyone or know more than anyone. I'm just a humble mom who wants to be a high school history teacher. But I can't stand to be silent when such a great man has died. He was eloquent, and I needed to add some of my words to his."

Helen put the page down beside her dinner plate. "I'm going to take my seat now, and we can have our dinner."

Her three children simultaneously applauded.

Helen started to seize up. Daniel went to her, putting a hand on her shoulder. When she raised her head, he kissed her forehead.

"I keep asking myself," said Tom, "where do we go from here? And I ask myself who is 'we'? Is it just another word?" He looked at his mother. "I don't want to get gushy, but thanks."

"You can get gushy all you want," Helen said. She raised a fork. "Let's not let this meal get cold."

❦

The Cold Is Set on Fire /

The Brownsons watched the news on the TV: fire and smoke pouring out of buildings, gaping cavities where store windows had been, glass-littered sidewalks and streets, people running, people holding boxes and cartons, fire trucks and firefighters aiming hoses, police and soldiers, many soldiers. A war zone, Baltimore was under curfew. Somber politicians intoned pieties about the evils of civil disorder. In Washington, troops stood guard around the White House.

"Vietnam's come home," said Herb.

"That's one way to put it," replied Daniel. They had been watching the events for sickening hours but could not pull themselves away from the bad spell of it.

"It's what I said yesterday. But I've thought more because all there is to do is think, and I haven't thought enough." Tom's words sounded more like a plea than a statement. "How could the murder in cold blood of someone who stood for everything decent and who showed so much courage feel to anyone who was part of him the way black people are part of him? He was their leader. Politics doesn't amount to anything like what he amounted to. Anything. I know that laws have been passed, and it's laws that can change lives and try to make this society fair, the way Mom quoted that word, but Reverend King was like hope made real. He was a true man of God."

"He was," said Helen, "he was, he was, he was. But sitting here now and watching this, what I'm afraid of is that other people are sitting in front of their TVs. They're seeing these people looting and setting fires and destroying all this property—stores that people have put their whole lives into—and they're going to say that black people are worthless, that all the bad things white people have said are true, that all the blame and contempt are justified." She shook her head. "It makes me feel awful in a whole other way. There's his death. There's this terrible trouble in the city. And then there are people looking at this and saying, 'I want George Wallace and segregation forever.'"

"How can you ask the people in the city," said Star, "to turn away from what they've experienced? How can they feel when they look at Wallace, or Nixon, for that matter? I can imagine smashing a window. I can imagine it feeling good."

"Anger's not a hard thing to imagine, is it?" Herb extended a hand toward Cleo, who had ambled into the room and started to brush herself against his pant leg.

"It's not, but that's not the point," said Helen. "The point to me is to hold on to what Reverend King was about. My professor has talked about him and I've read his speeches, and you can see that over time he got clearer and clearer about what has been happening here, how we spend our wealth on wars, how we believe cars and swimming pools and closets full of clothes are the end-all of life, how racism is a sickness. But who will get up and say people are sick?" Helen tossed her hands up. "I'm going to start crying again. It feels as if that's all I know."

The TV droned on with more "up to the minute" reports. Some people had died.

"There are children there too," said Star.

"They're throwing Molotov cocktails into those buildings," said Herb. "I've read about them—an easy-to-make incendiary."

"I want to turn this off," said Daniel. "I want to go outside and look at the sky and give thanks for my sitting here in this house on this street, but—and there is a but—for whatever it's worth, I'm going to sit here because I was allowed to be here and these people haven't been allowed much of anything. So they're taking something that feels like theirs. And in a way, it is. And I am their witness to liberation and hopelessness." He put his hands out, palms down, and looked hard, as if inspecting them. "What good that does, I can't say."

Cleo, after much rubbing against Herb's pant leg, started to purr resonantly, a depth of cat pleasure. April sun shone through the living room's mullioned windows. They sat there transfixed, transfigured, and helpless, yet more sadly real to themselves and to one another than who they had been only a few days ago.

⋙

The Days Were Breaking Him /

The Negroes rampaging through the streets outside the White House and in Baltimore, Chicago, and many other American cities were not part of what Lyndon Johnson called the "Great Society." That phrase was something Johnson used in a speech but that he intended to create through the aegis of legislation passed by the federal government. After John F. Kennedy's death and the landslide victory over Goldwater, the time was ripe to pass the laws that would help all people and pick up where Franklin D. Roosevelt and the New Deal left off: Johnson was an acknowledged master of getting Congress to do his bidding, but the spectacle of thousands of people running amok, destroying and pillaging, was not a matter for legislation. Or if there were to be legislation, it would come from the Republicans and would be repressive.

The Republican Party paraded various shibboleths, as parties were wont to do, but to say the party existed foremost to keep the wealthy comfortable with their wealth would not have been out of order. Johnson understood that very well, since he had used various government levers to make money in the broadcasting field in Texas. He had become one of them, one of the wealthy, but his Texas hill country origins could never touch the origins of those who had been born into money or those who had turned moneymaking into their life's purpose. He was raised among poor, hardworking people, and a vestige of them remained within him.

How this played out in the American experiment was hard to pin down. What did great mean? Joe DiMaggio was a great ballplayer. Van Cliburn was a great pianist. Marian Anderson was a great singer. They, however, were gifted individuals, not a nation-state. To apply the word to a country was to take a heady but dangerous step into national emotions. What was the measurement for this greatness? Was the Roman Empire, which was built on slavery and exploitation, great? Didn't the Nazis tout the greatness of their Reich? But, as he tried to explain, he meant the word in an inclusive, welcoming sense—room for everyone to use his or her abilities and not be held back. And he was applying the adjective not to a nation or empire but to "society."

The rub was the amorphous nature of that society. Given the variety of rural and urban landscapes, ethnicities, religions, business enterprises, and educational institutions, and given the uprootedness that many Americans took for granted—the restlessness that went with the promises and possibilities—positing anything like a coherent society that could be willed into greatness through legislation seemed laughable. And that's what his political opponents, who still despised the New Deal, were quick to do: blame the overreaching government for every shortcoming they could imagine. They aimed to take their power back and assert it. As long as there were entities to demonize, the work of the ruling class could proceed without interruption. Lyndon knew the power of popular animus; how loathing, not love, was the fulcrum of politics.

Johnson was not one to weep, but he had every right to as he watched the nation avoid urban anarchy at the price of rifle-bearing troops. Was this the vision the United States offered the rest of the world? Was this the clarion and cornucopia of the near-mythic American democracy? How many lives were destroyed in the free-floating distress? Were the TVs and bottles of liquor being looted the sadly laughable symbols of the whole American exploit? Were civics a mere sideshow from the workings of power? He, Lyndon Baines Johnson, was someone who believed completely in the validity of governance. Yet what if that notion, as it embraced a kind of official betterment, was an illusion? He pushed the question aside as best he could, but the question would not go away. And he, who could smell the vile, billowing smoke in his White House office, knew it.

Everyone Knew Which Show Came on at Which Time /

If you were out on the streets on Sunday night in Baltimore after Martin Luther King Jr. was assassinated, you could be arrested. Some were, but many more did what they normally did on a Sunday night, which was stay home and watch *Bonanza* on TV where, in a domestic yet male milieu, a seemingly endless number of Western adventures occurred, with various people nursing grudges against the Cartwright family who owned the Ponderosa, a vast tract of land near Lake Tahoe; various women getting entangled with the Cartwright sons, women who were dance hall performers or school teachers or widows or bank secretaries; various crooks who were scheming to steal mines or cattle or payrolls or horses or land or timber; various personal dilemmas that involved alcohol, corruption, maltreatment of animals, blackmail, mental distress, injustice, and cowardice; various Indians appearing who were deserving of sympathy or contempt; various people turning out to be not who they said they were because they were former convicts or flimflam artists or congenital liars; or various disagreements that ended in gunplay, because this was the West and the six-shooter the ultimate arbiter.

Bonanza went on for an hour, so there was time for the drama to unfold and reach something like a plausible resolution. The following week there would be another drama, and that too would reach something like a plausible resolution, and then the week after that, stretching into years of shows so that a careful viewer could feel the characters aging even as they were somehow timeless, caught in the web of their circumstances and their characters, be they the judicious patriarch, the well-disposed mountain of a son, the hot-tempered son, the more or less smart son, or various other characters who passed through and exemplified human traits, right down to the Cartwrights' Chinese cook who, because he was Chinese, exemplified a degree of Asian wit and patience.

Each Sunday night, a scripted version of America appeared and the hours passed the way hours would have passed anyway. Could those hours have gone elsewhere? Need they be entertaining? And what remained after the hours with the Cartwrights passed? Was there some residual feeling in the viewer, or was there only another mortal penny deposited in the collection box of oblivion? And did the army troops and police on the streets of Baltimore miss the Cartwrights as they stood on street corners and maintained what Richard Nixon came to call "law and order," which the Cartwrights were enforcing in their sometimes rough but basically fair-minded manner, justice being served one way or another—which was more than could be said for those Negroes caught up in the curfew enforcement who were trying to get to work and would lose pay or maybe their jobs but did not receive any sympathy from the troops or police, who were only doing their jobs.

What wonderful neatness each television offered! In a designated period of time, a rise and fall would occur that was as predictable as the fizz of soda pop yet different each time, the finite world being full of infinitely different people. No one in the Brownson household cared about *Bonanza*. If they did watch TV on a Sunday night, they watched the *Smothers*

Brothers Comedy Hour, which aired in the same time slot as *Bonanza* and featured various rock and rollers and comics and two brothers—one, the straight brother possessed of reason; the other, the sometimes antic, sometimes querulous, sometimes stubborn brother—who sparred and offered needling remarks about the vagaries of human behavior. Genial troublemakers, they were a latter-day version of court jesters, the court being the TV network executives who had the final say about what did and did not get said. On *Bonanza*, for all its wordiness, the actors could have been mimes—such a TV "show" being a semblance, a seeming, a pretense leading one anodyne day, week, month, and year into another, a mule train bound for the legendary realm of Nowhere Special.

∝∞

Mother–Daughter Special /

"I need to talk, Mom. Now."

Helen was peering into a kitchen drawer. Sometimes she felt that such searching was the main gist of her life, that on her tombstone should be written: "She lost the star that was part of the Christmas cookie–making kit." Meanwhile, she also wondered how many years ago Sharon, who incrementally was becoming Starflower in her mind, had made blue jeans her daily uniform. Also, long necklaces made of glass beads. And a perfume that wasn't exactly a perfume, but what Sharon called an "essence." Lost and found, lost and found—and there was the knife she was looking for! "Sure thing. Just help me make a Waldorf salad. Chop the celery and apples. Break up the walnuts so they're smaller pieces but not too small."

"I'm your daughter. I know what 'too small' is. But I have to tell you about today. I'm not gonna cry or anything, but I'm upset because it seems the world is coming down on me especially." Starflower took the serrated

216

knife Helen had put on the kitchen counter. "I talked with Mr. Klausmeyer today, you know, the assistant principal. I told him that some other kids and I thought we needed to do an assembly to honor Martin Luther King Jr. He told me that was a good idea and that he'd talk to the principal about it. I told him that sounded fine, but I wanted to do something soon. He gave me that look of irritation that grown-ups give you when you've messed up their line of patter."

"Line of patter?"

"You know, the words they use to push you aside without actually telling you to just get lost."

"Maybe he will talk to the principal and do something. Stranger things have happened."

"You're an optimist, but then something else happened. I went to my locker at the end of the day to get my books and someone had written 'Nigger Lover' on my locker."

"What? What did you say?" Helen's voice quivered as her body became rigid.

"That's what someone wrote on my locker with a black marker. What I told you. I went down to Mr. Klausmeyer and he said, 'Twice in one day,' being jovial with me. I told him what someone had written, and he made a face and said that was 'defacement of school property.' He asked for my locker number and said the janitor would come and clean it off, but I told him I didn't want him to clean it off—that I was proud of who I was, that we should see how some people in this school feel, and that we shouldn't pretend."

"You told him that?" Helen sat down heavily in one of the kitchen table chairs. "What a daughter I have."

"He told me that we were not going to send a message to the 'student body'—he loves that phrase—that it's okay to deface school property. As he put it, that's 'not a negotiable.'"

"And how do you feel now, standing here and telling me this? Do you need a hug?"

"I do, but what bothers me is the old thing. How I'm like a half-person. How school makes me small even though I don't want to be small. I want to stand up and be counted, but all I can do is write my editorials that most of the kids never read."

"Perhaps some of what's happened will change them," said Helen. "Perhaps they'll start to think about how other people feel."

"Could be, but everyone just does what they want to do. A few people who have been brought up by people like you and Dad are different because you raised us to think about other people. But you know what?"

"What?"

"I know you like this house and everything, but I really wish we didn't live here, because even though it's pleasant here, it's nowhere. I know I say that over and over, but I'm disgusted and miserable." Star put an arm up across her eyes.

Helen looked away but spoke. "I feel like Mr. Klausmeyer. And it's not a good feeling."

"Do you hear what I'm saying?" Star dropped her arm.

"I do, but it's not simple, our being here. There are a lot of factors."

"I'm a factor too, right?"

"You are," said Helen.

"I don't want to mess up your life, but look at mine. It's only gonna get worse. I'm not wanted in that school."

"I need to talk with your father."

"I need to get out of that school."

They both, as a token of coexistence, went back to the making of a salad. Helen felt that any remaining walls in her head were once more being breached. That was uncomfortable but, as she knew, at once obscurely and keenly, to the good.

A Dearth of Good News /

"Before you go downstairs and hear what Sharon has to say about her day, I want to tell you what I went through," said Helen. Daniel had taken his tie off and was switching from his cordovans to a pair of beat-up loafers.

He looked at her with weariness, wariness, and love. "Shoot."

"I went, as you know, to an interview here in the county at a high school for a position as a history teacher—US history, to be exact. Also, two classes of geography. I was interviewed by an assistant principal. It seems to be a day for assistant principals, as you will hear from your daughter. Anyhow, I met this assistant and the head of the social studies department, also a guy. After a few stiff pleasantries, they started commenting about how I hadn't taught in a long time and, even though I've done my student teaching through the master's program, I've been away from the classroom, and asked what I thought about teaching 'today's students,' as they put it. I told them that I've raised three, two are in high school right now, and I thought I had a pretty fair idea of 'today's students' from raising them. At this, the two gentlemen raised their eyebrows and looked not so furtively at each other. One of them said that was well and good, but that 'today's students' presented 'significant challenges.'"

Daniel stood up and went over to the closet to deposit his shoes. "Sounds like they wanted to load the dice and see how you responded."

"What it sounded like was that I appeared to them as a mother who'd been out of the loop and had no business trying to get back into the loop. I told them I was ready for challenges. Then they asked me how I would deal with students who challenged 'the status quo,' as they put it. I said, "How do you mean that?" And they said students who presented behavioral problems that stemmed from 'societal issues.' At this point I didn't know exactly what they were talking about, but I assumed what they were getting at is whether I could deal with students who might not be 100 percent flag-waving Americans, though they didn't say that. Maybe they just meant that kids smoke pot. But this is all just a prelude to their saying that the department was all-male, and how I would feel about that."

"And you said that you love guys. The more the better."

"No, I didn't say that. I said that I was a professional and would act professionally. But what I wanted to say, and maybe should have said, is: 'Why are you asking me this?' But I didn't think quickly enough, and I realized that I didn't want to work in that school anyway. They asked me more questions, which were nuts and bolts about my education and teaching philosophy, and then asked me to ask them questions. So I asked them how much dialogue about the war they encouraged in their school."

"You decided not to fool around."

"First, they froze, but then it was like alarms went off right on their faces. The assistant principal started to talk about how this was a democracy and all points of view would be tolerated, which meant he wasn't going to answer my question. Being the polite person I am, I thanked them for the interview and got up and left."

"Lots of reasons for me to love you, but now I have another." Daniel took a few steps toward his wife.

"Hold off on the love for the moment. I'm still angry and something like humiliated. They wanted a guy and I wasn't a guy, and it wasn't much more complicated than that. And you know what?'

"Let me hear it."

"Guys can go to hell."

❧

A Hell That Never Left But Also Came Home /

"Hey, this is your token Negro friend calling his token white friend. Which is one more friend across the color line than a lot of folks—black and white in our fair city—can say. My cousin Tough is amazed I have one. He thinks I should have a seat in the United Nations."

"I—"

"No need to protest anything. Just leave that to us, though we have lost our heart."

"Where—"

"I'm calling from the edge of the so-called 'riots,' which means I'm at my folks' place, which is a Negro neighborhood that has been left alone. Sort of the semi-ghetto as opposed to the true ghetto."

"But—"

"Hear me out, and then you can talk. Fair?"

"Fair." Tom sat down on the little upholstered chair next to the desk on which the downstairs phone rested.

"I never experienced agony. I broke an arm playing lacrosse and I've had a couple of women tell me they lost interest in me, but that was kid's stuff. Martin's death was hell right inside of me. I sat there, trying to take it in, that feeling of darkness—the worst—but right away my head went to a state of mind that's not unusual for my people: What did we do to deserve this? It's a pointless question but, you'll grant me, one that makes too much sense. He goes out on the balcony of his motel room to take a breath of air, and some white man shoots him. Is that America? Can we adequately explain the vulnerability of being a black person in America? Because that gun is pointed every minute, and there are many different guns. Some are slow guns that kill you slowly, and some are real guns, like what happened to Martin. So later, after I stopped crying and I talked with some people, I wondered whether the so-called 'riots' would happen here. Would people set fire to the very places they traded in and sometimes the buildings they lived in? Was Martin's death just an excuse to go steal a new Philco or a bottle of gin? Was all this nonviolence just a load of crap, the way the Black Power guys have said it was, just trying to get along with the white folks and persuade them that black folks weren't gonna make any trouble? What can you say? If you put people in cages, they want to get out. And those buildings in the ghettos of Baltimore, those buildings are cages where black people live their lives and do the best they can, but they know, oh they know, that the whole white world wants to keep them in their cages because that, in the eyes of the white world, is where they belong—in cages. White people won't say it of course—not that anyone's asking. When I hear white people on the TV talk about how black people shouldn't act like this and should somehow just sit there and take it, take the grief, take the agony, take the misery on top of all they've taken ever since they set foot on this miserable continent, how do you think I feel?"

"I—"

"Remember, you don't have to say a word. I know you've got your own troubles. In fact, I'm wondering if I might go to one of these meetings you've started going to. The notion of people getting together and being quiet in a church, that's one of the most white-folks ideas I ever heard. But I kinda like it. So maybe we'll be in touch. And if you think I rehearsed what I just said, I did and I didn't. Every black life is a speech waiting to be given. Goodbye, Tom."

The line went dead. Tom held the receiver like a foreign object, an irreconcilable thought in his right hand, then put it back in place but didn't move. There was no going back from the Reverend King's murder, but going forward seemed a joke—forward to what? To the endgame of fatality, to the violence that had become too real? Every last thing felt broken: futile questions and then more questions.

Questions and Their Ever-Partial Answers /

Since he worked downtown, it did not take long for Daniel to drive into a neighborhood where there had been—to use Helen's word—trouble.

He had watched the TV compulsively and read the newspaper, but the investigator in him wanted to see the actuality—an impulse not much different from the boy asking the adults steeped in their mysteries to "Show me." And the city was his city, where he had chosen to live after going to law school at the U of B and for which he had feeling, for what Helen called, however laughingly, "the Baltimore in the heart." Yet he was able to define the city rather than the city defining him. He could move about. He could do, more or less, what he wanted.

The houses the black population lived in were usually row houses, block-long structures erected as working-class barracks but never called that, and which nominally offered a family more than a tenement offered. There were no trees on the blocks he was driving through. No shrubs or bushes, only asphalt and concrete: The earth was elsewhere. Daniel knew that many of the people who lived in these houses had come up from the South, where they had been close to the earth. If they had been allowed to own land and farm fairly, many of them never would have left. But fairness was not—as Helen pointed out in citing Robert Kennedy's speech—what the nation was about. He didn't need one of Helen's history books to understand that these people were the targets of long-standing malice.

He pulled over to a ruined storefront, some mom-and-pop grocery. The odor of charred wood greeted him as he got out of the car. Everything of value seemed to have been stripped from the premises. A few busted light fixtures were dangling from the ceiling, but in places there was no ceiling. Fire had taken the roof down. There was only the injury, the waste and the desolation. No doubt white people had owned that store but not lived there. They retreated from the city at day's end, the way he retreated.

An old black woman holding a broom was standing out front. Daniel walked up beside her. Staring into the netherworld of the destroyed store, neither of them spoke for a time.

"You out here as a tourist? Sightseeing?" The woman did not turn to Daniel, but he was the only person to whom she could have been speaking unless she was talking to herself.

"I wanted to see for myself," he replied. "I work in the city."

"But you don't live on this block, that's for sure. Only what's left behind lives here." She turned to Daniel. Her hair was gray and she was stooped. "And when you get as old as me, you're doubly left behind. Time does that. Time is one hard ticket."

Daniel nodded.

"You see this?" She pointed the handle of the broom at the empty storefront. "White folks is evil and black folks is evil. Take your pick. I give you credit, though, for showing up. You got some interest." She lowered the broom handle and leaned on it, as if for support. "You believe in the Lord?"

"Sometimes."

"There ain't no 'sometimes' with the Lord. You do or you don't. Jesus wasn't about 'sometimes.'"

"I don't believe enough."

"That's not for me to measure. A person could darken up till there was no sky left in the person. A person could look at what we're seeing and wonder why the Lord bothered to make people. And there's worse than what we're looking at. I reckon you know that."

"I was in the war in Europe."

"Then you seen worse." The woman turned the broom handle so it faced her horizontally, holding it with both hands as if she were a tightrope walker. "I got to be going. There's a heap of sweeping needs to be done. This is my home. I got my pride."

Daniel watched her proceed very slowly down the sidewalk. A minefield, he thought. A minefield.

A Field of Vision Enlarges /

"I don't want to screw tonight, so if that's the only reason you're here, you can go home. I'm tired and Travis has a cold, and that makes me worried. And I look at what happened in the city and I wonder what's going on; is this what my husband died for? We're off telling the Vietnamese what to do, and look at us." Sharlene got up and went to the refrigerator. "If you're staying, I can offer you a Coke."

"I'm staying, but I'll pass on the beverage."

"Suit yourself." Sharlene pulled one from the gridlock of cans, bottles, and jars. Tom had pointed out to her one day that she had three half-finished jars of mayonnaise. She had told him to mind his own business. "I like to drink from the bottle." She smiled. "But I don't think I can keep doing what I'm doing." She took a swig. "You know what I think?"

Tom set his elbows on the kitchen table. He was getting used to the smells of the place—instant coffee and the Utz potato chips Sharlene set out in a bowl, only to get stale. "What do you think?"

"I want to go to school. I want to learn why people do the things they do. I know you left school, and you probably think I'm too stupid to go to college in the first place, being a waitress and all, but—"

"Whoa!" Tom put up his hands to ward off further words. "Have I ever said a word about you being stupid? Do you think all I think about you is sex? Don't you understand that when I sit here and talk with you, it's real in a way that nothing else in my life is real? That you've touched me?"

Sharlene looked carefully at him. "I'm putting my stuff on you. That's not fair. I'm looking to you the way women look to men to somehow make things okay, the way they bounce their feelings off men like a rubber ball off a brick wall."

"I'm a brick wall?"

"No, you aren't. You're coming from some place I really don't have a clue about. Or I have a partial clue and want to learn more, but I don't think life is gonna let that happen. There's this war that's scrambled my life once, and I don't want it scrambled again." Sharlene took another swig. "How's your draft status doing?"

"I've sent in the form to declare myself a conscientious objector. The draft board will take it from there. I can respond if they deny me. I can appeal. And then they can have a hearing about me. And then—I don't know."

"My neighbors, the guys I grew up with, they'd just call you yellow. That's part of what ate at my husband. He didn't want anyone to think he was yellow."

Tom leaned back in his chair. He thought what he thought every time he came to Sharlene's, how strange and good it was that life had brought him to this kitchen, how he'd been right to leave school. "I really don't care what anyone thinks. I've told you. I'm sort of finding out about myself. It's weird, but maybe that's how it has to be; maybe you have to be in something extreme to ever wake up. Otherwise, you just shuffle along. Keep passing the ball to the next guy."

"So when the government says where do you get off living here if you aren't willing to fight for your nation, you're gonna have an answer for them?"

"I'll tell them that war is never the answer. That in the long view, which you can call 'God' or 'justice' or the centuries of human beings, war doesn't make anything right. War makes things worse. War is a perennial abomination."

"You know, I went to Sunday school. That's like a Bible word, and I know enough to know that no one thinks that way now. It's not practical. I bet in other countries, they'd just take you out and shoot you."

"You're cheerful—but if I'm thinking what I'm thinking, then someone else is thinking it too."

Sharlene came over and ran a contemplative hand through his hair. "I could almost go back on what I said about screwing, but not quite. I just want to sit here with you. It's not like I'm happy or the world's happy, but something's getting lit up inside."

⌖

Inside Stories /

John Tobin held the lecture room door open. "Hello, ma'am. How are you?"

"I know you mean well, but ma'am makes me feel ossified. I have a million things on my mind, many of which are unhappy. Do you want to hear them?" Helen pointed to two empty seats. "But I'm being rude. The world is definitely too much with me. How are you?"

After he let Helen sit, John sat and turned a bit—the seats were narrow—toward her. "To tell you the truth, Helen," and he paused, as if struck once more that he had managed to say her name, "I've been upset about Reverend King. As a man of God, he was trying to bring us together. He spoke his faith and lived his faith. For someone, some white man, to shoot him like that, I won't say it was like what they did to Jesus, but it made a kind of death real to me. Like he was a martyr. I know my faith is supposed to help me—and it has—but I feel as if I was naive, like a child, like I didn't know something I should have known. About evil. That it's real."

"I could start crying right now because, although I'm not religious, as I think I've told you, you just said some things that have been terribly on my mind. I feel the way you do, as if there were something I didn't cherish enough and now it's gone." She saw puzzlement and concern on John's face. "And I'm ashamed."

A male undergrad a few rows in front of them started laughing. "No shit!" the guy next to him exclaimed. He started laughing too.

Others, thought Helen. Always there.

"I want to be a chaplain in the army. Did I tell you that? After I go to the seminary, I want to join the army and be a chaplain. It's not like I hope the war is still going on, but if it is, I'm going there. The men need their chaplains."

"For such a young person, you have strong thoughts." Helen opened a notebook she had extracted from a large macramé pocketbook, last year's Mother's Day gift, chosen by Sharon but purchased by all three of her children. "My kids have thoughts like that too, but—here, now—each of you has to sort out these matters. But history knocks on our door whether we're ready or not, doesn't it?"

The laughing subsided. One student, he was shorter and had a beer gut, slapped his pal on the back. "Damn right!" he crowed.

"I know that we say, 'Life goes on,' because it does, but it's an awful cliché that I've always hated because it doesn't say anything like the truth—what the feeling is, how 'going' can feel like being out of control. I mean, listen to this. I wrote this down in my notebook from something someone just wrote: 'Lyndon Johnson's refusal to run for a second term is a clear admission that the policy in Vietnam already responsible for twenty thousand dead American soldiers and countless Vietnamese, is indefensible.' What gets me is that word *countless*. Like those Vietnamese are pebbles or grains of sand. But they aren't. Go tell the people in this room that they are anonymous, that they are among the 'countless.' Go tell those boys in front of us who seem to feel everything is funny." Helen pulled herself away from the page. "I'm sorry. You're just a young person who's being kind to an older person." Helen could feel John flinch, a tiny movement back into himself.

"I don't know those guys, but most guys I know, like the guys in my fraternity, blow everything off. They aren't remotely what you would call 'political.' They're okay with other guys fighting this war. They don't want history to mess up their lives, and they sure as heck don't want to spend any extra time thinking about it."

"Like we're doing?" Helen tried to smile through the catch in her voice.

"Like we're doing. And I understand what you're saying about the war. But if it's still going on, and if I can be a chaplain, I'm going. I don't want my talk to be cheap. It's my duty."

Helen could imagine him in front of a congregation or group of soldiers, preaching. He had that firmness in him, what he called "faith." She found herself envying him, she who had resisted any calls—including her husband's—to religious devotion. He wasn't thrashing in a sea of his own confused device. And what lifeline was she looking for? Immunity? Shelter? Resolution?

The professor had come up to the lectern—a beat-up wooden relic. "There aren't that many weeks left in this course, and I've got a great deal to talk about. More, really, than I'm going to be able to say. There are too many books, too many thoughts, too many events for me—and you—in this history." His words, spoken very deliberately, seemed to Helen more a confession than an explanation. And a rebuke.

❧

Rebukes Considered in Time's Ill Light /

What sort of society murdered its prophets? A society, as Ho Chi Minh could testify, that did not want to hear its prophets, a society for whom prophets were a bother and a threat. Better to kill such a person. Martin Luther King Jr. was explicitly a man of peace who proposed the largest of revolutions—humankind loving one another. For all the beauty of the sentiment, a beauty Ho could acknowledge, King's was an unhistorical vision laced with spiritual eloquence. A pipe dream. The challenge was to make something definite happen.

Within the hard realities, conundrums remained. When—to choose one—someone was murdered like King, gunned down, how many bore the guilt? Society was collective, but unanimity—as Ho observed with the Soviets—was a lie and, as with Stalin, a nightmare. The answer for the individual cut both ways, responsible and not responsible, but inevitably, prophets, those who stubbornly opposed the status quo, stood by themselves. No mediation or palliative was possible—something most Americans, marooned in their material progress, did not understand. King paid with his life; Ho was ready to pay with his. As King's death showed, the precipitous moment was always waiting.

In the words of a noted American writer in 1968, the United States was "a hateful, convulsive and chaotic civilization" that was "closing in on you from every side." Ho had every right to ask what sort of "civilization" promoted hate? Among the many failures of the West was the automatic imputation that there was, in the first place, something called "civilization." Who said? What ethics underlay this "civilization"? Colonialists, imperialists that suborned and enslaved whole populations? Sanctified the economic war of each person against each other person while allowing a few to make fortunes? Vilified others because they lived elsewhere and had other customs? Assumed that might automatically made right? The list was a long one.

What would Ho have said to the minister from Atlanta, Georgia? Ho supported war, to say nothing of merciless revenge. Was there a bridge from his world to King's? How could the Americans throw away a person such as King, because that was what they did: They threw him away to the hatred and anger that were encouraged in speeches, conversations, platitudes posing as common sense, even in jokes, every murderous day.

Who cared what was in anybody's heart? What did that matter? King insisted that it did matter. For his pains, he was shot. Ho brushed aside all talk of hearts and consciences. There was a graphic situation called "colonialism" and the prejudices that attended that situation. No one told the Americans, whose Declaration of Independence Ho admired, to pick up where the French left off. The Americans believed communism of any sort was the end of the world, but it wasn't. Nothing human was the end of the world. That was a conceit. Time was so much larger than any notion.

Ho came from a culture that understood that. King came from a biblical culture that cultivated both pity and apocalypse. He raised his voice to a heaven that could shake with retributive wrath and that concerned itself exclusively with humankind's muddled, free-will path. A light, however, beckoned. Even from the darkness of slavery and the folkways of brutality, a light shone that would not go out. You could call it "hope." You could call it "wishful," but it offered something Ho did not grasp or thought was merely idle. To Ho, such religion was a form of duping, another ruse, more stifling fantasy.

Ho did not create the arrogance and contempt that drove the mechanisms that supported the plantations, factories, and banks that ate his native land alive and reduced his people to chattel. King did not create the mix of fear and loathing that assumed its prerogatives were God-given. What bitter knowledge was granted each man! Yet neither was embittered. Death held the decisive card, but when the riddles were unraveled, there stood an essence that had nothing to do with any trumpeted standards or some hallowed, impermeable goodness. In their very different ways, they had believed but knew they were not the last word. A fallible, yearning margin remained.

What, If Anything, Remains After the Songs Are Over? /

"Shouldn't there be more songs? Feels awfully short to me. Sort of a rip-off." Herb held up the record jacket that showed two young men, Paul Simon and Art Garfunkel, known to the world as "Simon and Garfunkel," in a pensive mode.

"Maybe they try too hard. Maybe they're perfectionists. It's not like rock and roll, where you let it rip. They're thoughtful." Star was on her back on her bedroom floor with her legs in the air. She had recently taken up "something like yoga."

"Maybe they're too thoughtful. They can't write enough songs because they're so thoughtful."

Star lowered her legs. "You should do some of this. You're too self-conscious about your body."

"Telling me about being self-conscious is going to make me more self-conscious."

Star raised her legs. "Where did they get that album title? *Bookends* is so pretentious."

Herb placed the album on Star's bed. "Let's play 'What's next?' Remember how we used to when we were little?"

"Of course. I remember almost everything. I think there's someone like me in a Greek myth. Here goes. It's gonna rain later tonight. I can feel a quiver in the air. April showers."

"Simon and Garfunkel will disappear in a sensitive cloud of thoughtfulness."

"Bobby Kennedy will be elected president, even though I want McCarthy."

"Richard Nixon will say something so hypocritical that our father will put down the paper and start to sputter about that 'worthless son of a bitch.'"

"The Beatles will go on forever."

"The war will go on for what feels like forever."

"My brother Herbert will start smoking pot."

"My sister, Sharon, sometimes known as Starflower and abbreviated to Star, will become a foreign correspondent for *The Sun*."

"Make that the *New York Times*."

"Walter Cronkite will tell a joke and Tommy Smothers will read the news. Will people be able to tell the difference?"

"Hold on there. We're trying to be realistic. And speaking of that, I hear from a close source that Ruthie wants you to press the point with her."

"She does?"

"Wake up. I've tried to tell her you're just a gangling dope, but she won't listen."

"Thanks for the praise. And where are you at?"

"Waiting for a real man to come along."

"Any candidates?"

"Robert Redford. You know, as in *This Property Is Condemned*. I'd like to be that property. Some blond guys really do it for me. Then again, some dark-haired guys do it too. I wouldn't mind if George Harrison knocked on my door. His eyebrows slay me."

"Any more predictions?"

"We'll get to like the Simon and Garfunkel album and wonder why we didn't like it so much when we first heard it. We'll walk around humming 'Mrs. Robinson.' Mom will ask us what we're humming."

"Here's to you, Mrs. Brownson."

They began to sing—an upbeat tune about an unhappy woman. Their voices rang out—a glad, healing thrust. Mrs. Robinson's troubles were not theirs.

◎

Troubles Compared to Problems /

Helen and Daniel, silent, bewitched by the day's wretched headlines, were halfway through their morning coffees. Tom—who had been reclassified 1-A but had not yet received his notice to report for the pre-induction physical or received a response to his letter declaring his desire to be classified as a conscientious objector, and who had started using the adjective *surreal* to describe dealing with the government—was upstairs sleeping. Star was writing in her diary and said she would be down in time for a glass of OJ before the school bus came. Herb was putting more grape jelly than necessary on his rye toast.

"So, Mom and Dad, how is it that everyone is always talking about 'problems'?" President Johnson spoke on the news last night about—and I quote—'the massive dimension of the urban problem,' by which he means, I assume, among other places, Baltimore, Maryland." Herb waited for his parents to rouse themselves. They were parents; they were supposed to respond. That was what they signed up for. "Does that mean he thinks there's an answer to Baltimore? Like something you might come up with in math class? Or does it mean something else?" They lowered their sections of the newspaper: Before them was the son they had brought into the world seventeen years ago and who, the attending doctor informed them, was "healthy but not perfect." "I know I may be kinda philosophical for this early in the morning, but I've been wondering."

"It's good to wonder," said Helen. "We raised you to wonder. Heaven forbid if all you did was take orders."

"No problem on that count, Mom." Herb liked saying "Mom." An anchor of sorts.

"You're asking us why social situations are framed as problems? Is that right?" Daniel laid his paper down so it rested awkwardly on his cup and plate.

"I'm asking whether human stuff is just human stuff. Did they have problems a couple of centuries ago? Did kings think there were problems with their subjects? Did the British parliament think there were problems? There were conditions, right, like "the poor" or "the destitute," but those weren't problems, were they? Problems are sort of new stuff, right? Modern-life stuff. Or am I off base?"

"How do you come up with this?" asked Daniel.

"I spend some seriously bored hours in classrooms, so I think a lot."

"How wonderful school is." Helen smiled faintly. "What am I thinking of doing with my life? Spending each day in a public high school? I must be out of my mind."

"You're not going to bore anybody. You're going to make them think." Daniel reached over to touch his wife. She recoiled slightly.

"To try to answer your question," said Helen, "I think that most people, who after all are working people, want the government to do something to make people's lives better. That's what FDR was about. And the government can make people's lives better in some basic ways, as in helping to bring electricity to rural people. Or helping people save some money for when they are old. But I think what you're getting at is whether conditions that have been bred by the complexities of history, like the city of Baltimore—which means slavery, race, religion, industrialism, local folkways, immigration, prejudice, and fifteen other factors—can be solved like a problem, and the answer has to be 'no.'"

Cleo strolled into the kitchen, looking for a lap to jump into. "First one up feeds Cleo" was the family rule; she was looking for love rather than a handout, though the two did blur.

"As to cities like Baltimore," said Daniel, "I have to say as a lawyer that it's not enough to pass laws. You have to be able to enforce them. And people are individuals who are making individual decisions."

"Like where they live," said Herb. "Like in some godforsaken suburb."

Helen and Daniel glanced quickly at each other, registering another small touché.

"So," Helen went on, "when we couch everything as a problem, that opens us up to be unrealistic and then disappointed, and then we start blaming the government, as in, they made a promise and didn't keep it."

"But if we don't aspire to help people, then the government becomes what it was before FDR—a way for the rich to get richer." Daniel brought the fingers of his hands together—a judicial gesture.

"Gotcha," said Herb. "I'm thinking I won't vote until someone comes along who says something like what you guys just said, which means the person would have to not be a politician."

Helen rose and pointed at the kitchen clock. "The bus!" she shouted, trusting her voice would reach to Star's room. Then she said to Herb: "You know what else LBJ said? He said that in cities like Baltimore, 'human tragedies and crime abound.'" She put her hands on the top of the back of her kitchen chair as if bearing down on it. "He understands. That's what makes this all the harder. He's not a stone."

"Nixon," said Daniel "is a stone. A stone smiling for the TV cameras. But proud of being a stone."

<hr/>

Stones That Can Be Borne /

The thin, gray-haired man across the oak desk from Tom wore a white dress shirt of the sort you could buy three of in a package, blue-green work pants, and beige canvas shoes. Tom recognized him from the meetings he had attended, though the man had not spoken. The two of them were sitting in the office off the meeting room, a not very big space with many mimeos, small posters, and typewritten pages hanging from several bulletin boards.

"Ray Moore. Pleased to meet you, Tom." He extended his right hand.

"Tom Brownson, Mr. Moore. Thanks for taking time to talk with me."

"You can call me Ray. And I'm glad to be meeting with you. Meeting is a big word for the Friends." He smiled a slightly lopsided smile. "I'll listen and you talk. The only thing I want you to keep in mind is that I'm not a draft lawyer. I'm just a Friend."

"Got it. My dad's a lawyer and has put me in touch with some lawyers who are counseling guys. But what I want to talk about isn't exactly that. It's how I'm feeling." Tom paused and looked at one of the bulletin boards. He focused on a poster that had the words "Take Action" in bold letters. "I've attended a few meetings, and I've been moved in ways I have a hard time describing but that I want to try to talk about, because something has started to happen to me, something that probably has been triggered by the war but something that I think has been within me forever that I didn't know what to do with. Sitting in silence has made me feel how much I value being left to my thoughts and not having to talk about things I don't want to talk about. In school I was what you call a 'jock'—a guy who's good at sports, gets by in his studies, doesn't have a hard time attracting the opposite sex, and sort of floats along. My parents went along with that picture. I mean they raised me to think for myself, but I didn't particularly want to think for myself because, for one thing, when you're on a team it's about the team. No one likes a ball hog."

Ray Moore gave an encouraging nod.

"My dad started going to meetings here and I was curious. My dad used to take us to church for Christmas and Easter, but he stopped doing that and never talked about why he stopped, maybe because we kids were all getting older, but he stopped. But he would say other things sometimes about how God mattered and you couldn't really have a world without God, that people wouldn't know how to justify themselves, how they would get too lost. When he started going to these services, I wondered. I could tell something was going on with him, although he doesn't talk much about his feelings, maybe because he was in the war and saw a lot of bad things. I don't know, but when I went here, I started to feel that I could stand for something larger than I was, yet personal. So much in our world is negative, even peace is presented as being against war, but I started to feel, just sitting there in the silence and listening when people talked—"

"And you talked, as I recall."

"You remember? Yeah. Once. But mostly I've just sat there, because that's what you do."

Ray smiled again. "We do a lot of sitting. That's true."

"You do." Tom didn't smile. He was afraid of losing his thread. "I felt that there is a bigger picture than the one I've been carrying around. I don't just mean God. I mean stuff that we take for granted; I mean about how we act that things have to be a certain way but they don't. Like there doesn't have to be war. There doesn't have to be so much hatred. If the light is in everyone—and I think it is; I mean that must be what people are for—then it seems a matter of recognizing that."

"You've been doing some serious thinking. Have you talked about this to anyone?"

"You're the first. I wanted to talk to someone who was a Friend. But I need to say a little more, which is that when I dropped out of school, which was a couple months ago, I really felt lost and disgusted with myself for being lost. My parents have tried, and here I was just sort of taking up space in school, not really interested and getting tired of being a boy throwing a ball around. I left. But what I've started to feel—and again it's just starting, but I guess things have to start somewhere—is that I don't want to live dead inside me. I know that might not make sense, but to me that's how I need to say it, how I need to be alive inside me and what I've felt here and some of what I've read about the Friends—who I didn't even know existed, which embarrasses me—about how "the human and divine may commune," which is a phrase I've remembered from a book I've been reading, makes sense to me." Tom halted. He felt drained but pleased he had spoken. Trying to get all his feelings into one word at a time was hard. Whenever he had to give a talk in front of a class, he got nervous. This was like that.

"You think we may be for you. And you think you want to find out more about who we are."

"Yeah, that's a fair way to put it."

"Good. You've seen a few other young men at our meetings. The war is making some people think about their conscience and the place of conscience in this world. I was raised by Friends, so that sort of thinking comes naturally to me, but the phrase the government uses—conscientious objector—squarely puts its finger on conscience. To me it's identical to what you're talking about. Living without an active conscience is not living. It's doing what you're told to do because—what is it people say?—you want to go along and get along."

Tom shifted slightly on his seat. He felt better—not relaxed but better. "I know this is stupid, but do I sign up somewhere or something?"

"No tricks up our sleeves." Ray Moore pulled at his shirt cuffs as if to show there were no surprises in store. "There's a mild process to joining our community, but the main thing is to keep coming to meeting. Are you reading the Bible?"

"Some about Jesus, what Matthew and John have to say."

"That's excellent. God is present and available. That's how it was with Christ, and that's his message for us. We don't have to despair. We can feel

God's presence within us. We can be peaceable. Grace is given to us freely. It's our task to live it, to raise up the good, to abide with our convictions."

Tom was silent, letting Ray Moore's words settle within him. "You know, I can't believe I'm sitting here, talking to you and hearing you say these things and me saying things too. But that's what was bugging me. I was just marking time, like I was in jail or something. It's not like I have a million words to say, but thanks."

"Fine, but one more thing, Tom."

"Yes?"

"Talk to your father."

The Son of the Father /

"Apparently you aren't going to the sunrise service."

"I thought sex in the morning was a sunrise service."

"I think that's what's called blasphemy."

"Not a Jewish word, is it? One more Jewish sanity. But repentance is near. I'll take a hot shower and wash my sins away."

"Better make it a long one." Helen reached out and mussed Daniel's hair. "You're going longer and longer between haircuts. Must be the boys are influencing you." She mussed a bit more. "You can't fool me, though. I'm sure you've got Easter on your mind. You took the children to church once upon a time."

"At this point, I'd say Sharon and Herb are both teenage atheists. Tom is trending in another direction. I suppose thinking that Christ had a conscience and so does our son is sufficient."

"And you?"

"Hard to know what to do with a miracle. That's always been the rub for me. Where do you go with it? After Christ came back, he didn't hang around for very long."

"Heaven and life-everlasting was the story I heard. Secondhand of course." Helen tugged at the sheet to cover herself up more.

"That story has never done it for me. I've got too many bad pictures in my head. Hard to see those blown-apart corpses ascending on angel wings."

"And yet."

"Kind of you to say that. I need breathing room but never know what to do with it. The war was a long time ago. The world is always saying, 'Get over it.'"

"Yes and no."

"More kindness on your part. The thing is that I do believe in miracles, in the sense that nothing has to obey some immutable law."

"You're disputing gravity?"

"Somewhat. That's why there's God, something beyond the rules and regulations. A power unto Himself."

"And God is a guy?"

"If he were truly omnipotent, he would be a woman too. Hold all the cards."

"I like that idea. Both sides. Cosmic balance."

"I'm going to pull that sheet down and bother you some more."

"You've got more in the tank?"

"Miracles never cease." Daniel kissed his wife on the forehead and pulled the sheet down.

Down in the Wartime Dunes /

"Are these kids who are getting beat up at Columbia University, is that about the war?" Chuck rubbed his eyes. "I gotta start getting to bed earlier.

241

I stay up late because that's when things quiet down. Or I gotta run away. Any thoughts about where? Maybe you want to run away too."

"San Francisco," said Herb. "Anywhere out west sounds great. See something different, better weather. But, no, I don't. It's not that things are perfect—my brother's sort of like a boarder the way he goes in and out, like he's not my brother, like he has too much on his mind—but I don't want to run away. But to answer your question, I don't think it's about the war. It's about the university wanting to take over some land and the students being opposed."

"They look like they got their asses kicked. A billy club can hurt you pretty bad."

"Not as bad as a bomb."

"No, but it's one more thing that brings the war home." Chuck had a window seat on the bus and looked out at the cheery April morning. "Amazing how much we human beings fuck things up. Why don't we just listen to the trees? They leaf out when it's time to leaf out and drop when it's time to drop and sleep through the winter. Smarter than we are."

"Maybe you should run away to one of those communes where they live in the woods. But you know—to bring up something else—I've been thinking that by this time, there should be a quiz show about the war. You know where they ask questions and people give answers."

"You mean like, 'Can you identify acronyms or name the operations?'"

"Yeah, yeah, exactly." Herb paused some moments to summon up the requisite TV personality. "Hello, folks; our contestant today is Chuck Carranza—high school student, informed citizen, and fair-weather patriot. Question number one will focus on military operations. So, Chuck, we all are familiar with the delightfully named Operation Rolling Thunder that rained death on many Vietnamese, including civilians, but we have undertaken many other operations and come up with many fascinating names. Here's a list. Can you name which one is not an actual war operation?"

"I hope so, Mr. Quiz Master." Chuck tried to look earnest, which meant trying to cross his eyes.

"Okay, Chuck. Operation Junction City."

"Nope that's a real one. I read about it."

"Operation MacArthur."

"Read about that one too. And I think I saw some photos."

"Operation Barrel Roll."

"I'm not sure about that one. Maybe a bombing campaign?"

"Operation High School."

"Obviously that one is not for real. No one would implicate a venerable institution like high school. Rah, rah!"

"You are right, Mr. Carranza. And you get an all-expenses paid trip to South Vietnam. Not to be confused with North Vietnam, the way some people confuse South Dakota with North Dakota."

"Can I put that off for a few years?"

Herb shook his head no. He sighed. "We're fucked up. You know that? People are dying."

"In a year or two, we can do it too," said Chuck. "Right now, I'm gonna get back to looking at my friends the trees."

❧

Trees Outside Windows, Cars Going Down the Street, People Eating Submarine Sandwiches /

"Harry Little's is just right, isn't it? Subs. Cold cuts. Maybe I should work here." Sharlene leaned toward Tom and snatched him by a wrist. "Are you listening? You're so moony."

"I can't step in here without starting to salivate. And I'm listening. I've got a world on my mind. Including you."

"Me?" Sharlene did not let go and leaned closer. "Can you smell it? I've got on something French. Very fancy. From Hutzler's."

Tom made a show of sniffing. "Nice." He sniffed again. "One more way you can push me over the edge. I'll add it to the feelings I didn't know I had, which is getting to be a big category, like the Quaker stuff I told you about and the reading I've been doing and Reverend King getting killed and what happened after that and even just being in my room by myself."

"Don't get too real on me."

"Why not? Look at what you've been through. It's some of why I'm half crazy about you."

"Only half crazy?" Sharlene opened her mouth and moved her tongue invitingly. "But you're still growing up." She took her hand off and rustled around on her chair. "They could get some more comfortable seats here." She rustled her tight-skirt butt more. "But I'm still growing up too. I got a kid, but I'm still growing up. How can that be? Probably I should be embarrassed. But I want you to ask me a question, and the question is: 'What do you want to do with your life, Sharlene?'"

"Fair enough. I'll listen and chew." Tom angled half the long sandwich to his mouth.

Sharlene gave the bracelets on her left wrist a jangle, a trying-to-settle-herself motion. "I want to be able to take care of myself. That's what I want to do. And I don't have a clue about how to do that. I can say that to you because I know you won't freak out, like in, 'She's a mom and she's just thinking about herself.' But what I think is: 'How can I take care of Travis if I don't know how to take care of myself?' And when I think about what I just told you, it frightens me but excites me too."

"Are you looking for an answer?"

"You don't have to hand me a diagram, if that's what you mean. You're kinda up in the air yourself, waiting on the government."

"But I'm starting to know what I want to do, no matter what the government does."

"You do?"

"Yeah, I do." Tom pointed at Sharlene's uneaten sandwich. "You might want to eat. Considering what you just told me, you're a growing girl."

"That's what my mom always said. I wish I knew what kind of girl I was. But I know it's all been way too tight. It's not a big thing, but I'm gonna start community college in the fall. I told my folks, and I told my in-laws. They were what you'd call 'skeptical.' Like I should just stand still and make my waitress money and be with Travis and that would be my life. But I can't do that. And they're happy to have Travis around when I'm off at school. He looks a lot like Tom."

"Tom?"

"That was my husband's name." Sharlene slumped a bit. "You didn't guess that? Why I never said his name to you?"

"That's what's called a coincidence."

"Yeah, my life is full of them. Diners, sub shops, guys with long hair, guys with short hair, me saying nothing in bed, me screaming in bed."

"I think that's great about you going to school. I'm all for it."

"That's why you dropped out?" Sharlene took his wrist again. "You're full of it. You know that? You're trying to be good. And that kinda breaks my heart."

❧

Heart of Persevering Sadness /

When John F. Kennedy was killed, one thread of faith that formed the American psyche was snipped. His death wasn't the first assassination of a president. Whitman's elegy continued to put Lincoln's death firmly in a certain number of American hearts and minds, but however gripping Lincoln's murder had been—the act itself, the hunting down of the assassin, the funeral train—it had all been a long time ago. Kennedy was young and offered the nation a sense of invigoration that, true or false, was appealing to many. The sheer violence of the scene was what would come to be called "traumatic." One moment he was smiling and waving and then he was gone, testimony to the power of a rifle. And the instantaneous aspect that exemplified his death, exaggerated and pushed into unreality by the murder of Lee Harvey Oswald on television, the grimace—there for all to see—of a man being gunned down, was shocking.

Anyone who cared might imagine what it was like for his family, for his widow and children and especially his brother who stood immediately behind him in the family order. The eldest brother a pilot, had died in World War II on a mission whose outcome depended on an untested technology. The assassination was death again, but without any foreground. Here was death that seemed utterly fantastic—where was the killer?—but wasn't. Here was death that could have been someone acting alone or a series of resentments and covert manipulations that made for the ineradicable moment, the one that people held onto for a lifetime as they told others where they had been when they learned of the president's death. A Passion had occurred, but there was no Redemption, only the news-riddled days following one another in heedless succession.

A Potomac of ink had been spilled about the Kennedys, some of it mythologizing—the JFK presidency as Camelot—and some of it demythologizing—pointing to Jack and Bobby as little more than Boston ward heelers. Other unscrupulous characters, such as Richard Nixon and Lyndon Johnson, were eager to lance the Kennedy mystique. Such were the ironies and legends that infested politics while Americans went about their daily round of duties, yet considering, as the Brownsons did, a shifting array of politicians they would never meet yet were all too real. Though democracy claimed to be a direct form of government, there was a ghostly, impalpable quality to it brought on by the TV's deluge of informative noise.

Death proved the reality of a life, however. Robert Kennedy came to realize that all too well. To say that his brother's killing was not part of any known script was not to traduce history—consider Lincoln—but was to assert the potential brevity of a political trajectory. Now the trajectory of his career rested in his own fallible hands. He confided to several that his death by assassination might well be in the cards and was not beyond indulging in black humor, as if the Fates had already spoken. No stranger to tragedy, he cited Aeschylus in his Indianapolis speech.

Crowds responded to Bobby (as Robert Kennedy was known) as if he were Elvis or the Beatles, literally tearing at his clothes. He was the living remnant right there in front of people, and while he radiated the Kennedy aura, he was his own person—more vulnerable than Jack, yet willing to take on and transfigure the grief of the nation. His brother's death freed him to change as he saw fit to change. There was little use in playing to a script if the script could be destroyed in a second. He remained politically shifty. When he sought to dodge the question of his authorizing wiretaps of Martin Luther King Jr.'s phone, he invoked that all-purpose end-of-discussion: "national security." He had seen, however, more of the world since his brother's death, and what he had seen affected him. When he came back up from a mine shaft in Chile, a locale he insisted on visiting, he remarked, "If I had to do this, I'd be a communist too." An American politician wasn't supposed to say that—ever—but no American politician had gone through the ordeal Robert Kennedy had gone through.

∞

Through the Days the Echoes Expand /

Being the one who almost always took in the mail, Helen had taken to imagining how she would feel when a letter came from the Selective

Service. The phrase "it's just a matter of time" took on a new resonance yet was puzzling. The "just" ameliorated nothing. How was time a "matter," something material? Yet the truth was clear—an inevitability, each day ponderous. Elsewhere, decisions were being made.

When, one overcast late morning in April, a letter arrived, she found herself staring at the envelope as if she somehow had believed it would not come, as if, as in a fairy tale, she could wish so hard that reality would accede to her. She couldn't help but know there was a world beyond her front door. As a teacher, she hoped to influence, however modestly, that world. Yet she also had felt that world would not intrude on her and her family, that there would be a tacit congruence, an agreement between that world and the lives dear to her. Now, with the slight weight of the envelope in her hand, her unreason was manifest. No hiding, no avoiding, no pretending; her love felt hopelessly private.

She did not call up to her son, who kept very late hours and was probably sleeping. In all likelihood, the letter informed him that he was being summoned to a pre-induction physical. He had written the draft board about his wanting to be declared a conscientious objector but had not yet received the requisite form, assuming they would ever send the form. The task of the draft board was to supply the military with young bodies, not consciences. Who knew how much attention they would pay to their own rules and regulations? And Tom had come to his decision so quickly—a few Quaker meetings, and he had experienced this peaceable insight. It was not hard to surmise that the draft board would look quizzically at him, thinking his decision little more than a dodge. That was the common phrase: "draft dodger."

She put the letter down on the front hall desk, thought again of calling him and again ruled it out. Better to let him do this on his own. This was not a college admission letter. Better to let him sleep. Since coming home from school, he occupied a different orbit, pulled by a different gravity.

He was still her son—she could easily see in his face the child he once was, willing but not too willing—as he struggled. Yet, with society's imperatives, his childhood seemed much longer ago than a decade or so. Always he had been the child who kept the most in, who rarely confided in her. As a boy, he had put it straightforwardly: "I like to do things more than talk about things."

This is not what was supposed to happen was the thought that played over and over in her head, almost a musical motif, something with a life of its own. A stupid thought, one indifferent to the manias that drove tribes and nations, but there she was—first and last, a mother, a woman who resented giving up the child she had brought into this world, nourished, watched over, adored, helped to educate, and, yes, worried about. She had not raised him to murder or be murdered, yet both loomed in that envelope, both fates as tangible as the paper that composed the envelope. How was it that her maternal feelings counted for so little? Was the inference that she, as a woman, was a child, someone who didn't know any better, who didn't understand the importance of resisting communist aggression? Her feelings were precisely that—female feelings, and hence worthless.

Tom had told her that he was reading more now than when he had been in college. "Reading all sorts of stuff—Thoreau, Vonnegut, some Hesse that Star gave me, even the Bible." He had smiled his full-on smile, the one where she felt his inner buoyant self. She told him how good that was, but then they both were silent, understanding how little the world beyond the front door cared about what he read or who he was becoming. She felt then what she felt now, that a great, insupportable weight lay on her chest and was crushing her.

Standing there in the hall, she knew she had to move in order to preserve herself. She had been putting off some errands—the shoe repair, a blanket she wanted to donate. She needed to do some grocery shopping. Tom would pick up the envelope at some point and tell her what it said. "All in good time," was the phrase. One more nostrum she had no use for but that made a terrible, self-satisfied sense.

❦

A Sense of the Senseless /

"Herbert said you needed to talk with me." Helen stood in the doorway of her daughter's bedroom. Sharon sat on her bed in her usual getup: jeans and a Mexican peasant blouse whose front featured two stitched-on red flowers, perhaps done by hand, perhaps by a machine. Her feet were bare. She was going to be seventeen in September, and once more Helen had the feeling that her daughter was a woman, not a girl, and that many women her age around the world were already married and bearing children. Two or so years ago, Sharon had been wild, going after boys, asserting her female power, but she stopped, withdrawing, not dating or even talking about it. "The whole thing is stupid" was her summary comment when Helen brought up her lack of a social life. "I'd rather attend to myself" was her daughter's only further remark, accompanied by a sly smile.

"I got suspended from school."

"You what?" Helen did a double take, moving forward a step and then back.

"I threw some soup on Michelle Baxter. I was in the hot lunch line because I wanted some soup, even though it's watery and never hot enough. Anyway, Michelle, who considers herself one of the school's pillars, came up to me and told me she knew who wrote 'Nigger Lover' on my locker. She said I wrote it, that I did it to get attention, that I was a sick troublemaker who only caused problems for everyone. That I wanted everything to be political, and people were tired of me." Starflower looked around absentmindedly. She picked up one of her stuffed toys—a dinosaur. "I know this must sound unreal. I don't know what to tell you. I had this cup of vegetable soup on my tray, and I picked it up and threw the contents at her. I told her she was a nasty bitch too. The soup mostly landed on her chest, which is Michelle's big claim to fame. She's called 'PT,' for 'perfect tits.' She started screaming and yelling, calling me bitch and whatever, and some teachers ran over—one of the Phys Ed guys and a math teacher, Mrs. Ferguson. They calmed Michelle down and told me to go to the office, which is what I did. The assistant principal, my friend Mr. Klausmeyer, who no doubt has had his fill of me, told me I had no business being aggressive, even though I told him she started it. I felt like I was in the first grade and there was a fight on the playground and the teacher was telling me how words can never hurt me. But they can. I mean, what an awful thing to say to me."

Her head reeling—a few moments before she had been thinking about making butterscotch pudding and the coming final exam in her African-American history class—Helen collapsed on the bed and extended an arm to hug her daughter. "I can't believe it."

"Neither can I. While it was happening, I felt like this couldn't be happening, that no one could be crappy enough to say that. But she hates me. And now she hates me more, and so do a bunch of other kids."

Helen looked for signs of tears. Her daughter's voice was husky but more filled with awe and disgust than sadness.

"And the outcome is that I have to apologize to her. Which I can do. It's not the end of the world, and throwing soup at someone doesn't exactly accomplish anything. That was stupid. I get it. I can apologize because I can do all kinds of things, but I have to ask myself what I'm doing in this school that doesn't want people like me, that just wants to go spinning on its dumbass, do-as-you're-told axis." Star gave the stuffed creature a hug. "I guess I should be embarrassed. But I'm not."

"It's not right that someone would say such things to you. And it's not right that the person in charge made no effort to sort matters out. What does suspending you accomplish besides putting you behind in your schoolwork?" Appalled on several fronts, Helen shook her head.

"I don't want to go back to that school. I know I have to. I have to finish the year. But I don't want to. I can't protect you anymore. I can't pretend it's okay when it isn't. If I can't be honest with you, who can I be honest with? We talked about moving. Right?"

Helen heard the timer go off in the kitchen—dinner rolls. Sitting there, taking in her daughter's words and beseeching look, she felt both feeble and selfish, as if she didn't deserve to have this child. "We'll have to do better, won't we?"

Star put the plush creature down but then stroked its tiny head. "It's like with the whole country: Something's gotta give."

⚭

Giving to Various Caesars /

"And what tidings do you bear tonight from your respective worlds?" Daniel asked. Some dinnertimes, he liked to play the paterfamilias.

"Not so great," said Starflower. "I got suspended from school for chucking a soup bowl at a girl who was saying nasty things to me. I'm not proud, but I'm not sorry."

"I see," said Daniel.

"I got the letter. 1-A. Physical slated." Tom spoke the words calmly. "No surprise there. I don't think the government goes in much for surprises. Unless they're really big ones."

"I aced a chemistry test," said Herb.

"I knew some of this and suspected other parts, and felt in the past hour or so that I was moving through a dream state," said Helen.

Daniel placed his cloth napkin—Helen insisted on cloth napkins—on his lap. "I guess my heartiness is ill-placed. I should have known better. And I don't know where to begin."

"Let's begin," said Herb, "with something unimportant. Telling about your grades is pathetic, but that's what school does to you. I don't even like chemistry, but I do like putting things together. But I don't want to become a scientist."

"Not to interrupt," said Tom, "but it's funny to hear you say about becoming something. I'm looking at the draft board letter and thinking one thing that's part of the equation, even though I know now that I don't want to be a soldier, is dying. That's a fact, right? Not being melodramatic. Just a fact. Ending not becoming. And yet—which is funny how it's woke me up—I'm becoming." He had been talking to each member of his family, moving his eyes from person to person. "I just don't know how I'm going to keep becoming." He lowered his head as if communing with his thoughts, but quickly picked it up. "But how could I? That's the point, isn't it?"

"It's like what grown-ups always ask you," said Star. "What do you want to be? And they just want some category. They don't want to hear about you. They just want you to make them comfortable. They had to fit in, and you have to fit in too."

"What's the success tip the guy in *The Graduate* tells Ben? 'One word—plastics.'" Herb picked up a fork for emphasis and stabbed the air. "Ben's a college graduate, but it doesn't matter because he's still a young person, meaning one step up from a cow—shut up, but moo once in a while to let us know you're there."

"Maybe that's what I'll do when I go back to school. I'll moo." Star opened her mouth wide and made the appropriate sound.

"You're finger-drumming on the table, Mom," Herb said. "That's not a good sign."

"Sorry. I'm trying not to worry but not succeeding. But I know," and she turned to Tom, "that worry doesn't help, which is a hard thing for someone born Jewish to admit. So how can I help?"

"You could overthrow the government," said Herb, "but don't let it get in the way of your making this noodle casserole."

No one laughed as Herb took another mouthful.

"I was talking today," began Daniel, "with a developer about a deal he's doing in Baltimore County, details. We got to talking after we'd wrapped up the legal side of things, which was pretty cut and dried, some title stuff I could do with my eyes closed, about what happened in the city, all those properties destroyed. And what he told me, and I repeat, is that 'it's a few more nails in the coffin,' meaning there is no way that banks and developers are going to help those people with those properties, much less help the people who live there. The services that were there, which may not have been great but were at least something, are going to disappear, and though other liquor stores will open or even reopen, the kind of investments that make for a positive place to live—the big grocery stores and shopping centers and medical complexes that people increasingly take for granted who live in Baltimore's suburbs—are never going to happen in those neighborhoods. The effects of slavery—and this is me talking, not my developer friend, who's not a bad guy, just another moneymaker —are still very much here more than one hundred years later. We can pretend they're not, but all the history that has isolated and ghettoized Negroes in this society and prevented them from, among other things, building the capital to get things done for themselves are still operative, and possibly getting worse."

"I like it," said Star, "when you talk about the real world. But it makes me even more depressed, because stuff that doesn't happen doesn't get in the newspaper and stuff that doesn't happen can be as bad as stuff that does happen. Even worse. Right?"

"Right," said Daniel. "That was my news tonight. Which I wasn't even going to tell you, since it's so much just the way things are that it's not news." Though he sat erect, one more gift from the army, he sagged inside. Another narrowing day.

"I'm not going to start bawling," said Helen, "but what I feel is that all this is like a mountain slide making its way over me. All I can do is make my casserole—though I'm glad you like it so much, Herbert—and listen. I had all these notions about how life was made for me. But that, my family, is *bubkes*, which is Jewish for "beans," which means very, very little." She set her lips in weary determination. "Tom, get the dessert puddings out of the refrigerator. I'd like them to warm up a bit."

∞

A Bit of Counter-Culture Levity /

"Travis sure likes it." Sharlene pointed to her son, who, as the center of attention, dressed in Oshkosh overalls and mini-sneakers, was shimmying to the strains of Country Joe and the Fish performing "I Feel Like I'm Fixin' to Die Rag," a free-spirited ditty that cast a jaundiced eye on the war in Vietnam. To the cheerleading "One, Two, Three," he sang his version: "One, Two, Free."

"I'm telling you, Sharlene, you got a musical kid here," said Carlene, one of Sharlene's two sisters. Introducing herself to Tom, she explained that "our mother liked the sounds of 'lene' and 'ar'" and that their other sister was named Darlene. "You'll need to buy him a drum set soon. I wonder who he takes after." She and Sharlene exchanged a brief, guarded glance. "Right. That's a bad question." She turned to Tom and patted the armrest on the couch she was sitting on. "Sharlene's told me about you. I wanted to see for myself."

Before Tom could say a word, Sharlene spoke: "What's going on first of all is this loony song Tom wanted me to hear. They don't play it on the radio, but Tom says," and she nodded to him to acknowledge he was there and probably capable of speaking for himself, "a lot of people know about anyway, like there's some kind of underground going on that people like me don't know about."

Tom got up and put the needle down on the song again. Travis clapped his hands. Tom bowed.

"I have to say that song's irreverent. I should kick you and that song out of here. I mean here's my son dancing to that." Sharlene's voice was amused-trying-to-be-serious. "He can't go around singing, 'Whoopee, we're all gonna die.'"

"I think it's cute. He's a song-and-dance man." said Carlene. "And he's just a little boy and it's just music."

Tom remained standing, preparing to play the song again. "Do you really think every guy over there feels reverently about the war? I bet you that plenty of guys know this song. You've seen the photos, the peace symbols they've drawn on their helmets."

"That wasn't my husband. He was gung-ho. He believed. You name it and he believed it."

"He didn't believe in you," said Carlene. She turned her head away from her sister. "I wish I had a cigarette." She looked at Tom, who had put the record arm at rest but left the turntable spinning. "You probably don't smoke. And my sister's always quitting."

"No, I don't. Sorry."

"A nasty habit's nothing to be sorry about. Between cigarettes and mints, I spend half of what I make."

"I heard what you said." Sharlene got up and went to her son, who was sprawled on the floor, happily exhausted. "And you're right. He didn't believe in me. He fooled around and he got bored with being married and having a kid and decided the war was a way to see the world and get some excitement. He didn't plan on getting killed, but probably not many guys do." She picked Travis up and gently straightened the part in his hair. "You're starting to get heavier, Trav." She made a sort of pirouette turn to Tom and put Travis down. "Now you know something more about me. That's what sisters are for. No truth goes unspoken. And I have been quitting cigarettes since I met you. And I've quit before. And I could start again tomorrow."

"Sharlene says you aren't going. I've read about people like you in the newspaper—guys burning their draft cards—but I can't say I ever met one. Maybe I need to touch you and make sure you're real." She got up and took a few steps toward Tom.

"I'm the one here who touches him." She put herself between her sister and Tom.

"That's fine," said Carlene. "Just move aside so I can ask him a question: What's going on inside you to make you do that? You know, step out of line."

Tom made the effort to look steadily at Carlene, to not act as if someone else was in his body, as if this was not happening now to him, Mr. 1-A. "If I answer you fully, we could be here a while, but I decided that I have to live with myself, that war doesn't solve anything and people have to learn that. I have to act on that, and the best way is not to go."

"You're not afraid to stand up, are you?" said Carlene. "The war's nothing to me. You know—more shit from men. What else is new?"

"I tell him the government's gonna fry his ass" said Sharlene. "They're just gonna say, 'What about all the guys who just did what they're told to do. Who the hell do you think you are?'"

Travis had wandered over to the stereo. "Play more song," he announced. "One, two, free."

⁓⁂⁓

Free to Ponder the Intangible and the Tangible /

"Are you going to keep attending the Quaker meeting?" Tom and Daniel were going over Tom's car with polish after soaping and rinsing it with the garden hose. "Because I am. I've talked with Ray Moore a couple of times. I should get the CO form any day. But I kind of wonder about you because we haven't talked, and you're the one who got me there. I wouldn't have gone if it hadn't been for you." The previous days of Tom's thinking about saying those words disappeared in the mild, late April air.

Daniel stood on other side of the car, examining the door handle. "You keep this foreign jalopy in good shape."

"Needs a new set of plugs, but I'll get there."

"Funny how the metal wears on these handles. Must be the air that does it." He folded the rag in his hand. "I don't think I'm going there again. I've thought about it, but I can see it's not for me. I'm glad it's good for you. I was surprised, but then when I thought about you, how you were as a boy, minding your own business, I wasn't surprised." He squinted, the midafternoon sun in his eyes, then pivoted slightly. "I need something a little more tangible. I think I'm going back to where I started, with the Presbyterians. That old-time rigmarole soothes me. Getting soothed may not be the main point, but you take it where you find it. You know I still have dreams, nightmares really, about the war, and some days those dreams leak into my waking hours. Your mother thinks I should talk to someone, but I'm a little leery of headshrinkers. Anyhow, I need something more solid—hymn singing and sermonizing. I need to feel God is in the house because—let's face it—I need Him. I was brought up to believe. It's still there in me. Like something you want and something you're convinced of at the same time."

Tom put his rag down at the peak of the VW's sloping hood and stared as if he had never seen his own car. He wanted to stop the moment and put a caption under it: "My Father Talking." Tom nerved himself up to speak, a feeling like in lacrosse, getting ready to shoot at the goal—now, do it. "You've never said much about what you went through, and I'm not asking you. I never wanted to hear war stories the way some kids do. I think I felt how deep the war was for you, but it's hard to say because I was a kid, and what did I know?"

"Probably plenty."

"Could be. Kids are like that. How they know."

"You certainly were. Taking things in."

"Yeah, well now it's another war and the government will do whatever they do, but it's not like I'm feeling big-time religious. I needed something that showed me something about who I am. And God's part of that. And so is the silence. And so is listening. And it just kind of all hit me, like I was waiting."

"Fair."

"I think I get it that you don't want to go there anymore. I actually told Reggie about it, and I think he's going to go. He's curious." Tom ran a hand over the top of the car. "What I'm wondering is how you are doing with this war, the one that's got my name in its file, the one that seems as though it'll never go away. Wasn't there a Hundred Years' War once?"

"You've heard me rant at the dinner table. What's worse is how it makes me not feel good about people. Any people. That we're hopeless, that we learn nothing. We make up purposes and go about our lives. All that does is just keep us busy." He looked away but then returned to the task. "I see quite a few sad things in my line of work—people deceiving people, people giving up on people. You add that to the war, and you can see why I might need 'A Mighty Fortress is Our God.'"

"Gotcha."

"I don't booze beyond the cocktail hour, but sometimes I have to say that I wouldn't mind drinking myself into a permanent stupor, because when I pick up that paper in the morning, it's awfully hard to read. Somehow, I expected more to come of what I did and what people died for beyond other people dying. I'm disappointed. A grown man, but I'm disappointed. We didn't have to wind up in this mess. We made it."

Daniel unfurled his rag and took a few brisk swipes at the side door.

"I'll keep reading about Gene McCarthy, though, and now about Kennedy. It's not all bleak. I know that. And look at you, how brave you are, how determined." Daniel felt the choke in his voice, too much feeling trying to get through a small opening. "What's happening to this country, the anguish and the effrontery, makes me wonder. And as you know, I'm trained to do more than wonder. I take careful notes." His voice fell to a whisper. "Maybe that's my personal treadmill. Being on top of things you can't be on top of."

Tom searched for something to say back but found only the caption: "My Father Talking."

∞

Siblings Talking for the Many-Thousandth Time /

"How's life with Ruthie?" Star and Herb were sitting on his bedroom floor, knees up against their chests. "As you know, I lost my virginity with Steve Hamilton when I was fourteen. Lost is a stupid word, though, isn't it? Like I mislaid it, like a pair of mittens. But Ruthie isn't Steve Hamilton, who was basically just doing a job. She's pretty loco about you."

"Glad to hear it."

"And Ruthie isn't a virgin. Same scene, getting it over with, though with a different guy. Some guys go around as if that's their obligation, or maybe they're like gunfighters scoring another notch. Steve and I don't even nod to each other in the hallways."

"Pretty obvious that I'm not in that league, not that I'd want to be. But there's something I'm almost afraid of." He put his hand on his sister's and thought for a distracted moment of the game they played as children, when they kept putting hands on top of one another. What was that game called? "I think about her all the time. It's like I could go off some kind of cliff with her. You know, day in and day out we're in school, and we're watching ourselves and watching everyone else and not giving up too much because we don't want to be taken down, and then there's this cliff that feels much more real than everything else."

"I could use a cliff like that. And maybe you're not so much afraid as anxious. I can get that. Could be a deep feeling that will get deeper. It sure beats throwing soup at some moron."

"How did the apology go?"

"She simpered. I think that would be the word. Mr. Klausmeyer officiated. We shook hands like at a basketball game, which is probably how he thinks about everything anyway. I can't imagine we'll ever say another word to each other. She's probably said enough about me to other people to fill a book. Now and forever, I'm the girl-who-threw-the-soup. Not that I'm ashamed. I'm kinda pleased I was so primitive." Star gave her brother a gentle prod to the ribs. "We've got to work on Mom and Dad so that they move and we get the hell out. One more year is more than I can take. I know Dad will say, 'Well, it's just one year and it's your senior year, and you'll be looking toward going off to college,' but I know I can't take it. I'm gonna have a hard time just making it till June."

"Convincing them is gonna be rugged." Herb looked at the wall opposite him where, among other posters, one of Jimi Hendrix resided, Hendrix looking down at his guitar, cool and amazed at the same time. "Maybe I can point to Chuck Carranza. Did you know he ran away?"

"Because of school?"

"Because of his shitty house, but school didn't help. He never fit in. You spend your life getting called 'Upchuck,' it sucks."

"We tell them that we're gonna run away?"

"Maybe."

"Maybe they just laugh at us, like we're acting like little kids."

"Then maybe we do run away."

"Where did Chuck go?"

"I think to Cincinnati. He's got an aunt there he used to talk about."

"Are you sad? Gonna miss him?"

"Yeah. We could goof together. Try to not let things get to us."

"I'd go to pieces without Ruthie. How can I go to another school and leave her? But how can I stay?"

"Feels like a cliff."

Star stretched and started to get up. "It is. But don't be afraid."

Being Afraid Was Not Permissible /

On one side of Ho Chi Minh's long life stood a small mountain of words—speeches given and received, articles written and read, Marxist tomes digested, pamphlets, and the old texts, those his father taught. On the other side stood war, those soldiers who before undertaking a mission against impossible odds were shown their coffins. How could a man stand between those two forces: the articulate air of language and the body's ruin, the fall into the silence of gone-forever?

He had believed the words, the communist sages who offered a way out of the maze of scorn, oppression, doubt, and fear he was born into. The phrases and slogans could be shifty, today's term of opprobrium turning into tomorrow's praise, but he was both nimble and grateful. What had the imperialists with their vaunted universities, banks, parliaments, and foreign offices offered him? Why did they expect him to stomach the indignities they meted out each thoughtless day? The answer was simple: He and his people were not real, at best exotic and at worst subhuman, possessions more than people, because the economy that ground them up was about possessions and was driven by profit. In that one word the nature of the Westerners was explained. What was the importance of this "profit" that so many lives must be sacrificed in its name? What did this "profit" do for the human race? Did it breed more compassion or love or caring or wisdom? The answer was plain about who was on the receiving end of the capitalist machine. Yet the capitalists barely identified themselves as such. To them everything was justified in the name of "profit."

Who gave them the right to take what they took from the earth? They had no such right, and though they might invoke their God, they did not care about such a right. They took what was there for the taking, including the "lesser peoples," as they liked to term them. The phrase came off their tongues easily, a mutual, unimpeded understanding among the powerful and those who represented the powerful. That those who used such a phrase were soulless was irrelevant. A soul wasn't money or rubber or tin. Their briskness, acumen, and moneymaking ardor showed they were alive and very well. Wasn't that sufficient?

Such people represented a nightmare of arrogance. Everything of value was on their side; the spurious excitement of their movies, magazines, motorcars infused their being, to say nothing of the quiet weight of all that capital. No nightmare resided in the advertisements' smiling faces—only comfort, glamour, and assurance. The Westerners had given themselves up to their appetites and expected to be applauded. Anyone who didn't applaud was, by definition, a malcontent.

The Americans who appeared after the French departed were a different sort of soulless, convinced of the genius of their amiability and well-meaningfulness, their fabulous freedom. They, too, had the money and machines. They could obliterate the whole terrain if they wished. That there were other people in the world continually surprised the Americans. Their own inspirational political origins were of little real interest to them. More to the point, their virtue needed something to oppose.

Any attentive reader of history came to understand how one nightmare begat another. On his side, Ho excused the nightmares that strife begat as necessities. Who had started all this grief? Who had reduced the multifarious magnificence of existence and the dignity of the old ways to profit? If there had to be seemingly endless war to prove to the imperialists that they were wrong, then there had to be war. Ho's gentleness was off to the side, beckoning at a near distance but still a distance. The world had not come that far yet. It might never.

Never To Say What Is within Is Unbearable Yet Commonplace /

"What are you planning to do this summer, John?" Helen found it a relief to ask a young person who was not a son or daughter about his life. Her classmate was a quiet revelation—someone going about his days without the thousand binding tentacles she knew too well.

"Thanks for asking, Helen." He grinned, proud of the ease with which her name now rolled off his tongue. "I'm going to sort of apprentice with a pastor in my hometown in Virginia, get more of a feel for the lay of the land, go over sermons with him and maybe do some pastoral visits with him, low-key ones. And get a sense of managing a congregation and a building and dealing with other ministers in the community." John shook his head in mild astonishment. "That already seems like a lot, doesn't it? But also, I'm going to do a little politicking."

"For whom?" Helen had no idea that John (he was now "John," not the formal "John Tobin" in her mind) had any active political interest. He seemed so completely in the category of "nice boy," she couldn't imagine him debating with anyone about anything. Or feeling strongly. But that wasn't fair. She had seen his face after Reverend King's death.

"I want to work for Robert Kennedy. Maybe that surprises you."

"Everything these days surprises me."

"I've been following in the newspapers what he's been saying. How he talked to the crowd in Indianapolis and how he didn't have to do that, how he could have been afraid but wasn't. And there wasn't trouble in

Indianapolis because someone talked from his heart. And I guess that's what I'm feeling, that he's someone who's talking from his heart. So as he goes around—and I know he's a politician and everything—I have the feeling he's connecting with people in ways that matter. And he's connected with me."

"He's a Catholic, as you well know." As she spoke, Helen pulled a book out of her bag, *The Negro in the Making of America*.

"I do, and I like that, how he's serious about his religion, how it's not just something he puts on for the purpose of winning an election. Christ means something to him."

"And you are going to do what?"

"Go door-to-door and talk with people. Help out in whatever ways I can help out. I talked to someone on the telephone. I guess I'll see." He tipped his head toward Helen conspiratorially. "I'm kinda excited."

"I'm excited for you. I've been following McCarthy more, because he stepped in first, but I talked to my family about the Indianapolis speech, and I agree with you. He didn't have to do that. He could have excused himself."

"What he's said is that 'we can do better.' I like that because it's simple and true and important. If we just say, 'good enough,' or if we don't care to begin with, then we lose sight of something, don't we?" A vision of declarative sincerity, John looked directly at her.

"We do." She put a hand on his hand. There were more feelings in the gesture than she in that moment could understand, but one was the confirmation a degree of age could give to youth. So much was quaking around her, not the least Tom's fate, but here was this determination to do something. What was she determined to do? The days swirled around her like leaves in the wind. "And what do your fraternity brothers think of your politics?"

"I haven't said a word." He gave a tight, skeptical smile. "I probably won't."

"A mind of your own." Helen lifted her hand. "That's commendable."

"That's kind of you, but I won't be much of a minister if all I do is follow others. If I don't see God and my fellow man with my own eyes, I won't be a help to anyone."

In the front of the hall the professor was making a show of arranging his lecture notes on the podium, a ritual devoted to bringing the lecture hall to order. "As I was saying at the end of our last class," he began.

"Immortal words," Helen whispered.

"Almost," John whispered back.

❧

Whispers, Declarations, Put-Downs, History, Poems, a Song /

Star stood before her high school in the early morning, Ruthie and Herb on one side of her (and giving off the physically-close-to-one-another vibe of being a couple) and on the other side two sophomores who worked on the newspaper and were against the war. Also present were Mr. Rackstraw, a history teacher, and Miss Gonzalez, a Spanish teacher. As teachers, they had been the negotiators with the principal and superintendent about the right of students and teachers to participate in the national strike against the Vietnam War (which, as Mr. Rackstraw pointed out to anyone who cared to hear, was not an official war). After numerous meetings, after which the two teachers talked with Ruthie and Star about what transpired, permission was granted to hand out a one-page summary of the participants' position, along with the right to strike by missing the first-period class. Students who missed the class would not be given a zero for attendance, nor would their absence otherwise be held against them. Miss Gonzalez laughed when she told the strikers that the administration would not condone any disruption or violence. "What do they think peace is about? Getting in a fight?"

Daniel and Helen both pointed out to Star that these two teachers had gone to bat for what they believed in and that they didn't have to do that. Star agreed but said she still detested the school. This morning, however, she was pleased to be standing there in the quiet moments before the buses and cars rolled in. And she wasn't standing there alone.

The piece of paper they were handing out was a rehash of editorials Star and Ruthie had been writing yearlong but had not swayed the student body in the least. Or maybe some people had listened but said nothing out loud. She yearned for someone to come up to her and say, "I know you're trying. Keep at it." Maybe life didn't work that way.

The first bus rolled up and a gaggle of students stepped down, some animated and some zombie-like, some talking with others and some buried in their own thoughts. Star thrust out her hand and announced, "National Strike Day. Here. Read all about it." She kept her hand out as students filed by—most ignoring her; a few making dismissive, get-lost faces; and one telling her to "Go fuck yourself," but in a low enough voice so the teachers didn't hear him. She knew the guy, a senior who had gotten in early to some good school and prided himself on his all-round uprightness. Star gave him a high-wattage smile and kept her hand out. A freshman girl took the paper, stopped, and whispered, "I'm on your side. I'd join you, but if my parents found out, they'd kill me." She hurried on.

A number of kids took the paper and made a show of crumpling it up and dropping it on the ground. Star wanted to say something but held back. This, as her father liked to say, was the human race. You better get used to it. She didn't want to get used to it, but she didn't have to give up either, because every seventh or eighth kid took the paper and nodded or said something like what the freshman girl said or, a few times, even stronger than that, like a girl in her physical education class who seemed to live to play volleyball and who took the paper and said without missing a beat, "I wish I had your guts."

During first period, the "strike" period, the six outside were joined by seven students, which meant thirteen participants out of six hundred or so students and faculty. Mr. Rackstraw read from a book by Bernard Fall about the French being in Vietnam and how badly that ended. Miss Gonzalez read two poems in Spanish and then in translation. She spoke about the poet, a man named Pablo Neruda. One of the students, a girl Star didn't know, read from some letters her brother, who was a soldier in Vietnam, had written. He wrote that "you can't believe what it's like here. Don't expect anyone who hasn't been here to tell you anything like the truth." The girl said her brother had three more months to go. She bit her lip, as if she were going to cry.

Star and Herb had decided to do "Where Have All the Flowers Gone" together, Herb on the guitar and Star singing. They had debated whether the song was too corny and whether people already had heard it too many times but decided the words were too important. They sang it once and then asked the others to join in. The assistant principal sat in a corner of the lobby on a folding chair and kept a careful eye on the proceedings. Occasionally he wrote something down on a legal pad he held in his lap. He did not sing along.

Along the Sociable-Suburban Path /

"Why does Becky Jansen give these Friday-night cocktail parties?"

"So she doesn't have to drink alone." Helen was searching through her jewelry box. "Do you think I should wear pearls?"

"I love you in pearls, you know that. And I'm sure most nights, Hank shares a drink with her."

"I'm sure he does."

Daniel pulled a pair of scuffed loafers out of the bedroom closet he and Helen shared. "It means I get to hear from him about boats, golf, and some of his Negro-phobia, which, when I comment on, he informs me that I'm a bleeding heart and gives me a genial smirk. Nonviolence seems the right path, but I'd like to deck him." He turned the shoes over and examined the soles. "I suspect our kids are right. We need to move and meet some other people."

"I'd say he means well, but I know he doesn't. Can you help me with the clasp?"

"Only if I get to cup your breasts first."

"Fair enough. Maybe later you'll be so frustrated, you can channel the energy into our bed." Helen held out the pearls. "I'd like that."

"I wouldn't mind myself, beautiful." Daniel lingered on her breasts, sighed, then raised his hands to do the clasp. "I went again today to a block in a burnt-out neighborhood. I was looking for this old woman I had talked to."

Helen turned around to face him. "That's how you're spending your lunchtime these days?"

"I have the picture in my head, but it's not really enough. I need to keep reminding myself. People walk by as if it's always been like that, burnt-out wrecks of buildings. A war zone. A phrase I don't use lightly."

"Any other perceptions?"

"You'll laugh, but I sat in my car and started to write a poem."

"A poem!"

"I said not to laugh."

"I didn't. I just exclaimed."

"It's not 'roses are red.' It's more like what a teenager would write. Or I think a teenager would write."

"You have a couple. You could ask."

"I could, but I don't think I'm ready to go public yet."

"Holding back even from your spouse, who just expressed carnal desire."

"You're on the lit-up side, and you haven't even had a drink yet."

"School's getting to me, end of the semester. I have a paper to write about Marcus Garvey and a whole world of yearning and heartbreak I didn't know anything about. And there's this classmate of mine, an undergrad who's earnest in that way that only a young person can be earnest, and it's true I get plenty of that around here already, but he's the real thing in his way, which is very decent, what they used to call 'upright.' And then there's the bushel of stress about our 1-A son and the lesser but real worry about my soup-throwing daughter, plus finding a teaching job where I'm not put on the spot for being a woman who wants to teach history but doesn't coach football, plus the supposedly greater worries about who the next president of this self-righteous, overbearing country is going to be."

"Maybe you could use a poem. Gene McCarthy writes poems."

Helen looked down at Daniel's feet. "You're not going to wear those are you? I put on pearls, and you're wearing a pair of shoes I want to give to Goodwill."

"I keep an eye on what shows up each week in the *New Yorker*. That's how poets are. Raffish, unaccountable, fond of old shoes."

"You have some vocabulary, don't you? And here I thought you were just a gumshoe lawyer."

"Well, think again." Daniel sat down on their bed and removed his shoes. "Here, take them. They've seen better days. But—" He picked one shoe up and dangled it.

"Something about the beauty of the accustomed?"

"Something. Maybe something that wants a poem." He let the shoe fall. "You know, when I was in Europe, I saw a lot of buildings that looked like what happened this month. Sometimes there were dead people in those buildings. Sometimes snipers. Sometimes I imagined the walls that remained standing had eyes, eyes that couldn't be closed, as if the walls were alive."

"I'm listening. And you don't have to throw those shoes away."

Away from Nothing but with Syrup /

One step into the kitchen and Herb shouted: "You made pancakes! A Sunday morning and you made pancakes! I love you, Mom!"

Star reached to take one from a pile on a platter in the center of the table. "She makes pancakes when she's depressed and she's trying to pick herself up and us up too. Isn't that right?"

"I don't want them to burn. That's my main concern at the moment. Whether I'm happy or sad, I don't want them to burn."

Lightly, Daniel shook the carefully folded newspaper he held out before him. "Someone out there is happy, and he's not eating your pancakes. I quote a Democrat candidate for president, one Hubert Humphrey: 'Here we are, the way politics ought to be in America: the politics of happiness, the politics of purpose and the politics of joy! And that's the way it's going to be, all the way from here on out.' And yes, there is an exclamation mark in there."

"He's delusional," said Herb.

"He's so trying to be happy, he's sad," said Star.

"If he thinks that's how he's going to win the election, he's wrong," said Helen.

"I like having a Greek chorus here," said Daniel. "Maybe Hubert could come by and help our son with the form he has to fill out about being a conscientious objector. Put in a sentence or two about happiness."

"Maybe he could see what a bad joke he is," said Herb. "He makes me angry. What is he thinking?"

"He's not thinking about someone like your brother, that's for sure." Helen turned off the gas burner. "Tom said he was going to put the CO form in the mail tomorrow."

"Make sure he sends it certified," said Daniel.

"I'll tell him and you tell him, and I'll leave a note out and maybe he'll do it. When I see him, he seems more than a little distracted. Is he in love? Or becoming a spiritual being? Or just his usual it'll-get-done self?" Helen sat down, put a pancake on a plate, and poured Karo syrup from a small pitcher. "I can feel this stuff rotting my teeth, but when I was a girl, I loved it. I still love it."

"More news from the front page?" asked Star.

"The police beat up a bunch of kids in Chicago who were protesting the war. There's a picture of them swinging clubs."

"Does Hubert," said Herb, "look out his window? Is there anyone around him to say, 'Hey, Hubert, things are kinda rough out there'?"

"And at Columbia?" asked Helen.

"Stokely Carmichael and H. Rap Brown have entered the fray," said Daniel.

"That's trouble for the administrators because they're national Black Power figures but probably good for the administrators, because now they can blame 'outside agitators.' Always handy to have some 'outside agitators' available."

"Someone could think you've become cynical, Herbert," Helen said.

"Come on, Mom. He's disgusted the way we're all disgusted. And each day we have to take it. Probably I'll throw more soup." Star raised her hands and mimed her tossing the contents of a bowl.

"I can understand why those guys showed up," said Herb. "It's a national issue. Here's this Ivy League school in the middle of a black neighborhood. What's it to them, to the people in the neighborhood? What's Columbia ever done for them?"

"Ever get the feeling that our lives have turned into a civics class that's taken a wrong turn?" Daniel put the newspaper down in the center of the table. "It's as I was saying to Tom not long ago. After my time in the big war, I thought, Well, that's done. Things will be clear from here on out. I'm afraid what we call 'politics' is too jerry-built for its own good." He tapped the newspaper as if in confirmation. "But we believe—amid riot, war, and assassination—that it's not confused."

"And here I am making pancakes," said Helen

"You're the one who knows what she's doing," said Star. "All these men the paper is full of never sit and appreciate what's on the plate in front of them. They need to be in the kitchen more."

They all looked down at the front page. A late-middle-aged cherub, Vice President Hubert Humphrey was smiling and waving to what was presumably a crowd.

May

EVERYTHING LARGE ENDING IN A BOX

Two Members of the Lonely Crowd /

"You're gonna need new ball joints, Mrs. Brownson."

"What's that?" Helen had brought her Chevy in for routine maintenance. She and Daniel had been going to the same garage for years: Jack's Automotive. Jack Fitzgerald stood in front of her—curly haired, cigarette in a corner of his mouth, and "Jack" stitched in cursive onto the front of his green work shirt.

"It makes it so you can steer."

"Sounds important. Soon?"

"Soon. Next week suit you?" Jack peered into a large, greasy notebook on the counter top that served as his desk. He put his cigarette into a plastic ashtray that advertised a local nightclub and took hold of a ballpoint pen.

"Tuesday's good." As Jack wrote, Helen stared down at the front page of *The Sun* that lay on the countertop. Students at Columbia University were being routed by the thousand police that had been brought in to end the occupation of several campus buildings. A picture of a student with blood running down his face accompanied the article.

Jack raised his head. "Kid doesn't look good, does he? Got what was coming to him."

"He could have been one of my kids."

Jack picked up his cigarette but then stubbed it out. "I got a nephew in Vietnam. He's humping through that damn jungle and hoping he comes back in one piece. I don't get these college kids, but they're part of the trouble, like the country's a soda pop bottle and someone shook it real bad."

Instinctively, as if to steady herself, Helen put a hand out to touch the photo in the paper. "My kids are good kids. They're idealists. They want the world to be a better place. And they can see that the adults who've been in charge haven't been the wisest or most honest people."

"Not like being in the army under Ike, if that's what you mean." Jack clicked his pen. "Tuesday at nine okay with you?"

"Tuesday at nine is fine. And I didn't mean to intrude on your life, Jack. I just see all these pictures every day, and I get sick."

"My wife feels the same way. 'When's all this gonna stop?' That's what she says to me. Like I know something." He pushed the notebook aside. "I know about ball joints; that's what I know."

"I'm glad you do. I sure don't. Let me write you a check for today." As she was standing there writing the check, she was still there with the picture of the bloodied young man. Did he get what he had coming to him? She knew the police loathed such kids, that to the police they were privileged brats who took their amenities and education for granted; kids who, compared to the police, had never worked a hard day in their lives, much less put their lives on the line. No wonder the police were violent. Why should they have patience with such people? They weren't being paid to understand whatever grievances were real to the students.

There must have been deans and such, though, who were paid to listen to students. But probably they had listened more than they cared to listen. Or they hadn't listened at all. Students making demands wasn't part of the approved scenario.

"Mrs. Brownson, you there?" Jack tilted his head in good-humored concern.

"I'm sorry. I went off into my mind. Happens all the time. See you next Tuesday." In a show of briskness, Helen took her purse and keys and strode toward the door that led into the spring sunshine. Once outside, however, she stopped, craned her face up, and let herself feel the warmth. She sensed Jack looking at her—Mrs. Brownson, who sometimes forgot where she was. That night, in recounting his day's work, he might tell his wife about her.

The Work of Being Here /

"You don't let much light in here." Herb gestured toward the pulled curtains.

"My light's inner these days." Tom tapped the top book in the pile beside him on his bed. He got up to exchange the handshake—a squeeze, knuckle tap, and slap—they had evolved over the years, the brothers' version of a soul shake. Herb was grinning, and for a second Tom got his childhood back, his younger brother eager to tell him something. "How goes it?"

"I was gonna ask you, but here's the story: I reached the promised land."

"You scored?"

"That's the locker room vernacular, but yeah."

"You know me— jockstraps and sports metaphors. I trust things went well."

Herb's grin got wider. "Better than that. We sort of went nuts together. It was what you'd call the basics, but that was pretty great."

"Something's been keeping the human race on this planet. Did you tell me who the lucky girl is?"

"Star's friend, Ruthie."

"Another troublemaker. I like it. Just watch out what you say."

"That our sister borrows T-shirts and doesn't return them? That she steams up the bathroom and takes days to wash her hair?"

"Everything is incriminating. Ask the government."

"Which brings up the topic of you."

"Look around. You see the signs of a conscience."

"If books can prove it, you're in."

"I doubt if books will prove anything, but they've made me think, which is more than college did. About stuff I didn't know existed."

"Stuff?"

"Other ways of looking at what we're doing. Big-picture stuff. It's not like I haven't heard the news around the kitchen table, but this is something else. The only word that fits is a word I never thought about, a word you never hear, which is *sacred*, meaning you don't want to be killing people. You want to understand how Jesus was about peace and how some people have lived it, people I've been reading about, like the Quakers, like Reverend King, people who understood that life is precious." Tom halted. "I didn't ask you to sit down. Do you want to hear this? You recently got laid. I should be setting off firecrackers."

"You're the mystery man around here, the elusive Tom. Yeah, I want to hear." Herb went over to the chair by Tom's desk. "I'm like the other people in this house—concerned."

"Yeah. I'm what Dad calls, when he's talking PI talk, 'a person of interest.' That feels weird. I was just another guy. And still am. Ask the army. But I'm not. You know what, though?"

"What?"

"I miss lacrosse. I had the operation and my knee's okay; I was gonna play on some team at school, probably not varsity but somewhere. That's kinda stupid, how I miss it, but that was the main thing I did. I went to the doctor about my knee, and he wrote a letter about it. He said I should give it to the army when I go for the physical."

"Sounds good. I mean you might get out on that count." Herb looked down. "Sort of like my famous foot."

"I'm not sure I'm gonna give them the letter, though. It doesn't seem right. It seems bullshit."

"Saving yourself is bullshit?"

"That's some of what's eating me up. If everyone passes the buck, nothing ever happens."

"Mom would lose it if she heard you."

"That's her life, not mine."

"And in World War II, if you were in Germany, Hitler would have killed you and not thought twice."

"I don't like Lyndon Johnson, but he's not Hitler. And even if Hitler had killed me, I would have had the satisfaction of my conscience. We're all going to go anyhow."

Herb stuck his legs straight out while gripping the side of the chair seat as if he were going to do something gymnastic. "I'm not gonna argue that one, but I've read my *Britannica*, and what causes wars isn't disappearing tomorrow. It's what guys do. What do they call the infantry? 'Grunts.'"

"I know you're thinking, What well is my brother drinking from? Or like I just got the secret decoder in the cereal box. But talking to this Quaker, Ray, who isn't like anyone, very calm and focused, and reading these books—Tolstoy, the Bible, the history of pacifism, because it has a history—and driving around and some sort-of-dreams I've had and even

278

being with this woman I met, who's on her own trip, it's done a number on me."

"There's a woman?"

Tom waved with one arm, a step-right-up showman introducing the main act. "A woman, my man. You know what I'm talking about."

∞

About Women and Books /

"Do you ever identify with a character in a book? Like it's you that's there in the book?"

Ruthie put down the half of a peanut butter and jelly sandwich she was working on. No one was sitting next to Star and her, which was not unusual. "Do you mean like which girl in *Little Women* was the most me? Or did I want to be Laura in the *Little House* books?"

"No, not childhood books. I mean now."

"Now I'm reading *Anna Karenina*. I don't want to be her." Ruthie picked up her sandwich and took a decisive bite.

"I identify with Franny, you know in the story by Salinger."

"I've read it. She cries a bunch and wants to see God. Do you want to see God?"

Star picked up the apple that Helen had given her as a "wholesome dessert." "It's more like I want to cry. And I could do it every day. Because I see all this suffering, all these photos of people shot and blown up and maimed, and the faces of the soldiers who look like they've been up for two weeks and maybe they have, and I don't know what to do besides having our little protest here but still feeling angry. And then inside the anger there's this wanting to cry the way that Franny cries. And I can't do it. The

279

tears don't come. I sit in my bedroom and wait, but it doesn't happen. It's like I'm one of the living dead or something."

"'Franny,' that's a hard story, like crawling across broken glass on your hands and knees. Like he wants you to experience her totally and sort of painfully. And, as if that weren't enough, there's the jerk guy she's with, who isn't really a total jerk, just a guy."

"I think my anger is more than throwing soup. It's like it could explode and I wouldn't be here anymore."

"That sounds scary."

"It is scary, but it's nothing compared to the pictures and news."

"I wouldn't say it's 'nothing.' In the story Franny gets so nerved up she faints. Is that how you feel? Now?"

"No. It's different. I'm wasting my time, but I don't know what better way to spend it. I go to school because I'm supposed to go to school. But it's like I'm just a little life on this sea of suffering. Nothing prepared me for it. My dad's vaguely religious, and my mom isn't at all. Tom's started hanging out with these Quakers, but he's got his own problems. And it's not like if I swallowed the Bible I'd be okay, because I don't think I would be. Though I don't know for sure. But it's like I could put a fist through a window any second and I wouldn't be surprised." Star looked over to a wall featuring a poster for the senior prom: "GET YOUR TICKETS NOW!"

"You need to stay close to me. Not that I know anything more, but you're my friend. I don't want you to hurt yourself."

Star turned back to Ruthie and gave her a light kiss on her forehead. "You're sweet, but the world seems okay to you. You're with Herb, which is cool. I'm alone."

"It is cool." Ruthie smiled. "But what bothers you, bothers me."

"I have too many pictures in my head. They won't go away."

"Do you think they went away for Franny?"

"I don't think Salinger is going to tell us. I read that he's like a hermit."

"Maybe if you nail things the way he did, you need to just take a break."

"Maybe. Right now, the bell's gonna ring. If I start eating this now, by the time I get to French, I can throw the core in a trash can." Star tossed the apple in the air and caught it. "If I start crying, I'll let you know."

$$\infty$$

Coming to Know about Unknowing /

Lying in his bed in his darkened bedroom, Tom felt the questions hovering over him, as if he could reach out and touch them. The foremost was easy but not easy: "Do you believe in a Supreme Being?" A person applying for conscientious objector status had to check a box, either "yes" or "no." Tom thought about the box as much as he thought about the question, which was not to disrespect the Supreme Being but to marvel at how such an enormity could be brought down to a check mark in a box. That seemed the human dilemma, however: everything large winding up in a box. The Country Joe and the Fish song was never far away, the line about your boy coming home in a box. There were boxes and there were coffins, but they were the same—and not ultimately, but in the first row of human happenings, the largeness and smallness of believing, of cosmic life and narrow death.

He could check the box in good faith, but then there was the second question about what is this Being to you? What, as the question stated, are your "duties" as they pertain to your "belief"? When he answered the question on paper, he tried to be concise, which was a challenge, because where his belief began was the experience of silence at the Quaker meeting, which could seem illogical to someone whose belief began and ended with the Big Guy in the Sky. Nothing more to be said, case closed, God is all.

281

Was God in the silence? Surely, for the silence opened the door. The silence was the receptivity that God required. No blather, no arguments, no assertions, no waving the Bible. First came the silence of people sitting there, waiting and looking into themselves because, as he quoted to the government: "There is that of God in everyone." That seemed plain—how everyone seemed to regard everyone else, people being alert to other people. A person was not a thing, and that was one reason killing was wrong: It made people into things. One of his quotes (he had accumulated dozens) was "War is possible in as much as men become things." That was not God's way.

Within the blunt questions were mysteries the government did not care about. The very notion of the nation-state examining his beliefs had a comic element. Here was another body to use in a war. Did the body have any thoughts? Did the body have a soul? Did it matter as long as the body could pull a trigger? And after the body pulled the trigger, what then?

What further piqued Tom's interest, and kept piquing it in the darkened bedroom, was the feeling, as he sat there in the meetinghouse, that everything was profoundly ongoing. Human matters hadn't been decided once and for all. The edifice was under construction for each person, and what he wanted to construct was someone who saw Christ's epithet as the "Prince of Peace" as something to emulate. That felt, to use the contemporary phrase, "mind-blowing." And in its quiet way, a power to match any worldly power.

Among the proclivities of his almost newborn soul, Tom had discovered—shining and glimmering—a great interest in striving. Here was the world as it always had been—Pilate telling Christ what the deal was and people going along with the deal and praising the deal because that's what life was, the deal, and you wouldn't want to be different or be left out or at least not have a smart opinion—and here was Tom Brownson, college dropout, fairly good lacrosse player, and easygoing fornicator, who wanted to go forward as someone who rejected the violence that (to quote) "has become the law of our species." Someone who recognized that the refusal to go to war (to quote) "flows from the sacred character of human life, from the fact that man is made in the image of God." Someone for whom (to quote) "there must be no limit to this striving for perfection in implementing the teaching of Christ in history." His feelings were as heady as the words. Where amid the dailiness of cars, six-packs, headlines, and bargains was "sacred"? How could there be such a word? How had he not heard about it? Had it been hiding? However haltingly, he felt answers stirring within him, and whether the government believed him was truly immaterial. He had seen a very faint dawn and was almost grateful to the war. "Peace has never been tried": That was one more quote he entertained himself with in the darkness. He didn't see himself as a hero but as a supplicant—another new word.

⋐∞⋑

Words to the Wise, the Half-Wise, Anyone Who Will Listen /

"When you start talking, you sound like you want to be a priest or something, like you've taken a really big bite of God." Sharlene examined her bright red, moderately long fingernails. "I hope you don't want to stop screwing. You've got a talent to make a woman feel good. But I'm glad to hear you talk some about yourself. I'm always yakking about me. You must think I'm desperate."

"No, I—"

"You don't have to be polite. I wish you hadn't cut your hair, though. It looks kinda homemade, like your sister cut it or something."

"She did. I'm going to a barber next week to clean it up."

"I liked putting a hand through your hair. You got nice silky hair for a guy. You know my sister got an eye for you right away. I told her to back off. She's got a man. He's not much, if you ask me, but she likes men she can boss around."

"Unlike you." Tom smiled pleasantly.

"You know how to come at me from the right angle, don't you? You act all simple and just going to live the Christian life, but you got plenty else in there. That's what makes you interesting. You got a lot floating around in there. Just like me. Maybe I'm a pacifist too. Who knows?"

"How—"

"I'm sick of my job and I'm gonna give notice. I gotta do something else. You have any ideas? There are months still before I start community college, and I gotta keep making money. Being a single mom is not what this world is built around. And I have to keep on the good side of my in-laws, which means I told them, 'Yes, I do see this guy I met, but he's nothing serious. Travis is my first concern.'" Sharlene drummed briefly on the kitchen table, a one-hand rat-a-tat. "Which Travis is, and you're not what I would call 'serious,' even though all this stuff about war and peace is plenty serious—like when those sergeants come to your door all serious and give you the news, and you're just standing there like you're supposed to drop everything because everything has just dropped on you."

"Do you think—"

"Do I think what?"

"Do you think you would have divorced your husband?"

"That's a funny question from a guy. Guys don't ask questions like that. Girls ask questions like that. But I know real well that you are a guy, which makes me sort of love you, how I can shove you in a drawer and leave you there as if I trusted you."

"You didn't—"

"Answer the question. I know." Sharlene touched her bouffant, a reassurance she performed many times each day. "Probably, yeah. I'm tempted to say definitely, but what's the point?"

"No real point. I just wondered."

"I got taken for a ride. I don't think he meant to, but he did. Maybe that's how it is between men and women, that the women get taken for a ride because they're women, especially when they're young and don't know anything beyond where the tampon goes." Another hair touch. "But I've been thinking about the war, and you know what? I've been thinking those Vietnamese people are probably people too."

"Probably?"

"You know what I mean. They're different from us on account of their being short and sort of brown looking, but all the same, they're people. Everything you hear makes them out to not be people. I guess that's part of what's going on with you, about your getting religion, how you must be seeing it's all people, and what are we killing each other for?"

"When did you put all this together?"

"When I'm making milkshakes and serving up hamburgers, I'm thinking. Wait till I get to college. I'll burn it up."

⌘

Burning Up the Charts /

"That's Moby Grape you're playing," said Star.

"It is. And you are?" asked the store clerk.

"A fan. Not as big a one as my brother," and she motioned to an aisle on the other side of the store, where Herb was flipping through albums. "But a fan, yeah. And you are reading?"

"*Billboard.* Record industry bible. Sort of goes with the job." He gave that good-natured head move that some guys did: Here-I-am-on-earth-and-I'm-rolling-with-it.

"You ever hear them live?"

"Have I lived in San Francisco? No. But I want to. Soon. My brother's out there. He paints houses and says he's got work for me. I'm just waiting." He shrugged—more good nature. "Meanwhile I'm selling records. My uncle owns this place."

The Hi-Fi Shop was a serious record store as opposed to the local department stores, which had un-serious record departments.

"I'd like to go. Hearing them live, hearing Janis or Grace Slick, women who sing their hearts out, I'd probably faint or something."

"Could be so many people around, you wouldn't even fall over. My name's Jim."

"I'm Starflower, Star for short." No hands were extended, just a bit of eye contact. Jim had a thin face, brown eyes, and longish brown hair, a seven out of ten on the Cute Meter.

"That's one happening name you got. What's keeping you from going?"

"I'm still in high school. Next year I'm a senior. After that, I'm free—more or less." Star looked more closely. Mr. Going to San Francisco looked to be in his mid-twenties. A man, not a boy.

"'More or less' can be tricky."

"Tell me about it." Star stood up a bit straighter. Part of standing up straighter was sticking your chest out. It never hurt when you were meeting a new male.

"You could go this summer. Check it out. I could get in touch with my brother. Tell him Star's on her way. He's probably got some floor space."

"Somehow, that's not what my mom would like to hear. When I walk out the door, I want things to be like I said. Nothing against your brother. Or you."

"I get it. Just what's happening these days. People with thumbs and sleeping bags."

Star felt an inner uh-oh. Not cool to be talking about your mother.

Jim pushed the *Billboard* to the side and put his elbows on the counter, the better to observe. "Mind giving me your phone number? I'd like to give you a call, you know, have a drink of something and talk. Not everyone who comes in here notices what we're playing. Some of the older folks hear rock and have a conniption. They don't want Beethoven to roll over." He smiled a thin smile that showed Star some wariness, maybe some smarts she didn't understand, maybe some standard guy-conceit. As smiles went, it merited contemplation and would be filed under the heading of "Reading Males."

"Sure, I can do that." Star pulled out the little spiral-bound notepad on which she doodled and wrote miscellaneous insights. Then she fished around in her bag for a pen. She usually had at least three.

Herb came over with a couple of albums. "Not to interrupt, but we gotta move. I'm supposed to meet Ruthie."

Star gave her best sisterly smile as she pushed a piece of paper toward Mr. Fast Worker.

"I ain't got no money / but I will pay you before I die" came from the stereo perched on a shelf behind Jim. Star nodded, as if someone had spoken directly to her. "Some guys," she said, pausing for effect, "tell the truth."

⮿

Truth Wears Perplexed Hats /

"Yeah, it's been a while. Several worlds of shit since we got together. I didn't join the Black Panthers, though. I did take some long walks where the so-called riots occurred. I'm thinking of switching my major to something like history or sociology because, although I get the basics,

I need to understand more about what's going down. My daddy won't like it, but I'll tell him I'll be a lawyer like your daddy." Reggie pushed his back into the wooden bench outside the Quaker meetinghouse. "You put your ass down on this, no one has to tell you to sit up straight. I stopped smoking weed. I figured when Martin died, what am I doing lying around in my own personal zone? Was that what his life was about? Tough tells me the world keeps spinning—no reason to stop having a good time. But it's not like I'm giving up women. Martin didn't give up women. It's not like I threw out my James Brown records."

"I stopped smoking too. Just didn't seem right."

"Well, you seem to be getting religion. I can't imagine many of your brethren we just sat with are big-time tokers. I have to say, sitting with a bunch of white folks who kept their mouths shut was a most refreshing experience. I think every black person should have it. You could charge money. I bet some black folks have been with this program already." Reggie gave Tom a playful shoulder punch. "And when someone talked, you felt they actually had something to say. Black folks tend to carry on in church because if they didn't let it out, they would have all died a long time ago. But to see white folks sit there and be modest and be focused on what you told me—'inner light'—I can't say anything prepared me for that. But when I get into white people's scenes, it's like being a foreign correspondent." Reggie mugged an earnest face. "And here he is: Our man in Whitesville."

"I never thought of it like that. Maybe you need one of those battered hats those guys used to wear in the movies. Cigarette hanging out of the corner of your mouth."

"Of course you never thought of it. You ever see a black man in that role?"

"No."

"Imagine *The Sun* sending a black man to do that, even though in France no one would have blinked. They got their own shit—strikes, the cops beating up on the students—but they don't have our peculiar racial history."

"Did you think about saying something in there?"

"No way. If I open my mouth, I'm going to be the representative Negro, which is the last thing I want to be. 'A Negro got up, and you know what he said?' No thanks. Most everyone was silent, and I can be silent too. Like I said, I liked it. I wouldn't be surprised if shutting up gives the Lord some room to operate in."

"I've been doing a lot of reading about that, about feeling closer."

"Good luck in convincing the US government. Can you imagine a bunch of politicians sitting in there, at the meeting? They'd lose it in five minutes. I read how these Quakers have been around for centuries. You gotta hope they keep passing it on."

"And do you ever go to church?" Tom moved his feet on the gravel in front of the bench, as if to make a design. Looking at his shoes, he thought about the times he went to church as a boy and how Daniel insisted he polish his dress shoes. "Church is special," his father had said. It did feel special, but they never talked much about it, more like they were going to some movie on a Sunday morning, the God movie.

"Not lately. Martin's death took me down a couple of big pegs. I know God's not up there keeping score, but the pain of it, the waste of that life— hard to go sit in a church and sing a hymn. Martin wouldn't agree with me. I know that. But that's how I took it. He had a faith I don't have. You read that speech he gave before the end. He expected to die. I wanted him to live out his life despite all the sick, hateful white people running around. I wasn't being very realistic, was I?"

"No, but it makes sense. How you felt."

"It does, but it didn't do Martin any good, did it? I don't know what would have done him any good. That nonviolent stuff, that's what he lived by. No surprise the answer was some cracker with a rifle."

"Reverend King was a martyr."

Reggie turned to face Tom, who had stopped moving his legs but had his head down as if examining the ground. "I don't think I ever heard anyone say that word. It scares me, because maybe you're right." He made a wheezing sound, like he was an old man short of breath. "But a martyr for what?"

⌇

What Moves Sideways, as If on a Game Board /

"Before we start this game of Scrabble, I think we should have a discussion about next year." Star gave her parents a level gaze, deferential but firm.

"That means," said Herb, "we should talk about not staying here so Star and I don't have to go to Dimwit High for another year."

"That bad?" said Daniel. He was turning the tiles facedown in the top of the Scrabble box that sat on the coffee table in the living room.

"If you're gonna ask me if I'll live," said Star, "I have to say, 'I'll live.' I know you guys like it here, where it's sort of like the country. But you know how I feel."

"What if I said that it's not moving back into the city that's the issue for me," and Helen looked at Star and then at Herb, "but not being sure where in the world I should live."

Daniel had all the tiles facedown. "You've got my attention, oh wife-of-mine." He folded his hands. He liked this role, being part of the Family Players.

"I want to live someplace where all sorts of people live together and are neighborly and where I don't have to spend my life in a car. I want to live somewhere where there's a market I can walk to and buy fresh vegetables each day and bread from a bakery, real bread."

"Sounds like France," said Star.

"These days they're on strike," said Daniel. "Even the bakers."

"Sounds like Utopia," said Herb.

"Maybe," said Helen. "Maybe I'm little more than the indignant quotient of my dissatisfaction, which I barely think about but follows me around each day, and I don't talk about it because parents don't do that. But as these months have gone by, I keep asking myself, 'What am I doing here?' I feel like sand eroding into the sea—gone. Maybe if someone offered me a job where I could start teaching in the fall, I would feel better, but, as I told your father, at the last interview the assistant principal asked me why I got a master's degree when I know people would have to pay me more, which would work against me. I wanted to scream at him, 'Isn't this a school? Aren't you about learning?'" Helen paused, fingered a tile, but didn't turn it over. "I'm naive."

"That's not a word I would use for you," said Daniel. "It's discouraging, but someone will see the light."

"You don't have to rally my troops," said Helen.

"I guess we sound selfish," said Herb, "immature."

"Or we're just telling you the facts," said Star. "Herb doesn't get the load of crap I get."

"This leaves us ready to play Scrabble," said Daniel. He shook the box.

"Not so fast, husband-of-mine," said Helen. "The house anchors me. Moving is a big deal." She pointed to the hutch beside her, full of dishes.

"It's just a house," said Star. "The world's full of them."

"As I've said more than once, I love you, my philosophical daughter. But what I'm trying to get at, and probably not very well, is that my only recourse seems to be self-centered, and I don't want that. It goes against how I was brought up and how I've wanted to live and raise my children." Helen drew her lips together then exhaled. "I think I may be hitting the American wall."

"What wall?" said Daniel. "This isn't Berlin."

"Come on," said Star. "There might as well be walls around where black people live. You know that. What about the word *ghetto*?"

"You're right and I'm wrong," said Daniel. "Good six-letter word, though."

"I can feel you steering us, Dad, and I expected this was going to be inconclusive," said Herb, "because you're the parents and we're the kids. We're not going to hold our breath until we turn blue, but you have to promise to keep talking with Star and me about this."

"As in, we're a family, right?" said Star.

"I promise," said Helen. "We promise; right, Daniel?"

"That's a seven-letter word. Extra points." Daniel offered the tray to his wife. "Shall we play as teams so we can exhibit team spirit or play as individuals and exemplify the basic economic unit?"

"Oh, Dad," said Star. "Give it up. Please."

"Okay. Here's the scoop. Your mother and I have been talking. I'll start looking at real estate. Maybe our dream house is out there beckoning. How's that sound?"

"Sounds like it can't happen soon enough," said Star.

They sat there, knowing in a few seconds they would start playing a game that would take them elsewhere, a simpler place of points and rules. A refuge.

The Inner Refuge Scans the Bureaucratic Horizon /

"Thanks for not opening the letter," said Tom. He had taken the envelope that Helen had handed him, gone upstairs to his bedroom, and come right back down. "They denied me. I'm still 1-A."

Helen opened her mouth; a brief wail came out.

"Don't worry. I'll request a hearing. Everyone has the right to a hearing to point out stuff that shows they should be granted CO status. I can bring a witness too. The Quaker I've been talking with, Ray, said he'd go. He's not a lawyer, but he has talked with two other guys and has gone to the draft board. It's probably better he's not a lawyer, because he's got a good sense of who I am and that I'm not bullshitting or trying to weasel my way out. He's a very level-headed guy. Credible. And he's lived a true life. You feel that about him. The life I'd like to lead."

Helen clenched her hands together. She was standing in the front hall, but she was on a rocking boat. She could get sick any second.

"I'm actually kinda glad to ask for a hearing because I want to talk to them, whoever they are. I've been thinking about myself and about how I want to be, and how I can't go along with what other people are doing, no matter what they say and how right they think they are."

"I don't need convincing, and I appreciate what you are saying. You know that. I just worry, as you also know, how much they will listen to you. You wrote very solid answers to the questions they asked, and they turned you down. Who knows how they feel about objectors? They can't feel very positively. There's bound to be distrust in their minds. If everyone were like you, they'd have no army."

"Pretty plain that not everyone's like me." Tom smiled his that's-the-way-the-world-is smile, one he'd been smiling ever since he was a boy and explaining to Helen about how he was going to do something. He was practical, so why wouldn't he be practical about what was going on inside him, even when it is was soulful?

"And?"

"And what happens if my hearing doesn't work out? Then I can make an appeal and they bring someone in to handle that. And then if that fails, I just don't go—and we see what the government does."

"I shouldn't say this is all too much for me, because you're the one who's going through it. But—" Helen noticed her hands were still clenched. They were starting to hurt.

"I didn't mean to put you and Dad through this. But like I said, I'm glad that Dad, for whatever reason—which I guess is about him being ever the investigator—decided to go to a meeting and that I went with him and that this door opened up for me that wouldn't have opened up otherwise. And I'm glad I spent nights driving around the city and went into a diner and met Sharlene."

"Am I ever going to meet her?" The boat's rocking slowed. The moments were starting up again, lulling.

"That's up to her. She's her own woman. I never know from time to time what's gonna happen with her. I like that, though. She's got a few breezes blowing through her."

"You've become more metaphorical. Is that from sitting up there and reading?"

Tom folded the letter and put it in the back pocket of his jeans. He put the envelope on the top of the front hall desk that also held the telephone and telephone books—Baltimore, the counties, and DC too, because sometimes Daniel had to call there about work. "The Bible's full of metaphor. Christ is sorta wild with metaphors. I was actually wondering if you've read much of the Jewish books."

Helen shook her head no. "Very little. But maybe I'll start. I seem to have a son who's discovered a vocation of sorts. I mean in the profound sense, the true sense. I could use some thinking in that direction. There has to be more to life than killings and beatings."

"You know what I'm gonna say. There is."

Tom smiled again and Helen felt her heart open, as if it were going to leave her chest in a spasm of love and turmoil.

Turmoil in Individual Portions /

"Hard to want to go to school on a nice May morning. I'll just sit here and eat six bowls of Kix." Herb reached for the box.

"Hard to want to go to school on any morning." Star drew the words out to better aim them at her parents.

"Kennedy won in Indiana," Helen announced.

"What's with him? Just because he's a Kennedy, he has to run for president? Is that how it works? A family enterprise?" Herb poured himself a generous portion of cereal. "McCarthy started it. Why not let him finish it?"

"You remember," said Helen, "what I quoted from his speech in Indianapolis. He's sincere."

Daniel, who had been immersed in the local news, got up to get more coffee. "He's sincerely ambitious, but you can't blame a man for that."

"Can't you? Isn't he in it because he's supposed to because of his brother? How he's another Kennedy."

Star got up from her seat. "Do we have any grapefruit? I could use a half grapefruit. I'm citrus-starved."

"You don't look starved."

"Can it, Herbie."

Helen swiveled her head to give both children a brief maternal glare. "Manners," she intoned, a one-word speech they had heard before.

Star opened the refrigerator. "School corrupts us."

"You got it," said Herb before taking another spoonful.

"Kennedy could go all the way. People like a name brand." Daniel poured a smidgen of cream into his coffee. "And it's true what you say about him being a Kennedy, how we're all bound to think of his brother, even if he doesn't want that, which I can't imagine he does."

"Don't say it," said Star. "I'll feel like I'm twelve years old again, sitting in Mrs. Schroeder's class, and some grown-up knocks on the door and talks to her. And she looks at us and before she can start to say anything, she starts crying, and we all look at her because that's not what teachers do, especially Mrs. Schroeder, who goes strictly by the book. Then she finally gets the words out about the president being shot and we all sort of look at each other, like are we supposed to start crying too? I don't even remember the rest of the day, whether they sent us home early or what. All I remember is Mrs. Schroeder crying. The world crumbled apart for me right then."

"And how did we go on from there?" Helen's voice sounded startled, as if the event were happening once more. "How did we?"

"I'll spare you one of my all-purpose clichés. Instead," said Daniel, "I'll point out that it's hard to care about these primaries. The power rests with the party bosses. That's why Humphrey is going to get it."

"So why—" Star began.

"Don't ask me to explain the anarchic yet checked-and-balanced nature of American democracy. I still have coffee to drink." Daniel made a semi-slurp.

"Every morning we have a little drama, don't we?" said Helen. "I love it. When you kids go away to college, I'm going to miss it."

Tom walked into the kitchen, neatly dressed, short hair parted on one side and combed, belt on his chinos. "Good morning."

"It's the day of your physical, isn't it?" Helen knew it was, the physical exam being an obligation regardless of his trials with the draft board. Getting the body ready.

"It is, and I'm out of here. Should be back in the late afternoon, but I'm working tonight too."

"Do you have the letter from the doctor?"

"Sure." Tom showed Helen an envelope with a letter from an osteopathic doctor attesting to the damage to his knee. "We'll see."

Everyone looked at him. Once more, the news stood right before them. The home front.

"Good luck," they chirped, each of them knowing the mention of luck seemed nothing so much as a feckless obscenity.

"Thanks," said Tom. "Down the rabbit hole."

Holes in Stories /

Mrs. Hanson, one of the office secretaries, looked in through the glass window that composed the top half of the chemistry room door, rapped on it, then opened it and walked over to where Mr. White was twenty or so minutes into a lecture-demonstration about the properties of "certain gases." After a few whispered words, Mr. White told Herb he was wanted "downstairs." "Not an emergency," Mrs. Hanson added as Herb rose from his desk. She had a fruity, breathless voice, as if she had just discovered the power of speech. On her left hand she wore a prominent diamond ring. Who, Herb wondered while heading down the hallway and stairwell and listening to her praise Mr. White as a "fine teacher, one of our best," could listen to that voice for decades?

After some waiting around, the door to the assistant principal's office was opened not by Mr. Klausmeyer but a state trooper who introduced himself as "Trooper Hurley." He wore a uniform that reminded Herb of what the Royal Canadian Mounted Police wore, or at least in books he had seen. His tall hat was in his hands. Beside Trooper Hurley was a man in a sports jacket and tie who introduced himself as "Detective Smith." Regular names for regular cops.

After Herb identified himself, the questions began. "Are you Chuck Carranza's friend?" "When was the last time you saw Chuck?" "Did Chuck talk about running away?" "Did he mention any people, such as relatives, where he might be going?" "Did he mention his Aunt Clara in Cincinnati?"

It wasn't as though Herb hadn't been thinking about what might have happened, though it seemed the police were slow on the draw. Anyone who followed the news knew that running away was a national pastime and that mostly it turned out okay: getting to someplace where the people were more likable and your home wasn't breathing down your neck. He also knew that it might not turn out okay, that there were wrong turns out there on the beckoning highway. Since his father was a private investigator, Herb had heard a few stories about what "missing" could entail.

"Anything more you can think of that might help us? We don't have much of a trail here to follow. No bus or train records. He must have hitchhiked." Trooper Hurley put his hat down on the assistant principal's very neat desk and ran a hand over the stubble that was his haircut.

"I don't know," said Herb. "We just kind of hung out. I knew Chuck wasn't happy with his scene at home. Like me, he read a lot, so he could have had some idea in his head about someplace he read about. But some of what he read was stuff like King Arthur that doesn't exist now."

The policemen gave Herb a dubious look, as if to say that Chuck's reading habits were not what they had called him in for. No doubt they wanted him to say something like, "Oh, yeah, he talked about visiting his Uncle Cyrus in Milwaukee. Same last name as Chuck's. I think I have the address."

After a few more questions that led nowhere, the policemen dismissed Herb with courteous nods and words of thanks. They both gave him their cards "in case anything came up," as in maybe Chuck would call him that night from a phone booth in Wyoming.

Mrs. Hanson told Herb he could wait the minutes in the office foyer before the bell for the next class. She indicated one of the wooden chairs beside a small table that held magazines about teaching and parenting.

Once more Herb savored the fact: Chuck had done it. He tried to imagine Chuck's mind as he put some clothes in a backpack and walked to a road, stuck his thumb out, and after a short or long while got into a car or truck. He must have been excited and relieved and nervous but curious, too, about what would happen next. School was one big dull schedule, but sticking your thumb out was not on any schedule—no one to tell you what you could and couldn't do.

Sitting there and waiting for the bell, Herb felt like an overgrown child. Chuck had opted for something besides fifty-two-minute periods and *Education Today*. But Herb knew there was more to Chuck's disappearance than wanderlust. Things were happening in that house that no amount of joking could make better. Chuck had said there were times when he wanted to kill his father. Would it help the police to know that? "Of course the Carranzas are concerned," the trooper had said, his sternly sympathetic look indicating that the world of adults was emotionally appropriate. But of course. Everything adult was great; that was why the world was in such wonderful shape. Herb had seen Mrs. Carranza with what looked like a black eye. Three girls walked into the foyer, full of prom talk. Herb hoped that Chuck was far away.

The Far Away Comes Near /

"What do you think?"

"About what?" Daniel scratched his chest. He was naked.

"Don't be dense. I'm not in the mood. About the army not reclassifying our son on account of his knee." Gingerly, Helen stepped out of her slip. "How the army doctor said that things didn't look too bad. And how when Tom asked about an examination, the doctor said that wasn't how the army did things."

"Unfortunately, that's true. The army does things the way the army wants to do things. If that doctor felt he needed a few more boys that afternoon or he just felt that every sort of medical excuse in the known world was landing on his desk and he was sick of it, then that was that. They can always wash him out in basic if his knee buckles."

"I was hoping."

"As was I. I thought we had a good shot."

"But as our son keeps telling us, it's not a matter of 'we.' It's his life."

"Something we can't argue with."

"No, but we can be plenty upset. Now it's about whether he gets the CO status or—" Helen took the few steps toward her husband. "How did you ever do it? Just the thought of Tom in a war makes me go to pieces. And you were in it for years."

"I put one foot in front of another. I didn't want to let down the guys around me. And as you know, I'm still in it." He put arms around Helen. "Probably I should put on some pajamas."

"Not necessarily." She moved more tightly into his hug but held her head back to speak. "As our daughter would say, 'Doesn't this all freak you out?' How our son may wind up as some desperado, wanted by the government, jailed?"

"We're not the only ones up against this."

Helen pushed herself away. "I hate when you say that. I don't care about others. I care about my son and my family."

"I don't blame you. I'm only pointing out the truth."

"I hate men and their truth. The government lies every day about how the war is going, and we're supposed to believe in truth."

Daniel walked toward the hook on the wall where his pajamas hung. He put on his bottoms and then sat down on the one chair in their bedroom, a caned relic they had bought at an antiques store in the Maryland countryside. "I don't want to get on a soapbox and hold forth. And I don't want to act as though I support this awful war, because you know I don't. I can barely get up in the morning when I think how we have the gall to believe we're saving people when we're killing them. But I know what it's like to be a man and be in the confines the world puts you in. And you don't. That doesn't make what men do any better, but there's a kind of pressure on every one of us, on Tom and Herb and me, and that pressure is deadly accurate. When I talk about others, I'm talking about, in part, the male condition and how that's like weather. It's not going away, and we have to acknowledge it as a long-standing and often unhappy part of life." He rubbed his eyes. "I'm tired, and the soapbox got the better of me. I apologize."

"I shouldn't blame you, because it's not your fault. But it is your fault." Daniel started to get up.

"Don't touch me. I'm too full of too many feelings. I kept thinking Tom would get out of it." Helen sat down on the edge of the bed and looked at herself in the mirror across the bedroom. "What a sight I am. I can see the headline: 'Mother discovers it's a bad world.' And here I am proposing to teach young people how one misery turns into another."

Daniel wanted to tell Helen that his bouts of churchgoing had something to do with what she was talking about, that they made him feel he didn't have to pick everything up, that acknowledging God's amplitude was something both consoling and inspiring. But that felt like a lot to try to explain at 10:30 in the evening.

"You know what? I want to go to church with you, the one where we were married. I need to hold your arm and walk in there and be there with you. My past and your past and our past. God will take care of Himself. He's gotten this far."

"I'd like that." Daniel's voice was level, not taken aback. This wasn't the first time a thought-feeling had flashed between them, a closeness that mocked definition. What a searching light love was.

 ∞

Searching for the Missing I

"Anyone wanna soft-boiled egg?" Star asked.

"Me," said Daniel.

"I do," said Helen.

"No thanks," said Herb. "Did you know we could have a jolly foot rug courtesy of the Jolly Green Giant for two dollars and two can labels or frozen package fronts? And did you know that Jell-O now has the just-picked taste of fresh fruit? Which goes well with the hand-stirred, slow-simmered Italian sauce of Chef Boy-Ar-Dee. Though I don't get why they need those hyphens, like Americans are too stupid to read the name without the hyphens, like we're babies. Like—"

"Okay, Herbie. I know you miss Chuck. I know you still want to do your impersonation of an immature teenage boy. But Chuck's gone missing, and it doesn't become you." Star took three eggs out of a cardboard carton that displayed some cartoonlike chickens and put them into a pot of boiling water.

"Happiest meat for sandwiches—Spam." Herb made a sour face. "You're right. I'm fucked up." He looked around. "Sorry."

"That's okay. Manners matter," Helen said, "but bad language is coming to seem less bad to me. Did you talk any more to the police about Chuck?"

"I've been thinking about him," said Daniel. "Hitchhiking is a hard one to follow, but someone must have picked him up. Putting his face in the paper and getting someone to see it could do something."

"He's not exactly news, is he?" Star was watching the egg timer, a tiny hourglass that sat on the counter beside the stove.

"One of thousands," said Daniel.

"But I miss him, and I feel a little anxious, because Chuck wasn't the savviest guy. He lived here since he was a little kid and never went much of anywhere. And now he's out there somewhere making it up. I was lying in bed last night thinking about him."

"I suspect," said Daniel, "his affairs have settled into something simple, such as pushing a broom for room and board somewhere in Colorado, and maybe some girl has her eye on him."

"He'd like that. He felt crappy here. Way down on the social totem pole."

"Join the club," said Star. "Eggs are almost there. Hold on to your appetites."

"I wonder why he didn't let me know when he actually did it. He talked about it plenty."

"Could have been pure impulse," said Helen.

"Do they ever find these people who run away?"

"They do, but usually it's not finding. Usually it's a phone call from the person or a postcard. Finding can be hard."

"But he doesn't want to be found," said Star. "That's what's out of whack. Who wants toast?"

"I'll take two," said Herb. "What I hope is he's having a great time. Meanwhile, I'm in chemistry class wondering how the clock can be so slow."

"Time can be like that," said Helen.

"Chuck's good," said Star. "I can feel it. He's probably out there with some hippies who've moved to the country. They take in unhappy high school kids and let them be people with chores—tend the animals, make soup, split firewood."

"Grow pot," said Herb.

"Grow pot," echoed Star. She and Herb locked eyes in amusement. So did Daniel and Helen, but their eyes were not so amused. They had a conscientious objector and possible draft resister in the house. They might have a runaway. Or two.

Two of the Concerned /

"I've been meaning to ask you a question. And you don't have to answer if you don't want, because I don't want to be pushy. But I wonder: What did you do in the war?" Tom was seated on a folding chair beside Ray Moore. One or two nights a week, they had been getting together and talking.

"I served in the merchant marine. I didn't kill anyone, but I helped the war effort." Ray spoke to the air in front of him but then turned to face Tom. "Hitler was a menace, a nightmare, but the underlying issue—the endless preparing for war and believing in war—gets pushed to the side in the pell-mell, the which-side-are-you-on. I wanted to stand up and be counted, help out, but I didn't want to hold a rifle. A certain number of guys were like me, guys who could see both sides, the fighting and the not fighting." Ray was silent for some seconds. "I had a first cousin who enlisted in the Marines. He died in the South Pacific. We were close. Grew up together." More silence. "My family said it was my decision to make. Part of me feels that, as a Quaker, I failed, but part of me knows how hard it is to keep your head clear." Ray raised a closed hand, unfurled his thumb and then one by one his fingers, as if counting: "Blame, contempt, fear, prejudice, the herd instinct. For starters." He looked at his hand with unhappy wonder. "The hard human stuff. But the militarism, that's not a word you see in the newspapers or hear on TV. It's a given. We have armies and we fight wars. End of story. And I'll tell you: It may be the end of the story." Ray looked away. "The funny thing is, I liked being on the ship. Being with the other guys and taking care of things—'shipshape' came to make sense to me. And being on the ocean, the expanse of it. But then there's what's in the back of your head: your death, sunk by a U-boat. Drowning. Thinking about your death—it keeps you honest." Ray looked down at his fingers as if surprised. "Or it doesn't. You're young. You brag and pretend. I heard plenty of that."

"My dad fought in the war. He says he'll never get over it. He's sort of spent his life going back and forth about God. I don't mean an atheist, but more like going to church and then staying away, not going for months, sometimes almost a year, and then dropping back into it like he can't rid himself of God. Like there can't be enough doors for him to go in and out of. Like he wants more than the church is giving."

"These days it's easy to feel we're not worth much. If we don't have God, where does our dignity come from? Ball games? Movies? Automobiles? Shopping centers? You'd think Christ was talking out of the side of his mouth."

"I get it, what you just said, how it's like a quote that I wanted to read to you. You know me—I'm full of quotes. It's from A. J. Muste—who six months ago I didn't even know existed—but then, since he was a pacifist, why would I?" Tom unfolded a piece of paper on which he had typed some sentences and began to read: "'We live in a time when the individual is in danger of becoming a cipher. He is overwhelmed by the vast and intricate technological machinery around which his working life is organized, by the high-powered propaganda to which he is incessantly subjected, and by the state-machine on which he is increasingly dependent and by which he is increasingly regimented in peace and war. In the face of such circumstances the individual must be able to believe in his own essential dignity and in his ability to somehow assert it.' But then there's this too: 'Yet who among us is not stricken with shame by the knowledge that he, too, is holding back the price of complete commitment that God asks?'" Tom put the paper down. "You said it and he said it, and it pretty much says it for me. I'm going to quote it to the draft board."

Ray squinted, a scrutinizing habit, no matter what was in front of him. "Good thoughts, though I can't say what it will mean to the board. You'll have to speak to it, show them how it's you. But then Muste was always speaking to it, so you have his example. He took some serious grief. Traitor, commie, coward, those kind of words." He paused. "Back then, even though I came from Quakers, I wasn't ready for those words. To do what you're about to do, you have to be ready. People will criticize you, ostracize you, even despise you."

Tom refolded the piece of paper. "Sometimes I feel like I'm preparing for a debate. Everything is about action, fighting wars and making money, and I'm sitting in my bedroom with the *Handbook for Conscientious Objectors*. It's like I'm becoming invisible—Mr. Inward. Or like I'm a seed that's growing into a plant. A little out there for me to even tell you this. You know—pretentious. But I keep telling myself how there's this light, how that's real, or at least could be real. If anyone I used to know, guys from lacrosse or school, asked me what I was up to and I told them, they'd shake their heads and say, 'That's cool,' which means not cool at all, which means 'Man, you have gone around the bend.' But there's something in me that's always been around the bend."

"On your own?" asked Ray.

"We're a pretty tight family, but I've had this sense of what I needed to do since I was little. Even when I was doing what other people were doing. I get that now. About myself. Thinking for myself."

"This is where the script indicates that the older person should counsel, 'Don't be too idealistic.' But that's the last thing I would say to you."

"Good," said Tom.

Tom Is Found Out /

"I'm thinking," said Daniel, "that the story about your giving the letter to the doctor is totally a fabrication, that the army doesn't work that way. If a medical doctor says something, it's wise for any army doc to take it into account and not get the wires crossed later. I covered for you because it's your life. I assume you want to go all the way with the CO business, and the last thing you want is to bail out because of a lacrosse knee. Fair?" Daniel lowered his glass of Scotch onto a side table beside the living room sofa.

"Not much gets by you. Not easy to be your kid." Tom felt something inside himself melt, like being called into the principal's office in grade school. "Beyond 'it's your life,' what are you thinking?"

"That you're sincere and headstrong. That I'm glad I wandered into the Quaker meeting, because I could have wandered into most anything. I wouldn't say I was in despair, but, as you know, I haven't been feeling real good. I've been putting one foot in front of the other for so long that my feet do it automatically. It's like they're way ahead of my head and heart and looking back and calling, 'Hurry up.' But I can't hurry. And my war keeps coming up because whenever I see the faces of those young guys on TV, I can see myself and the guys I was with, some of whom were older but plenty who were kids and plenty who never made it home. Who died in some strange, nowhere place. Like these kids in Vietnam. That enough of an earful?"

"I can take more." Tom leaned forward in his seat, one of the wooden chairs that flanked the living room fireplace, well-used heirlooms from Daniel's paternal grandfather.

"The political stuff gets to me too. We have two men running against the war, but you don't have to be a newspaper sage to see that Humphrey has the delegate edge. And Nixon! Nixon is like someone back from the dead and eager to make the most of it. Lazarus at Disneyland! To me he's always looked like a vampire. All he needs is a cape. Not surprising how I feel things will get worse. More fighting, more napalm, more bombs, more civilians murdered. And my oldest son a candidate to be in the miserable middle of it."

"For what it's worth, I'm not upset. The war's upsetting, but my head feels like it's screwed on straight."

"You may be living in what's been called a fool's paradise." Daniel picked up his glass and drained it—a gulp more than a sip. "I shouldn't have said that. I apologize. Part of me wishes you just had used the letter and let your parents off easy." He tried to drink again but remembered there was nothing in the glass. "Parents can be as selfish as anyone."

"What can I say? I've changed."

"I appreciate that. And I believe you, as your father sitting here and listening to you. In the long run, you are right, and maybe in the short run too. If no one stands up, then what is there to stand up for? It's all just palaver. Selfishness. You can understand why I've been sitting in church the past two Sunday mornings, singing along and listening to the minister. Trying to get there and be there—something more than me. Trying to let myself trust." Daniel put his head in his hands.

"Dad?"

"You don't want to know."

"But I do."

"War ruins people. We go on, but war ruins people. There's a part of you that's lost, and you're never going to get it back. You make do and you say it's all right, because you don't have much choice. But what war puts into your life is this hole, this absence that's about the death you saw and how death could have taken you but didn't. You're lucky. But you don't feel lucky. You feel that what you cheated has cheated you, because you've seen how cheap life can be, how poor a body is." Slowly he picked his head up.

Tom wanted to turn away but didn't. His father wasn't crying, but his face was wrought, stricken with what Tom took to be grief.

"I won't tell anyone—beginning with your mother—about what you did. It would be too much. Maybe we'll all live through this and can talk about it then."

❧

Then They Chose /

Ruthie and Herb stood pondering the candy selection in High's, a local convenience store. A tiered riot of packaged choices faced them.

"We fool around and that makes you want to eat a candy bar?"

"Why not?"

"Just trying to understand the female mind."

"The female mind is chocolate, but I can't decide. There are too many candy words in my head like *luscious* and *nougat*." She reached to get a Snickers but picked up an Oh Henry! instead. "And you?"

"If I eat too much chocolate, my stomach gets wacko. Has to be the right amount." Herb continued to scan the racks. "It's like there's a river of chocolate out there. All these candy bars and then boxes like the Whitman's Star and I used to give our mom on Mother's Day until she politely told us she couldn't stand the stuff. Chocolate must come from Africa, huh?" He grabbed a 5th Avenue.

"A lot of these I've never tasted. Maybe I should be more adventurous." She took hold of one of Herb's shoulders and turned him toward her. "You'll let me have a taste, won't you?" She stuck her tongue out and waggled it. "I like what we did in the car." She waggled again. "It's easier, though, for me to stick my hand in your pants and make something happen than for you to stick your hand in my pants and make something happen. Like my fuse is slower. That must be one of the problems between men and women. You think so?"

"I'm thinking that I still have the smell of you on my hand and how I can eat a candy bar and taste you at the same time."

"You're not as polite as I thought you were. Ever eat a Chunky?"

"Many. When I was ten, I could have lived on them. That thickness, biting down on it. Raisins. Very satisfying."

A little boy clutching a coin in one hand walked up beside them.

"I think we need to decide."

"Haven't we already?"

On the way out, Ruthie pointed to a *Newsweek*. The cover showed some students picketing at Columbia University. The caption floating in the air above the students read "Student Protest."

"I read this issue when it came to our house," said Ruthie, "the usual pearls of journalistic blah-blah."

"You sound cynical."

"It's called 'intelligent.'"

One of the students in the photo held a handmade sign that read "Legality Is Not Morality." "Do you think," said Herb, "old people are getting sick of young people?"

"You know what old people want. They want young people to do as they're told. It's what we hear over and over." Ruthie opened her arms wide to show the voice's extent. "And it's the same warning: If you step out of line, bad things will happen. We're blowing up a country thousands of miles away, and people are bent out of shape because some college kids have taken matters into their own hands. It's like Star and me dealing with Mr. Klausmeyer. He can humor us and stall us as much as he chooses because he's the boss, and we're supposed to respect that. We're supposed to wait our turn, except we're not going to get a turn."

"It's not just here, though." They were walking side by side, close but not holding hands. "It's all over. Paris, London, Rome, Berlin, even Czechoslovakia."

"And we're here in lovely Baltimore, where we have the honor of attending high school. I can't wait to leave. I'd like to be there at Columbia. They could take my picture and identify me as 'a radical coed.'"

"When in fact you'd be an outside agitator." Herb paused to look up at a late-afternoon May sky of dark clouds—thunderstorm coming. "I think I'll make up a T-shirt that says, 'Outside Agitator.'"

Ruthie stopped beside the car—her mother's Dodge Dart, available for "four hours and no more than that."

"Let's get inside and agitate," said Herb.

Agitations of History /

"Taking the test, it felt," John Tobin hesitated, "odd. Nothing against our professor. Nothing against the university. I'm thankful I had the opportunity to take the course. But as I sat there and wrote, I kept thinking about how many lives were buried in my words, lives I would never know, lives that were caught in a phrase I learned, you know like *peonage*. How many?"

"You thought that?" Helen stood beside him outside the classroom where they had taken their final.

"Well, yes, I did. Some of the things we've learned, like having a 'double consciousness' about African Americans dealing with white people and then being who they were in the world of their own people; it almost seems as if I shouldn't know about that. Like intruding or spying."

"What do you mean? I don't quite get you." Helen felt the earnestness that was there between them, but that was—as John sometimes reminded her—for God too.

"It feels like I'm opening something up that I couldn't possibly understand, but I have to try." He looked away and down to the corridor floor as if distracted.

"Do you talk with anyone about this?" A wonderment came over Helen akin to some of her recent talk with Tom about his 'Quaker principles,' as he called them. What America was she living in? The United States of Conscience.

"Not really. I thought I could tell you, though." He looked up and squared his shoulders. It was as if, or so it seemed to Helen, he was always reporting for duty.

"I'm glad you told me, because I need to tell you how I felt, that what came up for me was the violence, the lynchings, the railroad cars bringing spectators, the cutting up of bodies and selling the pieces as souvenirs. How could the nation call itself 'civilized'? How can it now?"

"Maybe we should go outside. It's a nice day out there." John smiled his courtly smile.

Helen thought how many people he would help with just that smile. It beat any bible. "Let's," she said.

They wound up sitting on a cement bench under a dogwood tree. "I love the flowers," said Helen, "but I'm shook up inside. I filled up a blue book, but I could have written more. I felt inadequate. That's what you're saying, isn't it?"

"Sort of. I'm a changed person from when I walked in back in January. When my wife and I have children, if we have a boy, I want to call him 'Frederick' after Frederick Douglass."

Helen felt something seizing up inside her. Again, Tom appeared to her, his conviction that seemed to be growing daily. She laughed lightly. "I hope your wife agrees."

"She won't be the woman I should marry if she doesn't agree."

His determination surprised Helen. As she sat there, she could see a thousand vicissitudes to come in his life, but what did they matter? And what US history textbook was she going to find that mirrored much, if anything, of what she had been taught? She could see the cartoon of a black devil hovering over white women, the work of racist agitators at the beginning of the twentieth century. Poison, pure poison.

"Are you there, Helen? Maybe I spoke too strongly."

"I'd like to get my oldest son to meet you. I know you're busy with the school year ending, and you're going home soon. And my son is sort of preoccupied. I should have thought of it earlier."

John leaned over, picked up a pebble, then dropped it. "Kennedy's going to win in Nebraska. That's the center of America, the heartland. He can do it. I know it."

Helen thought of a body dangling from a rope. "I wish him well. I wish you well too." Once more, several worlds of feeling washed over her, leaving her bereft but alert.

Alerted Actions I

"They were Catholics. That surprised me. To go into a draft board office, take the files, and then set fire to them—that took guts."

Ray waited a few seconds. "Catholics don't have guts? You might want to talk it over with the Kennedys."

"I know I sound stupid." Tom stared, as if for guidance, at the bulletin board in the room where Ray and he met. A new announcement about a potluck dinner had appeared. "But that's what I've seen—going to school in those uniforms, being taught by nuns, and being super obedient; the pope and all; and sort of superstitious too, how they're always crossing themselves. But these people are deep Christians. They're saying, 'Wake up.'"

Ray pulled a cigarette from a pack in his shirt pocket.

"What do you think," asked Tom, "about what they did?"

"It's symbolic, but who knows? Maybe they saved some guys in those files. It may have been more than symbolic. That's not you, is it, in those files?"

"I'm in Towson not Catonsville. My files are safe for the time being. But say more. I need to hear."

"Fair enough. Sometimes I worry about the Friends, that we're not passionate enough about Christ's example. We're too good for our own good. Well-meaning. The Catholic to-do—all those crucifixes—seems excessive to me. But—" Ray lit his Winston with a match from a matchbook. "Maybe it's not excessive; maybe they take Christ to heart in ways I don't. And I'm speaking for myself to you. It's not like I'm Mr. Quaker speaking for all Quakers. But there's something messy in how the Catholics go in for all that gore, and maybe that's it. Christ is messy, and really following him is bound to be messy. He's the countervailing force. He's what society can't permit. He's the lost cause that's the first cause. I can imagine Christ standing there and praying with those people as they watched the draft files burn. That's a scene right out of the Bible. But it's now. And I have to say that stuns me."

"It's an act of violence, though, isn't it?" said Tom. "Coming in there like that, getting hold of what isn't theirs, and destroying it."

"Yeah, it was violent." Ray tapped some ash into a little metal pail that served as the communal ashtray. "But that's part of Christ's story—the violence done to him, our reckoning with violence. What you and I have been talking about. Would you do what they did?"

"No, but yes."

They both grinned, but sadly—the joke of it.

Tom went on. "I wouldn't, because it was violent and because it was what you said—a symbol."

"And applying to be a CO isn't a symbol?"

"No," said Tom. "It isn't. It's who I am now. That's not a symbol. It's me. But I get what they're doing, because they're frustrated and they've asked themselves what can they do? What would Christ do?"

"Stand by and wring his hands?" Ray asked.

314

"No," said Tom, "he wouldn't do that. He'd talk and show people how wrong the war is, how Caesar is always Caesar, making up worthless reasons. How killing appalls God."

"He'd talk on TV? After a Chevrolet ad? But before *The Beverly Hillbillies*?"

"I get you," said Tom. "That's a big hiccup, isn't it?"

"One of them." Ray made a harsh, wheezing sound. "I need to stop smoking. But I'll tell you one thing. Every day I wish Reverend King hadn't died. I don't know if any of us understand what we've lost." He exhaled, a thin jet. "He knew Christ was more than a bunch of miracles, that he was teaching us how to live. But I'm talked out for right now."

In the silence, both men felt how the questions remained, presences that might as well be in the room sitting on chairs. When did the need to act ignite a person? How much futility could a person live with? Where was the line between disobedience and wrongdoing? How far down the road did you walk with Christ's example? Tom thought of the priests and others setting fire to the draft files. Pretty far.

⚭

Far from Khe Sanh, Dien Bien Phu, Hue, Saigon, Hanoi /

Lyndon Johnson liked to refer to the United States as "the number-one nation." Conditioned as it was by the malign forces of fascism and communism, his avowal was understandable. And there was his patriotic love of his nation regardless of other nations. Yet the assertion was ridiculous, as if nations were like the *Billboard* Top 100. With a little imagination, the president could have conjured up the likes of Herb Brownson and Chuck Carranza discussing in mock-serious tones what nations were headed up and what nations were headed down on this week's chart: "Once more

Britain's antediluvian class system has kept it out of the Top 10, while Algeria, as it feels its independent oats, is moving into the Top 40. Don't overlook perennial, delivers-the-yen Japan."

Was his assertion necessary? Was it provable? How? Weren't there domains in which the United States notably lagged behind? Had he consulted with any Negroes about how they felt about his boast? To Lyndon there was no boast, just fact. All that American energy amounted to something the world had not seen before and that the world was bound to respect. That was one reason he wasn't about to lose a war. Number-one nations didn't lose wars.

A skeptical eye might have pitied Lyndon and his countrymen. They carried around an enormous burden and an enormous anxiety. Lyndon, in that sense, was the nation personified. He carried the burden of America's honor, the nation's longings for both material and moral betterment, while he carried all the dark secrets that weren't that secret: a vindictive oligarchy that had no use for the huddled masses, and those members of the masses who were free to indulge their racism. He trusted there would be enough money to throw at everyone, even the Negroes; but the war in Vietnam took a vast sum, more than anyone wanted to look at, although the manufacturers of the helicopters, chemicals, rifles, and the endless supply needs of a distant army did not mind. They kept their heads down and their adding machines warm.

"Insecurity" was the psychological term that might have been applied to Lyndon and his need to be first. His teenage years had been hard. The opportunities he seized, to say nothing of manipulated, showed to him the number-one-ness of the United States. But at what cost? What was being proved? Who cared? What of the life of art and spirit that could not be measured and that wanted encouragement of a very different sort, the nurturing of sensibility and individuality? Was America number one in that department? After World War II, the CIA did assert that: America's cultural achievements showed the success of the so-called American way of life. Abstract expressionist painters who had worked in poverty and obscurity were trumpeted as signs of cultural prosperity. Irony be damned.

Art, baseball, Wall Street, Hollywood, automobiles: America had it all. Number One. No wonder the war in Vietnam ate Lyndon up. So much was in place in his mind and in the nation that his mind reflected. So much seemed to be working. How hard it was to believe that somehow America could fail, that there might be a lack of understanding, that mere willfulness could enter into what seemed unassailable calculations and rock-hard beliefs. How dare anyone pose a question?

But many did. The impulse to brand them as bad Americans, people who weren't part of the number-one-ness, tempted Lyndon, but he was not a demagogue. Even though people had been left out, as started to dawn on him when the Civil Rights Movement refused to die down, he believed in the emotional breadth of the nation. There was room to work everything out. He despised the narrowness of Nixon, who believed you had to marginalize some people so that others, more like-minded people, could live as they—orderly, law-abiding Americans—were meant to live. Negroes, hippies, and the poor could be neglected and, to be frank, persecuted via drug laws and avoidance of financial help. Why pretend, according to Nixon, that all Americans were good Americans? The Red Scare that had fueled Nixon's early career showed that. There were true-blue, real Americans, and there were the undesirables. Take your pick.

Lyndon Johnson resisted that equation, but he still inherited a war that wasn't winnable on any terms that would have meant anything. America was embracing air in Southeast Asia, an empty yet bloody gesture. Reams of earnest words went up in acrid smoke. What if number one was a curse more than a blessing, what if the hero was not a hero? Unthinkable and impossible and yet . . .

Yet Honesty Remains /

"Knock, knock."

"Who's there?"

"Harry."

"Harry who?"

"Harry up and let me in."

Tom opened his bedroom door. "Nice you still remember that one."

Star knocked on his chest. "I've got more, but I'll spare you."

"Welcome to the reading room. I can clear some space on the bed."

"I'll stand. Better for my posture. I've been known to slouch."

"A family failing. How goes it?"

"School sucks, although it could be worse, but I never know what that means—like it's not the Third Reich, so it's okay. But why I came knocking is that I want to know what's with this woman you're seeing. Who is she? How did you meet her? You're kinda secretive. And as your sister and repository of female wisdom, I thought I should know. Before you head out the door to wash dishes and go wherever you go afterward."

"Some nights I go to a cafeteria downtown and watch who comes through the door. I'll take you sometime. Baltimore at its demented best. But this woman is hard to summarize."

"I'm patient. I sit in school all day. They make us good at it."

"You know, I wasn't crazy about high school either. But this woman is someone you and I would never cross paths with, because she lives in the great lost sprawl of Baltimore. Which is somewhere very definite to her. Anyhow, she's a waitress, has a kid that I like, and we sort of click. She doesn't hold much back, and I like that too. She's not going through the motions, the way I felt at college how everyone was going through the motions, trying to do the right thing, get along, give the answer."

"Do you think I'd like her?"

"I don't know. She's different. There can't be too many hippie-chicks in her neck of the woods. It's still the 1950s there, but she's open. And I know you're open."

"I can't be open enough. I gotta get out of here. I love Mom and Dad, but I'm ready to leave tomorrow. I don't know how I can handle next year."

"You'll do it."

"That's just male bullshit."

Tom grinned. "Could be."

"I'd like to meet her."

"I don't see myself bringing her here. That would be a little weird. But, yeah, we could get together with you."

"Now I need to ask the big question: Where are you at?"

"Pretty peaceful. That sounds like a pun Herbie would make. What happens, happens. I'm not going, and I'm not running away. I played the part when I went to the doc and gave the army the letter about my knee and they decided I'm good enough. Who knows? But the more I read and think and talk with this guy, Ray, the more I'm convinced."

"What's that mean?"

"You always did ask the hard questions. I don't know. It's not like I was going into bars and starting brawls. Probably it means I need to go somewhere and do what the Quakers teach, let silence into my life and trust the inner light."

"That sounds good, but things could get hairy. Jail is 'somewhere,' and jail is hairy."

"You sound like Mom."

"There's worse people to sound like, but I wonder if I could do what you're doing. I think we all do. Does this woman you're seeing get what you're doing?"

"She lost her husband to the war. She believes in America, but she's starting to believe in herself, which means not so much believing in America."

"She's torn up inside?"

"Not many years ago, she was your age. Since then I'd say she's felt more than she wanted to feel."

"Seems to be a lot of that going around these days." Star looked at the books on the bed and then her brother. "You better get out of your boxers if you want to wash dishes."

Verbal Dishes for the Physical Feast /

"You ever notice how you always come to my house and I never go to yours?"

"Think it has something to do with your son sleeping peacefully in the bedroom down the hall and our being in bed together?"

"You're a wiseass, you know that? You act all light and good, all that conscience you got, but you're just another wiseass."

"You think so?" Tom turned to Sharlene and propped himself up on an elbow. He felt that deliciously drained, after-sex feeling. He'd never met such a very determined body.

"You take me seriously, don't you? I could cry about that. How everyone would tell me I was just shooting my mouth off: 'Shut up, Sharlene.' But there's something right in you. When you were a little kid, your mamma must have loved you plenty. What's her name?"

"Helen."

"That's a nice name."

"Actually, it is, but maybe I take you for granted. We sort of fell into each other's arms and maybe since I'm just hanging out in time and space and full of these big thoughts—what I call my 'peace and war folder'—maybe I haven't thought enough about you. I mean how you feel when I'm not with you, who you are."

"Jesus, where did you get your head?" Sharlene raised herself up against the bed's wooden headboard. She had told Tom how she and her husband had bought it at one of the "Jew furniture stores downtown." "I wonder what the government is gonna make of you."

"When you sit like that, your breasts drive me crazy."

"That's what they're supposed to do. And I'm not pulling a sheet over myself. Look all you want." She started to smile prettily but stopped. "Are you afraid?"

"I feel good in myself. The war's leaning on me, but I'm leaning back. Why should I be afraid?"

"My husband kept telling me he wasn't afraid; even when I didn't say anything, he kept telling me he wasn't afraid. That must have meant he was afraid. But he couldn't tell me because I was a woman, and a man can't tell a woman that because then he's not a man anymore." Sharlene bowed her head. "A whole world of sad shit. I try to keep it away, but I don't know. I really don't."

"Hey, not so bad." Tom reached over and touched her shoulder.

"You don't understand. I have this little boy and I want him to have a life, and that means not having a mamma who's some kind of ten-pound weight on him. I need to pick myself up, but there's shadows over me. I mean, my husband dying over there and how I'd already given up on him and he'd given up on me. It makes me disgusted with myself, like I shouldn't even be allowed to live."

"Easy does it."

"You're young. It's not like I'm an old lady, but I've already been through crap you couldn't begin to know, stuff that splits a person apart. Even though I feel your hand, and I love your hand because you're sweet and God knows I want that sweetness, I'm still off in my own country, Where-Sharlene-Got-More-Lost-Than-Found."

"Have a postal address?"

"Fuck off, honey."

"You know my hand can't stop at your shoulder."

"I do know. Some things just keep on rolling, don't they?"

"'Gin a body kiss a body / Need a body cry?'"

"What the hell are you saying?"

"It's from a Scots poem I came across. Robert Burns. From a book in our house. You know, when I'm not reading about God and everything. Though God made us bodies not just spirits, so He understood. This poem gets very naughty."

Sharlene inched over. "Tell me, lover boy. I can take it."

∾

It Doesn't Get Easier /

The minister's secretary, a suitably dowdy woman in a cardigan though it was a warm, June-just-around-the-corner morning, looked up at Daniel from the pile of what seemed to be letters on her desk. "Is the minister expecting you?"

"No, but I was in the neighborhood. I'm thinking of buying a house around here, and I'd like to chat with him if he has the time. I know it's the spur of the moment, but some moments are like that."

The woman said nothing.

322

"I like churches too. I like going into churches. Too bad most of them aren't open every day. What my teenage kids call 'the vibe.'"

Her muted brown eyes expressing doubt, she got up, knocked on the door that led to the minister's sanctum, went in for some seconds, then emerged to tell Daniel that though Reverend Hall was a busy man, he would be glad to meet Mister . . . "What did you say your name was?"

"I didn't, but the name is Brownson, Daniel Brownson. And thanks."

Her eyes continued to bestow doubt on Daniel—what dubious errand was this man on? But, attempting a polite smile, she waved him in.

The minister, a balding, unprepossessing man of sixty or so, was also wearing a cardigan. He motioned to a chair beside his desk. "Glad to meet you, Mister?"

"Brownson. Daniel Brownson. I appreciate your making time for me."

"I'm glad to. It's not every day someone comes in off the street to talk to me. I don't know if that's my failing or the society at large. I know it's not Christ's. What brings you to my office today?"

"As I told your secretary, I'm thinking of buying a house in this neighborhood and, as I told your secretary, I like to go to churches—"

"Any churches?"

"Well, I've mostly been a Presbyterian, and that's where I am right now. But recently I went to some Quaker meetings, and I've spent time praying with several denominations. You know how churches have a sign on the lawn that says, 'Everyone welcome.' I take that sign seriously. I'm not promiscuous, though. Far from it. I'm just a serious dabbler. Ecumenical."

Reverend Hall looked at Daniel with unfeigned curiosity. "That's interesting Mr. Brownson. I can't say I've met too many people with your approach. Mostly folks just find a congregation and settle down there." His words were measured, those of a longtime sermonizer.

"I can appreciate that, but I figure God comes in all sizes. In one way we're all on the same page as Christians, but then we're not. There are all these wrinkles. It's not as though I think God is following me around, especially since part of what I do for a living is about keeping an eye on people, but I like to think my attitude pleases Him. Good to be open. Good to soak up the Gospel wherever you find it."

"Have you always had this approach?"

Daniel leaned in closer to the minister, which caused the minister to lean back. "I was in World War II and saw the usual hell. I didn't lose my faith. I'm not like that. But I got shook up inside. When I hear a new minister or choir, I feel there are people out there, people I never met, who believe and are standing by it. That feels good because, to tell you the truth, and you're a minister, so I can tell you the truth, I have my shaky moments. And this war now, this Vietnam . . ." Daniel trailed off.

"What about the war?"

"Please don't tell me you're some true-blue patriot who believes that God blesses people killing people."

"Well, no, I'm not. But there are just wars. World War II was certainly a just war."

"I'd say so. But this war isn't a just war. It's a big nation trying to prop up a nation that is barely a nation while another nation is trying to reunite what once was a whole nation." Daniel paused. "I can't believe I said that so clearly."

"But it's complicated."

Daniel got up abruptly, his chair scraping the linoleum floor. "Actually, no. It's not. No one's talking 'complicated' in the Bible. Jesus doesn't say to the disciples, 'It's complicated.' I don't mean to be impolite, but good day, sir." Daniel strode through the minister's anteroom, nodding briskly to the minister's secretary, then through a hallway, then out the church's side door and down a gravel path to a small parking lot. He had acted badly, but all the top-heavy generalities—history, time, the world—coalesced in one semi-thoughtful word that blunted his soul and could steal away one of his sons.

There was God and there were people: How much he yearned for a One that could overcome the many.

∽

Many Rivers to Cross /

"You notice that evil-eyed waitress is gone? Must have moved back to Alabama." Reggie moved his plate of fries to the center of the table. "Have some. Not too many, just some."

"I'm surprised she didn't leave a note for you." Tom reached for the ketchup.

"Go easy there with the red stuff. But yeah, who knows? I may have been the man of her dreams."

"As my Jewish grandma would say, 'She should be so lucky.'"

"How's your luck? You hear from the government?"

"I go for my hearing the second week of June."

"You nerved up?" Reggie picked up a salt shaker.

"I'm looking forward to it. A chance to tell them how I feel and who I am."

Reggie tipped slightly to the side and gave Tom his best eyebrows-lifted, humorous appraisal. "Sometimes, I can't believe white people, which, by the way, is you. There's not a black person in this country who would look forward to explaining themselves to anyone in the government about anything. Black folks would not bet a penny on anyone sitting there and actually listening. You know, really listening, and nodding and maybe a little smoke over their heads to show they were doing something called 'thinking.' Oooh-weee!" Reggie exclaimed. "That's not gonna happen till the cow jumps over the moon."

"You think I'm naive."

"I'm not one for name calling. You are who you are. You showed me some of the best shots on goal I ever saw. Barely could see the ball. But I like to hear about this stuff you're reading and feeling, how God's talking to you through this one and that one. I told you my own life is shifting. But going to tell these people about your objections, that's just not how a black person would look at it. It's like the two candidates—McCarthy and Kennedy—and even though McCarthy is against the war, he feels just so white, like I could never know what goes on in his head, where Kennedy seems not black—I wouldn't go that far—but he seems like he gets it. He gets that there's been a ton of white folks who have never listened and another ton who have pretended to listen, standing around until some black man said his piece and then said, 'Git.'"

"I didn't know you were following the primaries."

"I'm not. What's it to me? It's everything because of the war, but I'm staying in school, and then I'll see what happens. They gotta end it one of these days, because pretty much everyone knows we're throwing good money after bad, letting more of our guys die, more of those people over there die. Damn." Reggie pulled the straw out of his glass but didn't pick up his Coca-Cola.

"I've been following them. Everyone in our house is."

"They're always selling some kind of promise, aren't they?" Reggie twirled his straw a bit, conductor-like.

"Easier for me than for you?"

"What do you think?"

"I think easier. But there's got to be some kinda light out there. Somewhere."

"You see what they did to Martin."

"Yeah, I do."

"Well, I expect the grief will keep coming. Could be that's too black, like in black-folks black, but could be not."

"That's why I want to speak at my hearing. Whatever happens, I'm standing up."

"You're a little simple, but you're one good man. I'm gonna cross my unlucky fingers for you." Reggie reached across the table and gave Tom a tap on the arm. "You're giving reality a run for its money."

~

The Reality of the Runaway /

"I got a letter from Chuck." Herb was washing; Star drying. Helen was at the kitchen table writing a to-do list on one of the short, unlined pads she favored.

"Wow. Where is he?" Star and Helen blurted the same words at the same time.

"The postmark was from some little town in Vermont. I looked it up in the atlas. It's hard to believe he got there from here."

"And what's happened to him?" Helen mouthed the words as Star said them.

"He's the 'mascot,' as he put it, of a commune. He just put his thumb out and decided to go where the rides took him. He wound up meeting some guy who was headed to this place, and the guy said they could use another set of hands. He's doing stuff like learning to bake and planting a garden. Hippie stuff."

"Just what I thought would happen," said Star. "It's like an underground railroad."

Helen stopped writing. "Are you going to tell his parents?"

"Somehow, I thought you might ask that." Herb turned off the faucet and faced his mother. "I don't have a return address. All I have are some sentences in Chuck's tiny, squiggly handwriting. He seems happy. Why should I contact the people he ran away from?"

"Because they're his parents."

"Mom," said Star. "You say the most ridiculous things sometimes. They're not God. They're two people who didn't do right by their son, no matter what they thought they were doing. He made a decision. Shouldn't we respect that?"

"I hope you two don't run away. I'd fall over."

"As long as you keep making that roast beef you made tonight," said Herb, "I'm sticking around."

"That's a very qualified response," said Helen. "I take it that you two don't buy what I'm saying about his parents, how they are probably sick with worry. I may call them up."

"That's your business," said Herb. "I just thought you two would like to know that I heard from my old pal. Hundreds of bus rides together. And he wrote one other thing."

"Which is?" asked Star. She placed the dish towel on her head as if it were a kerchief, put a finger on her chin, and moved one leg forward—all pert attentiveness. "Bet I can guess."

"Okay."

"He's getting laid. Am I right?"

"What do you think, Mom? Is she brilliant or what? No wonder they want to expel her from school. She knows too much." Herb reached for the dish towel, but Star moved away.

"This is where I go back to thinking about whether I need to buy more canned tuna," said Helen.

"Depends if it's on sale," said Herb.

"Depends if your family has had enough tuna wiggle," said Star. "I'm glad Chuck is getting some. He was kind of a geek, but he was cool too, how he could do those Lenny Bruce routines."

"So, as Chuck's best friend, it takes one to know one. But yeah, I'm glad. You know that song Cream does: 'I'm so glad, I'm so glad, I'm so glad.'" Herb executed a modest, one-foot-slightly-dragging shuffle across the kitchen floor as he crooned the words of an old bluesman.

"How can I think?" asked Helen, raising her pencil and pointing it at her son.

"How does anyone think?" said Star. "Badly."

"But it doesn't stop us from trying," added Herb. "Meanwhile, here's to Chuck." He lofted an unwashed glass. Star threw the dish towel at him; Helen went back to her list.

∾

A List of Tribulations Is Presented and Discussed /

What did Ho Chi Minh, an old, frail yet indomitable man, the epitome of armed revolution, make of someone like A. J. Muste—a dedicated Christian pacifist, famous for declaring there was no way to peace, that peace was the way—when Muste showed up on his doorstep in Hanoi in 1966 with two other clergymen? He was "received warmly," according to the press accounts. Previously, South Vietnam had received Muste coldly. Did the Christian look down at Ho's hands extended in greeting and see the blood on them—blood that was part of what the Vietnamese had the right to consider a never-ending struggle? Did he understand that for Ho, to avoid the struggle, to put one's head down and bear the weight of oppression, was impossible. Nations understood war. The United States, where Muste hailed from, had been forged in a war. To live a life where a person was demeaned for being who he or she was, a speck to be flicked off a cuff without a moment's hesitation—was that tolerable? What peaceful words could make that bearable?

329

Ho had spent a lifetime reading people—betrayal was always around the corner—and Muste had been, and was, a revolutionary in his way. Was that way hopelessly impracticable, a contrivance, a delusion, a relic of spirit to be tossed aside by the vanguard of Marxist-Leninism that Ho espoused? Ho's soldiers had killed many Catholics. They were "reactionaries" and a bevy of other epithets. They were oppressors, and if they didn't understand what they were doing to others, if they had been born into a milieu and faith that suited them and that they expected to go on for something like forever, then they were terribly wrong, and the soldiers who showed up at their houses in Hue with orders to "remove" them were only showing them that history had a right side and a wrong side. Guns enforced those sides.

Ho told Muste to approach Lyndon Johnson and tell him that Ho would be glad to receive Johnson in Hanoi and talk peace. When Muste came back to the United States, he wrote Johnson but never received a reply. Why would Johnson write back? Muste was off the map, some maverick minister who would be labeled a pinko by any self-respecting Republican congressman and many a Democrat. Ho knew that, but he must have enjoyed making the gesture. The great nation's president could visit the small nation's president. Ho knew the presidents of great nations didn't do that. Probably Muste knew that too, but he wrote Johnson because he was dogged, decent, and committed. No one made him go to Hanoi. He had a Christian conscience.

Muste was on the wrong side, yet Ho could respect him, a man even older than Ho, who had made such a long journey in the beleaguered name of peace. As an American, Muste could not understand the enormity that Ho had faced down, not just the power of two great Western nations but also the doubt that would lurk in the heart of anyone who had taken on what seemed an impossible task—ridding a nation of its powerful exploiters. Ho had his shifting backers in the communist world and knew how the nation game was played, that nations did not have consciences. Yet here was this Christian showing up in Hanoi, making a case for the sanctity of peace.

Listening was supposedly an Asian virtue, one Ho was willing to indulge. Muste was not a dupe, however, and Ho, who knew something about belief, would have been alert to the spark inside this man who had neither pretenses nor ideology, who sincerely believed in something so simple, so foreign to the fierce determinism of Marxism. The Christ that Muste upheld, but did not aggressively preach, was a very different sort of revolutionary, one who believed the upheaval began in the individual and ended there. To Christ, the Marxist belief in uniting the masses was meaningless. Souls did not belong to masses; souls belonged to individuals. But who could see a soul? Who could weigh a soul? How many divisions did the soul have in its army? The soul could be dismissed, and in the course of the twentieth century, it was.

People who persevere are uncommon. Blandishments can turn a person's head aside, accommodations, entitlements both major and minor. Or a person can simply say "no more"—exhausted, disillusioned, disgusted. What had Muste and his pacifism accomplished amid the bloody agonies of modern times? Ho could have taunted him, but Ho was resolute not fanatic. Given the exigencies of history and power, any wager on Muste was implausible. Yet the man would not give up.

Perhaps Johnson never saw the letter or someone crumpled it up and threw it away before it ever reached him or Johnson did see it and he crumpled it up. Peace be damned—which was where peace wound up, among the damned, as Ho knew too well.

Well-Wished, Dashed against the Rocks, but Rescued /

Helen reached under Daniel's pajama top and gave his back a nudge. He was a deep sleeper, possessed as he had told her more than once of an "untroubled conscience," which she told him more than once was the mark of a scoundrel. She nudged again harder.

"What time is it? Something wrong?" His voice was suitably hazy. He turned around to face her.

"It's around three. I wouldn't say something is wrong but it's not right, and I need to talk."

Daniel rubbed his eyes. "I was having some kind of dream. There were horses in it."

"You can go back to dreamland soon enough, but I'm not sure I should take the job that was offered to me."

"Because? I thought we went over this."

Helen turned onto her back and spoke to the ceiling. "Because when I asked the head of the department what textbook the school used, he said—and I quote—'What does it matter?' I don't find that reassuring. I didn't go through all this degree work to be subservient to a nameless textbook."

"Maybe he meant that textbooks are a necessary evil."

Helen stared at the ceiling. Their house was one of those mock-Elizabethan constructions builders went in for in the 1920s; the plaster ceiling was partitioned into squares by dark wooden strips. "Maybe. But maybe he meant my job is just to teach chapter 23, and one chapter 23 is as good as another."

"Maybe he's right."

"I knew you'd say that. You're so accepting."

"I praise your cooking every night."

"Don't be a lug. I'm upset. I want to tell the students things I've learned that aren't in any textbook. Black people barely exist in textbooks."

"Give the publishers time. They'll fix it. That's their job, right? To keep up."

"Did I ever tell you that you have an answer for everything? Did I ever tell you that drives me crazy?"

Daniel reached over and put a hand on Helen's chest. "Is this one of those times?"

"I'll call him up and talk with him. I can always withdraw."

"It doesn't look great. You signed a contract, didn't you?"

"To hell with contracts. And don't start telling me, 'as a lawyer.'"

"I wouldn't think of it. Anything else bugging you?" His hand moved onto a nipple.

"Watch that, buster. And yes, have you noticed that neither of your high school–age children is going to the prom?"

"So what? It's just a night when they go to a party and drink too much and make their parents nervous, and usually some girl gets pregnant. We can all do without it."

"Sharon stays in her room and writes and listens to music, as if that's all there is to do in the world. She hasn't gone on a date since I don't know when."

Daniel's hand began a soft, circular motion. "Your son Herbert is in love as far as I can tell. One out of two; that's not a bad percentage."

"You're Mr. Positive, aren't you? Going to put an end to the war today? I'm demented with worry about Tom, you know that."

"I do. I'm not immune."

"And all we can do is write our letters in support of his case and wait. I hate it."

"I'm not crazy about it either, but he's in good spirits. You can see that."

"He's got some kind of girlfriend too. Sharon's going to meet her."

"More power to him. What's life without women?" He increased the pressure ever so slightly.

"You're incorrigible."

"It beats dreaming about horses."

⬿

The Wild Horses of Feeling Will Not Be Corralled /

"What a sweet little boy."

"When he sleeps," said Sharlene.

Travis, who was building a tower out of wooden blocks, sat on the kitchen floor beside Star. Carefully he placed block upon block until the tower toppled over. He chuckled briefly with pleasure at its fall and then started building again.

"I want to have lots of kids," said Tom. He sat beside Sharlene on one of her kitchen chairs. The chairs were metal with pink Naugahyde seats and could have come from the diner. He'd gotten to like them.

"Let's hope your wife agrees." Sharlene winked at him. "I've got an announcement, by the way. I'm sort of rich. My husband had an insurance policy, and I've gotten some money. It took forever, but I can go to school in the fall and not worry."

Star looked up from Travis's handiwork. "That's great. Congratulations."

"Me too. Congratulations," said Tom. "You deserve it."

"I do and I don't. It doesn't bring him back in the important way, but in another way it does bring him back, which spooks me. Like he knew what was coming and had this policy." Sharlene reached for a cigarette from the pack of Newports on the kitchen table. "Anyone want one, which means you, Star, since Tom has given up most vices, though not all." She

334

smiled very slightly. "I wanted to smoke pot, but Tom tells me he's stopped. Just my luck to meet a do-right."

"He's getting awfully clean," said Star "I'm proud of him, though."

"I'm thinking well of him too. I just wanted to see what pot is like."

"I can help you out," said Star.

"I'll take you up on it." Sharlene lit up with a lighter. There were three lying around in the kitchen, which Tom had pointed out to her might not the best idea with a child around. She had told him to keep his opinions to himself.

"If I can speak for myself, ladies—"

"Nice lady," Travis announced and pointed to Star. "Nice lady." He took a swipe at his tower and over the blocks went. "Making throuble," he said.

"You can speak, Tom. Go for it." Sharlene touched her hair. Recently, she had stopped using hair spray. As she had noted to Tom, "Now I'm three inches shorter."

"I'm still who I was," said Tom. "I'm just more who I wasn't."

"You're so damn deep," said Sharlene. "Speak English."

"You asked for it."

"I did, but I'm a woman. I didn't mean it. Right, Starflower? God, I love your name. I'm gonna do that too." She paused. "I think of that insurance policy, and I go to pieces."

"He made a decision," said Tom. "I'm making a decision. Sometimes the weight is real."

Everyone watched as Travis carefully laid one block on another. They were alphabet blocks. He was putting N on T.

"You know how my husband died," Sharlene said to Star, "over there in the war. His name was Tom too. Isn't that strange? Of course lots of guys are named Tom, so it's not strange at all." She placed her cigarette in a glass ashtray with an Elks Club insignia on it. "What I'm getting at is how the big world keeps coming at us, day and night, and we sit here in my kitchen and talk. But the world never slows down, and we can't do a thing about that. It's something we have to live with, even if we don't want to. And I didn't understand that. I just thought I was flying around in my own airplane. Even when he went to Vietnam. Did I betray him? Or did he betray me? And why am I telling this to someone I've known for a half hour? I'm sorry."

"Don't be." Star was watching Travis, who had reached the fifth block, the level where the tower often tumbled. "I don't know. I want to change the big world. Because if it doesn't change, I don't see how I can live in it."

Travis observed his effort. No wobble. He considered another block.

"We always seem to wind up in a place like this," said Sharlene. "In back of the house of broken dreams."

"You," said Tom as he got up, "need to take poetry writing when you go to college in the fall." He went over to Sharlene, placed a hand on her head, which he pulled back gently, then leaned over and kissed her full on the lips, a popping, plopping sound.

Travis clapped his hands. Star joined in. Properly weighted, the tower of blocks stayed upright.

June

CORNERED BY THE UNSPEAKABLE

Upright Discourse while Pursuing Mundane Tasks /

"That's a lot of paint on your brush, kiddo," said Daniel.

"That's how I paint. Loaded." Star and Daniel were painting wooden lawn chairs. "Ancients," said Daniel when they started scraping and sanding, "but I'm not throwing them out."

"Fresh air. You can't beat it." Daniel paused and took a vigorous inhale.

"You always say the most Dad things. It's reassuring."

Another inhale. "I wouldn't want to disappoint."

"So, did you ever go to a Memorial Day parade? I know it's a big deal for some guys and I wondered, maybe you went before I was born or when I was little."

"The short answer is no. Some people—and I understand them— want to honor what they did. But I wanted to put it in a drawer and leave it there. You can't do that, of course. Your head isn't a drawer, but going out in public, that was way more than I could handle or even want to handle." Daniel dipped his brush in the white paint. "I don't like parades. I'd rather we saw a guy sitting on the curb crying. That would be better than any parade."

"Thanks," Star looked up from the chair and at her father. "You've always told me the truth."

"Oh, I don't know if I'm that good," and Daniel laughed.

They painted silently for a while.

"How are you doing in school?"

"I was waiting to see what topic you'd choose. Let's say that I'm trudging along. I don't like it, but I'm trudging. Sort of a good soldier."

"Ouch, that hurts." Daniel waved his brush a bit.

"Don't spatter," said Star. "Are you and Mom looking at houses? Mom's said she's open to moving. She'd be sad, but she said she can grow roses in some other yard."

"Your mother's quite the amenable soul. One more reason why I love her. We've looked together a few times, and I've looked around on my own. You know me—a looker and a poker. I've seen a couple places in the city that are in the ballpark. Summer's the time to move. It would be closer to work for me. For your Mom it would be sort of a reverse commute if she takes the job they offered her."

"I thought she was."

"I did too, but she's had some second thoughts. I'm afraid the school where your mother would like to teach may not exist yet."

"I guess I'm in that category as a student. But there's got to be better than what I've got."

Daniel turned a chair over to paint under the armrests. "The California primary looks as though it's going to be close."

"Another topic switch. You're so good at it. But it does look close. I'm still for Gene, but I have to say I've grown to like Bobby. He seems so alive. And he really likes people. You feel that. It doesn't seem that way with Gene. He's sort of distant, sweet but distant, thoughtful. It's not like Bobby's a dope, but he's sort of right there in front of you. You see all those people around him, and you can feel the excitement."

"Sounds as though you should write something for the paper."

"I've written my last piece. Ruthie and I turned it over to two of next year's juniors. I'm just writing in my diary these days. But you mean I'm being articulate. Thanks. Just trying to keep up my end of the conversation. I can't say I have anything constructive to say about Hubert Humphrey, however. Herb thinks Hubert has it in the bag."

"Your brother may be right. He often is."

"He's in love, so some of his head is definitely elsewhere."

"Your best friend and your brother, how does that feel?"

"Maybe I should become a matchmaker, but I didn't do anything. It just happened. Ruthie had her eye on him. And you know Herb—smart but socially oblivious."

"Unlike his sister who's smart and very un-oblivious."

"You got that one." Star looked over her handiwork. "I could do this for a living. Maybe I will."

℞

The Will unto Death /

As the first one up, Herb wanted to see who had won the primaries, especially California. He switched on the TV and then howled a long "No!"

He repeated the word, the same agonized howl, then fell to his knees as if struck. "No," he said in a lower voice, as if begging. "No." He struck the floor with both fists. "No," he moaned.

Daniel, Helen, and Star, who were up and stirring, ran downstairs. Tom heard his brother, got out of bed, and followed the others. There was the TV with its images and Herb's word. They looked at one another, hollow-eyed, then staggered toward the couch and chairs, too frightened and appalled to even clutch one another, too pushed into themselves. Herb remained on the floor, still hunched over.

"I can't believe it," said Helen. "I can't. It's impossible." Though her voice was distinct, she was talking to herself more than to the others.

Herb lifted his head. "But you can. Ever since his brother died, you can believe anything."

"But I can't," said Star. "Because this is too much. Like some evil is loose that won't go away, that's going to kill us all."

Daniel stared at the screen, the kitchen where the assassination had occurred, the man in custody, the reporters' strained faces. "It's hard to speak, to see the point of anything, like after Reverend King's murder. All it takes is a trigger." He kept staring. "And we all fall down."

"But isn't this what we're used to? I mean the killing," said Tom. "How many Westerns have I watched? Cops and robbers? War movies? And how I played as a boy. Bang, bang, you're dead." The TV spoke about updates.

"He's still alive," said Helen.

"But he won't live," said Tom. "I hate to say that, but it's like a play; and in the play, Robert Kennedy would die because John Kennedy died. He would die because America breeds vigilantes."

"Maybe he won't die," said Star. "You don't know."

"I don't but I do. This is an old story, but here, in America, it's our story, because deep down we don't want to get along with one another, because we aren't real to one another, because the great examples like Christ don't matter to people unless He's saving them and getting them to heaven. But they don't want to hear what He's saying about how to live, because that would get in their way."

"Maybe we shouldn't talk now," said Helen.

"Maybe," said Tom, "but I'm not just angry. I'm bitter because I really don't understand this place. America. Killing him like this, some guy in a kitchen with a gun, it's like a human sacrifice. Why do we think we are any better than the Mayans sacrificing people to the Sun God. Haven't we sacrificed Bobby? And how many others? How come we won't look at ourselves in the mirror? How come?" He started crying, a deep shake in his chest.

Softly, Star started crying. So did Helen.

Herb had his bowed head in his hands. Daniel went over to the TV and turned it off.

"They'll operate, and we'll hear later," he said.

For an amount of time that was hard to tell, because once again time seemed to have vanished, they were silent, a tableau in their living room, five characters not in search of anything, but bound to the wheel of events.

"This goes into my hearing next week. I don't care what they do, but I'm going to talk about Bobby." Tom wiped at his tears with the back of a hand. "I'll get some tissues."

He came back and put the box near his sister and mother. Herb still had his head down. Daniel opened a window to the quiet morning.

"I'm going to make coffee," said Helen. "I need it. Badly."

No one answered. For her this shooting was another confirmation of what she had been studying—how, as Tom said, people are sacrificed. How many times can you be battered, while sense and senselessness go back and forth? Do you give up? Do you become immune, indifferent, a shadow of a person? Do you find reasons? She could almost feel the broken pieces inside her, the insult to hope. She seemed at the end of words. A vast, humbling blankness. Perhaps—because everything felt "perhaps," felt equivocal, compromised, and uncertain—what she felt was akin to Daniel's God craving, some improbable yet beckoning depth, some wisdom steeped in suffering. She would ask him on another day.

The Day of the Train /

When the funeral train passed through, Daniel herded his family into his car and drove to east Baltimore. On the way, no one talked except for Star, who announced, as they waited at a red light, that she was Sharon "again" and that "Starflower died." No one replied. Each of them was like a wary animal, cornered by the unspeakable, staring out at the bricks and mortar, the other cars, the pantomime of dailiness.

Once there, they stood near the train tracks among a waiting crowd of whites and blacks, people of all ages. There, too, no one spoke. Everyone knew that everyone else felt the same—that was why they were there. Everyone knew they had come to honor the dead man and his family. Everyone knew there was no expiation, but by bearing witness, each person was acknowledging that he or she had been touched and that such touching mattered. In the background, the row houses, storefronts, and warehouses torched in April stood mute. If the buildings had voices, they might have said that it was easy to see how all this feeling would pass, how people would go home and have dinner and talk some but not much and then watch TV or read or maybe pray and read the Bible, but then night would come and sleep and the next morning and the opening-your-eyes sensation of being tied to something so much larger than a single life.

When the train came, the Brownsons instinctively held hands: Helen to Sharon, Sharon to Herb, Herb to Daniel, Daniel to Tom. None of them wept. There was only a stern, quiet pain, only the moment's gravity, the train passing by, holding that body.

His Body, His Wonderment /

Sometimes, toward the end of his life, Ho thought about his beginnings, not out of the self-indulgence of nostalgia but of wonderment. He had traveled far in the world at large, but all his journeys had centered on returning to Vietnam. Inevitably, his thoughts came back to where he had come from and who he had been, to the boy who flew kites, went for hikes, and listened to his father's teaching. He was the same body as that boy: larger and much older, but the same body with the same heart and eyes and feet.

The feet deserved the most recognition. How much he had walked! The hikes as a boy had been for pleasure, but most of the walking came from necessity. He had been poor—no carriages for him. There were poorer people, but so many times he had relied on his feet to get him where he needed to go—accompanying his father, going to school, and then becoming literally a foot soldier in the ranks of revolutionaries.

His feet had been sturdy. What a pity his life had not been devoted to the appreciation of such simple facts, the physicality of being alive. His head had intervened, which was what heads did. Still, he felt humbled by how stalwart his feet had been—complaining, to be sure, when he walked for too many hours, but ever resilient. As a man devoted to radical change, *ever* was a word he rarely used. He had sought to master time.

He had succeeded. No one could reckon the cost. A thousand voices might as well be speaking all at once. Simplicity, walking on the earth in all its glorious seasons, whether barefoot or with sandals, seemed beside the point, but he knew that was wrong. The point of revolution was to allow people to live their lives so they could find the simplicity that was theirs, so they could be free of the labels and bonds others imposed. Yet revolutionary

343

doctrine reveled in its special labels and bonds. Truth, as it searched out reality and insisted on its own vocabulary, remained as uncomfortable as a pebble in a shoe.

His feet remembered every step. Even in old age, he could list places and events, but he never could have listed each day's steps, only that he was driven forward. He lay on his bed in the little house that served as his official residence, a non-palace, and felt how death soon would take him. He wished to be cremated, his ashes scattered to the winds. The years that followed would do whatever they did with his nation. The years were like a river, full of turns and bends. As for him, he had not acted to gain historical fame. As much as he had been an actor, he had been a bystander while the Soviets, the Chinese, the French, the Americans acted out their own agendas. And what was that fame beside the tenacity that marked every step? What wisdom could match that? What revolutionary theory? His body had been more than a vessel. His life had been more than a page in a book.